Romantic Suspense

Danger. Passion. Drama.

A High-Stakes Reunion
Tara Taylor Quinn

Close Range Cattleman
Amber Leigh Williams

MILLS & BOON

A HIGH-STAKES REUNION
© 2024 by TTQ Books LLC
Philippine Copyright 2024
Australian Copyright 2024
New Zealand Copyright 2024

First Published 2024
First Australian Paperback Edition 2024
ISBN 978 1 038 90559 8

CLOSE RANGE CATTLEMAN
© 2024 by Amber Leigh Williams
Philippine Copyright 2024
Australian Copyright 2024
New Zealand Copyright 2024

First Published 2024
First Australian Paperback Edition 2024
ISBN 978 1 038 90559 8

MIX
Paper | Supporting
responsible forestry
FSC® C001695
www.fsc.org

Published by
Harlequin Mills & Boon
An imprint of Harlequin Enterprises (Australia) Pty Limited
(ABN 47 001 180 918), a subsidiary of HarperCollins
Publishers Australia Pty Limited
(ABN 36 009 913 517)
Level 19, 201 Elizabeth Street
SYDNEY NSW 2000 AUSTRALIA

Cover art used by arrangement with Harlequin Books S.A.. All rights reserved.

Printed and bound in Australia by McPherson's Printing Group

A High-Stakes Reunion

Tara Taylor Quinn

MILLS & BOON

Dear Reader,

Welcome to Sierra's Web! The nationally renowned firm of experts, college friends bound by tragedy, are all working on this one. This story has been germinating inside me for a couple of years. I saw it. I felt it. And finally, it came to life! Having been in there so long, it took a lot of me with it!

As you run for your life, you're getting my firsthand knowledge of sights and sounds in the mountain range that I look at every single day as I write. The Superstition Mountains, on the east side of the Phoenix Valley, are massive and hold lore and life and all kinds of magic. I've climbed to the top of the highest peak. I've been in the middle of the range with no cell service. I've visited a little town similar to the one in this book. I've stood at a mountain wall and tried to read centuries-old hieroglyphics. Right here in my Arizona mountains.

And a reunion—I had one of those, too. With my very first boyfriend. The first boy I'd ever kissed. Almost thirty years after our last young kiss. He looked me up on the internet just eighteen months after I'd driven by his town without stopping. A detour I took while on book tour. Thinking about him. We've been married almost seventeen years and love is still our driver. And my message? Believe in happily-ever-after. And most critically, believe in love.

Tara Taylor Quinn

DEDICATION

To Tim—I am so thankful for our reunion, and you.
I loved you then, now and forever. Tara Lee Barney

Chapter 1

He was stealing his newborn! Dr. Dorian Lowell ignored the pounding of her heart as she raced through the darkness toward the gray-hooded, hunched over man hurrying from the small stucco birthing center. Her frantic steps silenced by the grass, she ran full tilt toward the old red truck parked in a corner of the lot. The two-hour-old boy needed constant medical attention. He'd die within hours without it.

She'd seen Jeremy, the estranged father, pull in and head into the birthing center moments before. Had warned Security.

He was almost at his truck, not running like she was, but moving at a good clip, head down, shielding the newborn he held in both arms, upright against his chest.

If she screamed for help, it was unlikely anyone would hear her.

If she ran for help, he'd get away.

That baby's only hope lay with Dorian rescuing him before his father got to the truck.

Breath constricted by the panic tightening her chest, she crossed onto the pavement just steps away from the young, slim-framed man, hoping to reason with him. They'd all had a rough day, and he was overwrought.

As soon as he heard her steps, he jerked, straightening, and pinned her with a glare that was menacing in the moonlight. His eyes. She didn't recognize them. Two sharp pinpoints of warning...

It wasn't Jeremy! And in her peripheral vision, she noticed a second truck—Jeremy's truck—parked down a couple of spaces in the lot.

Too late to stop her forward motion, she upped her momentum toward the tiny baby boy the stranger held, her self-defense class of long ago taking over as she kneed the kidnapper, grabbing for the baby—not Jeremy's baby—at the same time.

Her blow was strong enough to make the hard-looking man loosen his grip for the split second she'd needed. With the blue bundle wrapped in one arm, she raised her other hand to the man's face, ramming her palm into the base of his nose. She felt a crack as he backhanded her upside the head, and, dizzy, stumbling briefly, she ran.

A shot rang out behind her.

Swerving in between cars, she just kept running.

FBI Agent Scott Michaels broke all speed limits as he raced across a desert highway to the small birthing center in Las Sendas, Arizona, forty miles southeast of Phoenix. Every second counted when it meant the kidnapper had another second to get away from him.

Six months of trying to track a series of newborn kidnappings, to find anything that linked them—other than the MO, a message board on the dark web and a hunch—and he might have just found his first real lead. The first kidnapping gone wrong.

A mistake made.

He had an eyewitness. A renowned physician who'd been leaving the facility late that night due to a complicated birth that had nearly killed both mother and child.

A heroic doctor, from what he'd heard. The woman had single-handedly saved another newborn male child.

There was already a BOLO out on the old red pickup she'd described with the California plate, and if there really was a God out there, someone would locate the vehicle.

It could crack the case that had been haunting him for months.

For a split second, just after Scott had turned onto the road that would lead him from the highway into the small town, he thought his non-prayer had been answered. At the first intersection, still on the outskirts of civilization, he saw a truck. Old. Beat up, just like the witness had described.

But as he drew closer, his heart accepted what he'd expected to see. The truck, while old, was black, not red. And not only was the guy behind the wheel not exhibiting any evidence of being in a hurry, he was wearing a white shirt, not the gray hoodie the witness had described. And a cowboy hat, which he tilted toward Scott, waving him to pass through the intersection without stopping.

Giving Scott a clear view of the Arizona plate. Not California like the doctor had reported.

Still, didn't mean someone else couldn't find the red truck. A few minutes later, with adrenaline pumping hard, he pulled into the birthing center parking lot, which was ablaze with red flashing lights. Showing his badge, he was inside within a minute, and being directed to the room where the doctor was waiting for him.

Each minute that passed was another opportunity for the kidnapper to get to another newborn.

Because there'd be another baby stolen that night.

The ring Scott's gut told him was behind the kidnappings had an order to fill and had just lost the merchandise. He'd seen the sale pop up on the dark web that morning...

Grim-faced and determined, he knocked on the door he'd been shown, and opened it before the feminine "Come in" had even been completed.

Opened it and stood there...staring.

"Dorian..." He couldn't remember her last name. It would have changed anyway.

But he remembered her. Far too vividly.

"Scott?" Open-mouthed, with a reddening bruise marking the left side of her face from the ear down the jaw, she stared at him. In wrinkled purple scrubs, with her red hair up in a bun, she didn't look like she'd aged at all in the fourteen years since he'd had her in class.

And...very briefly...in his arms.

"You aren't in the army," she said.

And she wasn't wearing a wedding ring.

"I was. Trained in law enforcement, made rank of sergeant, but wanted to fight crime on a broader scale." None of her business. Just as his plans in the past hadn't been. But that hadn't stopped him from sharing them with her. And then regretting having done so.

"You saved a baby's life tonight," she blurted, blushing. He remembered that about her, too. The way her fair skin turned red anytime she said anything that made her uncomfortable. "Or rather, your training did. I used what you taught me."

He'd been waiting to deploy, had been filling the time teaching a summer self-defense class at the community college. And she'd been...engaged.

To a guy who'd grown up with her, knowing her family.

By then, he'd already learned a hard lesson about him being on the outside looking into that kind of life. So he'd paid careful attention to avoid pursuing the instant attraction he'd had for her. One that had seemed to be returned, and on a level beyond the physical.

As if he really knew anything about living life on that level.

The younger version of the successful doctor had been impressively alert during his class, and he witnessed the exact same focus and attention to detail, the same ability to remember things, as she answered his questions about the thwarted kidnapping. She was able to describe her kidnapper, not only the size and build that closely matched the father she'd first taken him for, but the shape of his jaw, and the soullessly evil look in his eyes. She was certain she'd never seen him before. She'd already talked to the police, had sat with a local officer who'd responded to the scene and was also a sketch artist, but Scott needed other details. The kind you couldn't draw.

"Did he speak?" he asked. "Did he have an accent? Sound educated?"

"All I heard was a string of common swear words when I kneed him. No accent, but he slurred his *s*'s, like he had a tooth missing. And… I think he smokes. His voice had that raspy sound…"

If he could form a mental picture, he'd have more of an idea of where to look first.

"And he smelled like manure," she said. "And maybe hay. You know…like a farm…"

Bingo. Standing, he thanked her, looked her in the eye, and when he started to linger there, to smile his gratitude, he caught himself and immediately reached for his wallet, looking inside for one of his cards. Handing it to her, he told her to call him immediately if she thought of anything else, and, with a last directive to take care of herself, to follow police orders for her own protection, he turned to the door. He needed to get out of the small space.

Away from reminders of the things he wouldn't ever again let himself want.

But he looked back. Saw her watching him.

As if, for a second, she was remembering, too…

He refused to go back. Looked at her and said, "It looks like you might have a black eye by tomorrow." In a few more minutes it would already be tomorrow.

And he had an urgent job to do.

Find the kidnapper.

For three reasons now.

To save the babies yet to be taken. To find the ones who'd already been sold. And to make the fiend pay for that bruise filling up the side of Dorian's face.

What kind of weird fate brought Scott Michaels to investigate a thwarted kidnapping in Arizona? All the years Dorian and Sierra's Web—the firm of experts she and her friends had started—had been working with law enforcement, and he suddenly shows up at a crime scene?

It had to be some kind of warning sent by fate, issued to validate the choices she'd made so long ago. Reminding her why she'd made them.

With so many of the Sierra's Web partner experts finding love and settling down—with her own kidnapping the previous year still challenging her—maybe she'd been experiencing some weakening in her resolve to stay single.

Distracted by her initial reaction to seeing the man again, Dorian instinctively put on her professional face as Chief Ramsey came in to tell her that he would assign someone to escort her to wherever she was going as soon as she was ready.

"That's not necessary," she told him, emphatically certain of that fact. The bruise to her head, while painful when touched, and ugly looking, had been superficial as she'd had the advantage of being the aggressor in the second that the blow had been thrown. She'd been cut, right at the edge of her jaw, the result of the kidnapper's gloved hand jamming her earring into her skin, but overall, she was fine.

And she absolutely did not need one of Las Sendas' already overtasked police officers to follow her the two miles between the birthing center and the room that had been rented for her in the lovely old historic hotel downtown. All the Las Sendas law enforcers had been called in to work the attempted kidnapping, and they all needed to continue doing so.

She'd never forgive herself if they lost the guy because they'd pulled someone off the case to babysit her.

"This is the kind of thing Sierra's Web handles every day," she said, collecting the bag she'd dropped as she'd come out of the employee entrance at the side of the building and had seen the kidnapper leaving with the baby. "You've already seen how we work. Glen, our forensics and science guy, will probably be at the hotel by the time I get there. I'll be right back here in the morning, checking in on the patient I was here to assist with, and will be hanging around in Las Sendas as long as my partners think I can be of help to find the kidnapper."

"Still, this guy doesn't know you can't positively ID him," the chief said, but Dorian could tell the man was eager to keep his officers on the kidnapper's trail, as he should be. Major crime didn't happen in Las Sendas, which was one of the reasons the small town had been chosen to house the prototype birthing center.

"It's more likely he's going to be getting as far away

from here as he can, rather than hanging around for me," she reminded him, to assuage any guilt he might be harboring, as he walked her out to her car. After twelve years of being the medical expert on cases with her partners, many of them criminal cases, she knew the drill.

A thorough glance around the busy parking lot convinced them both that she was fine to walk to her vehicle. She saw him already heading to his squad car as she pulled out of the parking lot, shakier than she'd wanted the chief to know but eager to get to Glen.

Hudson Warner, Sierra's Web technical expert, was up and already working on the dark web site Scott Michaels had mentioned.

After giving Glen whatever he needed, Dorian was going to take a hot bath and put the night behind her. Or at least sit up with her newly-purchased-in-the-past-year handgun at her side for protection and watch old sitcoms until the sun rose.

She'd been abducted off a hiking trail sixteen months ago because she'd been unprepared. She was not going to let the fiend who'd taken her rob her of peace of mind.

Make her afraid to live her life.

When the idea of living life brought thoughts of Scott Michaels to mind as she drove, she allowed them to distract her. The self-defense instructor, former army sergeant turned FBI agent, had no idea that he'd brought a completely different moment to a horrible night. Seeing him again...she had no idea how she felt about that.

Had mixed emotions to the point of being slightly sick to her stomach.

She'd hurt a man she'd loved because of Scott. Had first started to lose her ability to trust herself because of him.

And yet...still got warm inside, just seeing his face again.

Her whole life, Dorian had been wise beyond her years, able to see clearly and make successful decisions, to remain practical in times of crisis, to be an asset to her family and those around her. She'd chosen her best friend, a man she'd known since she was born, to be her life's partner.

And then she'd met Scott, and, if not for the man's inner strength, she might actually have found herself in bed with him…

Turning the corner onto the road that led to Main Street, she saw an old pickup stopped at an adjacent corner ahead and for a second, her heart leaped to her throat, constricting her air. Then she got close enough to see that the truck was black, not red. And when she caught a glimpse of the cowboy hat the guy was wearing, she sat back in her seat, admonishing herself for being so jumpy, even as she gave herself some slack.

She'd been kidnapped and held for days. Not something she'd get over in a matter of months. Maybe not even years. And yet, when the baby had been at risk, she'd run straight into danger.

Still, she avoided looking at the driver as she passed the truck. Until her peripheral vision caught movement and she turned to see him staring right at her.

Her stomach jumped up to choke her.

She knew those eyes.

Gunning the gas, Dorian kept both hands glued to the wheel, her focus fully on the road in front of her. Reminding herself that if she didn't turn up at her hotel in the next ten minutes, her partners would have experts on the ground, looking for her.

The truck gained on her, coming up on her right, blocking her from making the turn onto Main Street.

Forcing her to continue straight on a deserted road that led toward the mountain.

Forcing her into darkness. Any second, it was going to run her off the road. No time for expert help.

She was going to die.

The thought was clear.

Suddenly it was as though she was in an operating room, looking at a patient who was coding. No panic. It was her job to stay calm. Aware. To make the best decision.

Letting go of the wheel with one hand, she reached into the pocket along the thigh of her scrubs, retrieving the card Scott Michaels had given her and, pushing her hands-free calling button on the steering wheel, rattled off the number on the card. Her partners would look for her, too late. But the next baby could still be saved. She had to let the agent know where his kidnapper was. She had to prevent other babies from being hurt.

"He's on my bumper," she blurted into the phone as soon as she heard the click that told her he'd picked up. "Black truck. Hampton Road." She pulled in a breath, maybe her last. "East." Another attempt to get air. "Past last turnoff…"

The truck's headlights reflected off her rearview mirror, blinding her, and then, with a jolt from behind, a crunch, her chin hit the steering wheel. She felt the sting, the split, felt a swoosh of air on an open wound. Moisture. Blood.

"What's going on?" Scott's urgent tone kept her gaze focused on the road. That was all. Blood. Pain. The road.

"Dorian! Talk to me."

"I'm…"

Another jolt. To the rear driver's side of her car.

Then, with a huge bump, the sharp explosion of the air bag against her upper body, she went careening off the road.

Chapter 2

Scott heard the crunch of metal. What sounded like hissing. "Dorian!"

Thug. Thuuggg. Flesh hitting flesh? Or something else?

His blood ran cold.

"Dorian!" Throat tight, entire body on red alert, he squealed to a stop in the middle of a deserted country road just east of town. GPS had mapped out local farms for him. He'd been on his way to the second one when his phone had rung.

"Dorian!" He called again and heard only hissing. They were still connected. He couldn't let go of that thin thread, of whatever clues she could give him.

Of the hope that she'd let him know she was okay.

Black truck?

At the sound of a grunt, he hollered. "Dorian!"

A groan was his only response. The sound of a car door opening.

And the line went dead.

Had she crawled out? Managed to escape? He wanted to believe she'd be fine.

But he didn't.

Dialing Chief Ramsey, the man with jurisdiction on a local incident, Scott relayed what he knew, including Dorian's description of the black truck.

Birthing center surveillance tapes had shown that Dorian had been correct, in that the truck used in the kidnapping was red. He told Ramsey about the black truck he'd passed on his way into town, a good hour after the attempted kidnapping. Ramsey let him know that a patrol car was close to Dorian's location and would be there in less than a minute.

As soon as the chief hung up, Scott dialed Hudson Warner, the tech expert Dorian had put him in touch with from her firm. He gave Hudson all the information he had, including the fact that he'd been on the lookout for a red pickup truck from the second he'd left the center's parking lot that night and hadn't seen even a newer model one. Warner was giving him Glen River's number, the partner who was just arriving in Las Sendas, but Scott disconnected midconversation when Ramsey's call came in.

"We've got her car," Ramsey's voice came over the line. "There's no sign of a truck and no sign of her, either."

"Trace her phone. She was just talking to me…"

"It's sitting here on the seat. Along with her bag. Handgun still inside it. Tells us she likely didn't have a chance to fight back. He can't have gone far, Agent Michaels. Either back toward town, and we'll have him, or he's got less than a minute on us heading out of town. That's a five-mile stretch with no turnoffs and I've got a car waiting for him on the other side. State police are here, too. We'll get him."

Scott wanted to believe the man. Wanted to believe that with her twelve years with her firm, Dorian, while a medical expert, not law enforcement, at least knew how to handle a fiend long enough for someone to get to her.

He wanted to follow protocol and let others do their jobs. But the kidnapper was his jurisdiction. And whether anyone else thought so or not, so was Dorian. His entire adult life, the only thing that gave him peace inside was giving his all to get justice for good people, and something was telling him she was one of the best human beings he'd ever known.

He'd seen it in her in the past—her faithfulness to her fiancé, her regard for her parents, the way she helped others in class—and it had been evidenced that night, too. She'd risked her life for that baby.

And had succeeded in saving it...

He hadn't even been all that surprised when he'd heard that she was a partner in Sierra's Web. While he'd never worked with the nationally renowned firm based right there in Phoenix, he'd definitely heard of them.

Her smartwatch...

She'd looked at her watch to read a text while he'd been questioning her. She'd answered the text on her watch, punching quickly, as though with practice, on the tiny screen, while her phone had been sitting right there. He'd asked why...

Her watch had its own separately designated line—with a number given out only to key medical personnel so that she could be reached anytime, day or night, no matter where she was.

Driving toward Hampton Road, following his GPS, Scott put in another call to Hudson Warner, telling him to ping Dorian's smartwatch. Because the watch was for Dorian's non-Sierra's-Web-related medical work, Hudson didn't know the number. But assured Scott he'd find it and get back with him.

Until then, Scott was going to drive every mile with hay in the vicinity. He'd walk every field if that was what it took. He wasn't stopping until Dorian had been found.

The kidnapper had her. It was the only logical explanation. She'd said he was behind her, as though he'd know exactly what she'd meant. She'd called him, and that night's case was the only reason she'd have done so.

Did the man sitting in wait for Dorian, taking her hostage, mean that he'd be too occupied to kidnap another baby that night?

Or was there more than one baby snatcher on the payroll?

Was Scott really after an entire kidnapping ring? Or just a single, severely demented man who'd managed to amass millions while keeping law enforcement completely in the dark?

Or was Scott wrong that the kidnappings were even related?

All questions that ate at him, insidiously, as he peered through the darkness, looking for a hint of fair skin. Keeping his foot on the gas pedal pressed down to the floor, he felt the tension grow in him, laced with fear, with every mile he traveled without success.

He was heading farther out of town. Ramsey, Sierra's Web, they'd cover the obvious. He was going for hay and manure in the same place.

Warner might or might not be able to help, but that watch, the number, gave Scott hope.

He had to save Dorian.

And somehow be able to use the night's horror to finally take down whoever it was who'd been terrorizing parents in several states for more than six months.

He had to do it or die trying.

She wasn't going to just let herself die. Hurting everywhere, Dorian promised herself that she would hang on long enough to help her partners, to help Scott Michaels, find the kidnapper of babies. She had to pay attention.

To note every detail.

She'd been unconscious when her abductor had pulled her out of the car but figured she couldn't have been out for more than a minute or two, if that, as she'd felt him yank her arms back and bind her wrists with some kind of twine that still bit into her with a nasty sting.

The ride on the floor of the truck, behind the seat, had been excruciating, to her head, her arms, her face, but thankfully hadn't lasted long. Had the truck been black? Not red? That didn't make sense, did it?

And then she'd been hauled from the truck and dumped in what she'd figured out was a lean-to, or maybe a barn that had partially fallen. She had a ceiling overhead, and at least two walls, maybe three, but could see sky and out-doors when she opened her eyes. Which wasn't often.

The guy—the kidnapper, she was pretty certain, judg-ing by the same manure-type smell she'd noticed in the parking lot of the birthing center earlier that night—hadn't checked to see if she'd regained consciousness. He'd just hauled her up, carried her to the inch or two of hay upon which she lay and dropped her there.

As far as she could tell, there were no animals anywhere around. At least not the kind that lived in barns and ate hay.

Anything else—the bobcats, coyotes and other natural life that were known to roam during the hot Arizona nights, looking for water—were out of her control and therefore, not worth worrying about.

With resolve firmed, she wiped away the sweat beading on her forehead by rubbing her face against the shoulders of her scrubs. And cringed when the bruised side of her face made contact with shoulder bone.

She was pretty sure her chin had stopped bleeding, but with her hands tied together behind her, she couldn't do more than touch her chin to her chest for evaluation. Her injured skin stuck more than slid as it made contact. Her blood was coagulating, and she took that as a good sign.

In her mind, she talked to Sierra, the friend they'd all lost in college, the reason Sierra's Web had been formed. And to her parents, who'd died in a car accident five years before. Told herself they were all watching over her. She had to believe that, because the thought of their love, something she'd known through tangible action on earth, gave her strength during those weak moments in the dark.

Strength of mind would see her through. And she fought to hold on to it by every means she had.

Focusing on the doing, rather than the fearing—as her parents had always taught her to do, and Sierra had done— she took stock of her surroundings.

Figuring it would serve her better to have her abductor think she was unconscious, she continued to remain completely still—other than the few hurried shoulder wipes and chin checks she administered whenever she heard her kidnapper's footsteps crunching gravel in a way that told her he was moving away, not approaching. Figuring, at those times, he had his back to her.

How long had she been there?

Twenty minutes? An hour?

How did she tell?

Feeling panic start to rise up in her again—far too reminiscent of the year before—she chanced another glance, her gaze staring toward her feet as she lay in the fetal position, and noticed nothing that would indicate time passage.

Using the previous year's captivity as knowledge to her benefit, she reminded herself that not everyone kidnapped to kill.

That her friends, her partners, were the best in the business and could succeed where others didn't.

That she had to do all she could to help them.

And that Scott Michaels was on the case, too. Maybe another expert on the ground. Right there in Las Sendas.

She was hot. But in that part of Arizona, nights only cooled to the high eighties. It had easily hit one hundred five in Phoenix and Las Sendas the day before, and would that day, too, she was sure. Once the sun came up. Even in the shade, she wouldn't maintain lucidity more than a day or two without water.

But there was hope.

A vision of Scott Michaels as he'd come in the door that night—Agent Michaels—flashed before her mind's eye, and she calmed. He'd been on the phone with her. Had heard the abduction. Knew where she'd been... Would call Hud...

Sierra? Mom? Steer me.

The kidnapper had driven over rough terrain to get her to her current prison. He'd gone off road.

Would anyone look where no roads led?

Did her smartwatch still have coverage? Scott knew she had it...

Thank God a text had come in while she'd been in the interview with him.

She could still hardly believe he'd been there at all, that Scott Michaels had been the FBI agent to walk through that door...

When weakness threatened, she let her mind stay on the image of the handsome self-defense instructor turned FBI agent, as she'd first known him fourteen years before. Tall, over six feet, muscled and lean, lithe like a tiger she'd once thought...his dark hair had been shorter then, military cut, but those blue eyes...they'd seemed almost like magic orbs to her younger self, reaching inside her as though to speak without words.

It had been the same that night, too. His hair was longer; there was bristle on his once clean-shaven face, and more lines around those eyes, but the way she'd felt during that brief second he'd met her gaze…almost as if they were meant to know each other…

She'd probably imagined it. Or was imagining it as she lay there, but for the moment, she wasn't sure she cared. That look, it lit her up and she needed all the light she could get at the moment.

If thinking about Scott Michaels was what it took to keep her inner fires burning long enough to figure out a plan of escape, then she'd willingly imagine away…

"I got it all worked out…" The words came to her from a distance, but grew louder, as though the speaker was coming toward her. Same smoker's voice. "We sell her. She'll be worth something. Kind of like bonus pay…"

Sell her?

Worth something?

Acid burned her stomach. She tried to draw in a deep, calming breath, but the pressure in her chest stopped the flow midstream.

Trying to find coherent thought, she flashed back to Scott. The baby-kidnapping ring he'd been trying to break into, to uncover and obliterate…

That was why he'd been there, at the center, in jeans and a dark T-shirt. He'd heard about the kidnapping and had come running. She'd been his first real lead. Was the only person alive that he knew who'd actually seen the kidnapper.

"I know. It's three hours to the border. All we gotta do is get her out of the country, and no one will know we ran into trouble. I'll get another baby and deliver it as planned—don't you worry about that." The voice came with confidence. There was no discernable accent. And the *s*'s still hissed. Paying close attention, then, she listened for anything that set the man apart, any identifier she could give Scott or her partners when she saw them again.

Because as long as she was alive, she had to believe she would see them again.

It was that or panic about the "sell her" part.

Her abductor sounded more educated than not. What else had Scott asked her?

The pauses in between conversation…she never heard replies. Was her abductor on the phone? Hud could trace that…

"Yeah, man, I swear, no one else saw me. We're cool. And about to make a little bit extra on the side…"

Man. The kidnapper was talking to another man. And it sounded like it was just the two of them in on the deal…

And then there was silence. Either the conversation ended, or her captor walked out of hearing range, on grass maybe? She hadn't heard the gravel crunch.

Didn't much matter. If the pair were planning to deliver a baby as planned, most likely that meant the next day, and they still had a three-hour trip, two ways, to make her gone, first—she didn't have until morning, or even enough time to wait for Scott, or anyone else, to find her.

She had to stop wallowing in emotion, rise above and do something. Almost as if her mother was right there on the hay speaking to her, Dorian felt her backbone stiffen.

She needed a plan. A way to take the kidnapper by surprise again, to attack and give herself enough time to get away, while possibly even having to do it all with her hands still tied behind her back.

No panic. Only thought that led to action.

Her legs had always been strong. And were uninjured. They were tied, too, but more loosely. The guy had made a mistake. Not noticing that she'd pulled her knees apart as he'd tied, keeping her ankle bones slightly separated.

Kicking off her shoes, she rubbed her ankles and toes, getting her socks down and away, which provided a little more give in the ties. Then, over the space of some painful minutes, she used dance lessons she remembered from grade school, got one foot turned in to the other, and into a ballet point, allowing the arch of one foot to slide along, and over, the protruding ankle bone of the other. With some severe muscle pain, turning the foot more, she pulled first the heel, at ankle height on the other foot, free of the tie and quickly got her arch and toes through. With one flick, she slid her other foot out of the rope's circle. Then, drawing from everything Scott had taught in self-defense class, she considered various kicks, to various body parts, that, if landed with accuracy, would allow a relatively small person to overtake a much larger one.

She practiced the kicks, uncaring if her captor noticed the movement. She didn't have all night. While she worked her legs, she started in on the ties at her wrist, too, with a vengeance. No matter what it took, she had to get her hands through those ties. She might do irreparable bodily damage, but she'd rather lose her skin, her normally shaped bones, than her life.

Or to have another baby lose theirs.

She had to get free. There was just no other choice now.

If she didn't, not only was another baby going to be kidnapped yet that night, but if the kidnappers got away, their business could continue in the future, too. She could not allow herself to be shipped off, or die, and let that happen.

Her parents hadn't raised her to allow such a thing.

Promising herself that she wouldn't fail, promising Sierra that she wouldn't fail again, Dorian gave everything she had left to keeping her word.

Chapter 3

Scott knew better than to let Dorian, or any woman, call out to him in a personal capacity.

His need to find the doctor was wholly professional. Her life mattered to all those she helped in the course of her work.

And she was the lead to his kidnapper.

Finding the man could put an end to a horrific six months of baby thefts.

Chief Ramsey's ability to organize both his men and the visiting law enforcement was impressive. Within an hour they'd combed every inch of the Las Sendas roadway, and, as Sierra's Web private investigators arrived, had started on four-wheeling paths through the desert as well.

With everyone else covering the grids Ramsey laid out, Scott stayed on his own course, searching out farms in the area—or any place where there might be manure or hay. Hudson Warner had experts on the computer, scouring hay sales, hayseed sales and vendors that had anything to do with hay, cows or manure used to fertilize ground. Didn't matter that it was the middle of the night. Warner had told him—it was what family did.

Dorian was family to her partners. The man didn't discuss his partner with Scott at all.

Didn't surprise him a bit.

And though he wanted to know more about the woman, he didn't ask. Not a surprise, either.

As he searched, he told himself he couldn't possibly hear Dorian's silent call. Just as he hadn't really sensed an affinity with her when she'd been in his class all those years ago. The way he remembered it had been like she'd needed something from him. And could give him something he'd needed in return. But he didn't trust the impression a bit. Back then, he'd still been in the early stages of accepting that he would always be the guy with a past good people didn't want to associate with. Born of parents that good women wouldn't want genetically attached to their own kids.

Had Dorian really been able to sense him back then, she'd have seen how lost he'd been, not some guy she'd be drawn to.

He hadn't become someone worthy of respect until after they'd parted, when the army filled the parental role he'd been missing all his life. And later, the FBI serving as his adult family had enabled him to give the world the best version of himself—finding justice for good people on a much bigger scale than policing in the army had allowed.

Somewhere along the way, long after knowing Dorian, he'd finally learned how to like himself.

A part of him wanted Dorian to know that. For no good reason.

They were ridiculous thoughts to thwart the frustration wrought by the unending stillness in the darkness surrounding him. Thoughts that kept hope on the table that he'd find her alive.

Determination filled him as he drove along dirt paths that served as roads, seeing nothing but the black shroud of night. What good was all his work if he couldn't save innocent babies who still had a chance to know the unconditional love of decent parents?

If he couldn't save the woman who'd brought him a touch of softness when he'd needed it most? Even if she hadn't known it.

Dorian. She wasn't Lily. He didn't even, for one second, think any differently. But she was like Lily in that she'd been raised by ethical, loving parents who'd instilled in her a sense of service and decency. Of accountability.

She'd been raised in a world where good won.

His heart had been broken when he'd learned the truth about his own place in that world. But he'd become a man through it. A man who didn't have to hide from himself or hide himself from anyone else.

A man who'd found real peace—and acceptance from others—with who he was.

He would not let a soulless kidnapper stop him. There had to be more to life than that. More to his life.

Rage gnawed at him as he bumped along, bottoming out his SUV, scraping metal against desert rock. He was an able-bodied strong man, ready and willing to help, but he wasn't finding the woman in need.

Or protecting the babies who would soon be stolen if he didn't find the woman.

This kidnapper, this monster, had become so much more than a case. Over the months of failure to save newborns, of meeting with grieving families, Scott's work to capture the kidnapper had become personal.

And now the man was imprisoning the vision of an angel from Scott's past.

Bile rose in Scott's chest. The phone rang. Distracting him from emotions that did not serve him, or anyone, well.

Hudson Warner.

The tech expert had been able to identify the number registered to Dorian's smartwatch. It hadn't pinged for over an hour, but the last known location was south of Las Sendas, at an abandoned homestead out in the desert.

He'd already sent the location to Scott's phone. And was alerting other law enforcement as well. The closest team was still almost an hour out.

Hanging up without wasting a second on thanks or good-byes, Scott touched his screen a couple of times and tore out for the location of the watch—just five minutes away from where he was.

Because he'd been out looking for hay. In areas that weren't already being searched.

He saw the half-fallen barn before he was close enough for his engine to be heard. And pulled off the road and down into a ditch the second he determined that if he went any farther, rounded one more corner, he could be easily detected by anyone at the barn watching the road.

After checking his gun, and the knife encased securely in his sock, he turned off the internal light so it wouldn't flash when he opened the door and slid out.

Precious minutes passed as Scott traversed rocky desert ground on foot, using the tall saguaro cacti, desert trees and scattered tall bushes as coverage. And then, as he lay on the ground, crawling through open space on his belly— trying not to think about the snakes that traveled the same hard desert ground in the same way—he saw it.

An old truck.

Black, not red.

And…the guy in the white shirt and cowboy hat. He couldn't make out any distinguishing characteristics. The moon's glow only gave so much. But the guy was leaning against the hood of his truck, one foot up on the bumper behind him, looking outward, as though waiting for someone. His jaw was moving. Could be talking on the phone.

As Scott crawled, more slowly, watching that the head didn't turn in his direction, he saw the guy spit.

Chewing tobacco. Not phone call.

Something one did while waiting?

On what? A phone call? Others to arrive?

Or was he just a guy who happened to cross Scott's path for a second time, who also just hung out chewing in the middle of the night?

There was no sign of Dorian. Didn't mean she wasn't there.

But it could mean that.

Could be this wasn't his guy. Her phone had pinged in the area and his gut was telling him he'd found his man. Cowboy hat and all.

Would have been nice if he'd listened to his gut when he'd first seen the guy back on the way into Las Sendas. He could have prevented Dorian from being traumatized further.

Maybe even prevented her death.

He couldn't think like that. Moved forward. She was alive. She had to be. She wouldn't go without one hell of a fight. And he'd given her some skills...

About a hundred yards from the barn, he saw movement. Legs held up in the air, wearing something loose enough to be scrubs, seemingly running wild.

He couldn't make out much else. Just the legs moving intermittently through the moonlight, but, heart pounding, he knew it was her. Pulling out his phone, he texted an SOS to Warner and then, upping his pace, knowing that the kidnapper could decide to get back to his prey at any second, he pulled out his gun and crept forward.

He couldn't shoot the guy, not yet, not until he knew

there was no one else on the property. If someone was in that barn, keeping watch on Dorian, the second his shot rang out she could be as good as dead.

Based on the crash he'd heard, and the scene Ramsey had described, she had to be in pain—a lot of it, judging by how she was thrashing—while the guy outside stood there and chewed.

One hundred yards became one hundred feet. Scott felt like he'd won the lottery when Dorian raised her scratched and bruised head in his direction. Her mouth dropped open. He could see her teeth in the moonlight.

He told himself she smiled as he continued forward with excruciating but necessary slowness, watching her for any sign she might give him as to what he might be crawling into.

A phone rang and he froze, not sure if it had come from the area of the truck, or through the opened barn. Since she'd turned her head in his direction, Dorian hadn't moved.

Was someone there, then? Guarding her?

He heard a voice, male. Couldn't make out the words. But he heard running, in his direction, had his gun ready. He wouldn't shoot unless he had no choice, to shoot or die, not until he could get a look inside the barn and be able to take out anyone in there, as well, before they could hurt Dorian.

Help would be on the way soon.

"What the..." He heard the words, the smoky voice, as, with horror, he watched the guy who'd been leaning on the truck reach Dorian, a gun to her head as he hauled her up and pushed her forward.

She didn't make a sound, or move her head, as though she knew not to give him away, and he stood, too, knowing he couldn't let the man take her again. The call…had it been a go-ahead the guy had been waiting for?

Go ahead to where?

For what?

It wasn't going to happen; whatever it was. He couldn't let it.

Where was Ramsey? Warner's guys? Anyone?

The guy moved quickly, and Scott had to be careful not to be seen—by Dorian's captor, or by anyone who might still be in the barn. Or on the property.

That missing red truck bothered him.

Keeping himself in shadows, he made it to a tall, three foot round cactus by the rear passenger side wheel of the truck, while the kidnapper opened the driver's door, pulled the seat back and shoved Dorian into the storage space behind it.

She fought back, kicking him, fighting for all she was worth, but within seconds was inside with the seat slamming back in place, holding her prisoner. Hoping that her continued ruckus had the attention of her captor, and anyone else in the vicinity, Scott ducked and made it to the side of the truck, then slid like a snake over the side of the bed, straining his arm muscles as he carefully held his weight, lowering himself slowly down, fitting around the junk inside, without giving himself away.

The engine started. The truck burst forward, even before he heard the door shut.

Dorian had angered her captor.

But she'd also given Scott the chance to get in the bed of the truck.

Smart lady.

With his mind on Dorian, willing her to be strong awhile

longer, he prepared himself to be ready for whatever was going to happen next.

He had his goals. Save Dorian.

And stop the kidnappers from stealing even one more newborn baby away from their parents.

Nothing else mattered.

The drive was longer, bumpier, more excruciating than before as her captor, with an arm along the back of the seat, had a gun on her this time as he drove. He'd been in a hurry, clearly agitated, and hadn't taken the time to re-tie her legs. Somehow, she had to use that lapse to her advantage.

Lying up against the back of the truck, she felt a thump as they hit the next set of rocky terrain on their route. A thump that came from the bed of the truck, not from tires beneath the truck. Something she hoped the driver couldn't discern.

Scott Michaels. *Agent* Scott Michaels.

He was back there.

He had to be.

Dare she believe it?

Since it gave her strength in the moment, she could.

She had to do whatever was necessary to hang on. To keep sharp and do, not feel. To focus enough to be ready for whatever came next.

To be able to help Scott and her partners. Not hinder them. To prevent more families with newborn babies from being obliterated by grief. To save the babies from...who knew what?

Scott thought they were being sold.

To whom?

Dare she hope that those little ones who'd already fallen to that fate, those Scott hadn't been able to save, were at least being loved by people so desperate to have a family that they'd broken the law to do it?

Or…better for the babies, but not the parents…what if the people buying the babies didn't know the babies were stolen? What if they thought they were part of a legal adoption?

She'd read about that…

Her heart cried out at the thought. There were no winners in a situation like that. Even the buyers were victims.

The only way to prevent the pain was to stop the kidnappers.

At any cost.

She slid more heavily against the back of the truck as the vehicle started up an incline. Imagining Scott right behind her, pretending that he'd found a way to lodge his body up against the front of the bed of the truck, she told herself that they could share strength through the metal separating them.

An hour passed. Maybe more. Driving up rough terrain. Unpaved roads. In captivity she'd been in the desert, at the base of the mountain range. If they were now up in the miles and miles of uninhabited mountains…

She held her head up from the hard floor as best she could while they bumped along, and still, she gained new bruises, flying up and landing on her shoulder as they hit a particularly bad rough patch.

Had Scott's body done the same? Risen up? Enough to be visible in the rearview mirror?

She feared the worst when the truck came to a sudden stop.

Scott was in the truck—and had been discovered.

Her heart beating a rapid tattoo, she was slow to distinguish another roar drawing close—an off-road vehicle approaching?

The "man" on the other end of the phone.

The accomplice.

Shaking, she braced herself. A woman with her hands tied behind her back against two men? She reminded herself she was prepared to do whatever she possibly could...

And then the truck door opened.

It had lightened outside. Dawn was coming. And her captor wasn't reaching for her.

"Did you get rid of the red truck?" The smokey toned voice sounded conciliatory. Not at all commanding. Which sent shards of fear through her. If her kidnapper wasn't the dominant one, what more did they have in store?

"Of course. It's at the bottom of Canyon Lake." The voice, male, more menacing than her captor's had been, came closer. "You fool!" The voice continued, near the truck.

"No, look, man."

A latch sounded and the seat back slid away from her a split second before her almost numbed, tied-back arm was yanked, practically from its socket. "Try anything and you're dead." The voice was harsh, but no more than a whisper right up to her ear, as her abductor hauled her out of the truck.

She had to do something. Might only have that moment.

Shaking, filled with fear, head aching and body weary, she stood there. Was she going to fail? Again?

Where was Scott? She'd wanted him to be in the truck, but she had no proof.

She'd seen him, though. Back at the lean-to.

Odd that of all the FBI agents who could have walked in the door the night before, it had been him...

There was more to be done...

Swear words flew around her as the men argued about

her, the man who'd taken her jerking her shoulder every time he responded to his angry partner.

The other man was older, bigger, bearded, but spoke like he was educated. Scott had asked her about that. To pay attention to such things…

"You've lost sight of one very clear point," the newcomer finally bit out, all volume gone from his voice. "You aren't being paid to think for yourself, to decide a new plan. The general wants a baby. Period. We aren't some sleazy operation here. We aren't low-life human traffickers…" The bigger man reached under his shirt.

A gun appeared in his hand, and before Dorian even registered what was happening, a shot rang out.

Chapter 4

As if in slow motion, Dorian stared at the still pointed gun as, at her side, her captor fell to the ground. The partner had shot her captor and she was next, his gun was pointed straight at her. Her gaze glued on that gun, the finger on the trigger, she saw it start to move, and then suddenly, leaving her standing there, the big man darted to the front of the truck.

Before she could move, Scott, a pointed gun in one hand, grabbed her arm with the other, pulling her with him.

She heard another shot. From beside her. Scott's gun.

Then one from farther away as he shoved her into the killer's four-wheeler. Instinctively, she dove across the seat so Scott could get in beside her, behind the wheel.

"Stay down." Scott's voice was almost unrecognizable to her in its anger. And urgency. On the floor, she felt the rumble as the vehicle started up.

With his gun still pointed, Scott drove with one hand, propelling them forward so abruptly she hit her head under the dash.

More shots sounded. From next to her, and in the distance. She heard the ping of metal against metal, just to her right, before they bounced painfully around the corner of a mountain peak, and then another. Winding around a dangerous cliff that, from her perspective on the floor, seemed too narrow for the vehicle to sustain them for long.

If they went careening over…

When she grew light-headed, she told herself to breathe. Kept her head down. And held on to the metal bracing the seat.

Scott had found her. Her partners, law enforcement wouldn't be far behind. Right? Even up there?

She just had to hold on.

And maybe pray a little.

Was that how Sierra had felt, right before she'd been killed? Like, if she just stayed strong, and prayed, right would win? Justice would be served?

If Dorian had only paid more attention to the last visit her friend had made to the clinic…had asked why Sierra had been there. She'd known Sierra wasn't due for any checkups. Had seen no sign of illness…

Sierra had been such a private person. Dorian had let emotion—her love and respect for the woman—cloud her judgment…

"We've lost him for now." Scott's voice called her back. Her gaze shot up to him. He'd slowed, was perusing the area as he drove, frowning, clearly worried.

While they turned and bumped over the rough terrain, and with her arms still wrenched behind her, Dorian got herself up onto the seat.

Scott gave her a quick glance, shoved his gun under his thigh on the seat, reached toward his foot, pulled a knife out and, barking at her to turn, cut the twine digging into the base of her hands.

"Did you hit him?" she asked above the rumble, refusing to wince as she moved her freed shoulders, flooding with gratitude for the man at her side.

"I don't think so. Not enough, at any rate. Maybe in the leg as he was jumping in the truck. He was still shooting after we'd rounded the mountain."

They'd managed to get away.

But only for the moment.

The man behind them wasn't going to quit looking for them. He couldn't. He knew they'd seen him. And that he'd pay with his life if they managed to make it back to civilization.

Scott's theory…kidnapping babies…multiple babies… he'd been right. There was some kind of horrible business being run right there in Arizona.

And a general was behind it all, pulling the strings. An army general? Some diabolical fiend who'd only served criminal endeavors and just fancied himself with the title? Or just a guy whose luck was about to run out?

"You okay?" he asked.

"Of course." Pain didn't count. Physiologically, everything was in working order. Inside…she feared she'd never be okay again. But that was emotion talking.

She couldn't trust it.

She had to fight the feeling…to do whatever it took to stay alive. "How about you?"

"I'm fine," Scott said, his gaze directed ahead of them, over the land they traveled—a flat, rocky prairie-type area, acres big, on a small mountain peak swallowed up by a huge range. The Superstitions. She'd been gazing at them with awe all the years she'd been in and out of Phoenix.

She'd had no idea there was an entire world up there, hidden behind the highest cliffs.

"Thank you."

Scott had risked his own life to save hers. He'd earned her undying gratitude.

While his driving wasn't as frantic, the FBI agent was still moving at a good clip. She thought maybe he nodded. "Don't thank me yet. We've slowed the guy down, for now, but he clearly knows these mountains. Far better than we do." He reached into his pocket and handed her his phone.

"Speed Dial, 2," he said. "Hudson Warner said he'd be tracking my phone. Hopefully we won't have long to wait, but just in case…"

With frantic fingers, Dorian got his phone on. Dialed 2. Nothing happened.

Glancing at the top bar, heart sinking, she had to tell him, "We have no service." And had no idea how long they'd been without it.

Then she told him the rest, too, about the phone conversation she'd heard outside the barn before Scott had arrived. The part about selling her and still taking another baby to deliver on time, too. His lips tightened, but his gaze didn't leave the road for even a second.

She could feel his frustration.

Tried to fend off her own desperation.

Another baby's life was going to be on the line within hours.

Their lives were in immediate danger.

And they were on their own.

He was out of bullets. He'd driven them to a spot where driving was no longer possible unless he turned around. Something he couldn't afford to do.

Pulling to a stop at the edge of the clearing he'd been winding through, Scott turned to Dorian. The reddened bruise on the far side of her jaw fueled his anger anew. "I can't promise to get you out of this," he told her, right up front.

Without breaking eye contact with him, she nodded.

Didn't even blink. "I know. But I can promise to do everything in my power to help you try," she said back, giving him a surge of…something that had no place in his life.

Warmth.

Like he'd fallen into the middle of some damned Christmas movie.

And so, to get them back into the real world, he just laid it right out for her.

"My cylinder's empty. We can't go back down the way we came. Not without risking a death trap. And, for the same reason, we have to ditch the four-wheeler. Makes too much noise. For all I know, he's got a tracker on it."

"Our best bet for staying alive is to go farther into the mountains, which we can only do on foot," she said, with another nod.

Like they were out having a cup of coffee.

Lily would have burst into tears when the first bullet rang out. And he wouldn't have blamed her.

Trying not to admire Dorian, he continued. "Good news is, we have the best of the best looking for us, aware that we're out here, and that the kidnapper is, too."

"My kidnapper," she told him. "No one else knows for sure yet, that you found your guy."

"Our guy." The correction came before he'd had a chance to analyze the words and hold them back.

Reminding him of his runaway mouth with Dorian in the past.

"You took him on single-handedly last night and won," he added, just to make sure that she understood he wasn't pairing the two of them up for any other reason.

And ignoring the part where the guy ended up kidnapping her later.

She didn't even glance his way. "It's hot, even up here

in the mountains, dry as hell. It's past time for breakfast and we have no food with us. Nor have we slept. Of more concern, we're out in the desert without water."

The doctor had spoken. Dire facts.

And yet, they were the exact impetus he needed. Rather than taking on whatever sick dudes were in his very near future in that first moment, he could leave them to the very near future where they belonged.

"I hope to have us out of here before we get too hungry." He held on to the possibility even though, realistically, he knew that they were going to have to find something to eat in the mountainous wilderness. He had a knife. Would have to catch and kill something. If he was lucky, a fish in a mountain stream.

Still, not an activity he wanted to think about.

"How are you feeling? Do you have a headache? Did he hurt you…otherwise?" His jaw clenched. He had to know.

"No headache. Just achy and sore, but nothing that's going to slow me down."

He held her gaze for long seconds, assessing her words, and, with a nod, trusting her to tell him the truth, he got back on track.

Opening the glove box, looking under the seat beneath him, he came up with a first aid kit, a flare and a couple of sticks of gum. Ripping one in half, he put one section in his mouth and gave her the other.

Dorian followed his example on her side of the vehicle and found a partially crushed, half-empty bottle of water.

"And a phone!" she told him, with an actual grin, as she held both up.

The smile left her face as quickly as it had come. But in that second…

He'd recognized the woman in his memory from the past. The one who'd put her arms around him...held him close...

They had his phone, too. And no service. But they could turn one off, saving battery, and have it later for a flashlight or compass as needed. And once Scott got them to safety, that phone she'd found could prove invaluable to his case. The near future, not the now.

After they'd both sniffed and then poured sips of water down their throats, careful not to touch their mouths to the bottle, Scott stripped off the button-down shirt that was part of his normal work attire, leaving him in a T-shirt more suited to hot mountain days. Wrapping their small pile of supplies in the fabric, he secured it all with careful folds and tied sleeves and slung it over his shoulder.

"We need to get to a water source," he told her abruptly, jumping out of the vehicle. Because while he wanted to hope they'd be out of the mountain before lunch, he had no guarantee of that, and survival came first. "There are streams running throughout these mountains. Our first goal is to find one."

She was right beside him before he'd taken more than two steps. "Sierra's Web just had a case in another mountain range not all that far from here," she told him. "It involved a missing child, and then a couple of law enforcement officers who were being stalked. I ended up on scene, to treat the female officer after several attempts had been made on her life. They stayed alive over the space of a couple of days by hiding in natural caves grooved out of the sides of the mountains—just like the Native American tribes lived in centuries ago..."

He didn't remember her as a talker. Figured she was more nervous than she was letting on.

And turned out, maybe he was, too, because, as they started to walk, to hike, he asked for more details of the previous case. Of which there were plenty. He was identifying with every one of them.

Right up until she said, "The two officers, they're both thriving. And getting married. To each other."

At that, Scott turned his back and started to climb the mountain in front of him.

Dorian hadn't known that a phone's compass still worked without service. Thankfully, Scott had and was using his app to keep them from wandering in circles as they climbed up and away from the four-wheeler and then farther into the rocky denseness.

"We need to step carefully, making the least amount of movement, and try to stay covered from view. My thought is to go up and then, on higher ground, head back in the direction we came," he said maybe an hour after they'd headed out on foot, as she kept pace right behind him. Turned out her rubber-soled work shoes were better for more than foot comfort during long hours of standing. They had good traction on the slippery rock face, too.

"I like that," she told him. "The closer we can stay to the area where your phone last pinged, the quicker my friends are going to get to us."

"The FBI and state and local law enforcement will be on the trail, too," he reminded her, with a quick glance back at her. Her heart lifted a second when she saw the almost grin on his face. It was more a light in his eyes than an actual turn up of the lips. But she recognized it.

Or thought she did.

Her mind had to be playing tricks on her. A coping

mechanism. No way she'd remember a glint in someone's eye from fourteen years ago.

She was a scientist of the human body. Knew better.

"I'm also hoping, with the higher elevation, we can spot the killer, be able to keep an eye on him."

Killer.

She'd been standing right there. Held captive by a man, hurt by him. As he was shot to death right beside her.

If not for Scott, she'd have been next.

She shook her head.

Dug her foot harder into the mountainside. "Hopefully we'll be able to hear him if he's still in the truck," she said aloud. Shivering, but pressing on, too.

It was what she knew. The doing. What she trusted.

Her mind.

Her Sierra's Web partners.

And…maybe, Scott Michaels, too?

Only because he'd saved her life.

Her thoughts bounced a bit as she walked. And then, as she nearly impaled herself on the sharp needles of a pear-shaped pad of prickly pear cactus, her mind was suddenly clear. "Hey, hang on," she said. "Give me your knife."

Without question, Scott reached under his pant leg and pulled out the blade she'd seen him grab earlier.

"Have you ever eaten prickly pear?" she asked him, squatting down by the massive plant as she carefully removed the pad that had almost caught her.

"I've had a prickly pear margarita."

She nodded. So had she. "We're lucky this is the time of year everything's blooming," she continued, acting as though she knew exactly what she was doing. "We aren't going to starve out here."

While she worked on the pad, she reached up for a red

berry at the top of the plant. "Start with that," she told him, handing Scott the piece of fruit while she went back to work.

"We can eat cholla and barrel cactus, too." She'd never had them. Or prickly pear, either, for that matter. She broke away the first piece of fruit from the pad, handed that to him as well. "That's high in antioxidants, fiber, minerals and vitamins," she told him, working on a piece for herself. "And, according to one of our nation's most respected health clinics, it's good for treating cholesterol, diabetes—" she got her own piece free "—and hangovers, among other things."

Standing, she turned, her piece of fruit almost to her mouth, to see Scott standing there, a berry in one hand, the piece of fruit she'd handed him in the other, staring at her.

"What?"

He shook his head. Took a bite of the fruit, and, eyebrows raised, said, "It's sweet." Then took another bite.

"My stomach's growling and I was just remembering an article I read in a professional magazine a year or so ago. Certain cactus fruit is becoming quite the star in a lot of different cuisines. Sought after in fine dining venues for salads, among other things. This is one of them. As opposed to the Agave…there, certain parts could kill you," she told him then, standing there in her dirty scrubs, with juice dripping out of the corner of her mouth.

Only to look up and see him staring at her again.

Self-consciously wiping her mouth, she continued to eat. But when she glanced over a third time, to see his attention more on her than the meal she'd provided, she refrained from taking the bite that she'd had on the way to her mouth. "What?" she asked again.

"I just…remember you."

The words hit her hard. Where she couldn't afford to be

touched. Until they'd found the kidnapper—the killer—
until they'd saved whatever babies they could, and gotten
themselves to safety, there could be no consideration for
matters of the heart.

And afterward...well...maybe they could be friends.
Like she was with Hud and Glen and Winchester, Sierra's
Web's financial expert partner...

"You were the best student I ever had. The way you took
everything in, processed, produced..."

Yep, he had her pegged. "My parents raised me to be an
asset to society, not a drain on it," she told him then, thinking they'd be done with it.

"I can't think of many people I know who wouldn't be
panicking right about now."

If he didn't quit talking, she might start doing that.

"To what end? If I give in to desperation, I weaken my
chances of succeeding." She was spouting pep talks from
her youth. Heard her dad's words. Her mother's. Silently
thankful that they were watching over her.

And she was desperately fighting Scott Michaels's effect on her, too. The man had ruined her life once—albeit
unknowingly—by engaging emotions that were counter-
productive. She could not allow him to do so again.

She wouldn't break another heart.

Or, if she had any way to prevent it, lose another life.

No matter what it cost her.

Chapter 5

He'd been on the hunt before. In life-threatening situations.

Alone, and not.

But Scott had never been on a job with a genius woman doctor who exuded caring and compassion, while she calmly solved a basic survival problem. Nourishment. Before it had even become a problem.

Not only was she finding nutrients to sustain them, by knowing which plants were safe to eat, she managed to get juice for them to drink as well. With his help, once he caught on to the process.

They ate, filled their squashed water bottle, drank, filled it again.

And moved on.

Up.

He'd known there were edible plants on the mountain. He hadn't known which ones. And hadn't wasted a lot of time worrying about it, either, planning to find a stream and fish. Figuring he could use the flare to start a small fire for cooking.

There'd been no sign of the kidnapper. He wanted to hope that he'd hit the guy well enough that he'd gone back to whatever hole he'd climbed out of for treatment. Scott allowed himself various moments over the next hour where he went with the thought.

But knew he couldn't let his guard down. The guy, or someone else who worked with the general, would be on their trail.

Other than some basic warnings as he foraged the terrain and prepared Dorian to do so behind him, he walked in silence.

Was mostly thankful that she did as well.

Even while he wondered what she was thinking.

It had been that way in class, too. It was like the woman had a treasure trove going on in that mind of hers, one filled with jewels that he had to have.

Fanciful.

Ridiculous.

Reminiscent of the foolish kid he'd been in high school, thinking he'd found a woman, and through her an extended family, who fully accepted him despite the baggage he carried.

At that thought, he glanced at his phone, and stopped.

They'd been hiking well over an hour.

"By my rough estimate, we've reached about where we were when the black truck first started up the mountain road, just at a much higher elevation."

The black truck. Driven by a man now dead.

Shot right in front of her. Holding her tightly enough that she'd have felt the push back of the blast. And she hadn't said a word.

Or shed a tear that he'd seen.

He'd seen her shaking a time or two, though.

Dorian caught up to him. Stopped, looking over the ridge in front of them. He'd been leading them back to the outside of the mountain range but wasn't so sure that had been the best idea.

"Should we head down? Try to get to a road before dark

and hopefully flag someone for help? Or, best case miraculous scenario, run into someone looking for us?"

He'd had the thought. Before he'd realized how long it was going to take them to reach their current point. He shook his head. "It's going to be scorching in another hour or so," he told her, assessing the steep slide of rocks directly beneath them. "And the more we move on the outer mountain face, the more easily we'll be seen. By our own people, yes, but by anyone out to attack us, too." He'd been fairly certain the kidnapper would have shown himself by then. Even just with the sound of his engine. Yeah, the guy had had a body to dispose of, but no way he was just going to let them walk out of there and identify him.

Not with a "General" involved.

More likely, he, or someone else, was hunting them. "Depending on his scope, and weapon, we'd be an easy take down without ever knowing he was there…" He said the words aloud because Dorian needed the information.

"We can't stay up here forever, hoping someone on our side finds us," she shot back, sounding a little cranky.

Lessening his tension just a notch for a second or two.

"Agreed. But we have no way of knowing if we've been followed. We head down now, and we could easily become target practice. We wouldn't have much hope of surviving."

"It could be the same if we continue forward," the good doctor pointed out with the practicality he'd admired in her in the past. "For all we know, he drove back to take care of the body he left behind and headed straight up from there."

Scott had been on the lookout for that possibility. And yet, every time he'd searched down the mountain during their trek, there'd been no sign of life, of movement of any kind. And that made him nervous, too.

"Which is why I think we should head from here farther

into the range but keep the same coordinates as well as we can. Find one of those caves you talked about. And take turns getting some sleep…"

An hour before, the possibility of such a plan had been last case scenario. He'd had time to think. To assess.

To come to terms with the situation.

"And move at nightfall," she finished his sentence for him. Frowning. Deeply.

"Which means we have little chance of preventing another kidnapping to fill today's order," he admitted what he figured they were both thinking.

"Unless someone on the ground, any of the teams involved at this point, are able to do so." Her words were soft. Gentle.

A reminder that there was always hope.

"I'm hoping my phone will at least ping to the location where he shot his partner," Scott said, thinking out loud. Welcoming the presence of a sounding board he trusted. "Even if he got back to the body before anyone found it, my agents will scour every inch of the ground. If the guy left one spot of blood, one footprint…"

"My partners will analyze every speck of earth, trace a piece of rubber, or even a tread, to a tire, to a service center, if that's what it takes. And hopefully get an identity on at least one of them."

Right. Sierra's Web. A firm of experts known to law enforcement all over the country.

How had a medical doctor become part of such an organization?

Instead of asking, he said, "Hopefully they'll have blood to analyze." Her personal life couldn't be his business then, any more than it could have been in the past.

Except…now that they would most likely have been pronounced as officially missing…and were planning to spend time alone in a cave, followed by a nighttime climb down the mountain…

"What about your husband? It's not my place to ask, but I'm assuming he's a member of Sierra's Web as well?"

It would explain her association with the firm.

She turned away. Was glancing toward the mountain range interior, or what was visible of it from their vantage point. "I'm not married. Look over there, on the other side of that ravine…just below the second overhang from the top…"

His gaze followed her pointed finger.

She wasn't married.

After a couple of seconds, he picked out the solid rock inset on the mountainside. Whether a cave that actually led into the mountain itself, or just a massive overhang that gave the appearance of one, she'd found decent shelter that should give them enough coverage to protect themselves, while still allowing a view of the immediate surroundings without them being seen.

In other words, about as safe a resting spot as they were going to get.

She wasn't married.

"Stay behind me," he said. "I'm going to hug the mountain as much as I can and single file, we'll be less visible."

He'd been hiking that way anyway. And she'd been staying in his path. There'd been no reason for him to reiterate.

Except to point himself to the track upon which he must stay. The job. Getting her to safety and then himself back on the killer's trail. The reminder set him immediately straight.

Scott set off, all instincts honed, determined to keep them that way.

And leave the fact that Dorian wasn't married to the ether.

* * *

Dorian didn't ask Scott if he was married. His personal state was none of her business. He'd said in the past that he had no intention of marrying or raising a family. And she'd noticed no wedding ring. But then many of the doctors with whom she associated didn't wear them, either. All the handwashing...

And she put her curiosity about his current matrimonial state down to a normal interest after reacquainting with someone one knew in the past. When the silence got to be too much as they hiked, when it started to allow her mind to feed her reasonable fears, she asked Scott what she could about his life. His most recent cases. His most memorable ones.

Because, alone with her unforgetable self-defense instructor for the first time in years, her thoughts kept returning to him. And every time they did, she knew a moment's respite from the dark weight boring down on her.

She found out the man specialized in kidnapping cases. Heard about a domestic situation. Something she could, unfortunately, relate to as she'd been called in on a few such situations that had ended up requiring specialized medical care.

Her foot slid out from under her, wrenching her hip. Catching herself on a boulder protruding from the ground, bruising the underside of her forearm, she slowed for a step. But didn't call out. Wouldn't slow him down. Kept her gaze focused on the cave she'd found, instead. The place they were going.

She didn't question him any time their destination was out of sight, either. Trusting him and his compass to get them to the natural rock room that would, hopefully, allow them some rest.

She'd been up twenty-four hours. Assumed he had, too. And he hadn't spent a few of them lying in hay, as she had. His body had had no chance to rest.

Not that she could convince herself that any second of her time in that broken down barn had been restful.

Still, as more than an hour passed and they finally reached their destination with no sign or sound of other human habitation, she wasn't sure she wanted to sleep there. Ever.

They both checked out the covered alcove, one at a time as the other kept watch, and determined that it would work well. It went farther back into the mountain than she'd figured, and with a shiver, she insisted that she'd take the first watch while Scott slept.

Hoping that they'd be rescued before she had to take her own turn. Looking at the back of that cave, seeing the darkness, had reminded her of the year before. The disturbed man who'd taken her because desperation had driven him over the edge.

When Scott shook his head, insisting that he'd keep an eye out, needing to get a significant lay of the land immediately surrounding them, she stood strong.

"You're physically much stronger than I am," she pointed out, a bit relieved at how normal her voice sounded. "And while I have had self-defense training from one of the best, it stands to reason that my trainer would still be better equipped than I. If it comes to a hand-to-hand battle with this guy, you have the better chance at success. We need you rested."

Straightening her spine, shoulders back, she prepared for argument. She was not ready to walk back into that dark hole and close her eyes.

No amount of fatigue was going to force its way past her current tension and allow her to sleep.

"Give me an hour."

Open-mouthed, Dorian watched Scott's back as he moved farther into the alcove, and then, she spun around, before he'd settled in, and determined the least risky vantage points for her to hold to keep the agent safe as he slept.

Chapter 6

Scott woke with a rock painfully digging into his hip. Holding a complete stillness he'd learned in the army, he listened, sniffed, and slowly came back to where he was.

With whom.

And sat straight up. The sun had risen high in the sky and was already on its slow way down. No way he'd only been asleep an hour.

Dorian wasn't in sight. His gaze shot around the cave as, moving like a panther, he stood. There was no sign of her.

Or of a struggle.

Fearing that the killer had her captive just outside the opening, waiting for Scott to appear so that he could take down both of them at once, Scott slid his knife out of its holster, and, holding it straight out in front of him, slowly advanced.

One flick of his wrist and he could take the killer out. As long as Dorian wasn't between Scott and the guy's jugular.

Keeping his back to the wall, he slid slowly along the side of the cave that gave him the biggest view of the exterior ground. And had taken only a few steps when he saw her.

Dorian was standing, her back and one hand against the side of the mountain, studying the terrain lower down, eating some kind of fruit.

Relief made him weak for the second it took him to pull out his phone and glance at the time.

"You let me sleep three hours." His tone was accusatory. Hell yes, it was. He'd trusted her to...

"You're the one who's most likely going to be called upon to keep us alive," she stated softly, with total calm. And then, still standing watch, her gaze making the rounds, she finished off the fruit and reached into the front chest pocket of her scrubs.

"You need to look at this," she told him, handing him the phone she'd retrieved from the four-wheeler they'd stolen from her kidnapper's killer.

"It's a burner. There's no owner information listed, just text messages. But he's going to be beyond murderous when he finds out it's missing and figures out we have it."

He took the phone. Quickly pushed the screen enough times to get to the messaging app.

Read.

And, with energy pushing at his skin, felt the weight of worlds on his shoulders when he looked back at her.

"We can't go back yet," she said. "Even if it was safe to do so."

"I can't get you any further into this."

But she was right. In his hand, he was holding possibly the best chance he was ever going to get of stopping something bigger than even he'd imagined it could be.

How many babies had already been ripped from their biological families? He had no way of knowing, but judging on the months that had passed, he figured in the double digits.

And how many more would there be in the months or years to come if Scott didn't succeed before worry that they'd been compromised caused the general to order the operation to simply pack up and disappear?

To continue their work elsewhere?

Location didn't matter to them.

Only secrecy did.

"I'm guessing the red dots might designate birthing clinics all over the Southwest," Dorian said, glancing at his screen, as he studied some kind of map.

Could be that. Or locations where potential drop-offs had been identified.

She reached over and, with one finger, scrolled to another image. "I think these might be customers," she said, looking at the list of lowercase letters that spelled nothing.

"They're all in sets of two," Scott agreed. "Like initials."

But none of it was as immediately compelling, igniting a fire within him, as the first message he'd read. "Someone was told to be at the mission at ten tonight," he said, looking at the doctor in her thin dirty scrubs.

And seeing a breath of fresh air.

Even as tension pressed the breath from his lungs.

"I think the mission is here, in these mountains," she told him. "I was kind of following our coordinates as we hiked, when I could see your phone. And if you scroll back a couple of months' worth of messages, you get almost the same altitude we were at when we first started hiking, but quite a bit east. Doesn't mean it's here. But the men were here. At a clearly predetermined meeting spot."

He liked where she was heading with the theory, but maybe because it gave him a chance to end the sixth-month nightmare? "They'd need to meet someplace close to pass off the baby," he agreed. "My guess is these high desert mountains were a meeting place for the kidnapper, and the middleman who was clearly his boss."

She nodded. "But wouldn't it make more sense, then, for the kidnapper to get the hell out of town? As in, drive across flat desert, in any direction, and meet up at any number of deserted areas where no one would ever see them? Where there's no chance of security cameras? Think about it... Why do you think we hear about bodies being found in the desert? Because it stretches for miles and miles, uninhabited land in every direction after you leave the Phoenix valley..."

Her passion grabbed him.

Her words were what hit him hardest.

They freed him from whatever stupor seemed to have slowed him since her return into his life. Allowed him to go with his gut.

"The mission is in these mountains," he said to her. "As you say, any direction away from the valley on land is filled with miles and miles of area where illicit activity could thrive. But that's not where they headed. And in the mountains, with the difficulty of traversing the terrain..."

She nodded. "I took a course on Arizona history when Sierra's Web first settled on Phoenix for our corporate headquarters. There was a ton of activity in these mountains during the gold mining days. And still believed to be a lot of gold up here. To the point that prospectors arrive here every year, hoping to find some. Which is totally beside the point except that there were some areas where miners clustered. They became like rustic camping towns. Some even built buildings..."

He'd been nodding while she was speaking. "There's actually one down by the east valley," he said. "It's like four or five roughly built buildings that are now a restaurant, shop and a one-room museum..." He was talking about a place he'd visited years before, but, in his mind's eye, was envisioning what could be a secret hideout. Something crafted from the remnants of a broken down, abandoned settlement. "There'd be some kind of path or trail from the place, out of the mountain," he said then, looking again at the coordinates on his phone.

Was he wrong to be thinking about testing his hunch?

Alone with an expert physician who had her own work to get back to?

Alive.

"We can't go back," she said then, as though following his thoughts.

"No, but if we head toward this place, if it really exists, right here in these mountains, then we're walking straight into the fire." He'd be putting her life in further danger.

"There's a baby drop-off at ten. Obviously, there were other newborn options on the kidnapper's list, which makes sense, and would also be something his killer would know…"

Her points were spot-on. This wasn't her first criminal hunt.

She took a step closer to him. "For all we know, he's already got a second infant…which, according to that—" she pointed to the phone screen "—will be delivered to the mission at ten."

Yeah, he got that. And knew, if he was on his own, he'd already be heading toward the coordinates of what they'd both figured could be the mission.

"So if we hit it tonight, after dark…"

She wasn't going to give him a chance to protect her.

And for what?

Their theories were all based on supposition. Fanciful, wishful thinking even. And yet, he and the men and women with whom he worked had solved more cases than not based on just such mental deductions. Evidence was gathered... as he'd been doing for six months. Theories established. They followed them as far as they could until new evidence appeared.

As it had the night before with the botched kidnapping that fit the method of operation Scott had already established.

Dorian finding the phone...

Even that made sense. The man he'd shot at had planned to kill off his problems and depart the way he'd arrived—in a four-wheeler that could travel off road in the desert, leaving little to no tracks on the hard ground, no trace.

He'd have succeeded, too, if not for Scott hot on the trail, and in the bed of that beat-up old black truck.

The killer would have had his phone safely stowed, in the event his kidnapper put up a fight...but the killer ran into law enforcement out looking for a kidnapper.

Because, as far as Scott knew, he and Dorian were the only two living people who knew that the kidnapper was dead. And that they were on the trail of his killer.

And so there he stood...with evidence shining up at him.

If he was with another agent, staring at that phone, there'd be no question that they'd follow their hunches. Climbing into danger, when necessary, was the job they'd signed on to do.

Being wrong was always better than not checking out every possibility.

He still didn't like it. His gut was in flux. Telling him unequivocally that he had to get to those coordinates that night. At the same time, it was warning him that he had to put the current life in his hands before the six-month long case. How could he find a way to get Dorian into protective custody, and then make it back up the mountain undetected? There might not be enough hours to do one, let alone both.

A sound in the distance interrupted the tension his thoughts were sending through him. "What was that?" he asked softly, but he knew.

"Sounds like an engine…" Dorian was backing up inside the cave as she spoke. Scott dropped to his stomach, sliding toward the edge of the small clearing of land in front of the cave. Hoping that the landscaping of desert brush would hide him from whoever might be driving down below, he peered into a vastness that angled downward for hundreds of yards.

"What do you see?" Dorian's voice had lowered, sounding strangely vulnerable to him.

Was she hoping for rescue?

As he sought out the source of the engine that was echoing in the canyon below, Scott found himself feeding on that supposed hope. He'd found his kidnapper, was on the brink of taking down the ring—everything was finally aligning…

"Get down!" He spat the words, his thoughts interrupted by the sight of the sun glinting off metal. "It's the black truck. He's back and he's coming in our direction," he added, not moving as he kept watch.

"He can't make it up here in that vehicle." Dorian's tone was calmer than not, stating what they both already knew.

"No. But it's imperative that we not give him any clues as to which direction to head up to find us," he bit out, barely allowing his chin to move against the earth as he spoke. "Are you on the ground?" He didn't chance a turn around to look.

"Yes. Flat. Sideways across the opening, just beyond the cave entrance, so I can see you."

Why that mattered—to her or to him—he couldn't worry about. The important fact was that her choices gave him confidence that she could act in a way that would help him help her. She was down. Inside. Just as he'd asked.

And was keeping a watchful eye outside, too.

Like a fellow agent, watching his back.

As he was still processing the thought, the sound faded in the distance. He'd lost sight of the truck. "He's made a turn away from us," he said, still perusing the landscape with total focus.

"I can't hear the engine. Are you sure he hasn't stopped, and is on foot?"

"Positive, for now," he told her, rolling away from the edge of the cliff to sit up between a desert bush and the cave. Still out of sight, just in case. Yet with the mountain at his back and a complete view around them. "Over there, I could still hear the truck, heard the engine sound fade away. Not shut off."

He heard movement, turned to see Dorian sitting upright, cross-legged, at the entrance to the cave.

"We're safe for now," he said, not allowing his gaze to linger on the captivating redhead. "Get some rest. You're going to need it later."

He had rudimentary charts to study, with only a small phone screen on which to do it. The killer's burner. It was smaller and cheaper than Scott's department issue, but it had 90 percent charge. Scott's, which was much more valuable to him for many reasons, being tracked by his peers, for one, was down to 75 percent. While it was offline, and couldn't be traced, he had it off to conserve energy.

He might only get one shot at reaching the mission, when the time came. He had to be as clear about where to head as he could be. Comparing coordinates he'd been following while they were hiking that day to the few he saw on various screens, he caught movement to his left. Glanced over to see Dorian still sitting upright in the middle of the cave opening.

"You've got to sleep," he told her. "Whether we head to the mission, or back down, I'm going to need you to be able to climb, to hike, as quickly as you did this morning."

She didn't look his way. Just kept staring straight out, into the vastness beyond, as though seeing something besides the desert mountain-scape.

"I'm relaxed," she told him. "And therefore, getting more rest than I would if I close my eyes right now."

The slightly lowering sun was shining into the cave's opening, alighting her face with a glow that was so perfect it seemed staged for the screen. He wanted to believe she was some kind of angel who could make the impossible possible.

But he didn't have that luxury.

"Close them anyway," he told her, purposely lacing his tone with authority. "That way you at least have a chance of drifting off."

If she didn't get some sleep, she was going to be a hindrance. He'd deal with it. Just wasn't as confident he could get her back without detection if he had to carry her.

Which could mean holing them up in another cave somewhere for God knew how long. He'd fail to save the baby due to be transported that night and could lose his chance at breaking up the kidnapping operation.

He could lose Dorian, too.

She had to sleep.

No other option.

He held his strong stance for several minutes. Giving her a chance to comply.

After a length of complete silence coming from the cave, gratified, he turned, ready to smile at the sleeping woman.

And saw her sitting upright, just as she had been. Staring right at him.

Chapter 7

"Why?" The word came at Dorian laced with some frustration.

"Why what?" she asked, calm as ever. But she knew.

"You're a doctor. You of all people know the importance of rest to the human body's ability to perform. We have no idea what's ahead. But we can count on there being a bit of physical exertion involved."

He was right, of course. Saying things she'd been sitting there telling herself. Apparently, stating the obvious was the only way she and Scott Michaels could communicate.

She had to sleep. Her emotions, her one weakness, were getting the better of her.

And she knew how to lessen their ability to debilitate her. Medically, psychologically, her brain knew the answer.

Sitting there in silence wasn't it. She was only feeding the fear.

"Sixteen months ago, I was out hiking with a friend... Camelback Mountain, you know it?"

She glanced at him, wanting to find something in common, to talk about hikes they might both have taken. And rave about the view from the top of Camelback.

To make small talk to distract herself...

He stared out at the view. "I've seen it from a distance.

Have flown over it. Never hiked it." He didn't sound in the mood to rave about gorgeous landscaping.

"We'd just come back down, were in the small parking alcove getting into our separate cars, and an arm went around my neck from behind. I was shoved into the back of my own car." She relayed the facts like a tale she was telling.

Might interest him, might not. No matter to her, either way.

Inside, she quaked. Every nerve on edge, she stared out at the mountains, the huge drop just in front of them.

Wanted to run and had nowhere safe to go...

A hand touched her arm and she jumped, hitting her head, and screamed.

The hand covered her mouth. Trapped the sound inside her.

Shaking, feeling her accelerated heartrate pounding in her chest, Dorian barely heard the voice.

"Shhh. It's Scott. You're okay." *Scott.*

Oh, God. What had she done?

Reacting so foolishly to a simple touch.

"I'm going to move my hand now. Just stay quiet."

She nodded. Embarrassed. Ashamed. Stared down, studying the hard rock and dirt surrounding them as though there'd be some cure there.

For her fear.

And her humiliation.

Warm fingers beneath her chin lifted her face, and she made herself find the courage to look up at the man who'd just witnessed something none of her partners—her best friends—had ever seen.

"I apologize," she said, pulling on every resource she had to bring out the doctor in her. "I thought talking about it would ease the paralyzing effect it was having on me. I miscalculated."

She'd put herself in counseling immediately after she'd been rescued. Had followed all protocols and been cleared months ago to end her sessions.

Standing beside her, he held a hand out, as though to pull her to her feet. She stood on her own. She would not continue to appear weak. But that hand, the warmth...just as she was wishing she'd grabbed hold when she'd had the opportunity, those fingers wrapped gently around her arm, just above the elbow, and she walked with him the couple of feet to the rock wall against which he'd been sitting. Slid down with him behind the six-foot-tall desert bush through which he'd broken viewing windows.

"It would help me to have the basics," he said. "We don't know what we might be facing over the next hours, and I need to be prepared for any triggers..."

His words were wholly professional. His tone sounded anything but.

The combination reached her in a way nothing else had. She was a professional. Her counselor, her workmates had all dealt with her on that level. And she was a human being who'd suffered serious emotional and mental trauma. Her friends and partners had met her there.

Somehow Scott Michaels seemed to reach out to both versions at once.

"He wasn't after me," she established right away. "He was after my friend. Other than keeping me locked up for days—and demanding some medical care—he provided food and left me alone. I was able to secure his cell phone long enough to send a couple of messages to my friend's cell phone. In a code we'd established when we were kids..." The most important part of the story at the moment. She'd be of use to him, not a hindrance.

"My team got to me, and then to my friend's deranged client just in time to save my friend's life."

"So last night…"

His words trailed off. Leaving her wondering if he was thinking about the way she'd risked her life again, to rescue that newborn baby. Or if she'd maybe lost her hold on reality a bit, having been cooped up in that barn.

"I was doing alright until I walked into the back of that cave." She told him what she figured he most needed to know.

The man lifted his arm, opening up his chest to her. "Put your head here," he told her, his tone more of a command than not. Still, he kindly said, "You need to sleep, and I can provide the security to allow you to relax."

He wasn't looking at her, but rather, was clearly focused on his watch duties. His gaze sharp, moving from one area to the next, resting long enough to make mental notes and then moving on. He didn't issue the invitation a second time. Just sat there with his arm up against the wall behind them.

Because she was exhausted, because she knew he was right and she could be the cause of a failure that ruined many lives if she didn't rest, Dorian slowly leaned over, giving more and more of her weight to the rock hard, but warm, strong and strangely comforting torso that had been offered up as her pillow.

The rise and fall of his breathing rocked her gently. The steady beat of his heart was womb-like. And when she closed her eyes, Dorian tried to focus on a mental vision of the organs in his chest, how they moved as they did their jobs. She tried to see blood being pumped and floating through veins. Instead, she floated back fourteen years.

Remembering a gorgeous and passionate self-defense instructor—one who exuded a compassion, a knowing that was deeper than normal—showing her how to keep herself safe...

He was sitting on the hardest case of his life. The hardest seat his butt had ever propped on for hours unending, too.

Both cheeks were asleep. He figured the condition was for the best, as the discomfort and numbness were constant reminders to the front part of him that kept wanting to jump into life. Every single time the woman sleeping soundly on his chest stirred at all.

She'd been kidnapped the previous year...

He just couldn't get past it. Couldn't find a way to settle the wrath that her words had instilled in him. That she'd been held for days...

And had had the wherewithal to get a phone and help save herself. Remembering a code from her childhood...

He'd never met a woman anything at all like her.

Intelligent way beyond his means, he was sure, but he'd been up against that before. He liked having someone on his team who could fill in his blanks. Who knew what he did not.

Dorian wasn't on his team.

They were just two people stuck in the mountains and running for their lives. Who also happened to both have risked their lives to save babies.

Maybe a team.

A very momentary one. Soon to dissipate. He'd head back to his office in Nevada. She to her probably luxurious home somewhere in the Phoenix valley.

Yeah, he liked that part. Them living a full state away from each other. Gave some distance for security purposes. No chance in running into her again once their short acquaintance concluded.

Scott tensed, hearing an engine again. For the third time. Not the truck. It was louder. Not as smooth. Had the killer found his four-wheeler?

Had the good guys found them?

In time for him to get to the supposed mission farther in the range? If he never solved another case, he had to get this one. Only the worst kind of fiend preyed on newborn babies.

The sound was still in the distance. But heading in their direction?

Pulling out his phone, he turned on the camera, focused it in the direction of the sound, in the gulley far below him, zoomed in as far as he could go...

"It's the four-wheeler we were in." Dorian hadn't moved, had given no indication that she was awake, but her words were clear.

And accurate.

He lowered his phone, not wanting even a glint of sun through the brush catching his lens, signaling their where-abouts.

"Move slowly," he told her. "Keep low. And get into the cave."

A few minutes later, when the distant sound of the engine stopped abruptly, he followed her inside. Gave her his guess as to the longitude and latitude of where the four-wheeler had quit running.

"He's at least two hours out," he added, "and that's assuming he spotted movement up here and is heading straight this way."

Dorian glanced at her watch. "It's another hour or so until dusk."

Sitting beside her, a foot of hard rock ground separating them, Scott kept his gaze outward as he nodded. "I'd say we go now, anyway, get that much of a lead on him, but he's armed and has proven that he'll shoot. I'm guessing at anything that moves at this point."

She didn't respond verbally. If she nodded, he didn't see.

"If you're still up for it, I think, once dusk hits, our safest bet is to head toward the mission," he said then. "If we're lucky, we save the baby. At the very least, we might find an actual settlement, with people who could help us get out of here. We can't go back the way we came. Not for now, at any rate."

He was thinking out loud.

And warning her at the same time.

He could be putting her life at more risk.

She was in trouble regardless.

The guy was clearly after them.

What he needed to get a picture of was her ability to hang tight in the face of more danger. They had to address the fact that she was not only a victim of a kidnapping the night before, but that the event had triggered trauma from the previous year. It he didn't stay on top of her emotional state, he could lose her.

"How's your friend doing? The one who was hiking with you last year?" From what he'd gleaned, the nameless woman had nearly been killed. Approaching the topic through the suffering of a third party sometimes made conversation less threatening in the moment.

"Good," Dorian said, her voice sounding so normal, filled with strength, that Scott turned to look at her. And breathed easier when she met his gaze head-on.

"She moved to Phoenix, opened a law office that is already thriving due to the numbers of clients that stayed with her in spite of the distance and is engaged to the lead detective from her case."

He glanced outward long enough for a perimeter check

but didn't stop his gaze from returning to her brown eyes. "Sounds like she's a lot like you."

She shrugged. "We were best friends when we were little. Lived next door to each other. Unfortunately, I was just a kid and couldn't be there for her when she needed me most. She pushed me away, and I let her…"

There was more there. He heard messages between the words. But didn't pursue them.

"You think you're going to be okay, moving on out of here?" he asked bluntly.

"I know I am. I fall apart when I have nothing else to do," she told him, head-on. "Never when I'm active. Just keep me busy, Agent Michaels, and you'll have a soldier worthy of your lead."

He felt like a grin should be attached to the words.

There wasn't one.

She'd lost some of his confidence. The truth hit Dorian harder than it should have. Than it would have had he been anyone but Scott Michaels.

The man who'd been her secret shame.

Two families that had been close friends for decades had been irrevocably changed by Dorian's secret, but hotly burning, attraction to the man when she'd been engaged to someone else. Her parents, while disappointed and worried about her, had stood by her when she broke up with her childhood sweetheart a month before the wedding. Brent's family, while polite on the surface, had not done so. Feelings had been too strong to ignore, drawing a line between sides, and eventually the families had drifted apart.

"Are you married?" she asked then, to keep her mind active, while her body couldn't be. And to get her head straight where the FBI agent was concerned. They had far more pressing matters than her heart issues would ever be.

And another woman's husband...that was the immediate shut down she needed.

"Nope."

Oh.

"My job consumes me night and day, a lot of the time. If a case comes up, I'm gone. Period. Doesn't matter if it's a holiday or I have reservations for a week of survival training...case comes first."

If he was giving her warning, she heard it loud and clear. If he wasn't...his life just seemed...like hers.

Which gave her the reassurance she'd needed. And another boost of strength as her heart settled back down beneath the blow of disappointment.

She glanced back out at the walls of rock and natural growth surrounding them in the distance. Was finding her vibe.

And then he sent, "You divorced?" at her, pulling her gaze back to him.

He didn't blink. His blue eyes, always seeming so intense to her, didn't waver.

She did.

The question was fair; her mind rallied. He'd found out she was engaged when they'd known each other in the past. She'd had tears in her eyes when she'd announced the news as she'd pulled herself away from him.

In the present day, just hours before, she'd told him she wasn't married.

Besides, she'd opened herself to his question when she'd asked about his marital status.

So she gave him the one word. "No."

That was all.

Chapter 8

With every muscle taut, his insides tied up in knots, Scott made himself sit in that cave for another half hour. It was just the possible culmination of a case that had been eating at him for months—the fact that he finally had a tangible lead—that was playing with him.

Not the woman sitting next to him.

It was only the forced downtime, the fact that they were trapped together with no outside world contact, that had his thoughts, his senses seemingly consumed with her.

"I come from bad stock." He heard the words come out of his mouth. Wasn't feeling any inclination to take it back, even recognizing the lack of a reason to share.

From the day he'd left for boot camp, he'd never mentioned his past.

The point had been to leave it behind.

Funny how he'd taken it with him, within him, every single day since.

"Excuse me?"

"Just…those who knew me back then tended to shy away when they found out my background. I wasn't a great kid growing up."

"Why are you telling me this?"

God only knew.

He looked over at her. "Just don't want you thinking I'm someone I'm not." Solid truth.

"Can I trust you with my life?"

"Absolutely."

"Then we have nothing more to say on the matter."

Good. He nodded.

Feeling like more of a fool than he'd felt in decades.

Because he wanted to say more.

"Time to get going," he said instead, standing.

To get back to the task at hand. To living the life he'd chosen for himself.

Focusing on the greatest thing in it—the career he'd built.

To that end, he headed out of the cave, staying low long enough to get a lay of the land, to see gray and shadow where once there'd been sun.

He heard movement behind him.

Knew Dorian was there.

"If you're capable, we need to head straight up and over," he said, taking in the steep climb, the best natural handholds and steps along the way.

"I'm capable."

"Then let's get to it."

He took the first steps.

And didn't look back.

They'd been climbing for a while. Used to working long, strenuous hours during medical emergencies—sometimes going a full twenty-four without sleep—the physical challenge wasn't the problem.

Spending every second worried about the possibility of a bullet flying out of nowhere and into your back was taking its toll on her mind.

Darkness was starting to fall. But not enough to make their movements invisible.

The only thing that seemed to calm her was focusing on the cute butt in front of her. Or rather, the enigmatic man to whom it belonged.

He was clearly an expert at what he did. As a co-owner of a firm of experts that employed hundreds of the best of the best in a wide range of fields, Dorian appreciated and respected his expertise.

But she wasn't in awe of it. In her world, he was one of many.

Normal.

So why did the man stand out so much? Seem so remarkable to her?

Other than a brief stop for a meal of fruit and cactus juice, he hadn't slowed his pace since they'd started out. Turned his phone on occasionally to check coordinates, but even then, kept walking.

"How much battery do you have left?" she asked after the third time he'd checked, as they changed course a bit. Heading more east than north.

"Fifty percent."

"We've still got eighty-five on the other phone." The killer's phone.

"And every time we turn it on, we risk him locating us."

"It's a burner."

"And if he has the IP address, and someone in his organization with clout, they could be tracking it."

"Someone with clout?"

"We could be dealing with a cartel."

Her heart thudded. She'd wondered, of course. "Clearly there's a hierarchy," she agreed, glad to be talking at least.

And because the conversation kept her mind occupied,

and fear at bay, she spent the next hour asking him more about various cases he'd worked. Finding common denominators with some of Sierra's Web's cases. Talking business.

"Wait, you're in the Las Vegas office now, you said?" she asked as they clawed their way up a steep incline by grabbing hold of plant roots.

"Yeah." He'd been checking each root before using it for weight-bearing, as though he knew that with the rocky ground, a lot of plants were ones that could survive with minimal roots and pulled out of the ground easily.

Darkness had descended upon them in earnest, but, rather than feeling safer Dorian felt more exposed. The moon's glow, up on the mountain, felt like a spotlight to her.

"We had a case there last year. Another stolen baby case, actually," She kept up the shop talk, finding energy, a semblance of goodness, in the similarities in their worlds.

Their life experiences.

As though they were connected that way somehow.

"The bounty hunter that helped a woman find her dead sister's baby," he said then, as though he'd known all along about Sierra's Web's Nevada case, and found the coincidence no big deal. "I didn't work the case, but I heard about it. Partially because of the way it all played out. The people involved."

He turned then. Met her gaze for the first time in hours. Even in the shadows, she could feel the force of that look. "I haven't ever worked directly with Sierra's Web, but I know of your firm, Dorian. I just didn't know you were a part of it."

She wanted him to feel as though their nearly conjoined lives meant something to him. To find something meaningful in the way they'd wound back into each other's lives.

Because she did?

He'd swung back to the next foothold, pulled himself up. And, as he'd been doing since they set out, he waited for her to occupy the space he'd just vacated, before moving on.

"They didn't even know for sure there was a baby," she told him.

Just as he didn't know for sure there was a mission. Or what the word represented in the cryptic messages. He was assuming a building of some kind.

He also had no way of assuring that they were actually heading toward it.

His comment earlier, him coming from bad stock, she couldn't get it out of her head. Because she couldn't figure out why he'd made it at all.

Had he been warning her that they might fail?

"This case...it's important to you." She was guessing, but pretty sure she was right. And suddenly had something that captured her full focus. As though it mattered more than any possible ill that could befall them.

Any trap into which they might be hiking.

"They all are."

"But this one's different." For such a confident, dedicated, successful man, he seemed off his mark.

As she was.

It took one to know one.

Words from someplace in her childhood psyche came back to her.

"Babies taken from loving parents...to end up being raised God knows how..." He'd started and then stopped.

As though any further words would make him sick to his stomach. Or fill with a rage he didn't need blocking his focus.

As though his words, his understanding, wasn't just business. It was personal.

And suddenly she got it. "Because you were raised without loving parents and your whole life has been affected by it."

His foot slipped. For a second, as he hung by his hands on a couple of roots, Dorian couldn't breathe.

His foot lifted to another, wider, rock jutting from the mountainside. He moved silently from there, to the next less treacherous yards along a ridge.

And Dorian, following right behind him, decided she'd said enough.

He had to get the woman out of his life. It was like she exuded some invisible, lethal callout to him that made no sense and had no good purpose.

She was wickedly smart.

Challenged him to be his best, for sure.

He'd had a lieutenant in the army who'd done the same.

But he'd never lost his focus or found himself pouring his sorry heart out to the guy.

As he turned to check on her, as he'd been doing, mostly surreptitiously, careful not to catch her eye, he felt another power pulling at him.

Mostly in the groin area.

Even in dirty, wrinkled two-day-old scrubs, lit only by the moon's glow, with her long red hair falling out of the ponytail she'd rebanded after she'd awoken, the woman was like a siren straight to his libido.

He'd been turned on before.

Pretty regularly since he'd hit puberty.

Some guys were wired that way.

He'd never ever had trouble turning away from the sensation. It was all part of being responsible with his sexuality. You learned to control those impulses. To divert them.

Self-control had never been an issue for him. Not even as a little guy. He might want something to eat, but he'd never cried out for food. Or anything else.

Not that he could remember.

He'd learned to ignore the hunger pains.

And so many other things.

So why in the hell was this one woman so hard to ignore?

One more step up and he'd reached the top of the highest ridge he'd been able to see while climbing. Expected to be met with another, taller mountain to climb ahead of him. Maybe after a bit of downward sloping. Hopefully at least a small valley with a mountain stream.

He made the last move and found himself on a piece of flat ground that reached for an acre, as best he could tell. Couldn't see much out beyond it around the entire perimeter. Thought he saw the shadow of a higher peak in the distance to the east.

Figured the perimeter was surrounded by ways down off the peak.

And turned immediately to give Dorian a hand up to flat ground.

"This is probably overkill, but I need you to drop down to your belly," he told her, watched as she did so, and then followed her down.

She was looking at him, her eyes glistening in the moonlight. Not with tears. He saw readiness there. Much like he'd seen in Afghanistan when he and a comrade were on their bellies at night in a war zone.

He'd known he was up for the task ahead of him then.

Hoped to God he could get the job done that night.

Because he had a woman on top of a mountain peak at least a mile straight up, in the dark, with a killer at their backs.

"Watch for rattlesnake holes," he told her. "They're one part of desert wildlife that are not usually out at night, and only attack when threatened, but if one is partially out of its hole asleep..."

He left the rest hanging there.

"I'm aware of the desert night life," she told him then, her expression serious. Mouth completely straight. "Mountain lion, bobcat, coyote, javelina, possibly bear..."

She knew the dangers.

Was prepared for possible hardship ahead.

Could he possibly have just read that last message from eyeball glints in the darkness?

Blinking, Scott looked straight ahead to the east. His coordinates—which could be no more than numbers on a chart that had absolutely nothing to do with kidnapping, babies, rings, killers or a mission—were pointing him in that direction. "We're headed there." He nodded straight. "Since we have no way of knowing what's just beyond the ridge, we're playing it safest by staying low."

If she nodded, he didn't see it. He'd already started to belly crawl. Heard her moving closely beside him.

He liked that. Her staying close.

Wanted to turn on his phone's flashlight but didn't dare. And kept watch on the ground he shimmied over, taking in the area she'd been occupying, too.

They made it to the ridge in minutes, with her head to his shoulder, half a crawl behind.

Motioning for her to stay back, he gave a last push of his foot.

Suspending his head out over solid ground.

And saw lights.

Chapter 9

Dorian waited for Scott's okay before scooting forward that last push to see the view just over the edge. His silence wasn't good.

If the killer was right there, pointing a gun at Scott, he'd have Dorian soon enough, anyway. If it was some form of wildlife, she might be just the distraction Scott needed to act.

After seconds of wondering what he was facing, figuring that if he was in trouble, she had to know in time to try to help, she joined him.

"Lights…" She hissed the word. Excited.

And scared, too.

"I can't tell what they're from." Scott's voice came softly. "If someone's down there with a telescope, they're going to see us descend."

"What if it's someone who could help?"

He came immediately back with, "What if it's the mission?"

She looked at him. Caught him watching her.

"We have to take the chance," she said, believing that if he was alone, he'd have already descended. "Either way. We have a chance to save a kidnapped newborn. Or we save ourselves and then get to work on finding the killer and figuring out what he's involved with. This is what Sierra's Web does every day. I swear to you—we'll find these people."

"I'm going to find them," Scott said, his tone sounding deadly. And then, with a nod, he added, "And would very much appreciate any help Sierra's Web can give me, if it comes to that."

He was already lowering himself to a piece of ground jutting out just below the ridge. Reached a hand up to help her down, too.

"It's not going to be very dignified, but I think the best way to do this is to sit on our butts and slide as much of the way as we can. Greatly decreases the risk of falling, and will also, I hope, help shield us from prying eyes."

"We could pass for animals, at least on first glance, if someone saw movement," she added, agreeing with him again.

So many times over the past twenty-four hours.

It had to mean something.

She didn't know what.

But she liked it. Being with someone who read circumstances as she did.

Which her partners did pretty much all the time...so why should Scott stand out?

Because he wasn't one of the six friends she trusted unconditionally? The six people in the world she considered family?

She brushed her thoughts aside. "We should each take some sips of juice," she said aloud. At her insistence, they had refilled their bottle every time they opened a cactus for pieces of fruit.

He slid the shirt-made small supply pack down his arm, opened it up. Gave her the first drink. And split another half a piece of gum with her. Which left them a half.

If they were lucky, and the lights below meant some kind of friendly civilization, they could each frame a quarter of that last half as a reminder of their strength, perseverance and—hopefully—victory.

Until the killer was found, and his organization exposed, Dorian wasn't going to be celebrating anything.

But to be most effective, she needed the help of her partners.

Scott, on the other hand, seemed perfectly capable of taking down an entire fleet of kidnappers, if that's what it took.

The way down was much speedier than the trip up the other side of the mountain peak had been. The lower they went, the more careful they became. Staying behind brush as much as possible. Traveling in one motion when they could.

When Scott suggested that Dorian straddle his backside, she did so. And through the tension of possible death, maybe even somewhat because of the heightened negative emotions at battle within her, she felt warmth pool in her crotch as she scooted behind him, opened her legs and wrapped them outside of his, as, with hands on the ground, she pushed herself up against him.

His hands grabbed her ankles, wrapping them around him, leaving the side of one foot touching his groin.

Which kind of felt...hard.

Before she could react, he was moving, using his feet to steady them as he lowered them down a steep, slippery rock incline. Still with her hands behind her, she tried to keep her butt lifted off the ground as much as possible, to carry her own weight.

What she wanted to do was wrap her arms around the man's chest, close her eyes and hold on.

She wanted to pretend that they were on some kind of pleasure jaunt.

And for a second, there in the dark, on her way down

into possible hell, she let herself imagine what such a sexy foray with Scott might look like.

Painted a vivid video in her mind.

And returned to the hot, dark, dangerous present with a jolt when Scott said, "It's some kind of settlement, for sure."

Glancing over his shoulder, she couldn't see much.

What looked like single lights scattered about.

But then she glanced at the screen he held, his phone's camera zoomed in. Things were blurry, but as he scanned the area below, she could see what appeared to be various buildings, scattered pretty far apart. Homesteads? Part of a mission? The pinpricks of lights appeared to be security lights, or widely scattered streetlights of some kind. They were too far up to be able to see more than roofs. Any lights that might be on inside buildings weren't visible from their vantage point.

There was a line running between buildings...what looked like...

"Is that a road?" she whispered rather than spoke, for no logical reason. They'd spoken seconds before.

Just...they couldn't get that close and be discovered.

"A dirt one, probably," he said. "It's too jagged to be paved. We need to get closer." With that, he patted her ankles locked in front of him, as though giving warning to hold on, and scooted down farther. Sliding some, on smooth rock, bruising her butt muscles when the terrain got rough.

Dorian held on. Kept watch as best she could in the moonlight.

Glancing at Scott's phone whenever he turned it on, she kept apprised of the area they were approaching. And of the time, too.

"It's an hour until drop-off time," she said aloud when

he came to a stop behind a tall, fully flowered Mexican red bird of paradise. They weren't going to make it.

Saying nothing, Scott unhooked her feet at his groin. Nodding to the right.

Another cave, more of a deep culvert, but large enough to obscure them from view. She had to move, lead the way.

Staying concealed behind brush, she went first. Crawled to the back of the culvert, behind a jutting rock face, and stood. Glad for the privacy. The hint of protection.

Not afraid of being trapped.

Her body was sore. Nothing that hinted at anything other than normal wear for the day she'd had, following the previous night.

Was it only twenty-four hours since she'd taken on a kidnapper and saved a baby?

Would she have done so had she known she was going after an actual criminal, rather than the distraught father she'd thought she'd been dealing with?

Scott, moving surreptitiously behind the desert plants immediately surrounding the culvert—reminding her of a soldier in a war movie—was using his phone to surveil the buildings that were still at least half a mile away.

The man was thorough. Diligent.

His dress pants were ripped in the back, halfway down the thigh, to the knee.

Her own clothes, while definitely ripe and wrinkled, were holding up well.

Scott turned then, ducking down as he entered the seven-foot-high opening—to stay behind brush to block any possible view of him, she figured.

"There's what appears to be a small town down there. Or at least a settlement of homes, which isn't all that uncommon out in rural desert areas."

She nodded. Could think of three of them off the top of her head.

"I counted at least ten homesteads…scattered throughout what I'm guessing are a couple of miles. There's one bigger building, a standalone, at the far north edge of the clearing. The road ends there. From what I can see, there's what appears to be a paved road heading east, toward the Globe-Miami area, a few miles up the dirt road. Hard to tell in the dark. But what I believe is paved road has reflectors along it, which I saw when a vehicle's headlights hit them."

His grave expression met her gaze then.

"You saw a vehicle." She said the words. Didn't ask them. Confirming what she knew she'd just heard. Taking a deep breath. "Coming or going?"

"Coming. A dark truck. Same size and style as the killer's. Doesn't mean it's the same one. No way for me to distinguish from here, but…" He came toward her, held out his phone.

Showed her a photo he'd taken.

Her chest tightened and she felt her pulse start to race. He'd caught the driver's side.

"It's got that broken running board," she said, forcing calming through a throat thick with tension. "I was staring at it when the kidnapper was shot…"

Adrenaline raced through her.

Accompanied by dread.

They were on the right path.

But would the two of them be able to survive against a possible operation of many?

"We need help." Scott put it right out there. "I still have no phone service. We're too deep into the mountains. I doubt there will be service down below, but I have to get down there and try…"

He didn't want to leave her.

And could not risk taking her down with him.

Most particularly since she'd just identified the killer's truck. A man above the kidnapper in the hierarchy. One who'd shot the baby snatcher for not following the general's orders.

"Put the burner phone on Airplane mode for now. Try to rest. Set an alarm for three a.m. If I'm not back, you sneak the rest of the way down this mountain range, on your belly if you have to, follow that road out of town to the blacktop and, once daylight hits, flag down a female motorist with kids to help you. If you can be patient for a police car to come along, do so. Do not turn on the service on that phone unless it's a matter of life and death. You could lead the killer straight to you. As you're moving, keep an eye out for places to hide in case you have to make a run for it. Rock is best. It's bulletproof."

He wasn't sugar coating a single word. He wouldn't insult her by doing so.

Every bit of information and training he could give her was one more chance to save her life. He took the bottle of cactus juice out of his shirt pack but kept the first aid kit. He'd be out among cactus, she was trapped in a cave, so the juice was a given.

And because he'd be out, and was less medically skilled, the first aid kit seemed like a given for him.

He unstrapped the knife holder on his ankle. Laid it down on the cement of the culvert, knife still inside.

"No!" Dorian's eyes were wide, the whites seeming to pop at him, as he looked up at her. "That's your only protection. You can't go down there, face off with who knows how many criminals might be down there, without any weapon at all. That's suicide. And...and...just plain not smart. If I do my job right, in the worst-case scenario that you don't get back to me, I won't need a weapon."

"You'll need to cut fruit. To eat and drink."

She shook her head again. "I'll use a rock. Lord knows my butt found enough sharp ones on the way down the hill."

The change in her tone of voice, the attempt at levity, the sense of control, had him staring at her. Hard.

He'd never not wanted to leave someone as badly as he didn't want to leave her.

And strongly disliked the idea of leaving her unarmed. If she got caught...

"Obviously, as a medical expert, I'm good with a knife," she said then, sounding almost as though she was teasing him. "But if it's me and either of the guys I've been up against in the past day, chances are good they'd be able to disarm me and use the knife against me. At least good enough that I don't want to take that chance."

"I trained you better than that." His words held more than was professional, too. Completely inappropriate and out of place.

As their gazes met, he wasn't sorry for the exchange.

"I need you to get back up here, Scott," she said then. "We know the men you're going down after are armed and prepared to kill. Please take the knife. Give yourself the best chance."

Because she was right, he picked up his knife. Strapped it back in place.

"I'm trained to kill with a single throw of the blade," he told her then. Thinking about her alone in the culvert in the dark, worrying.

She nodded. Came forward, as though to see him off.

He put up a hand to stop her, stepping forward, not wanting her even a little visible inside the hole where he was leaving her.

With her forward movement, his hand landed half on her breast. Her momentum continued, all happening in a split second, and Scott found himself keeping his hand over her heart as her arms came around him and held on.

"Stay safe," she told him, looking up at him. "And, Scott…for the past…" She covered his lips with her own.

Dorian lay on the floor of the culvert, allowing her to be safe, and to follow Scott's descent down the mountain with the burner phone's camera. Five minutes apart from him and she could still feel the warmth coursing through her from a kiss she'd owed him for fourteen years.

Finishing something she never should have started.

She'd meant to give him something to live for—not in an egotistical sense, just a positive, life-affirming pleasant activity. Or so she'd wanted to believe.

Maybe she just needed to know what kissing him full on felt like. In case she never got another chance to find out.

But as she lay on the ground, following his nearly indiscernible trek, she worried that she'd distracted him at the worst possible moment.

The most incredibly selfish thing she could have done.

Because she was Dorian Lowell—the woman who hurt others when she let her emotions rule her head.

Even for a split second.

The thought propelled another.

She had to see him again. To apologize.

Over the next bit, while she lay there on the warm, hard earth, her eyes adjusting to the darkness, Dorian made a deal with whatever fates might be willing to listen.

She asked for the babies' safety, first and foremost. And then, for mental guidance, for the clarity to know, not to feel, and the strength to act on the knowledge. And most importantly, she swore that she would work harder, do more, for the rest of her life, if she and Scott could have just one more minute together.

To make things right with a proper goodbye.

She couldn't lose him like she'd lost Sierra.

A spirit could only take so much.

Or so she reasoned.

She got no response.

Until…not quite an hour after Scott had left…she heard a very clear sound.

Gunfire.

Chapter 10

He was hit.

And he had no time to tend to the wound.

Surprised at how little the initial strike hurt, Scott stayed low, moving through the brush on the edge of a clearing behind the big building. Made it to his safe place. Feeling the warmth pooling on his thigh, midway to the knee, sticking his pants to his skin, he took note, and, reaching down in the cement confines of his storm drain, pulled his knife from its sheath.

He'd seen a dark shroud-covered figure with something in their arms, hurrying into the back of the building.

Ten o'clock sharp.

Had missed the lookout camouflaged as a totem pole in the dark.

There'd been no sound of an engine approaching. Or leaving.

No moving vehicles that he was aware of.

He'd been made.

At least as an unfriendly on the grounds.

Probably not as an FBI agent.

There was no reason for the killer to think that Scott, or Dorian, had had any idea about the mission, or that they'd found its location.

He'd know they had his cell phone, though. He'd have

figured that when he got back to the four-wheeler and found it gone.

At the moment, Scott had three choices. Continue forth, hoping that he could evade a single lookout long enough to avoid getting caught.

Head back up the mountain to Dorian.

Or give himself up for the purpose of taking down the enemy. And saving at least one newborn's life.

He hadn't seen an actual child, but the figure with the bundle…at the exact time that had been indicated…

No way that had been a coincidence.

And as long as he was alive, and able to move, Scott couldn't leave that baby at risk without giving his life to save it.

The choice was just that clear.

That simple.

And that hard.

He'd been training for just such a moment his entire life. Self-defense. Knife throwing. The army. Numbers of bodies weren't as important as finesse. Skills. Awareness.

And he had an advantage. He knew where they were. They had no idea he'd pushed himself feet first into a drainage pipe—had had it scoped out since he'd reached the clearing.

The pipe was there to divert water coming down the mountains after snow, or during a storm, from getting to the building. He'd seen several like them in the desert mountain communities surrounding Las Vegas.

At the moment, it was also serving as a decent pressure point to stem the flow of blood from his wound.

Three men, that he'd counted, had converged on the grounds after he'd been shot. All armed. One with a rifle, two with handguns.

There was no telling how many more were out there that he couldn't see.

Or who might be watching from a window in the building.

The drop-off was at ten.

Was there a pickup that night, too?

Unless the next drop-off, elsewhere, wasn't until morning? And the mission was a pit stop, much like a middleman, to throw law enforcement off the track?

That could mean Scott had all night to try to save that child.

Time to assess.

To plan.

To lull the killer and his kidnappers into a false sense of security.

Let them start to hope that they'd scared him off.

Or killed him.

Either way, it was best for him if they believed he was no longer their problem.

Scott had a lot of experience dealing with the lowlifes who preyed on others for personal gain. Guys like them would rather leave a body to the coyotes and other desert life that would consume it, than have any chance of evidence being found on their person.

Or in their immediate surroundings.

The smell of blood would attract desert prey.

His tight cement casing would diminish the scent.

And he had his knife poised in front of him, ready to slash anything that tried to reach in and get him.

Human or otherwise.

Unless he heard a vehicle approach, he had some time.

Would wait them out.

Maybe he'd get lucky and find out more about what he was up against.

He just had to hope that the damage to his leg was superficial enough that he didn't bleed to death.

Dorian was partway down the mountain before fear for her own life, as well as Scott's, started to kick in.

The emotion didn't slow her down.

She used it to her advantage. Let it heighten her senses. She stayed low. Kept her camera on Zoom at all times, surveying the entire perimeter before her.

She listened acutely.

And she fought back panic. She would not let her nerves prompt any mistakes. Or stop her from trying to save Scott's life.

There could be any number of reasons for someone to have fired a gun in a remote desert town. A coyote in the yard, for one. If there were farm animals down there, which she suspected based on some of the outbuildings, coyotes trying to get livestock at night was a real concern.

She'd seen a man killed early that morning.

While standing next to the same truck that was parked down below.

Scott didn't have a gun.

She might be his only chance.

To do what, she didn't know.

She was a doctor. She saved lives.

Who better to tend to a gunshot wound?

That part was all worked out.

The rest of it...finding Scott...getting to him without getting herself killed...those problems were left for the future.

She had to take one step at a time.

And the plan in mind was to get down to the clearing without being seen.

Period.

Nothing else mattered in her current timeframe.

She needed all senses tuned to the goal.

A slight breeze blew as she got closer to the valley, chilling the skin on her arms after a day of intense heat.

Dorian allowed that natural shiver. Disavowing any fright that could possibly be attached to it.

She was actually experiencing some positive feedback from her emotional cortex, an appropriately working limbic system. Until she saw shadows moving around the building Scott had scoped out as the place the killer had called the mission.

Men, she concluded, based on their heights and bone and muscle mass. Three of them. All armed.

She was going to get herself killed without helping a damned thing.

Which was exactly what Scott had been trying to avoid when he'd told her to stay put.

She had to figure a way to be of use. She'd die if she had to, but the death needed to accomplish something good.

The thought was strong. Pushing her to do more. Do better.

Sierra's death had led to the arrest of a killer who'd preyed on others before her. And to the end of an illegal gambling operation that had hurt hundreds, if not thousands of families.

She owed it to Sierra, to Brent's family, to her partners, even to her friend Faith who was happily engaged back in Phoenix, to learn from her failures—turn them into victories. To make the pain that they'd suffered because of her serve some good purpose.

To somehow make sure that Scott exposed his kidnapping ring, that no more babies were stolen and that those who had been taken were found.

Her whole life had prepared her for this second meeting with Scott Michaels.

She'd come full circle.

Keep an eye out for places to hide.

His words came back to her, as the various instructions he'd left her with had been repeating themselves in her mind ever since his departure.

She was afraid to use her phone that low down, particularly with men on the lookout. Worried that she might give off even a small moonlit reflection from the camera lens, she perused the area closest to her, and farther away, too. She couldn't make another move until she had a hiding place in mind.

Rock.

Bulletproof.

If Scott followed his own rules, and with her limited knowledge of him she thought he would, he'd have had a place scoped out.

Dare she hope he'd made it there?

Was he in hiding?

Frozen with knowledge, and no incoming revelations, Dorian lay supine in a mass of desert brush at the base of the mountain for several minutes.

Wasting time.

Wasting time!

Though her eyes had adjusted well to the dark, she couldn't find any rocks in her immediate vicinity large enough, or enough of an outcropping of them, to provide shelter. Hadn't seen any since she'd left the culvert.

Her heart thumped hard when she heard shouting down below. A male voice. Not close enough for any identifiers.

She couldn't make out the words.

Stared hard, looking for any sign of Scott. Of an injured body.

And blinked when a floodlight suddenly shone from close to the building directly east of her.

They were looking for someone!

Her?

Scott?

She wanted to hope he was who they were looking for. Meaning that Scott had escaped them? Would men be out patrolling if they already had their prey?

They knew she'd be able to identify the kidnapper. And the killer.

That she'd been with Scott.

They could have him, or have killed him, and be hunting her.

Or had those men over there merely heard the same gunshot she had and were out looking for the source?

The light was moving slowly over the complex surrounding the big building. Hovering near the brush farther east of her, not toward her—yet. She had time to find a better hiding place. A minute, maybe. Her blue scrubs would be a dead giveaway.

Could get her killed.

After taking them off, she lay on top of them, scooting herself into the brush. Feeling scratches on her skin.

Welcoming them as a sign that she was acting, not panicking. Doing. And through the bottom branches she peered out.

Her view much better from there, she followed the light as it traveled.

And found the hiding place as the beam traveled over it.

A cement drainage pipe.

Unless someone shot directly into the opening, or threw a bomb or something, a body inside would be fully protected.

Could Scott be in there? Dare she hope?

The beam of light seemed to hover for a second, but as she held her breath, the light moved on past. Straight toward her.

Burying her head, face down, with her arms over her hair, Dorian breathed in dirt.

And waited.

The woman had kissed him.

Why in the hell had she done that? Bringing an element to their association that had no good outcome.

Opening the can of worms they'd been managing to keep sealed tight.

Lying in his cement confines, trying to keep himself from likening his current habitat to the casket he'd very nearly been headed toward, Scott let his mind wander where it needed to stay alert.

He wasn't just thinking. He was listening. Watching.

He'd thought, half an hour before, that he was a goner as a searchlight had come at him, hovering, before moving on. He'd backed farther into the pipe before the light had hit. And had been ready ever since, knife in hand, to fight whoever came at him.

And he'd been thankful ever since that he'd left Dorian safely up in the culvert. And still hoped to get back to her before the three in the morning deadline he'd given her.

If nothing else, he had to make damned sure that she didn't climb down straight into the fire of armed guards. Even if it meant making himself an easy target to distract them.

At least they were in the open now. Had they been patrolling as they currently were as he'd drawn closer to the settlement, he'd never have approached.

Were the guards there on his account?

Why had the light passed so long after he'd been shot at?

Maybe they weren't there for him at all.

The floodlight had been a clear check of the perimeter. Making certain that all was well before someone else arrived?

Was a baby switch going to be happening soon?

Was he being too conservative, waiting as he was?

No way he was going to just lie there, keeping himself safe, if a baby was about to be passed over to a new handler and taken away to a location he might never find.

He couldn't be so close and fail that newborn child.

The bleeding had stopped on his leg. At least with the pressure on it.

He'd pulled the shirt pack off his shoulder when he'd settled into the culvert. Had been using it as a cushion for his head much of the time.

Grabbing it up, he bit into the fabric along the bottom edge and tore it. Then, bumping his elbows against the inner wall of his very temporary housing, he ripped the strip along the entire length of the shirt.

Holding it, he slowly pulled his leg away from where he'd been pressing it against the cement. Winced as pain shot so sharply up to his groin and down to his foot that he almost cried out. And with a deep breath, looped the strip of shirt under his leg with the one arm that could reach. He wrapped it around, and pulled one end up to his other hand. From there, he held on, gritted his teeth and tied.

Tight.

Tighter than he'd thought he'd be able to take.

The fabric would loosen some as he walked.

Giving himself no more time for feeling the pain, he used his feet to push his body forward, to the end of the drainpipe, and slowly, watching everywhere he could see, he put his head outside into the warm night air.

The three guards were still in the yard.

Talking to each other.

Planning an attack? Had they seen him?

One laughed.

Another lit up a smoke.

And Scott belly crawled his way out of his cement holding cell, rolling slowly down a slight incline away from the building and the men supposedly guarding it.

His leg throbbed and stung, but he wouldn't let the bullet wound slow him down.

He couldn't.

Lives were depending on him.

He couldn't let Dorian's last touch be a kiss goodbye.

Chapter 11

Maybe it was overkill, but Dorian didn't put her clothes back on until she'd dampened them with cactus juice and then rubbed them in desert dirt and growth. Multiple times. The filth went against every grain of decency she had.

In a profession where she washed her hands and arms for long periods of time multiple times a day, she was loath to even touch the slightly camouflaged material, let alone dress her body with it. But dirt was better than death.

She couldn't let light blue apparel be a walking warning to bad guys in the dark.

Not that she walked toward her goal.

When her camera picked up a lit cigarette in the mouth of a gunman, while those she'd seen earlier were clustered together, she decided she'd just been given her best chance to move. Belly crawling, she rubbed her elbows raw, heading toward the cement drainpipe mostly buried beneath ground. Occasionally, when she had enough cover to allow the faster progress, she raised up to travel on hands and knees. With every single move she made, she was looking out for pools of fresh blood, for tamped-down brush or earth from recent occupation. For any sign of Scott at all.

She'd reached the back side of the drainage ditch. Glanced inside.

And froze.

Scott wasn't there. And she prayed to God he hadn't been.

A line of what looked like fresh blood streaked from the opening into the darkness.

Meaning that if Scott had been there, he was no more. Had he been in the pipe when he'd been shot?

And hauled out to God only knew where?

Cursing the darkness that shrouded much of the ground around her, she looked for more blood. To no avail.

But just because she couldn't see any, didn't mean it wasn't there.

If that streak was blood at all, she reminded herself, with a calming, steady, professional breath.

And if it was, it might not be human. The reminder piled on top of the previous one.

Giving herself a second to get out of the limbic system and into the cerebrum, she focused not on what had been, but on what she would do next.

She had to go with worst-case scenario. Scott could be incapacitated. Either from a hit, or capture.

Which meant she was on her own.

Did she do as he'd suggested, wait until early morning, and head toward blacktop? Save herself?

Or did she try to save a baby that had possibly been delivered on schedule at ten o'clock? Right about the time that she'd heard shots being fired.

Chances were good that Scott had been taken out. The timing...

Meant nothing, for the moment. If there was a baby, if, if, if...

Scott believed that he'd stumbled upon a link in a baby theft chain. Could she just slink away without at least trying to collect further evidence?

Without trying to find him?

If he was alive, and in need of medical attention…

If there was a kidnapped newborn within her reach…

The question wasn't whether she saved herself or not. It was how she was going to be of service in her current situation.

Doing what she could to find Scott.

And, if she couldn't save the baby, then at least she could gather information and stay alive long enough to deliver it to the authorities.

She had a phone with a camera.

Needed daylight to snap a picture without risking immediate detection.

What would Scott do?

The question came. Followed by an immediate answer. He'd stay low. Keep himself covered. And get closer.

Easier thought than done. But Dorian didn't let herself consider the difficulties in her path, except to find ways to counteract them as best she could.

Moving slowly in the darkness, she searched for her next hiding place. Someplace closer to the building. No lights shone from within it that she could see.

Did that mean the place was unoccupied? That no baby had been delivered?

They could have the wrong building. The wrong settlement.

The *mission* could have been a code word for anything.

But the black truck. She'd seen it.

The killer, who'd been higher up in the chain than the kidnapper he'd shot point-blank, had been at the building earlier that evening.

Or at least his truck—something associated with him—had been.

And it hit her.

The truck had been parked beside a trash bin. A large one, with a wooden closure built around it.

To keep wildlife out, she assumed.

The door to the closure had been ajar in the photo.

Could it still be open?

And could she get inside?

Both the truck and the trash bin had been on the opposite side of the building from the mountain.

Which meant that she could get to them without passing the armed men clustered together in the yard.

Almost as though they were waiting on something. Rather than patrolling as she'd originally thought.

If she could get to the trash enclosure, and just huddle, she might see another vehicle arrive. Be able, from within the shelter, to get a photo. Maybe even of a license plate.

Thoughts solidified, Dorian crawled, on her belly and her hands and knees. She listened intently, still watching the ground for any sign that Scott might have been there before her.

Parts of her journey took her out of sight of the men in the yard, but as soon as they came back into view, she froze until she could make sure there'd been no obvious change in their positions. Still three of them. One still smoking.

As she drew closer, she heard the soft rumble of their voices.

And changed course. A bed of bougainvillea plants covered almost one whole side of the building. Their flowering growth was thick, completely covering the stucco structure they grew against, and reached six feet tall. They were closer than the trash bin. And would be covered in thorns.

No place anyone would think to look for a lurker.

Approaching the building from the back, she was up on

her feet for the thirty seconds it took her to reach the cement base of the mission—if that's what it was—and dive for the ground. She'd risked motion detector lights but hadn't seen any telltale metal hoods anywhere.

Out in the desert as they were, motion lights would be on almost constantly during the night as wildlife hunted and wandered freely.

Taking just a second to catch her breath, to remain motionless while she listened for any fallout from her action, Dorian belly crawled at top speed to the corner of the building, and then around it, to slide under the hearty plants.

She felt the scrapes of thorns on her forearms. Her face. But pressed forward. Stopping only when she reached the far end of their growth. On the opposite corner of the structure.

The men had moved closer to the mission. Were just feet away.

If they saw her, she was dead.

Lowering her face to the ground, she let her hair fall around her, concealing skin, and took a minute to catch her breath.

She had to reverse course. Belly crawl backward.

But she didn't dare move lest she make a sound, alerting them to her presence.

Heard someone telling an off-color joke. Followed by laughter.

Which broke off midstream.

What were they doing? Heading toward her?

She couldn't move to get a look.

But if she didn't...was there already a gun pointed at her?

"Looks like the mission has changed."

She knew that voice!

Oh, God, she knew that voice.

It didn't sound closer. If anything, it sounded farther away. Someone just approaching?

"We popped a coyote," the joke-telling voice said. "No reason to call a halt..."

"Straight from the general," the killer's voice cut off the other man.

"You all clear out first. Now. I'll follow with Zellow and the merchandise. Head to plan B..."

The voices faded, as Dorian's heart rate grew louder. Pounding through her head.

They popped a coyote?

Did that mean Scott was okay?

And nearby?

What would he want her to do?

How could she help?

By not distracting him.

He'd needed to know she was safely up in the culvert so that he could do his job.

He'd want her to just stay put. To wait until the killer's truck headed out so she'd be safe.

And just let the baby be taken to plan B?

If Scott wasn't close enough to hear what she'd just heard, he'd have no way of knowing what was going down.

An engine fired up in the distance, the sound growing dimmer.

The three heading out first?

Or had they left on foot? Hiking back to transportation hidden farther up the road, too far for her to have heard?

How in the hell did she know?

Wait...was that...?

Yes, the newborn's whimper was unmistakable. Most particularly as it grew more strident.

Suddenly, it didn't matter what she knew, or didn't know.

Scrambling out from the sharp branches covering her, Dorian saw a shrouded figure holding a bundle.

Then, filled with horror, she noticed the killer standing beside his truck, gun pointing straight at Scott Michaels.

"Who are you?" The killer, gun aimed at Scott's head, bit out the question, loud enough to be heard over the baby's wail. The hunched, shrouded figure at his side didn't move. Doing nothing to attempt to quiet the clearly distressed newborn.

Scott was at death's door. He understood that.

But the killer needed something from him.

Needed to know who he was.

Was he someone who'd just stumbled onto the murder of a kidnapper, and interrupted the killing of his victim?

How had he come to be where he was when that had gone down?

Had he talked to anyone?

Killing Scott was not about one baby. One deal.

It was about saving an organization that was lining pockets far and wide.

Scott had to find a way of taking down two criminals at once—one whose shroud, denied Scott the chance to see what he was up against—and save that newborn's life.

On a leg weakened by pain and blood loss.

Knife ready, and with a silent, "Now," he lunged.

The gun went off, sending a bullet whizzing closely by Scott's right ear as his knife slid into flesh.

A shriek sounded right next to the killer...the shrouded man...was a woman.

Scott's arm withdrew in a flash as the bigger body fell too close for comfort, and in the next instant, he dove for the waist of the shrouded body, hoping to protect the bundle as he flew flesh into flesh.

He had the second shrouded body on the ground, saw the bundle roll from an arm to the ground, and, too late, saw the second gun pointed at his head.

And realized that he was lying on top of a man, not a woman. One who was going to kill him.

"No!" He recognized the female voice that came out of the darkness. Didn't compute it. But wasn't as surprised as he might have been when a soft-soled shoe landed on the throat directly in line with Scott's vision.

The gun at his head fell to the ground, as the hand holding it went limp.

By the time Scott was on his feet, Dorian had the baby in hand, was unwrapping the blanket enough to survey the tiny body.

She'd barely met his gaze, with a tense nod, when he heard the sound of an engine. Dorian's gaze shot to the road in tandem with his, and then, her eyes wide, filled with too much emotion, she said, "Someone's coming."

Headlights in the distance obscured the one lane road from view.

Scott grabbed a key ring from the killer's pocket and took Dorian's elbow. "Come on," he said, leading her toward the building. After unlocking the door, he ran the key ring back out, snatched his knife out of the killer's left side and followed Dorian inside, closing and locking the door behind him.

She came out of a doorway as soon as he entered, her finger in the quiet baby's mouth. "Find an attic, a cellar, anyplace we can hide," he told her.

She nodded toward her knuckle. "This isn't going to keep the little one quiet for long." She'd given Scott a long look, first. Had gone pale at the sight of the piece of shirt tied around his leg.

He glanced out a front window. The vehicle was getting closer. Only one, so far.

They didn't have long.

And she was right. Hiding wasn't a viable option.

He couldn't get back up to that culvert as quickly as Dorian could. He'd have to get her out of the vicinity and headed back up to safety.

While he deflected.

"There's a back door," he told her. "I'm right behind you. Head straight for the culvert."

For a split second, Dorian looked as though she might argue, but when a whimper sounded from the baby, she gave Scott one last emotional look and ran down the hall.

Chapter 12

With the baby in both arms, held to her chest, Dorian ran as fast and far as she could, keeping a watch on the approaching headlights.

And when they drew close enough for someone to get even a glimpse of her, she dropped to the ground. She unwrapped the baby long enough to fashion a sling out of the blanket, secure the baby inside and tie it around her, talking softy, lovingly, to the newborn as she did so.

It wasn't a mother's voice he might recognize after nine months hearing it through the womb. But it was better than no voice at all.

Scott wasn't right behind.

She'd known when she'd left that he wouldn't be.

But she prayed that he'd make it back to them.

There'd been a lot of blood around the swatch of material around his thigh.

She couldn't think about that at the moment.

With the baby tied to her chest, Dorian dropped to all fours and began her climb, staying hidden in the brush. Watching all around her for signs of wildlife that might think she was breakfast. The best defense from them was to make noise. To call out in a mean voice.

Neither of which she could do.

Pausing to fill both pockets of her scrub pants with handfuls of rocks—a spray she could throw if need be—she continued upward.

Not looking back.

She couldn't.

If she saw Scott in trouble, or anything that led her to believe he was…she'd slow her own progress.

And worsen the baby's chances of escaping further horror.

But she couldn't help listening.

For any approaching danger, yes. But without that distraction, she was left with a silence that could, at any moment, be filled with gunfire.

"We'll be there soon," she told the little one in her care. Whether by the grace of God, or the swaddling against her chest and swaying motion of movement, the baby was quiet. Breathing evenly.

She assumed, asleep.

Forty-five minutes after she'd last seen Scott, she was crawling into the culvert. Her hands and knees were bloody. She suspected her elbows were, too.

She was thirsty. And knew the baby would need sustenance.

They were safe for the moment.

Not facing madmen with guns.

But they had a long way to go before they made it out of danger alive.

She took off her shoes, used them as the base of a cradle, set side by side, more than a baby's length apart. And as she gathered twigs and branches long enough to fit over them, and then brush to top them with, she felt the prick of tears in her eyes.

Blinked them away.

Several times.

And finally, was able to untie the sling from around her, lay the still-sleeping baby in the makeshift bed and cover the newborn with the blanket.

From there, she allowed herself one glance, through the phone camera, down to the compound below.

And saw nothing but stillness.

Darkness.

The sun wouldn't be rising for another couple of hours yet.

Desperation rose up, pushing at her from the inside out, and Dorian stomped her stockinged foot. Self-pity weakened her.

Made her less effective.

She ventured a little farther down a ridge to find a prickly pear cactus and slammed a rock onto the lowest pad, breaking it off. Back at the culvert, she used another, sharper stone to cut through the skin.

She sucked the first piece of fruit that filled her fingers and she grabbed and pulled.

Ate the second one.

By that time, she was watching, almost constantly, the mountainside leading up from the buildings below.

Made herself focus on useful activity.

She could feed the baby from the water bottle—had long ago learned how to feed a baby without a teat or nipple available. On more than one occasion, she'd referred new mothers to a national website that gave step-by-step instructions with pictures.

Not all babies were able to suck.

And while she squeezed juice to fill the bottle, she thought about the rest of the digestion process. The juice could likely cause more stool. Looser stool.

She needed diapers.

Figured she could rip off the bottoms of her scrubs and fashion something that she could tie around the baby's bottom.

Children had been born and raised long before disposable diapers were invented.

Before stores were around to provide cloth ones.

And…one step at a time…she was doing it.

Doing—not giving in to the fright and despair hovering at her edges.

But her hands were less steady. Her head starting to hurt.

As she grew more and more desperate to know that Scott Michaels was okay.

And that he was coming for them.

Scott's head was spinning—with information, a need to reach his colleagues, and, he suspected, a need for rest and sustenance after his loss of blood—as he made the last turn in his climb up the mountain.

The short, ten-minute walk took him half an hour. That included a five-minute stop to cut food and drink for himself and then consume it.

As the adrenaline seeped out of him, he was finding himself only capable of doing one thing at time.

Half dragging his leg, as well as the bag he'd filled to bring up with him, he came over the crest that made him visible to the occupants of the culvert. And they to him.

Dawn would be breaking soon.

Another day during which he needed to accomplish so much.

Miracles.

A day for which he currently had no plan.

Get to the cave.

Period.

His thoughts ended there.

"Scott!" He heard Dorian's voice before he saw her burst from the culvert, no baby in hand.

His thoughts cleared. As did his vision.

"What happened?" he asked, as energy started slowly to surge through him. "Where's the baby?"

"He's asleep," she said.

"He?"

"I changed his diaper. And fed him."

She sounded...different. Surreal. And...different.

A note to her voice he didn't recognize.

"Come on—let's get you in here and let me get a look at that leg," she said then, as though she'd woken from a twelve-hour power nap. As far as he could calculate, she hadn't had more than an hour in the culvert.

She stood there, seeming to almost burst with a need to move, but didn't move away from the opening of the space to let him in.

Instead, she smiled at him. Touched his face.

If he wasn't so out of it, he wouldn't have thought there were tears in her eyes. But he was. So he did.

"You made it back."

He didn't miss the whispered words, sounding to his haywired brain as more of a prayer than a statement.

And then, "What's that?" as he dropped the strap of the satchel he'd confiscated, among many other things he'd taken that he knew were important, but didn't care much about at the moment.

He swayed.

Knew he had to lie down.

And was pretty sure that when he did, the good doctor knelt down beside him and kissed his lips...

* * *

Dreams of Dorian…a younger Dorian…kissing him faded as Scott drifted into consciousness. He had no idea of how much time had passed. Where he was.

He started cataloging sensations even before he opened his eyes.

Hard ground.

Weight against him.

Leg throbbing.

He was alive.

Dorian!

He lay frozen, not wanting to alert anyone that he was awake. Not wanting to move in case the enemy didn't know he was there.

Had he made it to the culvert?

He'd been on his way.

Had stopped to eat.

Had been hurting. Badly. And feeling light-headed…

His lids shot open. Rock faced him from above. To the left, more rock.

And to the right…

Dorian?

Her eyes closed as her head rested on his shoulder, facing him.

So, he was still asleep then.

Still dreaming.

Except that…his leg was throbbing.

As was the arm on which the doctor lay.

And…there it was again…a whimper.

The sound that had awoken him.

The baby!

He'd made it back to Dorian!

He drew in air. Deeply. Held it there. Savoring.

He'd made it back to the culvert.

And Dorian and the baby were there.

The whimper came again and the weight against the right side of his body disappeared in a flash. Scott closed his eyes, needing a moment.

Dorian had lain with him?

Slept with her head on his shoulder?

Had anything else happened that he needed to know about?

Anything he'd done?

Didn't seem possible.

Not with the struggle he'd been having just to put one foot in front of the other before he'd lost consciousness.

He'd made it back.

The last thing he'd asked of himself.

And there was so much more to do.

Sitting up slowly, he expected dizziness. Had none.

Saw that his head had been lying on a pillow of leaves.

And that his body had been so cushioned as well.

Had he fallen on them?

Shaking his head, he turned around, looking farther into the culvert, and saw Dorian, with the baby in her arms, holding the water bottle to his lips.

His.

Had he dreamed she'd told him the baby was a boy?

Dorian wasn't looking at the baby.

She was staring at him.

Getting his bearings seemed pertinent. "What time is it?"

"Eleven."

Light flooded the culvert.

Eleven in the morning?

He'd slept for five or six hours?

And she'd slept with him.

At least for part of the time.

Pulling his legs up, he meant to stand—to head outside and take care of necessary business. Felt the pull on his lower thigh and saw the bare skin down to his ankle.

The bandage.

Glanced back at Dorian.

"I figured, since I had no anesthetic, the best time to take care of it was when you were passed out."

He shook his head. Felt a smile coming on for no good reason and held it back.

"You took care of it." Statement. Not question.

His mind calculated that it could only have been a little more than twelve hours since he'd told her he saw a vehicle in the compound.

It had turned out to be the killer's black truck.

Chuck McKellips, he now knew.

Right.

He knew a lot.

Details from the night before flooded down on him, and Scott stood up. Feeling ridiculously naked in his pants with one leg cut off.

"Where's the bag I brought?"

She nodded toward the leaves his head had been lying on. The satchel had been used as the base for the pillow.

As he glanced down, his eye caught an image off to the left, behind where he'd been lying. Back by a make-shift cradle.

Spread out, like medical tools on a tray ready for surgery, were all the items he'd retrieved from the mission before he'd headed back up the hill.

Grabbing the jeans and shirt that were going to be too large for him, he headed outside without another word.

Chapter 13

Scott was dressed in jeans that had to be rolled up at the cuffs and belted at the waist when he returned. Dorian, who'd finished feeding the baby and was waiting for her own turn outside, couldn't seem to stop looking at the man.

They were on the edge of a danger she'd never dreamed of—not even with all the tough spots her partners had been in over the years, with her own kidnapping the year before. She was facing down an organization that had power and money far beyond what she had expected.

Ripping apart untold lives as they walked in shadows, stealing newborns from their families.

She and Scott were two normal human beings without special powers against the evilest of powers.

A trapped duo.

One of them was injured.

And the other was caring for a baby.

"You found the clothes I brought you," he said, nodding toward the dark beige elastic-waisted pants and pullover top she'd donned after feeding the baby from the ready-made and still sealed formula bottles he'd had in that satchel. Along with a stash of tiny disposable diapers.

She stared at him, trying to rid herself of the woman who'd given in to temptation and lain down with her head on this unconscious man's chest and had actually slept. Dorian nodded and walked out.

Keeping low, noticing no activity down below at all, and seeing no vehicles, she quickly took care of business and headed straight back to the culvert.

Scott had wanted her on the paved road by dawn.

But with the quiet below, they should be able to head out. Get the baby to safety. And hopefully prevent yet another kidnapping at some other, as yet unknown birthing center.

At the very least, birthing centers across the Southwest, and probably beyond, needed to be notified to beef up security, keep outside doors locked. Not allow anyone but immediate family inside only if their name was on a pre-arranged list and they showed ID.

The doctor in her was in full gear.

Couldn't be said for any of the rest of her.

Scott was sitting in the back of the culvert, right next to the sleeping baby, phone in hand, when she dipped into the cave.

"I need to check the wound," she told him. "You didn't happen to save the cutoff pants, did you, so you can stay covered up?"

Asinine. Completely ridiculous. She was a doctor. Saw nudity all the time.

Growing hot, she forced herself to look at him, knowing that she'd just given herself away.

She couldn't look at his nudity and promise to remain professional.

Where he was concerned, she'd been compromised.

"I did," he told her. "But only because I didn't want to leave them out where anyone could find them. When we leave here, we need to get rid of any sign of our habitation, while leaving enough debris scattered around to make it look as though no one has been here."

Okay, good. He was on track.

She reached for the first aid kit and medical supplies he'd brought back with him. Didn't ask questions, expecting him to head out and change.

Instead, he stood, unbuckled his belt, unhooked and unzipped the fly and let his pants drop.

Everything in her froze.

Heated up quick.

And she saw the shirt that more than covered his groin area.

Taking a deep breath, refusing to let herself panic over behavior so unlike her, she focused on what she did know.

"I specialized in children's medicine," she told him. "But knowing we were forming the firm, I also certified in several other specialties and do regular rotations with top doctors from all forms of medicine specialties, which is what allows me to keep expert status in the field..."

She was rambling. But it was working. Putting mental space between them. Allowing her to focus on the torn skin she'd managed to repair and, most importantly cleanse, very early that morning, sealing it with butterfly straps.

"How deep is the bullet?" He remained standing. She didn't suggest otherwise. If there'd been fresh blood, that would have been different.

"I got it out," she told him. "It was a flesh wound. Just nicked the muscle. It needs stitches, inside and surface, to heal without scarring, but the butterflies are sealing the wound tight enough to keep infection out. There's no oozing."

She'd prefer that he be on antibiotics. And stay off the leg as much as possible. The salve she'd found in the supplies had been enough for the moment.

Hopefully they'd get lucky.

She bandaged his wound securely, but as sparingly as she could, needing to reserve supplies in the case of infection, or reinjury.

Both of which were highly possible with the hiking they had ahead of them.

She busied herself with putting away the supplies as Scott pulled his pants up. Checked on the baby, who'd eaten well, twice, and was sleeping soundly.

"His mother's milk will be coming in," she said then, getting emotional when she shouldn't be, as she assessed the even breathing. A distraught new mother, mourning her missing baby, fearing for him, desperate to find him, didn't need to be dealing with breasts aching for a baby to feed.

She cared about her patients. Felt empathy for them.

But it didn't ever get personal.

"Come, sit." Scott patted the pallet she'd made for him to lie on. And then had shared with him.

For a second, she thought he meant to talk about that. To talk about them.

As if there was a them.

He'd woken up with her head on his chest.

And she had no good or professional explanation to give him.

She went forward anyway. Took the seat he'd proffered.

Awkward or not, painful as it could be, she had to own up to her actions.

They needed the air between them as clear as it could be if they were going to be a successful team.

He'd pulled out his phone. Turned it on. The first thing she checked was battery level. It was crucial that they have enough to make one call when they were within service.

His battery was almost full.

And it hit her.

He'd come back for her and the baby. Not because they were still on the run.

The supplies...the battery...

But his leg...

"We can't stay here," he said before she could find words to articulate pertinent thoughts within the flying and wayward ones inserting themselves into her head. "But before we go, you need to know everything I know. In case you have to leave me behind."

Her gaze shot to his face.

His gaze was glued firmly on his phone.

"The vehicle you saw last night was one of the guards we'd seen earlier, coming back to find out why McKellips didn't show up at plan B."

She studied his face, because what she was currently seeing on the phone screen that seemed to be mesmerizing him was just a bunch of groupings of letters, symbols and numbers that meant nothing to her. "McKellips?"

"Chuck McKellips is the man who killed your kidnapper."

"The man you knifed."

"I hit purposefully. Enough to disable him long enough for us to get away, but not hit any major organs."

She'd figured that much out when she'd seen the knife hit.

Just as she'd applied expert pressure to knock out the man who'd had the baby, but not to kill him.

When Scott hadn't come right behind her back up the mountain, she'd feared the unknown baby carrier had gotten him. "I thought I got you killed by not telling you that the second guy wouldn't be out all that long."

He shook his head. "It's not my first rodeo, Doc." There

was a hint of teasing in his tone, and he finally looked straight at her. Meeting her gaze.

She wasn't sure what he was telling her. Knew that she had so many things to say that she didn't want him to know.

Scott looked away first. And she felt like a failure for not having had enough of her own common sense about her to have already done so.

"They spread out to find us, two outside, one in. I managed to knock out the one inside, drag him out the back, leave him on a trail heading to the road and get back inside before the other two got back. Praying the entire time that they hadn't found you."

"I was on my belly," she told him. "Climbing straight up here." Because…it seemed appropriate, letting him know that he could rely on her to make smart choices. As long as they didn't involve her body close to his, apparently.

"I was hiding when McKellips came inside, and when he didn't find his underling there, he ran back out looking for him. He found him, and then took off up the road…"

As Scott had obviously planned. The man was good at reading his enemy. And playing him.

"I heard McKellips talking to the other guy outside a while later. They got the guy I konked into one of the vehicles and were both heading out."

"Did they say where they were going?"

Scott glanced her way again. His eyes weren't telling her anything she didn't understand. They were filled with warning.

"What?"

"They were going to find another baby to fill the order. It was due this morning at nine. At a place they call the grocery."

Mouth open, she stared at him. Wanting to grab up the

little one behind her and run as far and as fast as she could. "A store?"

Scott shook his head. "My guess is it's some kind of private residence." And then he added, "They don't know who I am. They think I'm some lowlife who was hanging around Duane's place..."

"Duane?"

Those blue eyes met hers again. Almost as though they were holding her somehow. "I'm assuming he was your kidnapper."

"They think you're a friend of his?"

"They suspect I was. Trying to get in on the cut. But Duane didn't know the drop-off points. He doesn't know anything. He was just some guy McKellips knew in the past and recruited to do a few kidnappings."

"They figure me for having the baby, thinking I'm going to hold it over them, at least get some money out of it. They're writing that one off. And you, too. They think you're as good as dead. That now that I have the kid, I'll get rid of you."

He was watching her the entire time he talked. She didn't blink. Just kept holding on to him eye to eye and listening.

"They're alerting the squadron, whoever the hell that is, and everyone will know by now that if either of us are seen, we're to be shot on the spot. They can't let the general get wind of the mess Duane made of things. And they can't risk losing the mission as a cog in the wheel. If it goes, so does their team. And the money's more than any of them will ever see again in their lifetimes."

Sick to her stomach, she still held his gaze. And nodded. "That much."

Sucking in his lips, he turned back to the phone.

"Not knowing who the squadron is makes our task much more difficult." She put the obvious on the table.

"I have reason to believe there might be law enforcement involved." He dropped the words quietly, staring at his phone again.

"Or that there could be," he corrected himself. "I heard McKellips refer to someone by a series of numerals. Sounded like a police badge number to me. A small operation out of a municipality not far from Globe. I worked with them once, a few years ago. Recognized the numbers."

The man was smart. Focused.

Things she currently felt lacking in herself.

She proved as much by asking, "I'm assuming there's no service in the valley?"

He shook his head. "I found an office in the building… the place looked like some community center from fifty years ago, mostly decrepit and filthy, but there was an office in the back. Powered by a generator. After the two left to kidnap another newborn, I put my phone on a charger lying on the desk and went through the place."

"The supplies…"

He nodded. "There was a closet with baby stuff. I grabbed what would fit. Our clothes were in plastic, shoved in a bottom drawer of an old dresser in a small janitor-type room. I'm pretty sure these guys didn't even know they were there…"

"They'll miss the power bars. The baby stuff…"

He shrugged. "They'll know I circled back, is all. What's going to piss them off the most are these…"

Pulling his gun from his holster, he opened it, showing her fresh rounds. "Some not so bright person left them in the back of the bottom desk drawer."

He'd used his knife to pick the lock.

"I've got a box of them," he told her. "They wouldn't fit in the satchel. I hid them just outside the culvert." He glanced at the wall as that slipped out.

Because she'd gone through his satchel. Knew what hadn't been in it.

And she frowned. "Why did you do that?"

He shook his head.

"Scott?"

His silence didn't fit the hours they had ahead of them. "We can't do this without complete truth. And trust." She told him what she'd already decided for herself if he asked about that head of hers on his shoulder.

Or the kiss which she'd given him when he left the night before.

"I was...not doing all that great," he told her. "I fell. The box slid a couple of feet. I somehow thought it was the bullets or me getting back to you and I chose me."

Oh.

Oh! Her heart leaped.

And she said, "Do you remember where they are?"

"Yep. Already found them." Lifting his pant legs, he showed her a pair of socks stuffed full of bullets. "I'm not going to be unarmed again."

She wanted to argue. To talk about his wound and the extra weight.

Didn't trust herself to get it right.

And Scott, who'd turned back to his phone, didn't seem open to anything she had to say on the matter.

They were just going to have to trust each other with some things left unsaid.

Chapter 14

Scott didn't admit to weakness. Ever. Just wasn't his MO.

Instead, he worked through it. Took care of what ailed him on his own and moved forward.

So what in the hell was he doing, giving Dorian even a hint of the hell he remembered as his last moments before unconsciousness the night before?

Scrolling with his thumb on his phone screen, he came up with an answer he could live with. Accuracy not confirmed.

She was his doctor, tending to the bullet wound he'd received in battle. She'd need to know details in order to diagnose him, in the event of possible complications.

And to that end, she was also his partner over the next hours. There were things she had to know.

Landing on the screenshot he needed first, he handed her his phone.

She took it. Gave a cursory glance at the sequences of letters, numbers and symbols and shook her head. "What is this?"

"Those are confirmation of previous kidnappings and deliveries of babies for illegal adoptions." He swallowed. "I know this because of a site I found on the dark web several months ago. Your Hudson was going to work on it the night you were kidnapped. Those markings are code for dates and times."

"I'm guessing the yin yang symbol means the deal was executed successfully?"

He nodded. And then, weighted with the same gravity that had hit him the night before, he pointed to the four different intricate symbols that separated date and time in every single line.

"Are you familiar with those?"

She nodded. "Ancient Chinese, right? Guardians of the directions?"

He nodded. "Dragon means east. Bird south. Tiger west. Turtle north."

"North is actually the Black Tortoise…" She stopped. Handed back his phone. "They've got at least four drop-off locations," she said then. "This place—" she nodded downward "—is only one of them."

"And we don't know if it's north, as in Northern Arizona, or west as in Western United States…"

"Could be south, because it's down in the valley…"

Once again, she was on track with him. "Exactly."

"We have no idea what kind of scope this organization spans…"

He nodded.

"Did you find anything on the general?"

He shook his head. "But it's clear that McKellips, who is one tough dude, is intimidated by him."

He felt her shiver. Struggled to resist the urge to put an arm around her. Pull her close to his warmth. Even if only to give her enough false assurance for a moment of respite.

Which made no sense.

He wasn't a coddler.

And she wouldn't appreciate being coddled.

After effects from the gunshot wasn't quite out of his system yet, apparently.

He still hadn't shaken the initial rush of pleasure he'd had, waking up with her head on his chest. And he damned well didn't have the wherewithal to deal with that.

He got it. She'd been exhausted. Had taken care of the baby, of him. Built a cradle, a pallet for him—all in the dark. Building a second pallet would have taken energy she couldn't afford to expel. And she'd only had one satchel to use for a pillow.

For all he knew, she'd lain her head there to keep track of his heartbeat and exhaustion had just overcome her.

It all made sense. Except the way he couldn't get past waking up with her there.

Dorian stood, almost as though she could sense his growing desire for her, his awareness of her at the very least. Went back to check on the baby.

Giving him a breather.

That didn't last long enough.

She was back, sitting beside him on the pallet. Handing him a power bar. Unwrapping one of her own.

"We're going to need every ounce of energy we can muster," she said then, as though she had a plan in mind for them to head into.

"The minute we step outside this culvert, we're hunted targets," he told her. He'd sworn to himself that he'd get her safely home.

He couldn't change the facts.

"Sounds like we're hunted no matter where we are."

Yep. She got the full picture. He'd known she would.

Finished his bar in less than a minute, and rose. "You ready?"

"Yeah." Her lips said one thing. The stark look in those brown eyes gave another reply.

"We have to head to the road," he told her. "Our chances of making it back over the mountain, and then down without being caught, are slim. McKellips clearly knows that side of the range. My guess is that he either lives there, or has a place in the area, at the very least. He'll probably have traps set…"

"We have to head to the road because with your leg, and a baby, our chances of making it back the way we came are lower."

His leg wasn't a consideration. He'd make it, either way. But the baby…with cries echoing through a canyon…

"We need to stay up high as much as possible, keep distance between us and anyone on the ground hunting and stay low in the brush, behind trees, at least until dark."

She nodded. Was already packing things back into the satchel, while he dismantled their pallet. Leaving some pieces strewn about, spreading others around the area outside the culvert.

"We have to stay out of sight of anyone who could be in the other buildings we saw scattered about the settlement area," he told her as he returned inside to see her zipping the bag. He was stating the obvious. Thinking out loud.

Needing to make certain they were completely united on what lay ahead.

Their lives, the baby's life, depended on them being so.

He glanced over at her. "But it stands to reason, with a road leading to blacktop, there could be other homesteads farther down."

"Our side of the mountain has them," Dorian offered. "Just randomly scattered…people wanting to live off the grid." She reached down, he expected for the baby, saw her take up the blanket instead.

Watched as she fashioned a sling, tied it around herself.

"Can you come here?" she asked then, and he wanted to hold back.

Him and Dorian...with a baby...saving it was one thing... the idea of returning him to his parents, a given.

But...

She was waiting. Ducking as the top of the culvert lowered the farther back he went, Scott ended up kneeling beside the woman.

"We need him freshly changed and fed," she said then. "He's going to cry when I wake and change him unless you can distract him with his bottle."

She handed the small container—one of the dozen he'd found—to him.

And he...

Didn't take it.

"I've, uh, never fed a...baby."

Dorian's hands froze, suspended above the infant, as she looked over at her companion.

And saw an expression of complete blankness on his face.

Something so simple, and he—the instructor, the soldier, the FBI agent in charge—was afraid to take a bottle?

Had no idea what to do? Not even enough to bluff his way through?

He had to take it on. They had no choice. And no time for a tender family moment.

"What if I wasn't here?" she challenged him. "You wouldn't just let this little one starve to death."

She could very well not be there by the next feeding.

He'd had the wherewithal to grab the formula and the diapers.

"You want to do the diaper change or the feeding?"

He took the bottle.

And when she nodded, nudged it toward the baby's lips. The little guy suckled, Scott's big hand suspended above that tiny mouth. Dorian's fingers shook a little as she got the summer weight sleeper down over the tiny, sporadically moving limbs.

She and Scott…the baby…her heart was reaching.

She couldn't let it.

Focused her mind on fluid-ounce consumption, keeping track of feeding times, noting the amount of urine in the diaper. The lack of solid waste. Got the job done.

And then almost wept when she glanced over and caught the expression on Scott Michaels's face. It was like a painting…the combination of awe, and peace amid days' growth of whiskers…

She wanted to just stand there, to watch…to share it with him.

But he looked up at her, brow raised, eyes steady. Had she imagined the expression?

Needing it for some reason.

"You ready to go?" he asked her, the words, so professional sounding, slamming into her. Knocking the nonsense out of her.

"Of course."

With the sling already secured around her, she reached for baby and bottle at the same time, sliding the arm with the baby inside the sling. Settling him there.

Like the professional she was.

Scott, the satchel slung over his shoulder, turned, as

though to check on her, to make certain she was right behind him.

And the sound of a dislodged rock, tumbling down the mountainside, echoed around them.

Scott wasn't gentle about getting himself and Dorian flattened against the wall. They were in place in that first second. Frozen. Listening.

When no other indication of an intruder came, he motioned her to stay still and made his way to the entrance of the culvert. Dipped his head out just enough to scan the area.

With his hand down at his thigh, he waved her closer to him. Buried his face in the side of her neck. "I need to get a look over that ledge," he whispered. And handed her his gun.

With a nod, she took it.

And he took the scent of her, the warmth of her soft skin, with him as he lowered himself to the ground, and snakelike, slid out of the culvert.

Heart pounding, he counted two vehicles down below, at the office building.

And saw two men climbing up toward the culvert.

Shoving himself backward, feet first, in the dirt, he stood inside the culvert. "We have to go now," he whispered, taking Dorian's arm. "They're still ten minutes down. The ledge will hide us from their view, but not for long."

She didn't speak, didn't ask questions, just followed behind him.

Stepping carefully.

So close Scott could feel her there.

Her warmth egged him on to be stronger. More focused. Wiser.

He let it.

Keeping their bodies against the side of the mountain, he led them around a wall of rock, staying parallel with the culvert's entrance. One slow, steady, quiet step at a time. Keeping watch in front of him, while he listened behind.

Ignoring the pain in his leg.

The fact that the baby could cry at any time.

With no idea how many people had come back in those two vehicles, he had to assume the area was filled with them.

Had to assume that McKellips had made his delivery that morning as well.

And had brought the squadron back to clean up their mess.

Which meant getting rid of all the evidence.

Human and otherwise.

Half an hour of silence, bodies almost touching, they moved forward slowly. Until Scott came to a halt. Bracing himself as Dorian stepped into him.

He pointed to another small cave, looked for her nod. Got them there. And knelt to check the compass on his phone.

"We're parallel to where we were," he told her quietly.

"You think they saw us?"

He'd been wondering. "Either that, or in my pained state last night, I left some kind of trail." He'd been castigating himself silently. Just put it right out there.

"I should have stayed away," he told her. "If something happens to either one of you…"

"It would much more likely have happened already if not for the supplies you brought us." Dorian's tone was softer than normal. Warmer.

More personal.

"They know that we were there," she reminded him. "Makes sense they'd search every inch of land that served as possible escape routes."

He'd had that thought, too.

Which meant... "Another team could be heading up here. We have to keep moving. Even if it's in circles."

She nodded. "How's your leg?"

"Hurts like hell." There was no reason to deny the obvious. She'd just think him a liar.

"How much longer you think the baby's going to be asleep?" he countered back.

"We should get another hour, at least."

He nodded. Reached in the satchel for the full juice bottle. Handed it to her first. Sipped after her.

And liked the familiarity of having done so.

Chapter 15

Scott was looking a little flushed. Concerned, Dorian reached out to lay the back of her hand against his cheek and neck.

He stood completely still, staring at her, his jaw tight.

And she pulled her hand away. She shouldn't be doing that without a warning or explanation.

Touching him as though he was hers to touch.

"I'm sorry," she said. "I'm worried about infection."

His gaze dropping from hers, he turned and stepped just outside the small rock inlet, scanning their perimeter. Spent longer looking up at the climb atop the cave than eastward, toward the road. Or south, parallel to the way they'd been traveling.

"I'm going up," he told her, stepping back inside. "You and the baby can stay here, in the shade. I'll take my knife but leave the gun. I'm assuming you know how to shoot?"

She nodded. "All seven Sierra's Web partners took training and were certified shortly after opening our firm." She'd never shot anything but a target, though. And didn't want that to change.

Was about to tell him so but he continued. "There's a ledge about ten feet up, fronted with brush. It's as perfect a lookout as we're going to get. With the baby…" He glanced toward the sling tied to her chest and then away, shaking his head. "We can't hide three of us as easily as one. I need to see if I can figure out what we're up against. At least get an idea of numbers."

The plan made perfect sense. She liked most of it.

"Fine," she said, reaching for the tie on the sling. "But I'm going. You stay here with the baby."

His mouth dropped open as he stared at her.

As though she'd been speaking a foreign language.

His gaze moved to her fingers untying the sling. "Wait, what are you doing? No."

She didn't argue, just continued to implement her plan.

"You'll make him cry," he said then. "We need him quiet."

"If you'll come over here and let me get him tied to you, the chances of him staying asleep are excellent. The warmth and heartbeat emulate the mother's womb. Most any human would do." Not entirely factual, the any human part, but pretty close.

He didn't move.

"You're flushed, Scott. Whether you like it or not. You aren't superhuman. You had an untreated open flesh wound for hours and were climbing and sliding in dirt, among other things. An elevated temperature indicates infection. You need to stay out of the sun for a bit and rest your leg. I can carry one guy on this journey. I can't carry two."

With a nod he handed the gun to her.

She took it. Set it down while she stepped up to Scott, facing him. Thigh to thigh, and, holding the baby between them, his weight being supported by both of their chests, she transferred the sling ties from her hands to Scott's. Stood there, helping to hold the baby while he secured the infant against him.

When the newborn was settled and showing no signs of

waking, she picked the gun back up. Put it in the waistband of her pants and pulled her shirt down over it.

Glanced up to see Scott glancing at the strip of belly she'd just exposed.

As though he could find any part of her dirty, ponytailed hair, bruised jaw and unshowered body the least bit attractive.

"Keep your back covered at all times," he told her as she stepped up to the cave's entrance. Glancing back at him, she nodded.

And for a second or two, couldn't look away.

He didn't either.

It was as though he was urging her not to go.

But she had to.

And his silence told her that they both knew it.

The doc had told him to rest his leg.

He needed the baby to stay asleep.

Chomping to get his ass out of the cave and take on whoever was hunting them, Scott put his two most immediate challenges first, and, with the baby snuggled against him—curiously, not a horrible situation—he slid his back down the cave wall, as close to the entrance as he could get and remain in the shade, and sat.

Knife in one hand.

As a gatekeeper, his abilities were strictly limited, but he was at least able to see enough of the flat ground in the inlet outside the cave to keep watch from all approachable directions. And he was in a knife's throw distance if someone was unlucky enough to enter the area.

His leg throbbed. He hoped to God infection wasn't setting in.

And if it was, he'd have the good doc lance it and they'd move on.

There weren't any other options.

That throbbing, feeling as though it was in tandem with his heart, became like a metronome as he sat there. Counting beats until Dorian returned.

Senses acutely tuned, he listened for any movement of loose rock. The crack of a twig. A breath that didn't belong to him or the baby.

The hour was nearly up and Scott was standing, preparing to head up the mountain, baby and all, to find Dorian when she quietly appeared in his line of vision. She was on her belly, sliding over a ledge of rock at the edge of their little inlet clearing.

Her forearms were scraped. Bleeding lightly in a couple of places. Her elbows, too.

With her back flat against the mountain's rock wall, she stood and slid her way along to the cave.

He stepped back as she ducked in.

Sweat dripped off both sides of her jaw, and her clothes were splotched with dirt and dust. Her ponytail loose, falling to one side, she said, "Good call. The view was just what you would have hoped."

As though she'd just taken a two-minute stroll to glance over the edge of a mountain into a valley for the spectacular view.

If he'd been anyone else, and not on the job, he'd have hauled her up against him and the baby and kissed her right then. Right there.

Danger looming and all.

He handed her the juice bottle. She took it, but said, "I had juice up there while I lay watching."

Of course, she had. Dorian, always the doctor, could be counted on to tend to the needs at hand.

The circumstance might have put Scott off, threatened his masculinity even, if he wasn't finding the woman's abilities so incredibly attractive.

If he hadn't been smart enough to recognize their value and be thankful for them.

He saw her taking in the baby's face, and his breathing and posture, too, he figured. "I managed not to upset him," he told her.

"You'd have managed to take care of his needs if he woke up, too," she shot back, sitting down.

With the baby still attached to him, finding himself comfortable enough moving around with the small body tied to his chest, Scott went for the first aid kit.

Not the one they'd taken from the four-wheeler, but the much larger, stocked one he'd found at the mission. A soft-sided canvas zipper bag that had slid naturally into the leather satchel. Grabbing antibiotic cleaning wipes and salve, he approached Dorian.

She reached for them. "I can do that."

"You can't even see them all," he told her, sitting down directly in front of her. "I don't have a medical degree, but I think I can manage this," he held up his little stash. "Did you see anything?"

He couldn't just hang out in a cave like a sitting duck. He had lives to save.

Had to get moving.

Needed information to determine their next steps.

Dorian watched as he took first one arm, and then the other, cleaning every abrasion carefully. He didn't worry about passing muster under the supervision of a medical professional. He might not be versed on removing bullets from flesh, but he knew how to clean a wound.

After a couple of minutes, she seemed to be satisfied on that point and said, "I could see the compound where the mission was. Better with the phone camera. Took a bunch of shots for you. I think those two vehicles are the only two there. I saw two guys, didn't recognize either, have pictures of them for you, as well, walking up higher than our cave. I'm hoping that means that they didn't realize we were there."

"Or they knew we were but figure we're trying to get back out the way we came. Over the mountain. Better the evil you know, and all." He uncapped the salve, focusing on her words, not on how soft the skin was beneath his fingers. "Anything else?"

He needed more. What, he didn't know. Just didn't like the idea of having sent her up into danger only to bring back what they'd basically already known.

Other than a lack of any other obvious vehicles in the compound. That was good news.

And Lord knew, they could use some.

"I saw a place, a mile or two south of here…there were animals. Cattle, or something. A couple of roofs. And just looking out east, toward Globe, there were a few other scattered roofs, probably half a mile apart or more. Not in any kind of settlement or configuration. Just randomly stuck in the mountains."

He stopped, salve-dipped cotton round in hand, and looked at her. Filling with a much-needed burst of adrenaline.

"Did they look occupied?"

Her shrug didn't deter him much. "I couldn't really tell. But even if they're not, if we can get into any one of them, we might find more supplies. Or even some running water, assuming there's a working well..."

"And if they are, we have to be cognizant of the fact that any one of them could be employed by the general."

She nodded, without any hint of surprise.

As usual, they appeared to be already on the same page.

He kept thinking at some point there'd be a fork in their road. That their ideas and opinions would diverge.

"I zoomed in with the phone and checked every inch of land south of here," she said then, naming the direction they'd been traveling that day. "I saw no sign of any life at all. I'm really thinking those two guys earlier...they might be the only two."

He nodded, stood, satisfied. With the work he'd just completed on Dorian's raw skin, but also with his own ability to assess and guess with accuracy. As much as he didn't feel at all like the agent who'd shown up at the birthing clinic a couple of nights ago, he was glad to know he hadn't lost his job skills.

"They're figuring I'm like them, a criminal willing to do what it took to make the big money. They know they'd get rid of you, and so they'll figure I did. My guess is, they've been sent to wait for me to approach with the baby, wanting to make a deal." He put away the remainder of the supplies and felt a jab to his gut.

A foot.

And then another.

Shocked for a second, glancing down, he took in the downy bald head, the puffy cheeks and fully closed eyes.

And, with a jolt, told himself to get back on track.

To stay on track.

He wasn't playing a little "oh, look, I can hold a baby" game. He was dealing with life and death.

Making sure that the infant had a chance at the first.

Untying the sling from around him, he held it in place as Dorian had. She stood as he approached her and pressed against her, and she wordlessly completed the pass off as successfully as they'd accomplished it the first time.

"I'm guessing he's going to need to eat soon," he told her. Not mentioning the couple of foot jabs. They were in no way pertinent to the tasks at hand.

The woman, with all her lack of toiletries, looked...surreal to him...otherworldly...pure beauty.

He shook his head. Hoped he wasn't heading back to the lack of clarity he'd had during those last few yards up the mountain in the early hours of that morning.

"He's waking up now," Dorian said.

She might have shared more, but he stepped away from them, standing guard at the opening of the cave.

Just in case the two hunters came back down the mountain closely enough to discover the cave.

"You have my gun?" he asked then, and when Dorian nodded toward her waistband, he walked right over, all business. He saw her lift her shirt, and slid the gun from her side.

His knuckles against her side were just a hazard of the job, he decided firmly, shoving the gun into the holster he'd helped himself to the night before.

Holster and bullets...no gun that he could find.

He'd cataloged the information.

"As soon as he's fed and settled, we need to head out," he said then, back on lookout. "If those two really are the only searchers, and they're expecting me to show up, this is our best chance to get out of here undetected. And hopefully make it to a homestead before dark."

He wasn't sure how he'd approach that one.

They couldn't walk right up and knock on the door, for sure.

But knew he'd have to make that choice when he came to it. When he could assess the surroundings.

"They aren't going to wait around for me forever. They could feasibly still sell the baby, if they have another buyer ready. And even if they don't, they need me dead. My take right now is that they're betting on my need to blackmail them being the stronger one."

She had the little guy out of the sling. Had changed him. The pack of wipes he'd found with the supplies in the cupboard wasn't going to last forever.

As he'd done while he'd dismantled their cave abode that morning, he dug a hole with his knife, a rock and his fingers, and buried the used diaper. He left it open for the bottle she was about to empty into the baby's stomach.

"Do you think we can make it to the paved road yet today?"

Having to stay clear of the dirt road—McKellips's men were using it—meant the trek would be much longer.

And they had a baby in tow.

"I doubt it," he told her the truth. His leg was hurting like hell, but it would not slow him down. He'd find a crutch if he had to. Learn to run with it.

He asked for the burner phone. Looked through the plethora of pictures she'd taken.

Made a choice. Handed the phone back to her.

"I think we should head here," he told her. One roof. Smallish. Less chance of having to face a squadron running out the door. Hopefully, like many people in the Nevada desert, there were good people who were tired of the lies and rat race in the world, just wanting to live naturally off the land, with only natural dangers facing them.

She glanced up at him, babe contentedly sucking in her arms, and for a second there, Scott saw a wife. His child. And immediately turned his back.

Chapter 16

Scott clearly wasn't doing well. They'd been on the move for hours, stopping only to feed and change the baby, to eat cactus fruit and power bars and drink more juice. And while the FBI agent didn't slow down, he wasn't meeting her gaze anymore.

At all.

Like if he didn't look at her, she couldn't see his pale skin? Wouldn't know that something was wrong?

Her check of his face and neck earlier, in the cave, had indicated that he wasn't running a fever. The flush was gone. His lack of color came with its own information.

They were still traveling in the mountains, not always in sight of the miles-long road that led out of the mountain range, but parallel to it—their route much longer, more circuitous, due to the peaks they had to climb, or circle around. The need to keep cover—and to hike in the shade for the baby's sake—all played a part as well.

What had looked to her as a day trip from zoomed-in photos and aerial views from above was turning into something far more onerous.

And with Scott clearly fading, the journey felt almost impossible.

Would her team work their miracles and find them somehow? Was it ludicrous to hope for a helicopter overhead, sent by Sierra's Web to save them?

She looked for landing spots as she walked. To keep her mind occupied. To keep at bay the emotions that would weaken her.

To keep belief alive.

If she didn't believe in something, she'd be lost.

And she did believe that she'd do all she could to help save lives. So she walked. She assessed. She climbed, and, on occasion, slid. Insisting, when Scott offered to take his turn with the sling, that she needed him to be ready with the gun. To use his skills to keep them safe.

He'd insisted on carrying the satchel. No way she was giving the man any more extra weight on that leg.

Dusk hadn't yet fallen, but it was getting closer when Dorian saw Scott stumble. He righted himself immediately. Continued on without losing forward momentum. But she'd seen him wince.

His injured right leg had been the one to misstep.

"The baby needs real time out of this sling," she said to him then, no longer able to hold back. Telling a truth, but not the one that concerned her the most. She'd changed the newborn's positions regularly, and had refashioned the sling periodically, as well, allowing him to move more freely, so that his little body didn't get cramped. "I know it's early, but we should find cover for the night."

It would be their second in the mountains.

Her third away from home.

Seemed incomprehensible. Her life had changed so completely in just a few days' time. Far more than it had during her previous kidnapping, where she'd been largely kept physically comfortable, with enough to eat and drink, and in one place.

Seconds after she'd spoken, Scott spared a quick glance for the bundle covering her chest. Nodded. And continued taking them farther from the previous night's compound. And toward, she hoped, their salvation.

She was beginning to wonder if Scott was pushing himself so hard that the effort was affecting his thought processes.

Did she trust him to know best? Or was he so focused on forcing himself onward, blinded by pain, that he'd lost ability to discern?

He'd passed out almost as soon as he'd reached the culvert the night before. If he lost consciousness out there on a mountain ledge...what in the hell would she do?

He'd be fodder for coyotes...and worse.

She wasn't muscled enough to move him far...and to where?

With a baby strapped to her?

She was strong. Able. She acted rather than reacted. But she was human. Exhausted. Scraped up. And...

Scott had stopped at a little clearing, an inlet between the wall of mountain they'd just rounded and the wall straight ahead, then he walked to the ledge. She came up behind him. Seeing more of the valley they'd been following all day.

"Look, a little to the right." Scott's words held...something more than the deadpan tone from the past several hours...as he pointed.

An old shack—a good-sized structure—stood a quarter of a mile down.

And in front of it..."Is that a stream?" she asked, growing excited in spite of everything.

"Yeah," he told her. "I thought so a while back, but wasn't going to say anything until I knew for sure. We've been following it for the past hour or so. I just had to get close enough to see that it wasn't just a dry bed."

He could have told me.

The thought served no good purpose.

And yet, there it stood.

After pulling out her phone, she zoomed in on the shack. And her fingers started to shake. "I think there's a path leading out to the dirt road," she told him, showing him her phone.

Had the universe heard her call?

Her partner and friend, Kelly, would be more apt to believe such a thing.

"It's fairly grown over." He handed the phone back to her. And met her gaze full on for the first time since he'd turned his back to her in the cave when she'd been feeding the baby.

Not that it had rankled or anything…she gave herself a reality check with a taste of sarcasm thrown in.

He could connect with her or not. Didn't change their course of action. He didn't owe her anything.

To the contrary, she owed him her life.

"You okay?" He was still looking at her. With concern.

Dorian blinked. Nodded by instinct.

And then, meeting his gaze again—able to read from it as she'd been able to do from the first time they met—she nodded for real.

Broken, faded, cracked and askew, private property signs hung on various broken-down wooden fence posts. Scott, keeping himself and Dorian and the baby concealed as best he could in trees, tall desert bushes and brush, walked along the posted area, not ready to breach it until he was certain that the dilapidated gray building in the distance was really abandoned.

He'd seen all kinds of living conditions during his years as an agent, and couldn't afford to assume anything.

It was later than he'd have liked, with the sun having already disappeared behind the mountain, leaving the area in shadows. The baby had been fussy for a bit right after he'd eaten that last time, and while Dorian had been able to soothe him, and eventually get him back to sleep, Scott had been loath to leave their little inlet until he knew for sure that if he saw enemies, they'd be able to hide and have a better chance of remaining undetected.

The brief downtime had helped his leg as well. And had given Dorian a chance to rest. The woman never complained, but he knew her back had to be aching. The hiking they were forced to do was hard all by itself...having to accomplish it with a baby strapped to her...

"We could have to walk another mile or more before we get beyond these property markers to make it over to the stream," Dorian said from just one footstep behind him.

They could see the water in the distance.

Almost as though it was taunting them from the other side of the old, in dire need of repair, cabin.

He'd had a thought or two about lying down in the middle of the bed of water, closing his eyes and letting it soothe him for a while.

With his head propped on the bank, of course. No way was he checking out. But he'd give much for a few minutes of respite from the sharp burning in his leg. The pain was getting so great he was starting to have hot flashes.

"Hey!" A voice sounded out of the distance.

Behind the tall brush separating them from the house in the distance, Scott froze.

Had he actually heard an angel from heaven, calling out to him?

Scott rejected the thought. Took it as a warning that he was going to have to find a place to rest his leg soon. Eat some fruit and not burn it off immediately.

He needed to sleep long enough for his body to start to heal…

Right behind him, Dorian had ceased all movement as well.

"Hey there!" The voice came again.

He wanted to turn, to see if his companion was hearing things as well. But he didn't get a chance to do so before he saw the bent form coming toward them, waving her hand and smiling.

"I saw you out there!" the ancient voice said, with a waver and a crackle. "Figured you were lost."

Dorian's hand closed around Scott's elbow. Just held him lightly. Not squeezing tight.

Telling him that she wasn't afraid?

That maybe they'd found the help they so desperately needed in the form of an old spirit?

"My place is nothing fancy, mind you, and my fixings real basic, now that I'm here by myself with my Fred gone and buried, but I can still offer tea and sandwiches."

A couple of quick squeezes of his elbow prompted Scott to follow his own instincts and step out from behind the brush.

Just him, his forearm pressed against the gun beneath his T-shirt.

Dorian stayed behind cover. As he'd have instructed, given the chance.

"Thank you, ma'am, but we're dirty and shouldn't be coming inside. If you wouldn't mind just allowing us a dip in your stream?"

Standing in the open, he had a much better view of the

premises. Saw that a lot of the foot-high grass disguised the clutter strewn around it. Rusted-out pieces from machinery, broken parts of what looked to have been an old sofa, filled plastic bags.

Trash that the woman had been too frail to dispose of properly?

"Don't be shy, young man," the woman said. "You use my shower, my toilet, not that rock-bottomed river. It's got fish guts in it, you know. It does. Not proper for a little one like yours. I've been watching you with my beenoculars. Hoping you were coming my way. I don't get so many visitors here anymore. Now you all come right on in proper here, and I'll get some food on for you."

When Dorian stepped out into the yard, fully exposing herself and the baby, Scott knew their decision had been made. She was going in, whether he did or not.

Which meant that he was going in.

No way he was leaving her without protection.

The idea that he was thinking that she'd need protection from a little old lady who couldn't weigh more than a hundred pounds, and whose bones were obviously frail, gave Scott further indication of his need to take a breather.

He was human. And couldn't be so filled with his own determination and course, couldn't be so hardheaded that he'd refuse the help that they'd managed to find.

Which had been his goal all along. Finding help.

His plan had worked.

It was time to follow its course.

The structure, which appeared to have been a nice cabin at some point, was one main room with two doors leading to Dorian knew not what. But she was pretty sure she didn't want to know. There were stairs leading upward as well.

But from what she could see of them, she was fairly certain there'd be no point in trying to climb them—except perhaps to take in the enormity of a severe hoarding addiction.

Boxes in all different sizes, piles of shoes, a chandelier, stacks of books, of china dishes, folded clothes and many, many things that were unidentifiable due to the thick coats of dust on them, filled every available space. On what she could see of the stairs, and throughout the entire main room.

"Sorry for the clutter," the old woman said, her voice warbly, as she ushered them down a small aisle to a large table—three-quarters of which was also filled. "I'm in the midst of organizing and getting rid of things. For Fred," she said then. "He's not as much of a collector as I am."

Fred? The man the woman had buried? Dorian glanced at Scott. Recognized his frown of unease. She'd expected, as soon as they'd followed the woman inside, to find out how the woman communicated with the outside world, got her supplies, whatever, so that they could make their call for help.

She'd been hoping for a landline.

"Fred's your husband?" she asked quickly, wanting to keep the woman in conversation long enough, and quickly enough, for Scott to figure out what Dorian was strongly suspecting.

"That's right," the woman said. "Been married ten years now. I was just a teacher when he made me his bride, but I'm the principal now. Right here in the local school."

"In Globe or Miami?" she asked, naming the two closest towns to the east Superstitions.

"Miami, of course. School's just a mile down the road from here. My Fred, he works the mine, you know. Copper. He'll be home anytime now for supper. Always after the sun goes down. But don't you worry any—my Fred's a friendly sort. He likes company as much as I do.

"Have yourselves a seat," the woman continued as Dorian shared a longer glance with Scott.

His brow raised. She nodded.

"Go on now, sit," the woman repeated. There was only one chair, at the end of the table where the woman was standing, that was not piled higher than the table with clutter. "Just move that stuff down to the floor." The woman motioned toward the chairs closest to Dorian and Scott—chairs closest to the door through which they'd come. "I'll get it in a bit."

Other than the one small aisleway through the place, there was no floor space.

And then, before anyone could move, the woman said, "Oh, wait, what am I thinking? You'll need the bathroom first. It's through that door right over there."

Dorian needed a restroom. Just the chance to run water on her hands, wipe it on her face, to do her business without squatting in the dust. Glancing at Scott, who nodded, she walked over to him, untied the sling and, pressing against him, transferred the cloth to him to retie around himself. Trusting him to find out how best to get them out of there.

The baby whimpered as she moved away, and she started to take him back, but Scott shook his head. Motioned her toward the bathroom.

It might not be usable. Her lifted eyes and shrug were meant to tell him so. Whether he got the message or not, she wasn't sure, but she took his nod as affirmation.

"Ohhhh, let me get a look at that little one," the old woman was saying as Dorian got her first glimpse inside the door that had been indicated to her.

Shockingly, the room was…not as horrible as the rest of

the house. The floor, cracked tile, was stacked only along the walls. The countertop was covered with things, but not stacked up the foot or more of the rest of the house, and the sink and toilet areas were clear.

And relatively clean.

There was a washer, too, with the lid open, and a few pieces of clothing inside.

The shower, a stall, while cluttered around the edges, looked usable.

Maybe later, if she and Scott were still in the area, she could actually stand under the spray.

Wait! What was she thinking?

Before bed that night, she should be home and would be spending half an hour under her own rain-style spray.

Hurrying with her business, Dorian did take a few moments after sitting. She quickly washed her hands and face, and used a bit of the toothpaste from the tube standing in a glass to finger brush her teeth.

She'd just opened the door, was stepping back out onto the aisleway in the main room when she heard the woman say, "Oh, you'll have to wait for my Fred to take you to town. I never learned to drive."

And saw her hopes for a hot shower yet that night, fading.

As reality—the kidnapped newborn in her care, Scott's injury and being hunted by the worst kind of criminals—came crashing down on her once again.

Chapter 17

The woman's name was Grace Arnold. She had no phone.

She and Fred had had no children.

"Oh, there you are!" the woman exclaimed with obvious pleasure as Dorian returned to Scott, and took the baby from him. The little guy was still mostly asleep, but Scott had been holding him in the crook of one arm, rather than in the sling.

Just felt...better...at the moment.

"I have bologna or peanut butter and jelly for sandwiches," Grace was saying as Dorian took the baby from Scott. "I wish I could do better, but the man who delivers my groceries once a week hasn't come yet. He worked with my Fred at the mine, years ago. Helped him fix the well, too, just right before Fred died."

In the few seconds since Dorian's return, Grace seemed to have regained some of her faculties. Glancing at Dorian for confirmation of the possibility, he took her slight smile as just that.

"Fred's ashes were spread here on the property," Grace was saying. "Which is why I stay here."

Scott didn't find the idea a good one in any way. Even if for none of the obvious reasons, then because staying there alone, with her husband's ashes around the place, probably helped feed the old woman's fall back to earlier days when

Fred was still alive. She knew he was close. Just seemed to slide in out and of the reality of her husband's death.

"Her name is Grace," he said to Dorian then. And added, "Peanut butter for me, please."

He'd gained a good amount of information in a little time.

But unfortunately none of it brought he, Dorian and the baby any closer to being safe.

He had to get them to safety, even if he didn't make it there with them.

No second choice, no compromise on that one.

"She's offered to let us stay here with her until her next grocery delivery," he added, just to catch Dorian up on the fact that Grace had no immediate help to offer them. In terms of getting them out of the mountains.

Getting him on the trail of a killer named McKellips, and a high-powered kidnapping ring.

And away from the influence of a woman he'd hardly known but had never forgotten. One who seemed to speak to him without words.

He most definitely had to rid himself of that complication.

In the meantime, Grace had food and water.

Which, at the moment, was a good bit of help.

And she had kindness.

As the woman gathered sandwich fixings, asking about the baby, Scott excused himself to the bathroom, using every ounce of willpower he had not to limp on the way.

Grace landed a quarter of a loaf of bread, a knife and peanut butter and jelly on the table. Dorian, a big salad eater, was surprised to find her mouth watering for that bread.

Solid food. Wheat based.

Reaching down to start emptying a chair as best she could, with the baby strapped to her chest, she looked up as Grace said, "Oh look at these. Aren't they pretty now? The flowers on them!"

The woman was holding two plates that Dorian wasn't sure were clean.

"They're beautiful," she said, setting a shoe-sized plastic container on top of a pile of boxes.

"They're just lovely," Grace repeated, and then asked, "Are they yours? Did you bring these for me?"

And Dorian made another decision. As soon as she was out of the mountains, she was going to send someone up to help Grace. Assess her, at the very least. Depending on the woman's finances, maybe she could hire someone to stay with her. Or at least drive up from Miami once a day to check on her. Dorian would donate the money to pay for that if that's what it took.

The respite Grace was so kindly offering to complete strangers was worth that and more.

She'd just cleared a chair at the table, was sitting down, when Grace came over without the plates. "Your baby is just precious. Let me hold him while you make your sandwich." The tone had changed.

She sounded more like a principal in charge.

But that didn't make Dorian any more comfortable giving the baby to her. Most particularly not unless Grace was sitting down and would have her lap to help support the seven-or-so-pound bundle.

It was just occurring to her that Grace had said *him*, as though she knew the baby in the mixed-pastel-covered blanket was a boy, when the bathroom door flew open and Scott strode across the room, his gun in hand.

One look at him, his sharp gaze meeting hers, and Dorian was up and rushing out the back door behind him.

At first, she was thinking she should remind Scott that in Grace's day, it was common to refer to anyone whose gender wasn't certain as "him."

Until her mind caught up with the gun, and Scott's hurried, solid movements in spite of the pain they had to be causing him. The way he remained stooped, constantly surveying the shadows all around them, lit only by the window at the back of the house, commanding her to "stay low" as he jogged her swiftly from hiding place to hiding place, taking cover, even in the darkness, behind junk in Grace's yard.

Until she was reckoning with the pounding of her own heart.

The strike of fear tangling through her stomach.

Whatever Scott knew that she didn't, one thing was for sure, they were in immediate danger again.

And she trusted him enough to do exactly as he ordered.

Adrenaline helped him push through the pain, helped camouflage it, giving Scott almost normal abilities as he headed his small clan back north, toward the compound they'd left behind the night before. Hoping to throw off McKellips, or whoever else had been driving the truck that had turned onto the overgrown long dirt driveway leading up to Grace Arnold's place from the south.

He'd half thought himself paranoid when he'd taken a look out the bathroom window, just checking that there wasn't any sign of anything amiss on the side of the house he hadn't been able to see or evaluate before entering the building.

"Something wasn't sitting right with my gut," he told

Dorian as soon as they were far enough away for him to make a loud whisper without fear of being heard. "She called someone before she brought us into the house."

He'd figured that had to be the case as soon as he'd seen the headlights.

"Maybe she was playing us with the dementia crap."

"She's on the payroll of these guys?" Dorian's horror was evident even in an almost whisper.

He shook his head. He had no way of knowing why Grace had made the call. Could have been that she'd been told a couple had stolen a baby from the mission, that they were the bad guys. For all he knew, the old woman could be thinking she was helping to catch criminals.

Or she could be on the payroll.

Either way, by falling for her subterfuge, he'd almost gotten Dorian killed. And the baby back on the selling block.

"I told her our first names," he said then, blanching again at what had to have been the stupidest mistake of his entire career. Trusting that woman, even for a second.

Putting them all in immediately life-threatening danger...

"I'm sure mine's been on the news anyway," Dorian told him. "And yours, Scott...that's common enough to be anyone from anywhere."

He didn't respond, just continued pushing through brush in the darkness. Staying close to trees big enough to be shields from bullets if necessary as they started the climb back up into the mountain peak they'd left earlier, before heading south again. He didn't slow, even a little bit, for the first hour. Headed south down lower than they'd been earlier, but still a good way up. Got them past the coordinates at which they'd headed down to what they'd thought was the abandoned shack.

And then, in another inlet, similar to the last one they'd been in that afternoon, he stopped to give Dorian a chance to rest. "We have to assume that they know now that I didn't kill you. That you're still a threat. I'm planning to keep going for as long as humanly possible," he warned, as, moving away from her, toward the ledge of the clearing, he used his phone's Zoom function to survey the landscape below.

What he could see of it.

Grace's home, slightly to the north now, was lit. He saw no sign of headlights.

Anywhere.

Could only hope that she'd called one of the two men who'd been after them earlier in the day. That there weren't more men, a boatload of them, hunting the mountains for them.

"Hey, here, look," Dorian's voice, soft still, but insistent, called out to him. Turning, his entire being froze for a second, when he didn't see Dorian. Anywhere.

Adrenaline pumping anew, he strode toward where he thought the sound of her voice had come from.

Around the mountain?

She wouldn't have gone without him. Not even to pee, unless she'd told him so.

Reaching for his knife with one hand, and pulling his gun with the other, Scott rounded the steep jutting rock, expecting to see Dorian held at gunpoint.

Or worse.

Only to find...nothing.

"Keep coming," her voice called to him softly.

Without fear.

"You alone?" he asked. Knowing that she'd find a way to let him know if she wasn't. He couldn't help her by walking into a bullet.

"Fourteen years ago, the word I wanted so badly to say, I couldn't."

The response weakened his knees.

Doubly so.

That word had been *yes*. When she'd been walking out of his sight for the last time. With tears in her eyes. After having first kissed him, and then pulled away in the middle of it. He'd never forget her last words to him. "If I wasn't engaged, and you asked me to go to bed with you, my answer would be..."

She'd never finished the sentence.

And he didn't allow himself more than a brief memory of the past to come forth as he allowed present-day relief to flood him. *Yes.* She was alone.

"Can I come forward?"

She'd called him. But could still be relieving herself. Had just wanted him to know she'd slipped around the corner. Wanted him to keep watch.

"Yes, please."

Another couple of steps, and Scott saw why.

Dorian had stumbled upon a small cave. A real one that curved back into the mountain enough to allow them to turn on a phone's flashlight, however briefly, to survey their surroundings. To see each other.

To set up camp.

In a place far enough into the mountain that the temperature was at least ten degrees cooler than the heat outside.

The baby should sleep well.

They were on the south side of the mountain, rather than east, with no view of the area they'd come from or were traveling toward. But with a bit of finesse with rocks at the corner of that peak, he'd have fair warning before anyone even got close to them.

And with more brush and natural sources of noise—cracking sticks, rocks hidden under brush as Dorian suggested from a previous case her firm had handled—at the entrance to the cave, he'd be able to get a shot off if anyone breached the cave entrance.

With both of them working, it took another hour to get them settled inside. With a cradle for the baby and a sleeping pallet similar to the one Dorian had made the night before.

It was then that she told him what she'd shoved into the sling, at the baby's feet, when she'd run out of Grace's home.

The loaf of bread she'd had in hand as he'd come out of the bathroom.

Pulling out their filled bottle of cactus juice, she offered up that bread like a three-course meal.

They were in darkness again, to preserve phone battery, but with eyes adjusted to the dark, he could see her in shadows and wanted so badly to kiss her, to let good feeling take away the raging pain in his leg.

He cut off the thought as soon as it hit.

But still admired the hell out of her.

For the night, she'd found them a little home.

After dinner, while Scott did a perimeter check, Dorian fed the baby. Welling up with feeling as she listened to the rhythm of his breathing and swallows. He was such a little trooper.

Content just having his needs met.

And she couldn't help but fall in love a little bit.

The child wasn't hers.

Somewhere a mother who'd just gone through nine months of nurturing had given birth only to have her son snatched from the one place he should have been safest. She had to be grieving beyond what Dorian could imagine.

She glanced up when she heard Scott's two light foot taps after stepping over the rock crunch—which looked like river rock left over from rain and snow flowing off the mountain—at the corner before their cave.

Before he'd left, he'd handed her his gun and told her that if she heard approach without those two foot taps, she was to aim to shoot.

He was just a shadow as he rounded the inside turn to the back of their cave.

And her throat tightened. Tears had been pushing at her most of the night. Stress, she knew. And exhaustion.

And she wasn't done working yet.

But first... "Grace asked his name." While she'd been escorting them up to her house.

Scott had been right there. Had heard. She knew because he'd distracted Grace from the question.

"It's odd, caring for him, not calling him anything." Her words sounded pitiful to her. As though that newborn cared if he was called or not. He needed exactly what they were giving him. And nothing more.

The name calling...that was for her.

And not admirable. "I know his mother has named him," she added then, as Scott lowered himself down, sliding his back along the cave wall not far from the pallet she'd built for him.

Only one again.

This time because the back portion of the cave only had space wide enough for one. It narrowed considerably farther in where she'd put the baby's bed.

She wasn't allowing herself to think about that pallet. Or how she'd slept the night before. He'd been unconscious then.

That night, she'd figured they'd take turns sleeping, with someone awake to keep watch. Just as they'd slept the first afternoon they'd been in the mountains.

"It wouldn't hurt to call him something, just while he's with us." Scott's voice filled the cave so full her chest tightened up. "It's not like he'll remember."

He was right.

And his words brought a bit of a smile to her face. Gave her something positive to think about. "So, what should we call him?"

"I've always liked the name Scott." His words held a definite drawl. And they still didn't hold his normal decisive tone. As soon as the baby was in his cradle asleep, she had to get to work on Scott's leg.

Had purposely been conserving phone battery because she was going to need the flashlight…

"Might be a little confusing," she told him. "Scott here, Scott over there…who am I calling or talking about?" She smiled again. It felt good.

"So how about Michael?"

His last name.

Funny how the man who was never going to marry or have children was wanting a namesake.

But because it kept the smile on her face, she agreed with his choice.

Chapter 18

He couldn't remain standing for wound treatment. Had Dorian's life been at stake, maybe, but over the last couple of hours, every time he even brushed the leg against a twig, he felt tremors up to his hip and down to his ankle.

Even if Dorian just added salve to the wound before re-bandaging it—and he suspected the bullet hole was going to need more than that—he'd risk losing his footing and falling on her.

He'd seen some oozing on the bandage when he'd used the restroom at Grace's place.

Which likely meant infection.

So when she told him to give her access to the wound, and to lie down, he didn't argue.

He did wait until she'd turned her back to get supplies before pulling down his pants, lying back and making damned sure his shirt covered every part of his groin area.

Just to be certain, he grabbed the dirty T-shirt he'd worn on the first day of hiking and laid that across him, too.

If she found him prudish, he didn't give a damn.

And if, as he suspected, she figured out that he was finding her more woman than doctor, then at least she wouldn't know for sure.

Even with the throbbing he felt lying down, he was still

getting hard, just being in his underwear, knowing she was going to be bending over him.

Touching him.

Feeling like some kind of sick jerk, he swallowed. Hard.

"I know this is going to seem cliché, but I want you to bite down on this..." She'd brought the burner phone with her, had the light shining on what looked like a stripped clean stick that had been soaked in something at some point.

But was currently dry.

He took the stick. Stared at it.

Did not put it in his mouth.

"I made it last night," she said. "Just in case you woke up before I got the bullet out. And it's not just a movie thing. It'll help protect your teeth from gritting them too hard, which can cause damage to the teeth. More than that, it engages the thalamus, your pain receptor, with more than one message at the same time, which distracts some..."

She'd been talking while she unbandaged his wound. Ripping quickly enough that he barely had to bite as tape left hair. The intense focus with which she studied his leg, the interruption to her conversation told him what he'd feared.

He put the stick in his mouth.

Held it lightly between his teeth. Leaving more intense biting in case he needed it later. Noted the cactus juice taste.

Prickly pear again.

He'd told her that of the four juices they'd had the day before, he'd preferred the pear.

Could be why she'd chosen that particular fruit.

Could also have been that the prickly pear was all that had been easily and readily available to her the night before.

Dorian's gaze had never looked more serious as she moved the flashlight around, moving her head with it, as though some different angle was going to change what she was seeing.

More likely, she was taking in every single speck of the wound, determining just how bad a problem he presented.

He started to get tense. He knew that his muscles tightening wasn't going to help the process for either of them, and took the stick out of his mouth long enough to say, "You said it was just a flesh wound, Doc."

Her nod showed zero lightening of mood. "It's infected," she told him. "It went too long with that bullet in it, raw and open, with the dirt…"

"I'm not blaming your skills, Doc," he said then, caring more about her mental state at the moment than his own. If she was going to start blaming herself…

He put the stick back in his mouth.

"Bite down."

He did so. Without pause.

Felt light pressure on his thigh, around the wound.

Nothing that needed a stick in his mouth to endure. Unless that stick was going to lessen the pressure heading to another male stick in her near vicinity.

What the…

"The pus seems to be all at the surface," she said then, shrinking his male member right down. He missed the distraction, most particularly when she continued. "There's no apparent abscess, yet, which is huge. No sign of need to be overly concerned about tetanus."

Until that moment, he'd never considered that possibility. "I'm current on my shots," he let her know then. Wanting to reach up and wipe the frown from her brow.

Not sexually. Just…because she looked so worried, and he wasn't worth that. He'd be fine. He always was.

"I'm going to have to drain the wound," she told him,

gathering up something from beside her and positioning the light on some rocks she'd brought with her. One taller, one smaller to hold up the phone. Obviously, something she'd figured out the night before.

"It's going to hurt like hell."

He nodded. Figuring nothing was going to be much worse than what he'd endured the previous night, climbing up that mountain with the bullet in an open wound that was rubbing on his pant leg every step of the way.

"Counting down from three," she said, and then, "Three, two, one…"

It took every ounce of everything in him to keep Scott from yelling as the burning, shooting pain went up and down his leg. His fingers dug into the pallet beneath him. He was biting for all he was worth.

And her fingers seemed intent on killing him.

For a time there, as she let up while wiping the area and changing position slightly before applying pressure again, he wished he was already in his grave.

Or that he'd at least pass out.

One thing kept him there with her. The concern on her face.

That, way more than the stick, distracted him enough to keep him conscious.

"You okay?" she asked at one point, glancing over at him.

He might have nodded. He meant to.

He was certain he met her gaze full on. Trying to tell her that she was doing a great job. And that he was going to be just fine.

And then, as quickly as the debilitating pain had started, it was done. She was reaching beside her again. He braced himself for more.

"This salve will not only help prevent any further infection, it's also got some lidocaine in it. It will help with the pain. We're going to need to tend to this every four hours, for the next day at least, whether you like it or not."

He wasn't arguing.

Almost jerked upright when he first felt the solution being spread over his wound, but quickly relaxed as Dorian's tender touch soothed more than it hurt.

The bandage was more than it had been. Thicker.

It was going to hurt like hell, ripping all that tape off the hair on his leg. But...damn...he was already feeling less pain. If that was even possible.

Or maybe his thalamus was just too busy taking other messages. Like what a relief it was to see the lines leaving Dorian's forehead.

To notice the way her chin and cheeks had relaxed back to their normal positions, making her easily one of the most beautiful women he'd ever known.

Red hair, no freckles. Brown eyes, not green. Everything about Dorian Lowell was unusual. Different. Setting her apart in his mind.

Making her one of a kind to him.

He couldn't be blamed for noticing...

Good Lord, she was pulling his pants off over his shoe. The shackle he'd purposely left in place.

"I'm going to lift your leg."

What the...

He glanced down. She was holding gauze. Intended to wrap it around his thigh. He started to raise his foot.

"No, let me do it. I don't want that muscle flexed right now."

Yeah, well, he didn't want other things. And muscles couldn't always be fully controlled.

She'd already lifted. Used her shoulder to help bear some

weight, and there was her face, almost right smack in front of his newly exposed and very tender manly parts, only partially covered by his borrowed briefs.

There'd only been one size. He'd grabbed a few pairs. Had shared them with Dorian. There hadn't been any feminine undergarments.

Was she wearing a pair of the briefs, too?

The thought was the absolute wrong one, bringing him into complete, full on, ready mode.

No way she didn't know, with her hands down there, her gaze still focused, his region under that damned mobile spotlight...

"I apologize," he said, quite seriously. "With everything in me, I'm sorry..."

She shook her head, seemingly not in the least bit fazed. "It's a perfectly normal reaction. Don't worry about it."

The words should have shrunk him right up.

Might have done so if he hadn't, at that moment, glanced at Dorian's breasts—because...he was a normal healthy guy who was turned on and there they were, also in the spotlight as she bent over him—only they weren't just breasts in a bra and shirt. She wasn't wearing a bra. And her shirt was stretched tight as she reached back for scissors to cut the gauze.

Letting him see, with way too much clarity, that her nipples were hard as rocks.

And it wasn't the least bit cold in that cave.

He's a patient. He's a patient. He's a patient.

As Dorian opened yet another of the precious antiseptic wipes to clean her hands after taping off Scott's gauze, she continued the litany in her head.

He's a patient.

Except that—he wasn't.

He hadn't come to her for her professional services.

And she wasn't at work.

He wasn't a patient.

He was Scott Michaels. The man who'd upended her early adult life and shaped the rest of it.

The man who'd just saved her life.

And she was doing what she could to save his.

The fact that she was attracted to him didn't have anything to do with his bullet wound. Fourteen years before, she'd been turned on to the point of changing her entire future, disappointing so many, hurting people she loved, without seeing the man's hard-on.

But seeing it there…so many years later…after two days of fighting to stay alive with him, being hunted with him, caring for a baby with him…

Well, that was a cruel twist of fate.

She had to quit looking at it.

"You said it was a perfectly normal reaction."

Turning her back on *it*, she gathered up her supplies. Telling herself to take a sip of juice for her dry throat.

Returned the medical paraphernalia to the zippered kit. Put that back in the satchel. Just as she'd done the night before. If they had to leave on the run, things had to be packed and ready.

She heard movement behind her. A quick glance showed her Scott trying to work the jeans up over his bandage.

He needed to be dressed. Ready to run.

She didn't want the pants up.

But she needed them up.

In a sitting position, with his leg straight out in front of him, he was struggling. She'd told him no weight bearing for at least a couple of hours as she'd applied the last piece of surgical tape. She only had two more sets of closure strips and didn't want to risk having to go into the wound a third time.

Satchel zipped, she moved back over to her worst temptation. Focusing on the medical knowledge filling her mind. Back in complete, professional control. "Let me help with that."

And...slide.

The pants were up over the gauze. Her hand on one side, his on the other. Joint effort. He lifted his hips. She pulled before he did. Hard enough to get the job done quickly. As his left hand faltered, her bit of a tug ended up with a hand slipping from the jeans, her fist grazing...

Scott's enlarged penis.

Their eyes met. Held. She knew what hers were saying, traitors that they were. And even her mind, that which she could always rely upon to save her from emotional disaster, let her down. Played tricks on her.

Telling her that his gaze was communicating a mutual fire that was about to burn out of control.

If they let it.

Were they going to let it?

She continued to lock gazes with him. Silently. Unable to commit. Or to save herself.

She thought.

Until her mind presented words and she spoke them aloud. "I feel like I owe you one. For the past. Coming on to you like I did. And then stopping so abruptly..."

What was she saying? Her hand was there. Was she seriously considering...

"I don't do one-ways." His low, sexy drawl brought her gaze from his crotch back to his eyes. "Either we both go or no go," he said then, completely serious.

Fire burned within her. Through her. Lighting places she hadn't known she had. Her temporal lobe, her amygdala, was acting out. Having a hell of a tantrum. Careening out of control.

She tried to think. To reason. To think medical thoughts.

To bring herself back from the brink of sure disaster once again.

And said, "I thought I was going to die last year when I was kidnapped. My childhood best friend nearly did. And this week...it's like being in a die-fest...a messed-up world where roulette isn't a game. It's a reality."

The thoughts were clear.

And very clearly emotion based.

But rational, too.

More, they were stronger than anything else she had out there on the mountain, perhaps on her deathbed. "There's something about you," she said then, sitting there beside the man, his pants stuck just below the engorged proof neither of them was denying. "Before, and now. Maybe I need to do this. There's something I need to know. Something only you can teach me."

And knowing was the key to acting, rather than being acted upon.

"Are you saying it's a two-way, then? Because, I have to tell you, Doc, this is getting a little painful here."

The words could have filled her with guilt, her there, hovering over a bullet-wounded thigh. But his eyes, smoldering, without a hint of discomfort from his injury in their dimly lit depths, were showing her how very much he wanted what she'd started.

Years before, and then, too.

"I want it as badly as you do." She was honest with him. "Maybe worse."

"Not possible." His chuckle held little humor, and a whole lot of hunger that sent pangs resounding through her.

And still she sat there. Fighting to save herself. And him, too. Without coming up with any way having sex that night would hurt either one of them.

It wasn't like it would affect anyone else.

And in her life, there was no one who would even care.

"I have no desire to marry or be in a permanent relationship." She blurted the words.

"Already figured that one," he gave right back. "And ditto."

She could do it. There was nothing stopping her. And still, "I'm a total failure when it comes to emotional stuff. I get it wrong. And those close to me suffer."

The words might be all wrong. They felt right.

"Warning received." He chuckled again. Slid his hands up under her shirt, finding her hardened nipples. Sending wild sensations through her. Wiping away the world. Making her want to spread her legs and do things.

To do, and be done upon.

Not a one or the other situation.

Standing, her gaze locked with his again, pinpoint to pinpoint in the near darkness, she pulled down her pants. Stepped out of them. Feeling…powerful…in her borrowed underwear rather than embarrassed by them. She and Scott were in their crashed world together.

Sharing everything.

Relying on each other for life itself.

"You're killing me here."

"You have a condom?"

"In my wallet."

He couldn't get up. She'd forbidden it. After taking off her odd underwear she knelt down on the pallet beside him. Reached under his butt, taking her time at it, to get the wallet out.

Retrieved protection, was ripping into it when he said, "Shirt off, please." His tone was strangled sounding. And lest he suffocate, she complied. Feeling more powerful than ever as her breasts hung free before him.

His hands slid up her stomach, sending delicious chills through her. She reached for his briefs. Pulled down as he lifted his hips.

And within a minute, careful not to put any pressure on his thigh, had impaled herself on him.

She rode him, losing all thought, exploding, feeling him explode.

And then, still awash in residual sensation, she sat there, holding him within her.

Chapter 19

Scott was getting hard again. Normally a one and done, head to the shower kind of guy, he couldn't believe himself.

He was injured. Exhausted.

And ready to go again?

Dorian pulled off from him slowly, taking the condom with her. And when she returned to the pallet, she'd donned her clothes again.

He got the message.

Didn't want it.

He'd been able to flip his briefs back in place without lifting. Had done so as he'd realized she wasn't coming back for seconds.

Wondered if he'd ever left a woman lying in bed after sex, wanting more. Hoped not.

It didn't feel good.

Dorian knelt beside him. Grabbed hold of one side of his jeans with one hand, and gently lifted his thigh with the other. "Let me help with these," she said, softly, calmly.

Professional-like.

The doctor had returned. He didn't want her. In that moment, he didn't need her. He wasn't helpless. And while it might be best for his wound if he lay still for hours, the reality was, they could be up and on the run in minutes.

And he'd perform just fine. Get the job done.

He might pay later. Might have an abscess or some other physical price to pay for not babying his injury. And that was his choice to make.

He brushed her hand aside and got his pants up by himself.

And was thankful that her support under his leg made the process a little less uncomfortable.

"And now we rest," he told her, taking command of the operation because the case was his.

She started to pull away. "I'll take first watch."

He caught her arm. "We both need sleep. There's less chance of someone discovering us here tonight than one or the other of us failing tomorrow due to lack of sleep. We have no idea what's ahead of us, but we can count on it being arduous. We've got alarms set outside—I'm a light sleeper and have my gun ready in the event anyone invades."

She didn't pull away. Just glanced at him, not quite meeting his eyes, and said, "I need to feed the baby. He's starting to wake up."

Scott let go of her. But said, "I'm staying awake until you get back here. I need to know you're going to sleep, too."

He heard her rustling behind him. "I can sleep back here."

"Not comfortably." He leaned up on one elbow, saw her head turn in his direction. "You sorry?" he asked.

When she didn't reply, he had his answer.

He lay back down, trying to convince himself that her withdrawal was for the best.

The baby responded to stimuli as Dorian changed him. He ate well, burped, fell asleep right on target. And Dorian was too exhausted to fight with herself.

The back of the cave...too narrow. Since her kidnapping the year before, claustrophobia had been an issue. Therapy had helped. And her therapist had diagnosed that she might have the condition for life, too.

Wondering, in a half-aware kind of way, what type of long-term mental residue she'd develop due to her current situation, Dorian walked the few steps into wider ground. Thought about heading around the small curve and outdoors. Just for some air.

And a glimpse of a clear night sky with shining stars.

She glanced down at the pallet as she passed. Noted Scott's even breathing and, she was pretty sure, closed eyes. And just stopped walking.

He was right. They both needed rest.

And his chest was the only pillow that seemed to do the trick for her, out there in a world where they were being hunted by devils.

He'd offered it the first day. She'd helped herself to it the night before.

But couldn't seem to do it again. Afraid of what she'd be losing, what she'd be giving up, if she did so.

Instead, she stretched out on the cave floor, laying her head on the side of the pallet, almost touching Scott's shoulder, and promised herself that she wasn't getting weak.

She dozed, didn't think she'd sleep much, but came fully awake as strong arms pulled her up on the pallet.

He didn't speak. She didn't even open her eyes.

But fell asleep almost immediately.

Scott awoke, wide awake, each time Dorian got up to feed the baby. And stayed awake until she was back on the pallet with him.

He didn't welcome her back. Didn't hold her. He served his pillow duties and went back to sleep.

Three times.

Before sitting up straight as a gun blast sounded.

Echoing through the canyon beneath them. And then another. And the third, he was fairly certain he heard hit rock.

Which meant it had to have been aimed close enough to them for him to have done so.

Dorian, up beside him, jumped to her feet. Grabbed the baby, gently enough that if he awoke, he didn't cry, then tying her sling as she kicked aside brush and stepped into her shoes at the base of the cradle.

By the time she'd rejoined him, Scott had the satchel on his back and, gun in hand, had rounded the slight turn in the cave and was approaching the outdoors.

The baby was whimpering. They couldn't afford that, let alone a full-out cry. After reaching into the satchel, he handed Dorian a bottle. They had enough for one more day's feedings. He knew she'd have already counted.

Time was closing in on them. If they didn't make it out of the mountains that day, they might not make it out.

Not a usual thought for him. Yet, there it was, as he slid on his belly toward the ledge outside the cave, peering over, while Dorian stood around the cave side of the peak, feeding the newborn.

First glance from north to south showed him nothing but quiet mountain. Surreal beauty. The occasional roof he knew was there.

South to north, the same.

And then…a flash. Color. Phone out, he zoomed in. One man, slightly north of him, halfway down to the valley. Running south. In his direction.

Further along that coordinate above sea level was another man. Holding up something with both hands. Scott couldn't make out the body, his zoom was too blurred, but he figured it for some kind of animal.

They'd been awoken by hunters?

Legal hunters. Or at least ones hunting for prey that was most likely legal.

Or, as he told Dorian minutes later as they started their third day of hiking, "They could easily have been squatters, hunting illegally, but animal prey. Not human."

"You didn't recognize them, then?"

He shook his head. But had to add, "They were too far away. Too blurry." And also confessed, "My phone's back down to fifty percent battery."

"Mine's at thirty."

They were definitely running out of time.

The claustrophobia was getting worse. Dorian fought it with fact. With logic. Telling her brain what was happening to it, in a scientific sense, so that she could combat it.

Mind over matter.

And the matter was, she was trapped in the mountains, with guns at her back, and a babe in arms.

She was confined with a man she couldn't reason out of her.

Maybe because she didn't know him well enough? If she knew what he needed—as she'd known how badly Brent had needed to be the only man who'd ever strummed her strings—she'd know specifically how she'd be at risk of hurting him. And use that knowledge to stop the desire from flowing through again.

If the knowledge could also interrupt whatever strange nonverbal communication that had seemed to thrum through them from the first day they'd met, that would be a wonderful bonus.

With a solid goal, and a specific way to meet it, she had more energy in her step as she followed Scott along a mountain ridge, into another slight valley between two peaks. He'd said, with the hunters down below, they had stay up high for a while, which made for more strenuous hiking, but when they headed down again, they'd be much closer to the road than they'd been the day before. The paved road.

The good thing about the little valleys, besides easier trekking, was the natural cover the peaks surrounding them provided. They couldn't be seen from down below.

Stopping to change and feed the baby, to eat and replenish their juice supply—Scott feeding while Dorian insisted that he rest his leg, while she hunted and cut cactus—she welcomed the respite.

Along with the hope that resurged at the thought that the blacktop road had become the current goal, rather than a future one.

The journey was taking much longer than she'd thought it would, but they were alive. Relatively okay. And making progress.

She was feeling so much better she'd almost convinced herself that she'd overcome the earlier panic, until she returned to see Scott with little Michael in his arms and yearned to walk up and give them both a thankful hug.

They weren't hers to be thankful for.

And if they were, she wouldn't trust herself around them. How did one see they were blinded by emotion if they were blinded and couldn't see?

Somehow, from their very first meeting she'd romanticized Scott Michaels. Because she didn't know him well enough.

The thought came stronger than ever. So much so that as they started out again, with the easier walk ahead of them for a bit, she pressed forward verbally, too.

"When did you know that you didn't ever want to marry?"

She just put it right out there. A person's life choices were generally based on life lessons. The combination made them who they were.

"The first time, I was six, in first grade. The second, a year after I got engaged when she still didn't want to set the date."

Whoa. She stepped and restepped. Moving only about half a step. "You were engaged?"

"For a year."

Yes, they'd established that. But… "When?"

For two days she'd been looking at the back of the man's head for most of their time moving forward. That moment was the first time she was frustrated by that fact.

She was desperately in need of the information that he was only partially imparting. Without access to his eyes, how could she fill in the blanks?

And that, right there, was the reason she had to get him out of her. To find the key to expelling him. No way she could really read a man's mind through his eyes.

She of all people—a scientist, an expert in her field—knew that.

His answer was a long time coming. She was working on a repeat question when he said, "A year before you and I met."

"What happened?" Could it be that easy? She'd find her answers in one of his?

And…what woman in her right mind wouldn't set the first date possible to join herself to him? If she was the marrying kind.

"I pushed. She cried."

She waited for more. Tense to the point of irritability in her need to know. The valley's verdant brush was pulling at her ankles, she was sweaty, starting to stink, and the baby's sling was putting a permanent crick in her neck. "And?"

Tell me you got impatient with her. Gave her an ultimatum. Maybe she'd wanted to finish college first. Maybe she'd needed to get through medical school before being a wife.

"She told me that she couldn't marry me."

Now that, she hadn't expected. Brent had been in a hurry to marry, too. But when Dorian had told him it would have to wait until after she'd completed her residency, he'd been as supportive as always.

"Why not?"

Her need to know was all-encompassing now. Without justification to egg it along.

"Because she didn't want to risk having children with bad blood."

She stopped walking. Stared at his retreating back when he didn't even slow down. "Scott," she said as she caught up to him. He didn't turn.

"Why would she say a thing like that?"

It wasn't about her need to protect him from herself anymore. She'd never met a man with "better blood" in her life. Unless, "Does leukemia or something run in your family?" But even then...

"Nope, we're healthy as can be."

She scrambled to keep up with him then, as he seemed to find new sources of energy, propelling him faster forward. But she was just as fast.

And without a bum leg, she could keep up the pace longer. Caught up to him. "Why did she say that?" she asked, side by side with him. Glancing over.

His gaze remained steadily straight ahead.

"Because it's true."

No. No. No. No. No. Not good enough. She'd...they'd... he was attached to her somehow, by a string she couldn't identify. For his own good, she had to cut the thread.

"What makes it true?"

He still didn't stop. But Scott slowed to a more reasonable pace for both of them, considering the distance they had yet to travel, the climbing ahead of them, as he said, "My paternal grandfather died in prison. My maternal grandfather, best we can tell, dealt drugs to hippies back in the late sixties. My father is currently serving a life sentence for murder. My paternal grandmother had a substance abuse problem that eventually killed her. My maternal grandmother liked men and spent most of her life running off with one or another of them. And my mother is also in prison. She has quite the rap sheet for small crimes but is serving life as an accomplice to my father."

Her justification for questioning him disappeared as Dorian listened, her heart flooding with pain for his pain, and with an admiration she couldn't quell if she'd given her life to do so.

Pulling on his arm, she yanked him to a stop. Looked him in the eye, and, with all the command of an expert scientist in her voice, said, "You couldn't possibly have bad blood, Scott. You were born to people who obviously made very poor choices but look at you. With that start, with that baggage, with that example, you still managed to make the right ones."

Chapter 20

The woman was just being kind.

He'd saved her life. Of course, she'd spin him in the best light.

No need to convince her otherwise. It wasn't like they were going to see each other again once they got to safety. She'd be whisked off; he'd have to endure a quick medical check, and then he was going to be right back on the case.

Saving one baby was great. But there were too many more out there. Needing to be found. And needing to be protected from future kidnappings, too.

And, maybe Dorian had needed to paint him in colors she could look at more easily since she'd had sex with him, wham bam though it had been.

They'd reached the far end of the valley, which precluded further conversation at that point, anyway. Back to the hide and seek form of travel, sticking close together, speaking in whispers and moving from natural barrier to natural barrier, spending as much time out of sight as they could.

Always scoping out potential hiding places, just in case.

They'd been hiking since just after dawn—before six— and by noon he knew they had to start heading down. Much farther and they'd be circling around too far and would begin heading southwest. Farther away from the couple of small towns toward which they'd been heading.

Finding one last cave, to cool off and feed and change the baby, they rested for a couple of hours. Sitting upright, eyes closed, heads against opposite walls. She might have dozed. He doubted it. He planned.

The hours ahead. Anticipating ways a hunter could prevent them from reaching town. Planning solutions for each obstacle.

And moving on toward finding the general, too. The man was going down. Whether Scott was dead, or alive to participate. No way Sierra's Web or the FBI were going to let this one go. If nothing else, Scott had exposed the operation. Many of his colleagues, and, he assumed, all of the Sierra's Web experts, were more than qualified to finish the job.

He jerked upright.

What in the hell was he doing? Writing himself off?

No way in hell.

Standing, his leg stiff, but not throbbing nearly as badly as it had the day before, Scott grabbed the satchel, moved out of the last mountain domicile he'd share with Dorian and the baby and scoped out the safest route to head down the mountain.

Safe from physical harm, a landslide or slick rock that could send them catapulting. And safe from discovery, or capture, too.

By the time Dorian joined him, the baby once again changed and fed, he pointed out a jagged trail winding sideways at times, but that would get them down the mountain. He wanted her to know the route, just in case.

Told her so.

And at her nod, set off.

* * *

She missed Scott. Longed for the camaraderie of their first two days on the run. Recognized the futility of longing for anything, pursuant to her current reality.

Warned herself against any form of Stockholm syndrome—not relating to her captor, but to the captivity itself. And made it down the mountain without embarrassing herself further with phobia-induced chatter.

She did let Scott know that she'd filled a couple of formula bottles with cactus juice and was switching them out, two formulas to one juice. Just in case something happened to her and he was left to care for the baby.

Michael.

She'd denied herself the right to call him that. It wasn't professional.

Didn't seem to stop her thinking of him as such, though. Hard as she tried not to do so.

Scott was so worried about passing on his genes when, in fact, he was doing the world a disservice by not having a little Michael of his own. With Scott as a father, that human being would be pretty much guaranteed to make the world a better place.

When the man she wasn't supposed to be thinking about on a personal level came to a sudden stop, Dorian was so lost in her thoughts of Scott that she almost bowled right into him.

And then saw why.

"All points down seemed to lead me here," Scott said. "Now I know why."

They'd run into a rudimentary dam. Built who knew how many decades before. A cement wall taller than both of them put together. It ran from a wall of mountain to a huge swamp area.

"A retaining wall," she said. "To keep the snow and rain

rushing down the mountain from flooding something on the other side."

He nodded. Turned, and pointed to the north of the huge swamp. A huge drainage ditch ran along the mountain wall. "We'll have to head back this way," he told her, pointing in the opposite direction. "The brush is thick enough to give us some cover, but I have to tell you, I don't like it so stay close. At the first sign of trouble, head down into the ditch and into the tunnel."

He'd given her a hiding place, she knew. And, for the baby's sake, she also knew she'd use it if she had to.

And didn't ask if he'd be using it with her.

Keeping right behind him, she covered the top of the baby's head with the sling, using both arms to ward off branches as they walked through them. Avoiding prickers in some, and just more scratches along her arms in others. Scott did the same, holding branches for her as he could. Cutting through the thickest points.

They moved slowly, stopping often for Scott to use his phone to snap photos and enlarge them for both of them to study for any sign of a trap on the other side of the brush.

By the time she could see the end of the brush, and flat land, ahead of them, she was starting to believe, for the first time, that they had a better chance of getting home than she'd let herself imagine.

Mostly thoughts of being free had been suspended. They brought emotion that would get in the way, cloud her mind to what had to be done in the moment.

But as they drew closer to sunshine in the distance, she let hope flourish. The first ray of brightness nearly blinded her because she'd been looking upward, wanting the sense of freedom that blue sky up above used to give her from ground level.

Scott was the one who'd stopped.

It took her only a second to realize that his focus was on the ground.

At first, she just saw darker-than-dirt color in places. Some kind of plant life. But when one, and then another part of the small field started to move—to slither—she gasped.

"Rattlesnakes," she hissed on her last bit of air. Backing up.

Scott did as well.

Far enough away for them to determine that the snakes weren't looking to follow them.

"It's a trap," he said. "Those hunters I thought I saw… one was carrying a snake. I realize that now. The gunfire was aimed up into the mountains, as I first thought. I only heard one hit because they were probably shooting at different areas. Trying to lure us out, a warning to us that they knew we were up there. And the snakes…the men knew the direction we were moving. Knew, with the retaining wall blocking us on the other side, our route would would lead us here…"

"So we go back," Dorian said, as though the thought of it didn't take every bit of strength she'd ever dreamed of having. And she was healthy. Scott, with his leg…another trek all the way up…he might make that. And then what? The baby wasn't going to be well on a cactus juice diet for long. The diapers were only going to last for another day or two, if there were no major loose stool episodes, which the cactus juice would likely cause.

"We can't go back up," Scott said then, his voice barely above a whisper. "They've chased us down to this. They're fully prepared for us to retrace our steps. I can pretty much guarantee you someone is at the retaining wall right now, waiting for us. Or above it, waiting to shoot us from above. They still want the baby."

It was the thought of the killer ever touching little Michael, ever even looking at him again, that cleared Dorian's mind.

"Then we go forward," she said, and grabbed hold of Scott's hand.

Scott stood his ground. They'd had a rough three days. He could understand Dorian's panic. But there was no way he was going to walk them into...

"Rattlesnakes are by nature solitary creatures. They'd only be there if someone had planted them as you say," she said, looking him straight in the eye. "The only time they gather is during mating season, which doesn't start until late July."

She continued to hold his gaze. "They aren't an aggressive snake," she told him. "Unless they feel cornered. And from what I could tell there were fewer than twenty of them immediately at the entrance." He saw a shudder pass through her, or thought he did, but she continued. "And they seemed to be moving on their way. McKellips might have planted them there to stop us, but they don't know that and certainly don't have a share in his plan."

She still didn't look away. At which point, Scott laced his fingers through hers. He knew a bit about snakes, too. "You're suggesting that we step carefully, walk through them slowly, and..."

He'd seen what had looked like a wheat field just beyond the end of the forest of brush they'd come through. They could lay low in that long enough to plan from there, if they made it that far.

"Worst case is we get bit," she told him. "You might not have noticed antivenom in that kit you stole, but I saw it there. And I'm fully trained in treating snake bites. Beyond that, I'd much rather risk the mouth of a rattler than a killer's bullet."

They could end up with both. He didn't bother saying so.

Nor did he tell her, when they made it back to the edge of the brush, facing the small clearing, that he was going to pick her up—baby and all.

He just did so and started walking.

"What the hell!" Dorian unleashed her fury on Scott the second he put her down, on her butt, in the wheat field. "Let me look at your legs," she said in the same breath, her gaze trying to take in every inch of both legs from the knee down at once.

"I'm fine," he repeated for she'd lost count of how many times. Once for each step he'd taken in that quagmire. "Look, see?" He lifted his pants legs. "You get bit by a rattlesnake, you know it." When the man had the audacity to put his finger under her chin, lift her gaze to his and then grin, she almost bit him herself. "I'm feeling better right now than I have since I was shot," he told her. "What a rush...something like out of *Indiana Jones*, wouldn't you say?"

He was sweating. Carrying her and the baby had taken too much toll on his leg. But it was hard for her to stay angry with a man who was feeling so good about himself.

Most particularly one who didn't find himself worthy of fathering kids.

"We need to keep moving," he said then. "They're only going to wait so long for us on the other side. And a snake or two could have followed us."

"One could have come in ahead of us, too," she pointed out, irritably, but with a keener eye on the ground around them. "And McKellips, or whoever is in charge, has to have planned for the chance that we'd have continued forward through the snakes."

"Not necessarily," Scott said, sounding sure as he crawled

along in front of her. "He's going to assess from his own perspective, figuring out what he'd do. I was ready to turn around."

"No way you would have walked back there into a barrage of bullets."

"No, I was going to get you safely ensconced, and then go hunting. In either case, we're going to hang out in this wheat field until we find a way out of it without being exposed. And pray that it isn't watering day. If this field is watered normally, we have a one in fifteen chance of getting drenched, but since it's past late afternoon, I'm giving us a fairly good shot."

She crawled silently for what seemed like hours, but was probably only thirty minutes. Watching the ground, and Scott. Keeping her movements as small as possible so if someone was watching the hay, any movement would seem normal with the slight wind that was blowing.

They'd lucked out on that one.

But then a valley, at the mountains…most days there was at least a breeze. Hot as it might be.

After a while, the snakes weren't such a concern anymore. And Dorian found herself staring at Scott's butt in front of her.

Remembering sitting on the front side of that body…

And forced her thoughts to the baby tied to her chest. He was going to need to eat again soon. Glancing down at him, she was surprised to see him wide awake. Watching her. It was the first time she'd seen his eyes fully open.

She smiled at him. And continued to crawl.

A few minutes later, as dusk was falling, Scott stopped. They were in a middle of a row, where a couple of plants didn't mature, giving them some space, but one that wasn't obvious to anyone looking out over the field.

"You plan to wait right here until dark," she guessed, what she should have already figured.

"It's about time for Michael to eat."

He was right. She took the diaper he handed her, before passing off the dirty to Scott and then took the bottle. From the outside looking in, one could be forgiven for thinking they were seasoned parents.

At the thought, a longing hit Dorian. Hard. One she'd never let past her defenses in the past.

"As long as we're surrounded here, anyone coming after us is going to be detected before they get to us," Scott said, his timing perfect for getting her out of a hell of her own making, and back into the one they had a hope of escaping. "If that happens, you head away as quickly and low to the ground as possible," the FBI agent continued. "And I engage with however many bullets it takes."

There were holes in the plan. If he was hit...

Silently, she stared at him.

"We're in a pickle here, Doc," Scott said then. "You got a better plan?"

She tried to find a plan. Any plan at all.

And only came up with one.

Leaning forward, she pulled him over, leaned forward and kissed him full on the lips.

Long and hard.

Like she'd wanted to do in the past—had started to do, before she'd come to her senses, shocked at herself—and had pulled away.

That late afternoon, with no easy way out, she didn't pull away.

She held on.

And on. And on.

Chapter 21

Scott broke the kiss, but he didn't move away from Dorian. Sitting side by side—him facing one side of the row, her the other—their thighs almost touching, they could each keep an eye on an opposite side of the row, maintaining cover of all four directions.

He remembered the night before, instead. The way she'd frozen him out after they'd had sex. As though he'd taken advantage.

When she'd made the first move.

And beyond that, their situation absolutely did not support any activity that took energy away from that which they were going to need to save their lives.

Nor could he afford the distraction.

They'd both stipulated, openly, that they weren't looking for, or even open to, any kind of relationship flourishing between them or with anyone else, so there should be no hurt feelings.

And yet...the way she'd turned from him the night before...had rankled.

Not hurt exactly. You couldn't hurt when your heart wasn't involved. But...he'd admit it. To himself. He'd been put out.

And told himself, as he prepared to pose a question to

her, that he was going to ask just to pass the time until it was dark enough for them to make a run for their lives.

He queried, "I know why I'm doing life alone, not shared, so…why are you?" Not quite the words he'd intended, but they sufficed.

With a sigh, she looked down at little Michael, sleeping as though he hadn't a care in the world. Scott was pretty sure he'd never been that peaceful. Not even in the womb.

Almost as though she could read his thoughts, Dorian looked up at him. "You want the short version?"

"Is there a long one?"

Her shrug said little.

"The long version," he opted. With nothing but stalks of hay and hard dirt to look at, he figured he could use the diversion.

"My parents were both gifted in their fields," she told him, and he got that he was getting a longer version than he'd envisioned. Way longer. But with nothing better to do, wasn't averse to listening. "I was an only child, born to them in their early forties. They taught me from my first memory that I was to use my mind to better the world. Didn't matter what I was good at, just be my best at it. I was to do, not be done upon. To act, not react. To keep my head about me."

From what he could tell, the woman she'd turned out to be must have pleased them immensely.

"I met Brent when I was two and he was four. Our parents were all members of a local group sponsored by an international organization for people with higher-than-average IQs. The group's quest was to use their minds to serve others. As Brent and I grew up, we also became members of the group…"

Brent, her fiancé. He wasn't sure, suddenly, how much more he wanted to hear.

He didn't stop her, though.

"We started dating, officially, our freshman year of high school, though we'd been telling each other since we were five that we were going to get married someday."

Yep, he should have stopped her. Thoughts of Lily came pouring back. The only child with a close-knit family with close-knit friends. Scott's advent into her life in high school had messed everything up. Until, ultimately, she'd chosen to dump Scott and marry the family friend...

When Scott realized his thoughts had had time to spiral on him because Dorian had quit talking, he looked over at her. Prompting, "And?"

When her eyes pinned his, he swallowed hard, but didn't turn away.

"We were engaged when I met you."

That was it. As though that explained everything. It didn't.

"And?"

Dorian glanced away, shook her head. He thought she was done talking, until she burst out with, "My emotions are not in sync with my mind. They're... I don't know... immature...is the best way I can think of to describe them. I ended up not only breaking Brent's heart, but hurting his parents, and mine, too."

"How? What did you do?"

"The things I felt around you...they were based on nothing. We weren't even friends. They made no sense."

She'd felt things, too. He'd wondered. So many times.

Knowing that it made no difference to the outcome. She'd done the right thing, getting away from him.

She'd fallen silent again. He offered no prompts.

The conversation had grown...difficult.

He left it there.

* * *

She couldn't just leave him hanging there. It wasn't fair. Not after he'd explained his own life choices. She'd yet to fully explain hers.

Not in any way that would lead him to her reality.

Glancing off, down her end of the row, seeing again that there was no light, no movement, coming at them in the near darkness, she glanced back to see the baby still asleep and said, "I'd never felt anything like it for Brent. I told him so, hoping that we could work on it, do something to, I don't know, spruce things up. We'd known each other forever. We just needed to see each other in different ways…" She'd done her research before having the conversation. Had a list of possible actions to take.

Hadn't even made it to number one.

"He said that if I felt that way about another man, and not for him, then our relationship was doomed before it began. Feeling horrible about myself and my wayward emotions, I offered his ring back. He took it. And when my parents still supported me, and his did him, sides were taken, and a lifetime of friendship slowly eroded."

"So, you didn't love him…"

Her gaze shot back to Scott when she heard his words. "I did love him!"

"As a very good friend." His gaze was barely visible and seemed to glint truths.

"A brother, even," she admitted. "Not quite, but pretty close."

"You were ripe for any guy who paid attention to you, or you found good-looking and had cause to contact you physically, to show you that. It's certainly no reason not to trust…"

Shaking her head adamantly, Dorian cut him off before he could finish.

"He wasn't the first person I hurt," she told him, ready to get it all out so they could move on away from her, with her choices firmly established, just as his were, between them. "The first was Faith, the woman who was with me when we were kidnapped last year. I was her soul mate. Her rock. She had a really rough life, to the point that we had rescue codes. And when she was ultimately taken away from her mother to live in another state, I just let her go. Never tried to find her. To let her know that I was still there for her..."

"Childhood friends slip away, Dorian. You have to know that. It's a natural part of life when families move."

Pressing her lips together, she told herself to just rip off the bandage. "Sierra was my best friend. I knew something wasn't right with her, but because she was a private person, because I needed her friendship and was afraid I'd piss her off, I didn't push. Had I done so, she wouldn't have been murdered. My emotions steer me wrong, Scott. They're unreliable. Immature. I can't trust them. And I won't let my lack hurt anyone else. End of story."

"Sierra?" His tone had changed. Softened. Like he was on her side.

Which was ridiculous as there were no sides.

"Sierra's Web," she said. He'd said he was familiar with the firm. The story of Sierra was right on their website. And often mentioned in news stories.

"You named your firm after your friend whose murder you blame yourself for?"

She'd hoped to be done. It was getting dark. The baby would need to eat again, and then they had to be off. Hopefully to the blacktop, a passing car and maybe even home before dawn.

It was either that, or not make it.

To get things moving, she gave him the quick rundown she'd thought he already knew. "We were all friends with her. All had noticed things, different things, and when she went missing, we took our collective thoughts to the authorities. Our information led police to her rapist and his bookie killer."

"So you aren't the only one who noticed things…"

"No, but if I had followed my professional code, pursued the facts sooner, I could have saved her life." She couldn't say more about Sierra's clinic visits. But there was no doubting the facts.

And the fact was, it was time for them to move on.

From the conversation.

And the hay field.

The perimeter of the hay field was being guarded. They'd almost reached a clearing and Scott couldn't lead them out of there.

With his head flat on the ground, he'd seen the lights shining into the growth. The first time had come just a few minutes after they'd started the last leg of crawling themselves out.

And now, with the clearing in view, he caught the taillights of a running, but stationary vehicle. He had to assume that McKellips's team had guns posted on all perimeters.

There was only one chance of getting Dorian and the baby out of there alive.

He was prepared.

Reversing course, motioning for Dorian to do the same, he backtracked far enough into the hay to be able to speak softly without fear of immediate discovery.

Whether or not McKellips knew they were in the field

was immaterial. The killer knew they were somewhere within his mountain or in hiding on the ground. He wasn't going to quit looking. He had time on his side, as he didn't have a baby to feed, and he apparently had the manpower to pretty much guarantee his success. Scott wasn't willing to risk Dorian's or the newborn's life by trying to retrace and get back up the mountain.

He'd led them right into a well-laid trap.

With adrenaline pumping through him, his gut filled with certainty.

But he had something to do first.

"What did you see back there?" Dorian asked as soon as they were once again sitting as they'd been earlier. Side by side, facing opposite directions. Albeit in far tighter quarters. No dead stalks to give them more space.

"A flash of light," he told her. The truth. Not all of it. Not the worst of it. Not until she listened to him about something else that had to matter. That *would* matter if she made it out alive. "In the meantime, since we're back here waiting again, let's get back to that conversation…"

"What conversation?" Her tone remained low, as it had been all the while they'd been hiding out in the hay, and yet it sent a certain warning with it.

The same freeze he'd been met with the night before?

He didn't have time to take the hint.

"Yep, that's the one. I've been thinking about what you said—I think you're wrong, Doc." Never, in a regular day of his regular life, would he have said such a thing. Regular life was a thing of the past.

"Excuse me? You think my life choices are wrong? What gives you the right to judge?"

Good. She had anger left in her. The will to fight.

And he didn't have a lot of time to defend himself. The

longer it took McKellips to find them, the more troops he'd call. The writing was on the wall.

They'd done their regular checks for phone service all day. Still had none.

He could no longer rely on any hope that his team or Sierra's Web was going to find them.

"I think your assessment of circumstances is skewed by personal involvement and preconceived notions about yourself. Or an inability to see outside yourself."

Her glance in his direction was sharp. When she didn't argue, he pressed forward. "I've been thinking about what you said. Your reasonings. And it sounds to me to be more of a case of you not being able to understand or explain your emotions in a way that makes logical sense to you, so you see them as a flaw."

What, he'd become some kind of psychiatrist now in the waning hours of life?

Or something more was guiding him. Mixed in with behavioral analysis training. He chose to go that route. What did it hurt at that late stage?

"The instances you use as proof… Brent, Faith, Sierra… all circumstantial, Doc. You were engaged to a man you loved but weren't in love with. Those were the circumstances. Faith's childhood…circumstances. Sierra…a set of tragic circumstances. Those lives came into close contact with you, but you didn't cause the circumstances."

He could go do his job much more easily if he could do so with the assurance that he'd be leaving Dorian with a new lease on life.

With the hope of having a personal partner, a child, of her own.

Of having the things he'd never had.

Of having it all.

He could go feeling good about himself.

"I'm guessing Brent took his ring back, not because you were attracted to someone else, but because he knew you weren't in love with him. I can pretty much guarantee that any man you're in love with, who loves you in return, will love you for your mind and your heart and will eagerly welcome the occasional loss of cerebral response, take on the risk that you might miss a fact now and then, when you're caught up in the emotion of the moment. That's what love is, and does, Doc. And the lack of perfection you seem to find as a fault...it's called being human."

She sat there. Staring straight ahead at the hay just a foot from her face. The baby asleep against her.

He couldn't look at the little one, again.

In his mind, he'd already passed the newborn over. He was trusting Dorian to get him back to his parents.

"Any man?"

Dorian's softly spoken words had his head swinging in her direction. Her gaze caught his before he could stop it from happening. Moments careened down upon him.

That first kiss all those years ago. Seeing her again, scraped up, in the interview room at the clinic. Her feet kicking in the barn with moves he'd taught her. The sex. The kiss she'd planted on him earlier, just before they'd headed out to the clearing...

"But not you." She wasn't asking.

His eyes had adjusted to the darkness. He'd seen the question there, when she'd first turned toward him, through the shadows. That was his take on it. And the question wasn't there any longer.

Taking a breath, he finished the job he'd crawled back to do. "Not me."

He had to convince her. To set her free.

"I'm as selfish as they come, Dorian. Every single thing I do, I do for myself. With myself in mind." Total, undeniable, ugly truth. One he'd never have admitted under any other circumstance.

"I visit my parents in prison, flying to two different states, several times a year. They live for those visits. And I don't give a damn about that. I don't go for them. Ever. I go for me. To remind myself of who I will never be. Every choice I make, it's with one thought in mind. Me. Being the me I can live with."

He stopped, evaluating the solid truth in his words, coming up with total certainty. And then finished his task with, "My whole life has been about me taking care of me. I'm not capable of loving others."

He might have faltered on that last bit. He didn't test himself again. Didn't have time. "Let's head out," he said, last task done, ready to implement his final plan.

Without waiting for her agreement, he turned and started to crawl.

Chapter 22

Dorian wasn't ready to move forward. With every knee and hand moving forward, she grew angrier at the man whose butt was less than a foot in front of her.

The idea had been to appear as one movement, not two. A deer, not human. She couldn't think about what the day's turmoil had done to Scott's leg. There'd be time later to examine that.

In the meantime, how dare the man sit and tell her that she'd misjudged herself, but think he saw himself clearly?

How dare he offer the possibility of more to her, and then retreat, taking the one thing she might want?

She wasn't saying she did, but...what the hell?

The anger buoyed her. Made her a little less aware of the sharp ache in her neck, and the stinging in her hands.

Who cared about an irritant like physical discomfort when one had more important things to consider—like ripping into a man for...what?

Hurting her feelings?

For his own lack of clarity?

Or...or...pretending he didn't want her?

They were yards away from the clearing. As Scott lowered down to his belly again to scout, she remained completely still, ready to put a knuckle into Michael's mouth if he started to stir, just in case. She would need to pacify him so he didn't give them away to anyone who could be close by, until they knew the person was a friendly.

Or, at least, someone not out looking for them.

How would they know?

Grace had been a hard-learned eye opener.

Still down on the ground, Scott scooted around toward her, motioning her down to him.

Leaning forward, so that her ear was close enough to hear his whisper, she thought she heard him say, "I need you to listen. To do. Period."

Pulling back, she stared at him in the darkness. Saw pinprick glints in his eyes. And nodded.

"The stream we were following from up above is through this row to your left. You are to leave now, take the first row break you come to. It's about ten yards back. Follow the break, crawling as we've been doing, down to the water. And then, staying low, and along the bank, step in and move at the pace of the water, no slower, no faster, to keep the rush of water from sounding against your legs. If someone comes, you go under, baby and all, and stay down as long as you can without risking the child's life. While you're under, you move, in various directions, coming up for air, and going under again..."

While her heart thundered and her mouth hung open, she saw him move again, fidget some, and then he was handing her his knife. "Strap this to your ankle. And don't hesitate for one second to use it."

She who hesitates could lose her life.

His words from self-defense class so long ago came flooding back to her.

As she had back then, she nodded. Took the knife. Moved little Michael as little as possible as she strapped the weapon on. Trusting Scott fully to have her future safety in mind. To teach her how to protect herself.

"If you can swim across the river, underwater, do so as soon as possible. About half a mile back, the river butted right up to the mountain. Get there. Find a place to hide. And keep hiding until you're rescued."

Reaching into the satchel, he then pulled out the last bottles of formula. "I can't help you with diapers, they'll be soaked, but stick these in your waistband, and pockets."

He waited while, with trembling hands, she did so. She had questions. But she needed all the information first.

With his whisper turning urgent, he said, "Good, now go. Stay in your head, Doc. Do." He didn't wait for a response, just turned around and started to crawl away.

"Scott!" she hissed, going after him. "Scott."

He didn't slow down. Didn't even glance back.

And she got the message. Whatever he was doing, he had to do it alone. She and the baby would hamper him. Slow him down. Get him killed.

Just as he had that first night at the mission, he was trusting her to stay safe until he came back to them.

She had her instructions.

Turn around. Stay low.

Get to the water.

And with her heart in throat, and also with Scott, she did as he'd ordered.

Scott had nothing but the plan on his mind. Getting it right. The test of his life was ahead and there'd be no room for error of any kind.

As he crawled, his mind went over the plan.

Create every distraction he could. Make it appear as though there were two adult bodies in the field. Draw all manpower in the hunt to the hay field. Have all eyes on the continued ruckus he created. Attack, move through the hay, attack. He'd recorded the sound of the baby crying the night before. Had about 20 percent battery. He would have to make certain that he utilized the limited capacity of his ace in the hole in the most effective way.

The baby was McKellips's guarantee of a paycheck. Getting the kid back would likely save his team.

Certainly, that baby would be the killer's only hope of saving his own ass. And if McKellips made good, his team would likely be protected as well.

McKellips wasn't going to have anyone fire at any target that couldn't be clearly seen, lest the baby get hurt.

All Scott needed was enough diversion to get all eyes off the water, away from the mountain, long enough for Dorian to get to safety.

From there, his plan was, ultimately, to set the field on fire. Drawing first responders. A load of them. With the water source right on the edge of the field, preventing the flames from jumping up the mountain, a perimeter could be dug around the field, preventing spread in the valley.

A burn off not completely unlike ones that farmers did sometimes to refertilize their ground.

The fire was his last act. When Dorian had had ample time to escape. And he was staring death in the face.

Scott didn't hope to save himself. Didn't have any plan to do so.

If he made it out, he'd be thankful as hell. If he didn't… he couldn't waste a second worrying about it.

He was the bait. The sacrifice.

It had come down to Dorian's and the baby's lives. Or his. He'd made his choice. Felt right, knowing that he'd have lived his entire life, and gone out, a good man.

Beyond that, he wouldn't—couldn't—go. Just as when he'd been overseas, a young soldier sent to battle enemies that went beyond the scope of any training he'd had, he focused on what had to be done.

Not on what would happen to him.

He would not die as his parents and grandparents had lived. Breaking laws and oaths, sacrificing others, to live.

Nor would he cling to those in his life, as his parents had also done. If they'd been willing to sign away their rights to him, he could have been adopted out.

They'd been more interested in the welfare money received on his behalf. And maybe of their own selfish love for him.

And he was not going out with them on his mind.

Figuring, based on her earlier progress, he'd given Dorian enough time to reach the water—thinking of her and Michael swimming away to safety—Scott lay on his belly, aimed low.

Ready to slither like a snake to his next location.

And shot.

She was in the water, wading slower than she'd ever walked, hugging the bank when she heard the first shot. Freezing in place, Dorian listened. A couple of long minutes later, she heard another shot.

And then, only yards away from her, the click and static of a radio.

Dear God, was she being rescued? Had Scott known?

Too frightened to show herself just yet, she held the baby's head to her chest, ready to duck underwater, and hardly breathed as the river flowed slowly by her.

"All, I repeat all, hands to base. Just heard the baby cry in the hay field. I want all eyes in there finding the merchandise. And if the woman happens to be alive, get rid of her. That's an order."

McKellips's voice sent chills through her. Followed by nausea.

And reality crashed down on her.

Scott had set a trap for them, more ingenious than the one they'd set for him. He must have recorded the baby crying. It was the only way McKellips could have just heard...

Tears flooded her eyes, and she stymied them. She couldn't afford so much as a sniffle. Stood still, praying Michael stayed asleep, ready to slide them both underwater if he so much as twitched, as brush moved, twigs broke and the sound of more than one big body moved farther away from her.

All sound ceased, other than a barrage of gunfire in the distance, and still, she remained still. There'd been at least two men in the mountains. For all she knew, there could be a dozen or more by then.

Another gunshot, she heard a masculine note barely floating to her through the air. McKellips sounding victory?

Scott hit? Giving her some last warning?

About to move, she stopped when she heard the rhythm of the water change to her left. Something clearly in the water. More than one something. For a few seconds, it sounded like a waterfall over there. Or a dam burst.

Preparing herself for an onslaught of water, she was left staring as only calm waters came at her.

The last of the hunters, those in the mountains, had crossed the stream.

She'd bet on it.

They were the last of the bunch.

At their backs.

She was free to run. To head into the mountains and hide. To wait for rescue.

And there was no way in hell she was going to just slink away and let Scott Michaels die like trash.

They were closing in on him. Floodlights had flipped on after his first shot. He'd seen poles, had expected as much. Just kept moving. Detonating.

During the time he'd allotted for Dorian to make it to the water, he'd watched the flashlights and crawled around inside and outside the field, planting bullets in hills of dirt in various locations.

He'd shot two of them. The first had brought the flood-lights, and two sets of footsteps running.

That's when he played the recording of the baby cry-ing. Using an app that amplified it, but made it sound like it was coming a distance away from him.

By the second shot, there were four sets of feet on the ground.

He was now counting six. All teams of two. Like the hunters that morning.

He believed that, with McKellips, there were seven. And was fairly certain the killer had assembled his entire team. At least the parts of it that knew about the foiled kidnap-ping.

If the operation was as large as Scott suspected, and as was indicated by the website and the ledger he'd copied the other night, the general in charge had to be someone with clout, somewhere. Someone with a load of money by this point, too.

Someone in a position to have made certain that Mc-Kellips would disappear if he found out the man had been compromised.

So...the six-member team...someone, probably McKellips, was keeping the news small. Mitigating fallout.

At that point, they'd have all hands on deck to search for that baby. It was the only thing that made sense. The woman who'd been kidnapped... McKellips could have been saving her life for all anyone knew. Seeing a woman in distress, shooting to protect her.

Then some wild man comes out of nowhere and takes her again. McKellips's only crimes would be not reporting the murder, tampering with a corpse, with a crime scene, and not reporting the second kidnapping.

Nothing that would lead to a newborn kidnapping ring. Or illegal adoptions.

The hunters were systematically combing the hay field, circling in closer, leaving him less and less wiggle room. His only chance of escape was to get by one of them.

The floodlights limited possibilities.

His best bet was the same way he'd sent Dorian. The river. It was dark, with trees hanging over much of the bank, blocking any hint of moonlight. He could disappear underwater in the event of flashlights.

But he didn't want to risk leading McKellips to her.

He had to travel upstream. Meant swimming underwater until he got far enough out of earshot that his body against the current didn't create a surge.

He could do that.

And go in farther upstream, too.

He continued to move slowly. Had one more bullet he needed to shoot. The one farthest from the water. But footsteps were getting so close, he couldn't shoot without giving away the location of his gun.

He could shoot the leg. Then the next, and the next. Which would definitely give up his location and bring a barrage of bullets down upon him. They wouldn't shoot to kill, though.

Not until he gave up the baby.

Which he wasn't going to do.

Damn sure they weren't ever going to let him walk out of there. Baby or no.

"I think I got something here…"

Scott heard the voice. Continued to belly crawl. Pulling with his elbows, pushing with his feet. Staying in shadow, beneath blades of plants, as much as possible.

A radio crackled, and then, another voice, "I've got something over here, man…a diaper, and it wasn't here five minutes ago…"

The feet coming at Scott ran down the row next to him, so close he could have tripped the guy. Was just passing on the option, when he froze again.

"Attention!" The female voice commanded what she'd demanded. Loudly. Clearly. Through a megaphone?

"This is Captain Michaels with the Phoenix police. The FBI is here as well. You're surrounded. Come out with…"

"Scott!" Dorian was there beside him, on her hands and knees, with the baby strapped to her chest, looking…just as he'd last seen her, though wetter. "Come on!"

He didn't question, didn't need to know at that moment. With the satchel still on his back, he followed the woman and child to the river.

Chapter 23

As soon as they were in the water, Dorian took her place behind Scott, not even pretending she knew what to do next.

She'd saved him.

That had been the end of her plan.

He took them upriver, mostly swimming.

With the summer heat, the water was like a tepid bath and little Michael woke up but didn't cry. She fed him as soon as they were on dry land in a low mountain cave. And found some dry diapers in the satchel, too.

She wanted to wait for his sleeper to dry before moving, but Scott had said they didn't have time. He wasn't meeting her gaze.

Hadn't talked to her, other than to give directions or check in on how she was doing, since she'd found him.

"We've got to go back up tonight," he told her, standing at the base of the mountain. "And head down on the other side of the dam."

She didn't see how he was going to make it. Not with the way he'd been dragging his leg around on the ground for hours. Wasn't sure she would, either. But didn't say so.

"Following the dirt road out is no longer an option. We'll head out farther west instead. And run into the north-south blacktop at some point."

It could take days. He didn't say so. Neither did she.

She just started hiking when he did. Watching the baby. Watching him.

And trying to believe that as long as they were still alive, they had hope.

Scott realized the futility of pushing too hard when he heard Dorian's foot slip behind him. She was a doctor, not a triathlon athlete. And she'd been carrying the extra weight of a newborn for days. With nothing to eat but cactus fruit.

Granted, their supply was plentiful. They'd been switching between the four different kinds of plants that Dorian knew for certain were healthy and safe. And had different health benefits.

But as the moon reached its peak and headed downward, and he and Dorian were only halfway up the mountain, he knew he had to call a halt.

He needed intel. And then they both needed sleep. One thing was certain, McKellips wasn't going to just give up.

He might be calling in backup. Or, if his supposition was spot-on and the man didn't want to alert anyone else of his kidnapper's major screw up, he and his men would sleep some.

Which gave him and Dorian a little more time.

Just depended who all was on McKellips's payroll. And who he might call on in an emergency.

The hunt for the man and baby was clearly a crisis. A life-and-death one.

As an inlet came into view, leading back into a smaller cave, one that was deep enough to provide decent protection, he called a halt.

Built a cradle and pallet as though he'd been doing so for years, as Dorian fed and changed the baby with their last dry diaper. And he arranged the unused, river-soaked diapers on warm rocks along the wall for drying.

Their own clothes had been dry within half an hour of leaving the river. Arizona's dry summer heat was a real thing.

The first aid kit they'd taken from the four-wheeler hadn't fared well. The one he'd stolen from the mission was waterproof. He hadn't known. But was thankful as, dropping his pants, he got a look at the stained off-color gauze around his thigh.

The fresh blood didn't please Dorian.

He'd figured it was there. Had felt the injury open a time or two.

Lying on the pallet, too tired to care whether or not his shirt covered limp parts, he didn't speak as Dorian tended to the wound.

But was thankful when she announced, "There's no sign of infection right now."

It could come. The river water would have been on every doctor's list of things to avoid. He felt her reapply salve. And strips. Before beginning the bandaging process. They'd be out of gauze, too. If not in the next seconds, then by the next bandage change.

Just as they'd run out of formula sometime the next day. Even switching it out with cactus juice, the baby milk was running out.

As were the diapers. "Good call, leaving a dirty diaper…" he said then, sounding woozy, even to himself. But only because he was allowing himself to relax for a minute or two.

The second he heard any sound of approach, he'd have his gun out and be ready.

He'd rather have his pants pulled back up first.

"But the Captain Michaels thing?" He had to ask. The question was there…

"I heard a radio transmission, that the baby had been crying in the wheat field." She'd finished with his leg. Helped him get his pants up.

Neither one of them so much as paused as they went over his penis and he zipped them closed.

"You recorded him on your phone, right?"

Looking up at her in the shadows, with eyes adjusted to the darkness, he realized, "You just did all of that wound cleaning without your phone."

"I didn't know if I'd find you, so used the name Michaels, as a clue to you. Turned out, watching the circle of men closing in, finding you wasn't the issue. Getting them away from you was."

He could see that. Still didn't…

"I used palm leaves to make a megaphone," she told him. "Set them, with the burner phone, and my recording timed to start, far enough from you to give us a chance, and then hightailed it, at a crawl, over to you…"

She'd saved his life.

Good. They were even.

Holding out an arm, Scott waited until Dorian had settled down beside him, her head on his chest, and then let himself sleep.

Dorian didn't wake up in fear. She awoke slowly, with a sense of relaxation, and as consciousness descended more completely, didn't move right away. The steady rise and fall of Scott's chest, the strong, healthy heartbeat were…nice.

More than nice.

She'd been up every two hours in what was left of the night. Could see bright sun shining in a small corner of rock around the small cave's bend.

Didn't even think about the day bringing rescue. Instead,

she got up, used the quiet time to carefully check her surroundings and then tend to her own ablutions and returned to see Scott changing the baby.

She squeezed fresh juice into an empty formula bottle, rinsed out with juice, and then fed little Michael while Scott tended to himself, and then cut up breakfast for them.

It was routine. And a sense of well-being settled upon her. For the moment, only, she knew. Her life had begun to consist of only the current moment. They couldn't live as they were for long. She only had one more bottle of formula. And three dried disposable diapers that she'd have thrown away if she hadn't been desperate.

A diet of only fruit wasn't good for her or Scott, either. They'd finished off the power bars the day before. It wouldn't be long before their digestive systems reacted to the fruit overload.

All stuff she knew. Just didn't worry about on that early morning. After days of the same, she'd grown weary of the effort it took to be bothered by things over which she had no control, things she couldn't change.

While Scott went back out to investigate their surroundings in daylight, to determine their next moves, Dorian dismantled their pallet and the baby's cradle. Rearranged the satchel some. Holding out the medical supplies she'd need to change Scott's dressing before they headed out.

She was tying the little one to her chest, ready to go find Scott when he came back in. Handing her his phone. "Look," was all he said, but his demeanor, the tone of voice, all different. Stronger.

One glance and her pulse picked up.

"A road," she said, glancing from the phone to his face, and right back to the phone again.

"Paved and about a mile down the mountain," he told

her. "It could mean cell service. But even if we're too far out for that, I've seen two cars pass over the stretch already, and it's early yet."

"What about trucks?" she asked. Every vehicle they'd seen since they'd been in hiding, all driven by their hunters, had been trucks.

"Not so far," he said. "But it's not like we're going to head down there and just stick our thumbs out at the first passing vehicle," he added. "We find a hiding place with a good view of what's coming up the road. We observe. And then we pick a vehicle that is most likely to carry law-abiding people and we flag them down."

"How do we know who's law-abiding?" Thinking of Grace, in particular, she had to ask.

"We don't." His statement, so matter-of-fact, sent the day's first tremors through her. "It's all guesswork."

He thumbed through his phone again, then, held another photo up to her. It was blurry. Beyond blurry. But she made out enough. "A police car," she said, recognizing the aerial-view number displayed on roof.

"If we can, we wait for another one to pass by. If not, we look for a woman with children, for instance. Or, better yet, women with children. Maybe four women, heading out to lunch. Young couples. A vehicle full of young dudes, with at least one of them holding a basketball…"

He grinned at that one, and she smiled back. Silence fell as they watched each other. Until she broke contact and said, "I get it."

There were no guarantees.

And the only things certain were that they weren't safe and could die.

Sobering, she straightened her shoulders. "I need to tend to your wound." There were no guesses about that one. Her tone of voice must have communicated as much because Scott immediately dropped his pants but remained upright. "My muscles hurt like hell, but the wound itself feels less tender today," he told her, while he stood, looking at his phone.

With the baby strapped to her chest, maintaining professionalism was a given. Helped by the fact that Scott couldn't have been less interested in her kneeling beside him with her head at crotch height. He didn't care. She didn't look.

The wound appeared better than it had to date. Some of the coloring was still concerning, but the skin was already pulling together. She applied antibiotic cream, rebandaged and wrapped and stood. "I'm ready when you are," she told the man she still trusted with her life.

Her attraction to the man, and any feelings she might have for him, were what couldn't be trusted. Whether she believed what he'd said about her past being circumstantial, not a deficiency in her, or didn't believe him. One thing was clear to her. Aside from feeling drawn to Scott in the past, her current situation could clearly be the result of a form of Stockholm syndrome.

She almost said as much. Just to make things clear between them. With words, not just looks and actions.

But when he set off without looking at her, she followed behind him silently, thankful that she could.

The woman's touch was an addiction that he had to avoid at all costs. Scott told himself he was just reacting to days in hiding, living with death on their doorsteps every minute of the day, being responsible for two very precious lives, while still aware of all the other babies in danger. And all the babies in misplaced homes whose biological parents were grieving them.

An hour had passed since he'd avoided embarrassing himself by staring at a blank phone screen so his gaze didn't wander, reminding himself of the danger they were in. Reliving the night before, planning for the day ahead, Scott was still thrumming with an awareness of the woman walking the path with him.

She was everything he'd ever admired in a person, all in one. To the point that her physical beauty, which was definitely noteworthy, took a third-row seat to everything else.

He wanted to believe that once Dorian and the baby were safe, he'd be back to normal. His desire to be close to her, to hear her voice and see her face, would fade. His gut wasn't convinced on that one. But the possibility hung there.

Heading back down the mountain was much quicker than climbing up. Doing so on an angle made it easier on his leg. The vegetation was different on the western peak, thicker, with more leaves. By midafternoon, Scott was finding a total influx of adrenaline again.

He was going to get Dorian and the baby to safety. Nothing else mattered.

They'd made it to mostly level ground, were close enough to the road to find a hiding place. He'd seen no sign of hunters.

And he had bullets in his gun.

"Do you have phone service?" Dorian's question sounded with a note of the hope he'd been trying to keep in check. So he didn't make a mistake.

She glanced over his shoulder, so close he could feel her sweet warmth, as he turned on his phone. "You do!" She exclaimed, right there, next to his cheek, and he wanted to turn his head and kiss her.

The desire plummeted as his phone screen went blank.

"Your battery's dead," she stated the obvious. "And I left the burner phone in the hay field."

What kind of fate did that? Got them right to the winner's circle, only to make them stand outside it? The part of the plan where they had service and called for help was deceased.

It was a setback, not a fail. Scott shook his head, pocketing the evidence.

He was too close to believe that they wouldn't make it.

Warding off a strength-sucking downward cycle, wanting to hold Dorian up, too, he focused on the good. They'd made it out of the mountain alive.

"We see a paved road. Another hour and we'll be in hiding someplace close to it," he stated the plan again. A reminder to her, and to him. And then, when he started to reach for her, to pull her against him, as though to make some silent open-ended promise that he'd get her home yet that day, he shook his head and headed toward the closest cluster of desert brush.

Good intentions or not, he had no business making promises he wasn't sure he could keep.

With a nagging pain in her shoulder blade, a crick in her neck, Dorian put one foot in front of the other. And, when necessary, one hand and knee in front of another. The farther out from the mountain they traveled, the more important it became for them to stay low. Out of sight. For their movements to appear animal like to anyone up on the mountain looking for them.

Michael was moving more, crying some.

"He's got to be tired of that sling," Scott said, as they sat within a cluster of flowering bushes.

Rocking the newborn, trying to quiet him, Dorian, who'd

just fed and changed him, nodded. And then added, "It's also the cactus juice in his tummy. I knew it was going to affect his stool, but that's better than no nourishment." It was all a matter of choices.

You made the ones that kept you and others alive, first. And then?

Any man. Scott's words from the night before in the hay field had been rankling for most of their travel time that day. In spite of her best intentions. He'd said any man who loved her in return. But not him.

It looked like they were at the end of their journey. Scott had picked out another cluster of flowering brush, much like the one they were currently in, nearer the road as their final destination. From there, they'd pick the vehicle that would, in all likelihood, get them back to their teams. And then home.

She wanted that. So badly. Home. For all three of them.

But she didn't want to never see Scott Michaels again. And with him in Vegas, and her in Phoenix, that likelihood loomed.

The baby's discomfort seemed to have passed. His eyes closed, he gave an occasional dry sob in his sleep.

Another second or two and Scott would be announcing that it was time to head out.

As he studied the landscape, she studied him. She might not get another chance. Was incredibly saddened by that thought. "Why not you?" The words pushed up out of her.

He turned. Met her gaze for maybe a second before returning toward the road. "Why not me what?"

She had a feeling he knew. And knew to leave it at that. Pressure built in her. "Why any man, but not you?"

"It's time to head out."

Dorian put a hand on Scott's arm. "Not you because you

couldn't love me? Or not you because you could, but think you're not good enough?"

He turned to her then, his gaze professional. Sharp. "Really, Doc? Now?"

His demeanor changed hers. Made her more determined. "Can you think of a better time?"

Moving slowly, carefully, Scott resumed his crawling position, the satchel balanced in the middle of his back, instead of swinging under his stomach as he sometimes wore it. And Dorian slid into acceptance mode. Blinking. Refusing to allow tears to flood her eyes, as she, too, got back up on hands and knees.

Scott glanced back, checking to see that she was ready, she knew, as he always did. "I personally can't imagine any man that had your love, not loving you back," he said, and then, without waiting for a response, turned around and started to move.

"Just for the record, I can't imagine any woman who loved you ever thinking you weren't good enough."

Had they just issued declarations of love?

For a second, Dorian got all giddy and shaky. Open to the possibility that her life choices could change. But the larger part of her, the woman who knew all the things that she knew, figured there'd been no intent to admit to loving each other. Whether emotions had grown between them or not.

They'd been thrown together, with a bit of past connection between them, and were merely clinging to each other because of circumstances.

They were simply two like-minded, savvy, independent professionals who'd just issued their parting shots.

And her heart was going to have to accept that.

Chapter 24

The second he saw the police car, with the familiar emblem on the side, Scott's adrenaline surged with such force he said, "That's the one," and went immediately into action.

He'd worked with Creekville law enforcement on a case a couple of years ago. A larger municipality in the Phoenix valley, Creekville had a thriving diverse population with a low crime rate.

"Why would someone from Creekville be up here?" Dorian's question reached him as she followed him into the culvert at the side of the road, staying by the drainage ditch as he'd instructed while they'd been waiting for what he'd determined as the best vehicle.

"Best guess, looking for us," Scott said, and stepped out of the culvert and up to the road. Raising his hand with his official ID wallet displayed across the palm.

Police would likely stop for anyone flagging down help. He was hoping his insignia would give the officer some warning that, with an agent in trouble, there could be imminent gunfire.

As he'd expected, the car, still an eighth of a mile away, slowed and pulled to the shoulder of the road.

The officer, Sharon Luthrie, her name badge read, was already out of her car, and reaching to help, as Dorian stepped up to the road with the baby.

"Let me take him for you," the dark-haired, slim woman said.

Scott had already pulled open the back door of the car. "That's okay," Dorian smiled at the officer as she quickly ducked under the roof. "He's asleep," she added, sliding over so Scott could jump in beside her.

With an intent, assessing look, the officer shut the door behind Scott, climbed back into the driver's seat and sped off, sending an alert of their rescue out over her radio. Seemed to be listening to a reply through an earbud. Gave a response.

And Scott's entire system froze. Recalibrated. Shifted to a higher gear than he'd ever known before.

Looking at Scott in the mirror, the young officer, clearly unaware of what she'd just revealed, said, "Agents and officers all over the state have been looking for you two. I can't believe I just drove right up to you."

She signaled a turn with confidence. As though she knew exactly where she was going.

"I've been on vacation out of state. Was just called back this morning to help with the search."

Scott felt Dorian's fingers touch his arm behind the sling.

He'd captured a Creekville car via his phone just after dawn. When he'd seen the road. Large ID number clearly on the roof—462. Luthrie, as an obvious reply to a question on the earbud, had just identified her vehicle as 462.

Keeping his expression bland and facing the officer, Scott pushed against Dorian's knee. From the rearview mirror things had to appear as though he was exhausted and relieved.

The woman had just signaled a southeast turn. Not north,

or west. Either of which would have taken them away from the compound. To a city and safety.

"I'm assuming there's some kind of substation set up?" Scott asked, sounding as friendly as he could get under the circumstances, keeping his knee pressed against Dorian's.

Knowing in his gut that something was horribly wrong.

She hadn't been called in until that morning?

"There is," she said. Making the turn, still on blacktop. But Scott had a sick feeling they'd just turned onto the blacktop toward which he'd originally been headed. The road that connected with the dirt road out of the compound. The direction fit.

"Any sign of McKellips or his crew?" he asked, purposely letting her know he had some information about the case. Whether Scott died in the next minutes or not, the jig was up. His agents, Dorian's partners, were not going to just let them disappear.

He had no immediate plan, except to keep Sharon talking. Unaware that he was onto her.

What he needed was a miracle.

"McKellips?" the woman asked, shaking her head. "I just know about some guy named Conrad Boring. The kidnapper who had Dr. Lowell. Until now, no one even knows for sure you two are together, or if either of you is still alive. But like I said, I just called in this morning. Am just arriving in the area. I'm not even officially on duty yet. I was just heading to temporary mountain headquarters when I saw you. That's where we're heading now."

She sounded friendly. Reassuring. Calm. Professional, even.

She knew facts about the case. Was, in all likelihood, a working officer in good standing.

Completely unaware that she'd just cooked herself. Car

462 had been the zoomed, very blurred photo he'd shot that morning.

He had to stop the car. Get them out of it. Killing the young woman seemed like the only way. But he risked the car wrecking and killing them all.

A glint in the distance, half a mile or so up the long straight road, caught his attention. A bumper. High up.

On a dark vehicle.

The black truck? Filled with McKellips and his six goons?

Scott had no time left.

Dorian hadn't been sure she'd made out the 462 on the photo that morning. She'd thought 482. And had known that was too close for comfort.

Scott's pressure against her knee confirmed her fears. And sent alarm shooting through her in waves too sharp for her to calm.

She had to think. To do. Holding Michael close, her heart was breaking. For him. For all three of them. Their little family.

Scott was going into battle against those killers…fear engulfed her.

She started to shake. Couldn't figure out a plan. Or how she could help. She focused on Scott. Afraid he was going to jump into action at any second.

Tried to be aware.

To catch any clues he sent her.

To help him.

He tapped her arm. And then pointed to the floor. Still looking straight ahead. He held three fingers out, down low. Pretending to check on the baby, she watched them count down. Three. Then only two.

Then one.

Shielding Michael, Dorian dove for the floor as Scott, reaching for his knife, slid forward in a one-second, fluid motion.

"We all die here and now, or you have a chance to live." She knew she was listening to Scott. But could hardly recognize the steady, menacing, determined tone of voice. Glancing up, she caught a glimpse of his arm reaching around the driver's headrest.

Around the officer's neck? Had to be the knife in that hand, because the hand she could see had a gun buried in the dark hair that was all that was visible to Dorian.

"You're going to stop this car, open the back door, and then, with hands up by your head, lie flat and kiss the ground, or you're dead," Scott said then. "Reach for your gun and you're dead. Are we clear?"

"Yes, sir. Please… I didn't mean to… I fell in love. Was used. And then threatened…"

"Now!" Scott hollered the word so loud that Michael jumped. Started to cry.

Before Dorian even had a chance to kiss the baby, to try to soothe him, the car jerked to a halt. The door opened next to her head; Scott slid out. She felt the car dip slightly, heard a door slam and with a sharp turn—to avoid a body?—the vehicle sped out so fast her scalp slammed into the door.

"Scott?"

Was she with him? Or had the cop managed to cut him off somehow? Was she about to be turned over to killers?

Michael's cries grew. But she couldn't help him.

Not until she knew…she leaned forward, had to get at least a glimpse.

"Stay low." The command was loud. But no longer filled with death threats. And all Scott. Dorian's eyes flooded with tears. She let them.

Didn't know how to stop them.

"If you can, slide up and buckle in, but keep your head below the window." He was yelling, over the sound of the baby's frantic cries. The car bumped and hurtled. As though Scott had gone off road.

Before he'd even finished talking, Dorian, with one arm propped on the seat, was sliding her butt and the baby up to the fabric of the front seat. Lay there for a second, with backside up against the satchel Scott had left on the seat. And very clearly, knew one thing she could do to help him. Pulling the last bottle of formula out of the satchel, she quickly affixed the attached nipple and quieted the infant.

Scott drove like a bat out of hell. The words of a song flashed along with the cactus he barely missed as he turned yet again, keeping the car behind trees and tall brush as much as possible. Knowing his chances of escape, of getting out of the day alive, were growing slimmer by the second.

His only hope was to find a spot to stash Dorian and the baby, without McKellips knowing that they were no longer in the car with him.

And to drive long enough, keep McKellips and his men on his tail long enough, that Dorian got herself to a hiding spot. And eventually to the road.

To flag down a car that fit the parameters he'd already given her.

A bullet sounded in the distance. He didn't bother shooting back. Not until someone was close enough to him that he could actually take out a windshield.

Or more.

There was a chance, depending on how many were after

him, that he could take them down one by one. He had five bullets in his gun.

Last he knew, there were seven of them.

As the baby's cries quieted, and an eerie silence seemed louder than the road noise in the car, Scott stabbed his blade into the headrest next to him.

"Take the blade," he told Dorian.

And in his peripheral vision, saw the blade disappear.

The woman was a godsend. Followed all instructions. Kept her cool. Did all anyone could ever expect of her and then some.

She'd be alright. A sense of peace infiltrated the tension pushing through his skin.

He'd taught her all he knew, and she had a mind that would not only remember every bit of it, but one that could figure out how to adapt, to adjust, as she used the information. If it was possible for anyone to get that baby safely home, she was the one who could do so.

He was nearing the mountain, but the trucks—he'd counted at least three—were gaining on him. He had to get around a couple of peaks at least to be out of sight long enough to dump Dorian.

The car's undercarriage hit an object. He was pretty sure he'd put a hole in something. Could be draining fluid that, when gone, would stall the car.

He swerved. Scraped the side of the car against rock.

Swerved again, sliding in the dust, and saw a six-foot rock abutment.

"On the count of three, open the door, and run as fast you can. Behind the rock. You know what to do from there."

Scott's throat thickened. So much he couldn't say other things.

"One. Two… Three." Stabbing his foot on the brake, he

heard the door open, then close, and shoved his foot to the gas, getting the hell out of there before anyone knew he'd driven into the range.

As he peeled out from behind the peak, Scott knew he'd just committed suicide. His detour had given McKellips time to catch up to him enough that the truck, with its four-wheel drive and bigger wheels, was going to overtake him sooner rather than later. But Scott didn't give up.

He wasn't going down a loser.

With his foot pressed to the floor, and sweating two ton, he turned, and swerved, turned and peeled out straight ahead.

For ten minutes.

Twenty.

Watched his mirrors as he careened over rocky desert ground. Saw the convoy getting closer.

Within shooting range.

Heard the shot. Glass breaking.

Felt fire in his left shoulder.

Kept driving.

Thought he heard sirens. Knew he was hallucinating. That he'd likely triggered the police car's warning sounds. Was blaring his whereabouts...

And just kept driving.

Trembling, hunched over the baby, Dorian sat in a small indenture in the mountain, just beyond the six-foot boulder where Scott had dropped her. Knife at the ready. She'd only ever cut a person for surgical purposes, to save lives, but sat there reminding herself that she knew exactly where to slice to do the opposite.

As minutes ticked by, her own life didn't matter. She wasn't sure she could take another life to preserve her own. But for tiny Michael...

The silence became a roar in her ears, as she wiped away tears she couldn't afford to shed. They'd lead to dehydration in the ninety-degree temperature. Sounds of the police car's engine had long since faded into the distance. And then, the louder roar of multiple engines had, too.

Dare she venture out?

Aim for the culvert by the road where she and Scott had hidden to watch for vehicles? Did she trust herself to choose one that wouldn't get her and the baby killed?

Or that would return the baby to hands of traffickers?

It's what Scott would advise. She had one dry diaper. No formula. And a horde of men who'd be hunting her when they didn't find the baby with Scott. Her options were to try to get back over the mountain—with the baby at least a two-day hike—and then out of it along a miles-long stretch of dirt road. Or flag down a car for help.

He'd told her what to look for.

First responders were off the list.

She had to get to that culvert. The choice was clear.

And so, after a quick meal of cactus, cut from a plant at her foot, and filling a second bottle with juice, she held the newborn close to her chest with one arm, settled the satchel in the middle of her back and set off on a three limbed crawl. No reason she couldn't use her fourth. She'd been doing so while wearing the sling for days. It would make balancing the satchel easier.

But holding on to that warm little body gave her a strength beyond anything physical. Or logical. And so she drew on it. Filling herself even while she further depleted what energy she had left.

She would get to the culvert. One bush, one cluster of bushes, one bruised knee at a time. Scraping her already raw palm. Switching hands, and doing it some more. She didn't rest much. She couldn't bear to sit out there alone, without Scott. Was afraid that if she stopped, panic would take over and she wouldn't start up again.

And then, reaching the last cluster of six-foot-tall flowering plants, Dorian crawled inside, huddled in the branches Scott had broken to fit them earlier, closed her eyes and breathed. Shaking, she held Michael, felt him stir. Knew that he'd be waking soon.

Knew, too, that she needed to have a bottle ready to put in his mouth, to keep him quiet, when he awoke. It was a given, already established routine. She knew what to do and she did it.

Do, don't be done to. Act so you aren't acted upon. Act rather than react.

Her parents' words were like a litany to her as she sat there with branches poking at her hair, her back, feeding the baby. Trying to decide if she should change his diaper or save the last one in case of a cactus juice stool situation.

She could fashion diapers out of the scrubs she'd stashed at the bottom of the satchel the day Scott had brought her pants and a shirt to change into. Out of her underwear, even.

Laying her head against the branches sticking into her, allowing them to hold her tired weight, she held the bottle for the healthily sucking baby and closed her eyes.

Longed for…escape.

For Scott.

Was he even still alive?

He'd have come back if he could.

Tears trickled from the corners of her closed lids. She didn't care enough to wipe them away. She should have told Scott that she loved him.

Stockholm syndrome aside, she'd been drawn to the man fourteen years before with such undeniable power that she'd broken off her engagement over it. He'd thought himself forever marred by biology, and she'd failed to prove to him that he wasn't.

She'd failed to do. To show him how very valuable, how wonderful and worthy, he was to her. She'd told him he was a good man.

He'd told her he was selfish.

And…she'd done nothing. Just let things linger unsaid.

She could make diapers out of her sweats.

Or take a nap, first.

The baby's sucking stopped.

Eyelids popping wide, immediately, Dorian saw him lying there in her arms, sound asleep, tiny toothless mouth open, with the nipple still touching his lip.

He was content. Secure.

He trusted her.

As Scott had.

Do.

She had to go choose a car.

Do.

The word wouldn't let go of her. Wouldn't let her give up. Or wallow.

There were things she hadn't done. In the faraway past and in the recent past, too. Because she wasn't superhuman. She was one woman. Who couldn't do it all.

Who did a lot.

And could do more.

She had to go choose a car.

Up on all fours, Dorian settled the satchel on her back, kissed the top of Michael's head, and…

Was that a siren?

A *rash* of them?

Remaining in position to move, she peered out from between the branches camouflaging her. Saw the vehicles, some unmarked, pulling up at all angles along the road.

Froze.

Had McKellips found Scott? Knew that he didn't have the baby? Called in more troops? Did he have an entire police force on the payroll?

Was he that desperate to save himself with the general?

Or was the general in charge now? With powerful people behind him?

Was their operation that lucrative?

Pulse jumping through her skin, her thoughts flew while she remained completely motionless. Listening to the high-pitched warnings piercing the air.

She was one woman with only a knife. Didn't matter how well she knew the human body, or where and how to slice…she couldn't take down multiple attackers at once.

She had to retreat.

Get back into the mountains. Live on fruit and juice and diapers made out of leaves if it came to that.

Raise a caveman.

They'd grown up strong in the past…

"Dorian Lowell, Doctor, this is the FBI—if you're out there, let us help you. You're safe." They had a real megaphone. Were approaching from the road.

She didn't budge. Was afraid to blink lest she alert someone to her presence.

No way they were getting Michael. She couldn't lose another loved one on her watch.

"Dorian?" She heard Scott's voice. It didn't sound right. "We got them."

No. They had him.

"It's Hud, Dorian…" They had a recording?

"And Win…"

"Savannah, too…"

"And Kel… You're safe, honey. The baby is safe."

"And Glen…"

"And Mariah, sweetie…you know you can trust me with Michael…"

Michael.

Only one other person knew that's what she was calling the baby.

Only one other person knew it had been her way to let him know she was there.

Scott Michaels.

With tears streaming unchecked down her cheeks, and the newborn strapped to her chest, Dorian crawled out of the brush, leaving smudges of blood in the dirt.

Chapter 25

The paramedic wouldn't leave Scott's side. "We need to go, sir. You've lost a lot of blood and the hospital's an hour away..."

Scott didn't care if he lost the use of his left arm, he wasn't leaving the site until he saw Dorian and the baby. Knew they were safe.

His own team had already tried to convince him.

And had accepted that they weren't going to get him to budge from the case until he'd led them to Dorian.

It was good to be known that well.

It was family.

They'd pulled a car up as close to the culvert on the side of the road as they could get. He'd had to stay seated. Had nearly lost consciousness when he'd tried to walk.

But he wasn't going anywhere with his charges still out on the run. He was the only one who knew where Dorian would go. How she'd hide.

And how she'd survive.

He'd called out to her. Her partners had.

If they had to go farther into the mountain to reach her, he was the only one who...

"We've got her!"

He heard a voice before noticing the commotion. All six of the Sierra's Web partners took off at a run across the desert. Followed closely by members of Scott's team, and paramedics.

"Now, sir?" The uniformed medical man beside him didn't touch him. Didn't attempt to take a hold of his arm and guide him away. He'd done that once. Earlier.

It hadn't gone over well.

"Not yet." His throat was dry. He ached...everywhere. But he hadn't seen proof.

Motioning someone to stand by Scott, the paramedic—Bruce, he thought—walked away to talk on his radio. And was back a minute or so later, while Scott continued to stare in the direction everyone had run.

"Here, Agent Michaels, does this do it?" The man was holding out a phone.

Scott reached for it. Nearly passed out from the pain. Glanced at the screen.

Dorian, with the baby still strapped to her, in the arms of her partners. A big, family circle of arms, all wrapped around each other.

And baby Michael. He looked again at the sling. And the tangled ponytail of red hair.

"That does it," he said, stood, intent to go under his own cognizance.

And felt himself floating away.

"Is Scott okay?" Walking slowly, with Win's and Hud's arms around her for support, Dorian approached the road-blocking barrage of law enforcement vehicles. She'd already given up the newborn. Kelly was ahead of them, walking faster than Dorian could, to get the baby to the ambulance waiting to take him back to Phoenix. To the birthing center where he'd been born.

Where his mother, who was having preeclampsia issues, was still a patient. Hunter's return—Hunter, not Michael—was expected to help her recovery in a major way.

None of her partners, those holding her up, literally, and those walking behind her, had answered her question.

"I heard his voice," she said then, feeling confused. Unsure of herself.

Had she heard him?

Or had she just imagined him calling out to her?

She stopped walking. Looked to the two sets of concerned eyes on either side of her, and then, glanced over her shoulder, too.

"Agent Michaels," she said, finding strength from somewhere to give the tone that would let them know she meant business. "Is he okay?"

"We don't know." Kelly their psychiatry expert came up to stand in front of her. Making eye contact. And Dorian's bravado slid away.

Along with the strength in her legs. She felt the grips from the men beside her as they stabilized her.

"Tell me," she said.

"He's been shot, Dor. Through the back, left shoulder area. No indication yet on internal damage. He's lost a lot of blood. Was breathing on his own, but clearly struggling to stay conscious. And refused to leave the site until you were found. They're on their way to meet a CareFlight copter to get him to Phoenix."

Her knees strengthened then. Enough to allow her to keep walking. Albeit slowly.

Scott was alive.

He'd brought his mountain mission to a successful conclusion.

The baby, Hunter, was on his way home.

She'd done what she could do.

And that would have to be enough.

Scott's entire body hurt too much to move. He was… somewhere. Felt like he was encased in something. Tied up maybe?

He had to open his eyes. Figure it out.

Didn't want to alert anyone that he was awake until he knew who would benefit from the knowledge. His side or the other.

If only the annoying beeping would stop, maybe he could gather more clues.

And the stench. Like someone overdosed on Dorian's antiseptic…

Dorian!

His eyes shot open.

And saw all three members of his team, along with his unit chief, standing around him.

He was in a bed. Strapped down?

What the hell?

Glancing into four concerned gazes, he looked down instead of dealing with them. Saw the white gauze tying his left arm to his chest. Wrapped all the way around him. Not just taped there.

And frowned.

"My leg was shot," he said, remembering. So why was his torso tied up?

Where was Dorian?

And Michael?

"There's a little muscle damage there, but not much," Tommy, his second-in-command, said. "The wound had already healed too much to stitch. Leave it up to you to get trapped with a gorgeous doctor." The man's grin was familiar. Scott relaxed a tad.

"Dorian?" he asked then, eyeing his unit chief.

"She's fine," Bonita Holmes assured him, with her no-bullshit voice. "Scraped and bruised, but already back at the office, from what I've been told."

Back at the office?

"How long have I been out?"

"Two days."

Two days? He'd lost two days of his life and didn't even know it?

And Dorian was back at the office.

Not at the hospital.

That felt all wrong.

Yet, it was right, right?

His head throbbed. And he was tired.

Exhausted.

"Where am I?" he asked, to make certain he had some bearings next time he awoke.

"Once you were stabilized, we had you flown back to Vegas," Bonita said, as Ashley, Henry and Tommy all looked like they were about to do something asinine, like cry.

And he figured he might as well know. "Am I dying?"

"No, sir, you most absolutely are not," Ashley spoke up. "The bullet was lodged in the outer lining of your lung. It was touch and go at first, but Sierra's Web called in an expert who was able to extract it without puncturing the lung. You're going to be just fine."

The bullet from his leg traveled up to his lung? Didn't make sense.

He shook his head. Big mistake. "Dorian got…bullet…" He heard his voice. But wasn't sure he was still awake.

And, surrounded by his family, let himself fade off.

* * *

Dorian had thought, when she was rescued, that she was free. Instead, there she sat, with a bodyguard, McKenna Meredith, in her office. McKenna had retired from field work the year before, ran their bodyguard unit, but had insisted on taking Dorian's case herself.

Which was really Scott's case.

And now Sierra's Web's.

On the morning of the third day since her rescue, Glen Rivers, forensics expert, partner and friend, walked into her office. Nodded at McKenna before looking straight at Dorian, and said, "Ballistics have come back on the bullet that killed Chuck McKellips."

"And?" she asked, knowing that him telling her was only a courtesy. At the moment, with Scott unconscious, she was the only viable witness to a high-powered national case—not an expert working the job.

"It's a match for Scott's service revolver. He managed to get the fiend."

"And he didn't remember that?" Scott had been conscious when she'd been rescued. She knew now that she *had* heard his voice call out to her. That he'd insisted on being at the scene, in case he had to help find her. He'd know where she'd hide.

"He didn't mention the shooting, if he did remember. He was in bad shape," Glen repeated what she'd already been told. Sending another weight to the growing pile in the pit of her stomach. "The man was hell bent on using what strength he had to find you."

She'd heard that before, too.

Glen's sympathetic look flashed briefly as he turned and left her office.

From the second she'd crawled out from under the brush,

Dorian had been under the concerned and watchful gazes of the six people who knew her better than anyone ever had.

Her Sierra's Web partners.

They had questions about Scott Michaels. About her and Scott. About what had happened between them during their days on the run. Personal questions. She could almost feel the queries on the tips of their tongues.

But no one asked them.

And she had no answers for them.

She was pretty sure that she was in love with the man. Didn't completely trust herself to be discerning. And was absolutely not going to talk to anyone else about what had happened between her and the FBI agent in the mountains until she had a chance to speak to Scott.

If she *was* really in love, he should be the first to know that that little complication had arisen.

At the moment, they had a bigger problem to contend with. A killer dead. His henchmen unidentified.

An old woman with dementia who kept confusing Chuck McKellips, who'd helped her out ever since her husband died, with said husband.

And no idea as to the identity of the general.

By the time the FBI had gotten to the mission, it had been bulldozed, with a perimeter dug around it filled with water, and torched. Clearly part of a well-thought-out exit plan. They'd found the officer Sharon Luthrie dead from a single gunshot wound to the chest, tossed in the debris.

What they did know was that Dorian's and Scott's identities had been all over the news in missing persons reports, as part of what everyone had assumed was a manhunt for Dorian's kidnapper, with them as his victims. They'd originally assumed, when they found McKellips's dead body, that Chuck McKellips was the kidnapper. Dorian had quickly set them straight on that. Her kidnapper's body had yet to be found. Until Dorian had mentioned the general to her partners on the way to the hospital, everyone had thought the case had been solved.

And because she and Scott had been in the news, they had to assume the general knew who they were.

No one was sure whether the general knew if McKellips had mentioned his existence within earshot of them. No way to tell if the general knew Scott and Dorian were aware of his existence. But after the terror of the previous days, no one was willing to risk that he didn't know.

The joint FBI and Sierra's Web team working the case had determined, unequivocally, that she and Scott could not be in the same place at the same time until the general was identified and locked up. They weren't going to give the unnamed leader a chance to take them both out.

They'd further proclaimed that having the two of them even in the same state was too close.

Luckily, by the time the experts had reached that conclusion, she'd already brought in the surgeon who'd operated on Scott, and had been a microphoned observer of the surgery itself.

Since then, she and Scott had both been placed in protective custody. Separately. In two different states.

Made a troublesome thing like a pretty strong possibility of a declaration of love a moot point.

And it wasn't like anything was going to come of her feelings, real or not, anyway. Scott was firmly ensconced in Las Vegas. His team was his family. Her home, her firm, her partners, and now her childhood best friend, Faith, were all based out of Phoenix.

And he'd said, *any man*, but not him.

He'd made his feelings clear on the matter.

Besides, love or not, she was not at all ready to seriously consider the idea that she might change her own life choices as far as her future was concerned.

In spite of emotional involvement, she'd managed to help Scott keep the baby safe. And…maybe…emotions could be dealt with to the point of—if not exactly relying on them for guidance, then at least learning to accept and live with them…but…

"You ready to do another cognitive interview?" Kelly popped her head around the corner of Dorian's office. "They want me to take you back to that officer whose body they found this morning. Luthrie."

"Of course," she said. Her steady gaze indicated her need to communicate her willingness to do whatever it took to find the man who'd ruined so many lives for his own financial gain.

To save any babies in current danger, and to recover those who'd already been taken.

To help Scott finish the job.

Even if that meant relieving the terror a thousand more times.

Chapter 26

For all his physical trauma, Scott was working from a chair in his hospital room by the afternoon of the third day after he'd been shot. With officers stationed at his door, he listened through headphones as he watched a series of cognitive interviews with Dorian. The most recent had been recorded that morning.

Focus on the words, the information, came naturally. He'd been absorbing her insights and impressions for days. Relying on them. Working together, they'd saved at least one baby's life.

A time or two, as there'd been a pause in information, moments of silence, he'd experienced an uncomfortable lurch. She was looking at the camera, at him, answering questions as they were posed to her. Was reliving time spent with him.

And yet, she was so far out of reach.

Agonizingly so.

As she started speaking again, and he immediately tuned in to every nuance, every word, he brushed aside the sense of longing as nonessential. A residual feeling from being shot.

He'd be himself once the case was solved. The general caught. And the babies all accounted for.

Some of the earlier interviews he'd listened to that afternoon had been reminders of what he'd already noted in his reports. Accounts of things accounted for. Validation of his information.

But the current one—regarding Sharon Luthrie…he hardly remembered the woman. She'd been the officer on McKellips's payroll. Scott remembered threatening her, leaving her face-planted on the ground. Stealing her car and careening off into the desert.

He hadn't remembered her telling Dorian she'd take the baby, as Dorian got into the car. He did as she said so, kind of, peripherally, but not clearly.

Because of his blood loss, he knew. There were definite holes in that afternoon. Doctors had said he might never remember all of it.

He'd remembered shooting McKellips, as the man had pointed a gun through his truck window. He'd fired, not so much to save himself from a kill shot—he'd figured he'd already had that—but so that the killer couldn't escape. He'd needed his team to find out who McKellips was. And more importantly, had needed the killer to lead them to the general.

He remembered being in mind-numbing pain, fighting to remain conscious, as he waited to hear that Dorian had been found.

"So, you're on the floor of the backseat with the baby, and Agent Michaels, Scott as you call him, is leaning through the open partition, with his arm around the officer's neck—you think, he has a knife, you think to her throat, and he gives the officer an order to stop the car, threatening her life if she doesn't comply?" Scott recognized the voice coming from somewhere off camera. He'd been listening to it all afternoon. Kelly Chase, Dorian's psychiatry partner, he'd been told.

"Yes." Dorian's eyes were closed, but she sounded strong. Sure. "That's right."

"What does she say?"

She didn't say anything. The thought popped into Scott's head, as he watched Dorian frown. "Yes, sir."

What? Leaning forward, Scott froze for a second as his bandaged chest and arm rebelled against the movement, and, staring at Dorian's face, watched her mouth move as she said, "He asked, *Are we clear?* She said, *Yes, sir.*"

"And then what?" The offscreen voice came again.

"She says, *I didn't mean to... I fell in love. Was used.*" Dorian's lids flew open and she was staring right at Scott. "I think. I'm pretty sure that's what she said. She was saying something about being threatened but Scott yelled *Now!* and the car lurched to a stop..."

Holy hell. Staring at the screen, Scott rewound. Needed to watch every nuance of Dorian Lowell's face. To hear her words, in context, again.

And then stopped the tape. Reached for his phone. Pushed Speed Dial.

Sharon Luthrie hadn't been in it for the money. She'd been in love.

"Hudson? I need a deep dive on Luthrie's personal life. Yesterday."

Still watching Dorian, feeling her, growing more confident as he studied her stilled expression, he felt the familiar adrenaline coursing through him.

They were closing in.

His gut told him so.

And what it was telling him about his chemistry with the doc?

That was going to have to wait.

Dorian heard from her IT expert partner, Hudson Warner, late that day that the intricate look into every aspect of Sharon Luthrie's life had turned up a couple of prior relationships, but nothing in the past couple of years. At all.

Disturbingly so.

Along with weekends where she seemed not to exist. No texts, no phone calls, no streaming services or credit cards used. Once in a while, that would make sense. But for almost a year, it was two or three weekends a month. Even her car's GPS system showed up empty.

The woman had been in love. And then threatened?

The likely conclusion, apparently drawn by Scott and passed on and agreed upon by the team, was that she'd been having a secret affair.

With a married man?

A woman?

Two members of Scott's team were on the ground in Arizona, talking to everyone who'd known Sharon. Hud's team was tracing her steps immediately before she'd started disappearing for weekends at a time. Glen's forensics experts were going over McKellips's home with a fine-tooth comb.

Law enforcement was combing the mountains and surrounding areas, on all sides of the range, for any sign of McKellips's team members. The blurred photos on Scott's phone were all they had to go on, but they at least gave an estimation of skin color, body shape and a decent approximation of weight and height.

And for all anyone knew, another baby was being stolen, while they all sat in their offices, or worked the field, in relative comfort.

Eating healthy meals. On time. Sleeping on mattresses in air-conditioned comfort.

As Dorian ate a late supper of cobb salad and homemade wheat bread in her office with three of her partners—and a police officer stationed at the door while McKenna grabbed a nap across the hall—she kept thinking about Scott.

Her time with him.

Nights lying on rock and brush, with her head on his chest. She'd slept better those nights than any since her return.

All the conveniences of normal life had been stripped away, and she'd found...more.

Something that lasted when everything else was gone.

When all that existed was the moment between life and death.

Certainly, she would have bonded with whoever had saved her. But she hadn't just connected with Scott over their fight for survival.

She'd found parts of herself through him.

Her phone beeped as Kelly and Mariah discussed a shared client and Dorian glanced down to see the Text icon showing.

Tapped and opened the message.

A picture of Hunter, eyes open, looking up at his mother, with his father sitting on the bed with them, his arm around them both.

Blinking back tears, she smiled.

And knew there was no one else in the world who'd understand the mixture of joy and grief washing through her, except Scott.

She had his cell number. Not only from remembering it during her times with his phone during their fight for life. But because it had been included on the interoffice memo delivered to every Sierra's Web partner when the firm had partnered with the FBI on Scott's baby kidnapping ring case.

Quietly pushing the contact information she'd entered for him, she forwarded the picture.

And tried to be content with his returning message.

Job well done.

As in, over.
He'd moved on.

Scott's team got a lead regarding a political rally Sharon Luthrie had worked a couple of years before, right around the time she'd started mysteriously disappearing for weekends.

Hudson's tech gurus followed up with multiple internet searches, including social media services, collecting hundreds of photos from the event.

They scanned them for facial recognition of Luthrie, and assigned others to go through them one by one with the naked eye, on a physical hunt for any hint of the fallen dirty officer.

By the time Scott was discharged from the hospital the next morning, and, at his insistence, was taken to the office rather than heading to a hotel with his protection duty, a man had been identified as someone of interest. Several people had turned up photos that contained Luthrie in the background, talking to the man. A political donor, Colin Evart, who'd been known to back several major candidates.

Judging by some of the expressions on Luthrie's face, they hadn't just been discussing business. The way she'd been looking at the unmarried entrepreneur, the smiles in some of the photos, made it pretty clear that she was, at the very least, enjoying their conversations.

While Scott hadn't officially been cleared for duty, his unit chief was allowing him to call shots from his desk, as long as Scott agreed to head to his hotel with his detail at lunchtime for a rest.

Scott sent one of the Bureau's Arizona agents helping with the case to find Colin Evart and bring him in for questioning. He'd watch, and participate if the need arose, via teleconference.

Winchester, Dorian's financial expert partner, had his people looking into money trails. Starting with any monies other than her regular pay that might have been deposited into Sharon Luthrie's account in the past eighteen months. And following out from there.

They'd be delving into Colin Evart's finances, too, as soon as they had legal access to them.

And then, since Dorian had initiated contact between them, he texted and asked if she'd be up for an interview with Grace Arnold. He knew the expert physician had been in the office every day since her release, working steadily to help find the general.

Before heading with her detail to whatever hotel they had her stashed in at night. The exact location of her temporary lodging was need to know only, and he had no need to know.

Not professionally at any rate.

His phone vibrated in his hand, signaling an incoming text, less than a minute after he'd hit Send.

Of course, he read.

Two words. No lines to read between.

The answer he'd sought.

And it wasn't enough. He needed more from her.

You sure? He thumbed the response back. He was asking a lot—for a victim to face one of her attacker's known consorts.

Absolutely.

I'd like the interview to take place at the Sierra's Web offices. With Kelly Chase. His thumbs flew quickly from letter to letter. Using Autocomplete whenever possible. As though, if he didn't get things out with speed and alacrity, he'd lose her. Maybe lifting her out of her environment, and away from McKellips's influence, will help free up something more.

He couldn't ignore the sense of a weight easing away from his chest as he connected with the doc.

But moved through it.

Until he saw Dorian's response. Seeing me might help, too.

He'd had the exact thought. Had left it unexpressed so as not to put undue pressure on Dorian.

The way she'd seemed to read his mind, or at least to be on the same thought wavelength as he was, had followed them out of the mountains.

His relief, though illogical, was palpable.

And he typed one more time.

I miss you.

Dorian read and reread the text what seemed like a hundred times, as she waited for Grace Arnold to arrive.

She responded in kind. And deleted.

Typed that she hoped he was okay, and deleted that, too.

As she ate lunch with the partners in the office, brought in by their receptionist who'd been with the firm since its inception, and caught up on the case, she heard that Scott had been sent to his hotel to rest.

And left her phone alone.

But when word arrived that he was back at the office, and doing well, she picked up her cell again.

I miss you, too. She hit Send without a second's hesitation. She was done fighting with herself about it.

He'd been brave enough to put it out there.

She couldn't ignore the gesture.

And she couldn't lie to him.

Nor could she get him out of her mind as she listened to Kelly interview Grace Arnold late that afternoon. The woman recognized Dorian. Called her *dear*. Asked why she hadn't been in church on Sunday. And how her little girl was feeling after that cold.

She remembered seeing someone in the brush at the edge of her property, after Kelly prompted her with a description of the incident. Said that she'd fed *those folks*.

Spaghetti and meatballs. Fred's favorite.

Dorian knew the questions were establishing a groundwork for Kelly to work from—a level of lucidity—as the psychiatrist determined the best way to proceed to extract the information the team so desperately needed from her.

Grace was the only person they knew of who'd had dealings with Chuck McKellips. The only one who could lead them closer to the killer's crew.

Other homesteads interspersed throughout the area, roofs Scott and Dorian had seen on camera from atop the mountain, had either been vacant, or the owners had claimed ignorance of the mission and its work. The agents had not been completely convinced that no one knew anything, but it had been very clear that no one was going to say a word.

Could be they were all on McKellips's payroll.

"How did you meet Chuck?" Kelly's question came casually, without a word of warning to Dorian.

"Chuck is a nice boy. He helps me." Grace, sounding as kind as Dorian remembered, smiled.

"How long have you known him?"

"I'm sorry, honey, known who?"

"Chuck."

"Oh, Chuck…such a nice boy."

"Have you known him since he was a boy?" Kelly wasn't lightening up on the woman at all. Maybe not her usual method, but this time, a member of her family, her firm was involved.

"A boy, yes. Such a nice boy."

And on it went. Kelly let Grace guide the conversation to a point. Following the woman's mental wanderings. But always bringing them back to Chuck McKellips.

Half an hour into the conversation, Grace said, "This is fun, and so nice of you all to invite me for tea. And… I'm afraid I have to excuse myself. I need to go."

"Go?"

"To the ladies' room," the woman said, wiggling in her seat, clearly agitated.

Understanding how quickly the need to pee could hit, particularly at Grace's age, with lessened ability to hold on, Dorian stood. "I'll take you."

They'd had no tea. Had been sitting on couches in Kelly's office, with McKenna just outside the door, and as Dorian headed down the hall to the single-use bathroom reserved for clients, the bodyguard followed just a step behind her. Waiting with Dorian as the older woman disappeared inside.

Before there'd been any chance for the confused old woman to have completed her business, the door opened. "I'm sorry, dear, my zip is stuck. Can you help me please?"

With a glance at McKenna, Dorian reached for the front closure on the woman's pants.

"Oh, my, missy, we can't do that here. Not with gentlemen in the house…"

Afraid the woman was going to wet herself, Dorian stepped inside and closed the door, with the hope that, with them alone, she could get Grace to chat more freely. Scott was counting on her to make the difference. Nothing the woman said would be admissible, but once Scott got the "in," he'd find whatever proof he needed. She had no doubt about that.

And Sierra's Web would be right there with him, delivering whatever he asked of them.

Grace walked to the sink, not the toilet, leaning against it to turn on the water.

"Let me help with your zipper," Dorian suggested gently, from just behind the woman, preparing for a flood on the floor.

Tile, that would be more easily cleaned than the carpeted hallway and offices.

Grace turned, slowly, revealing the revolver, with a silencer, held steadily in her grip. "It's all your fault. Stealing that kid. I'm old. It's my time. I'll die, all roads point to me, and they'll never know what's still going on right under their noses."

For a split second, Dorian was working, a doctor with a patient having a psychotic break.

Until she saw the steely, hate-filled look in Grace Arnold's eyes.

Chapter 27

Scott was sitting at his desk when his cell phone rang. A second later, his desk phone pealed, as did those of his team members just outside his office.

Adrenaline pumping, he answered the cell. He'd seen the screen. Sierra's Web. His link to Dorian.

And was standing before he even saw every one of his team members up and rushing toward him.

Tommy got to him first. "I've just arranged a private jet for you," he told Scott, who was nodding, his one usable, free arm holding his phone. Whether the Bureau picked up the tab, or Scott would be billed for it, didn't matter a whit to him.

With the call ended, he dropped his cell into his left hand inside the sling and loosened his tie. Feeling the air cutting off at his throat.

"She's expected to be fine," Tommy said, hurrying beside him as his detail, getting briefed, followed closely behind.

"She has a bullet in her leg." He bit the words out. Could hardly sustain the fury—and panic—racing through him.

He'd lost friends. Comrades. Both soldier and agent. He'd lost Lily in a different way. And nothing compared to the despair roiling through him.

"I talked to Glen," Tommy was saying as they rode down

in the elevator. From what Scott had gleaned, as soon as they'd heard shots, every partner in Sierra's Web, as well Dorian's bodyguard, had rushed the bathroom to find Dorian bleeding and semiconscious, and the old woman, Grace Arnold, dead.

Kelly had been climbing into the ambulance with Dorian, when Hudson and the others had all called every number Scott had given them as contacts.

"He said the woman, Grace, was faking senility. She'd left a note on the toilet, detailing her deeds."

Chin tight, Scott nodded. Watched the floor number lights move, counting down. And was through the door the second that it popped open.

Protective team be damned.

The perp was dead.

His team, Sierra's Web, would be ripping apart Arnold's life to find the money trail. The connections. And hope to God, the babies.

He had to get to Dorian.

Men were after her. Dozens of them. All wearing handkerchiefs over their faces so she couldn't identify them.

They had guns.

Bullets flew through the air.

Dorian turned her head from side to side, trying to deflect the spray, to protect her head. As long as they missed her head, she had a chance to tell Scott she loved him.

And was carrying his baby.

Wait. No, she couldn't be pregnant, could she?

A bullet was coming straight at her. In slow motion.

She kicked up her leg, sharply, just like Scott had taught her and screamed for him.

"Dorian…ssshhh… I'm right here…"

She heard the voice. Felt a soft touch on her face instead of the bullet. But her leg wasn't right. Numb. Something tight was around it.

"You're safe." Scott's voice again. And then, "Thank God. Is she alright?"

"Her vitals are fine, sir."

She recognized the beeping then. The tone of voice coming from a woman.

And memory flooded back.

Grace. She'd kicked the gun. Knocked the silencer. And fire had rent through her.

She opened her eyes.

Was laying with her leg propped up above her heart. In a hospital bed.

And…there was Scott. Standing beside the bed. His hand gently rubbing her cheek. Pushing hair away from her forehead.

Was she still dreaming then?

But no, her mind was clear.

"Scott?"

"Yeah." He grinned. "You're back with me."

"I didn't know I'd left. And what are you doing here? How're your chest and shoulder?" He shouldn't be standing there tending to her.

"You were in surgery for half an hour, and I've been waiting for you to wake up. I'm sore as hell. As you will be soon enough."

She frowned. "No, Scott, you shouldn't be here. It wasn't her. She was in on it, somehow, the fall guy, I think. They're still out there…"

"Hudson's already found the money trail," Scott told her, sitting on the edge of the bed as the nurse checked various readings, typed on the computer and left the room. "Millions of dollars, all moving through Grace to offshore accounts. He's been able to trace various deposits to twenty-three illegal adoptions in the past six months…"

Scott was talking faster than normal. Hardly took a breath. Or let her get a word in. "Scott…" She tried to sit up. To get him to listen.

"All of the babies were taken right after birth, all from birthing centers not hospitals, and all but three of the children were being adopted legally, through another, legitimate source unrelated to this ring. My team's in the process of coordinating the rescue of the babies, the arrests of the illegal adoptees, and contacting the proposed adoptive families to see if they still want the infants."

"Scott!" Dorian spoke sharply. Needing him to listen to her.

And heard commotion in the hallway. Shards of fear shooting through her, she grabbed Scott's one good arm, clutched him tightly with both hands. "Duck!" she said, and then saw Hudson and a man wearing an FBI identification badge rush into the room.

"Another baby's been kidnapped," Hudson said, looking right at Dorian. "When they were wheeling you out, you were trying to tell us something…"

Another baby! Despair fought with anger. "Yes!" She gave Scott's arm a squeeze. "She intended all along to kill herself if anyone got close. There's someone else out there, someone running things. Someone close enough to Grace Arnold that she was willing to die for him…"

She'd barely gotten the words out before Scott's arm tensed in her fingers and, jerking away from her, he turned to the two men.

"Evart." He bit the word. "It just hit me. In Grace's house, I had to move things from a chair…" He swung back to look at Dorian, and then faced the men again. "There was a frame with a newspaper clipping. About a woman. Miranda Evart. It had been signed. 'Love, Mama.'"

Dorian stared at Scott. "In the fray... I totally forgot about it," he said urgently, looking at Hudson. "Check birth records. A mother would die for her child. What if Grace had a son before she married Fred Arnold?"

"Evart," Hudson said, rushing from the room, with Tommy right behind him.

Scott took a step toward them, glanced back at her and stopped.

"Go," she told him.

And smiled a little as he rushed from the room.

Even as uncontainable tears started to fall.

Colin Evart was adopted out as a child to a prominent family who raised him to understand the influence gained by being rich, and the personal power one carried to shape the world as they wished it to be if they were in possession of enough money.

He'd inherited several million dollars, but it had never been enough. There'd always been more to do, apparently. More lives to control through political endorsements. More money to be gained.

The political donor had been involved in all kinds of schemes during his nearly sixty years of living. The adoption scheme being just the latest.

He'd come up with the idea after Grace had reconnected with him when Fred died. He'd played on her guilt for abandoning him to earn her everlasting loyalty.

And the rest, he'd confessed to Scott and those watching the interview, had been almost too easy.

Until Chuck McKellips, a man who'd owed Fred and

Grace his life, had enlisted his deadbeat brother to make that last kidnapping, with the idea that they'd keep double the money in the family.

Even in handcuffs and chains, Colin Evart had been cocky. Seeming to think he had enough money to buy his way out of any legal problems that came his way. He'd declined to wait for his lawyer, as though there was nothing he could say that would keep him locked up. The man expressed no remorse. Not even a hint of grief at the loss of his mother.

And didn't remember Sharon Luthrie's last name. Saying only that the cop had come in handy.

It was the most nauseating interview Scott had ever conducted. He strode from the room, turned the case over to his team and left the Phoenix FBI building without slowing down.

Dorian had been discharged from the hospital, had been planning to head home with Kelly Chase keeping watch over her, and Scott couldn't get to her fast enough.

Over the past twenty-four hours, he'd spent what little time he had after work to rest, napping on and off in a chair in Dorian's hospital room. And had found more respite just having her close, than in any sleep he might have managed to get.

She'd become home to him.

He had no idea what that meant, in a real-world sense. They were independent loners. Both better suited to single life. She was here; he was there.

But when he saw her on crutches, through her front window as he took the walkway up to the front door in the gated community he'd been buzzed into, he finally had a moment of total clarity.

"I don't have to have all the answers," he told her as she

opened the door. "I've got some—you've got some—some we both have. Any way you look at it, between the two of us, we stand a good chance at figuring things out."

Mouth hanging open, Dorian stood there, speechless as the blonde psychiatrist he'd met a couple of times over the past few days stepped into view.

"I…think I'll be heading out," Kelly Chase announced to no one in particular. Grabbing her purse from someplace behind the door Dorian still held, she leaned in to give Dorian a kiss on the cheek and smiled at Scott as she brushed past him.

Dorian still stood there. Staring at Scott.

"You want me to go, too?" Scott asked. Because…he was who he was.

"No!" Stepping back, a little awkwardly with the crutches, Dorian made more room for him. "Of course not. I'm just…"

She stood there, leaning on crutches, and gave him a once-over, sling and all. Medically, more than in a man-woman way. As though to reassure herself, once again, that he'd gotten lucky and all vital organs were just fine.

"I'm in better shape than you are, Doc," he told her, shoving his good hand in his pocket. It was either that or attempt to pick her up with his one free arm, letting her crutches fall where they may.

She nodded. And then, her eyes getting that adamant look he'd grown to watch for over their days in the mountains, she said, "I love you, Scott. That's the answer I have. I debated about telling you. But when I was looking down the barrel of Grace's gun, and your face flashed before my eyes, along with words from long ago, telling me how to do that kick… I did it exactly as you'd taught me, lean and punch, knowing that if I survived, I had to tell you I love you."

Her stance, even on crutches, was filled with authority. Mixed with a bit of defensiveness. She most definitely wasn't going to apologize for crossing into territory he'd clearly marked with no-trespassing signs.

And all he could do was laugh. Out loud. Heartily.

Before he pulled his hand out of his pocket, lifted her up over his right shoulder as she squealed, and carried her toward the stairs.

Luckily, he'd fallen for a super smart woman. She was already directing him toward a bed before he'd made it halfway up the steps. He got there without mishap, but his chest was screaming at him, and his leg was throbbing a lot.

They fell to the bed together, Dorian leaning to use her hands to bear some of the weight, and then, with her still half sitting on his good leg, he kissed her. Full on. Long and hard.

Not caring a whit that his engorged penis was pressing up against her hip. He had it for her. Bad.

"I love you, too," he finally said when they came up for air. And then sat there, looking at each other.

A necessary break due to the fact that they were both in various stages of recovery from gunshot wounds.

"I don't want a long-distance thing," she told him, her face just inches from his.

"Me, either. I can put in for a transfer to the Phoenix office." Her firm didn't have another office. And her private practice office was there, too.

He'd miss his team. But they'd be in touch. And…they all had their own families.

Finally, he did, too.

"So…we're going to do this?" Dorian asked. "Be a couple?" She didn't look like she'd fall apart if he said no. But he could read the hope in her gaze.

"Yeah," he told her. "We're going to do it. And, federal lawman that I am, if I have my way, we'll tie it all up, nice and legal."

She threw her arms around his neck, managing, doctor that she was, to miss his shoulder, and followed him gently down as he lay back.

Her mattress seemed to be an extension of her. Welcoming him, harboring his aches and pains. Safeguarding their hearts.

Dorian's head planted gently on the right side of his chest. He heard her let out a deep breath. Scott lifted himself, taking her with him, just long enough to prop a pillow under her wounded leg. And settled back with an exhausted, grateful sigh. The last thing he remembered, as he started to drift off, was her saying something about starting a family someday.

And he fell asleep with a smile on his face.

* * * * *

Close Range Cattleman
Amber Leigh Williams

MILLS & BOON

Amber Leigh Williams is an author, wife, mother of two and dog mum. She has been writing sexy small-town romance with memorable characters since 2006. Her Harlequin romance miniseries is set in her charming hometown of Fairhope, Alabama. She lives on the Alabama Gulf Coast, where she loves being outdoors with her family and a good book. Visit her on the web at www.amberleighwilliams.com!

Visit the Author Profile page
at millsandboon.com.au for more titles.

Dear Reader,

As a kid, I had vivid, exciting dreams of teleporting to interesting places. That's why I fell so deeply in love with reading and storytelling.

Eaton Edge and Fuego, New Mexico, are fictional places, but they are tangible to me. I feel like I've walked (sometimes run) alongside these characters. I've lovingly prepared authentic meals with Paloma in her kitchen. I've jumped canyon walls with Wolfe and galloped through a snowstorm with Ellis. Like Eveline and Luella, I've come home.

So when I tell you how bittersweet it is to see this trilogy come to a close, believe me. I've known exactly how I wanted it to end...but it's still hard to say goodbye.

I have anticipated writing Everett's book since his steely introduction in *Coldero Ridge Cowboy*. I fell in love with the grumpy, exasperating cattle baron in *Ollero Creek Conspiracy*. One thing I did not anticipate was how soft this uncompromising man would become when confronted with a strong, powerful heroine like Kaya Altaha.

I give you *Close Range Cattleman*!

Happy reading, as always,

Amber

P.S. If you like Kaya and Everett's story, visit www.amberleighwilliams.com for some exciting extras—including deleted scenes, after-HEA episodes and recipes from Paloma's kitchen!

DEDICATION

As this is my tenth Harlequin romance and the
ten-year anniversary of my Harlequin debut,
I dedicate this book to you, reader.

Thank you for turning the page.

Chapter 1

"Hell's bells," Everett Eaton groaned as he crouched in the sagebrush.

Over his shoulder, his newest ranch hand, Lucas, bounced on the heels of his roughed-up Ariats and cursed vividly. "Jesus, boss," he hissed. "Jesus Christ."

"Calm your britches," Everett said as he examined the blood trail in the red dirt of his high desert country homeland. Among the signs of struggle, he saw the telltale teardrop-shaped prints with no discernible claw marks. He lifted his fingers, tilted his head and squinted, following the drag lines in the soil. "He went off thataway."

"Taking Number 23's calf with him," Javier Rivera, Everett's lead wrangler, added.

Everett swapped the wad of gum from one side of his mouth to the other. Standing, he shifted his feet and placed his hands on his hips. The trail disappeared over the next ridge, into the thicket of trees that surrounded Wapusa River, the lifeblood of his family's fourteen-hundred-acre cattle ranch, Eaton Edge and the sandstone cliffs that served as its natural border to the north. He nodded toward the mountain that straddled the river. "I reckon 23 dropped the calf during the night and the damn thing was lying in wait."

"Or smelled the afterbirth and came running," Javier guessed.

"He could have been out stalking and got lucky," Everett weighed. "Either way, he took it up Ol' Whalebones, ate what he wanted and covered up the rest."

"How do you know he's up there?" Lucas asked. His bronze cheeks contrasted with the paleness around the area of his mouth. His head swiveled in all directions as he tried looking everywhere at once. "He could be anywhere."

Everett eyed the back side of the mountain. It curved toward the bright blue sky. "You can hear him in winter. He's most active then. He doesn't go into torpor, like the bear. When Ellis and I rode out to check fences once the snow cleared after Christmas, we could hear his screams echoing off everything and nothing."

"Ah, hell," Lucas moaned. He gave an involuntary shudder.

Javier clapped him on the back. "You stay sharp."

"Watch your mount when you're up in these parts," Everett told him. "And make sure you're strapped. Got it?"

Lucas nodded jerkily. "Geez. Shouldn't the bastard have died like five, ten years ago or something? Ellis figures Tombs is eighteen. Mountain lions aren't supposed to live that long. Are they?"

"Not in the wild," Javier considered. He swapped his rifle from his left hand to his right, following the river with dark eyes. "Twelve years is a long life for a cougar. Could be another cat, moving into Tombstone's territory. Right, boss?"

"Maybe." Everett scanned the sagebrush, the canyons and the sandstone and couldn't chase the eerie sensation creeping along his spine.

Someone…or something was watching. "Mount up. I told the sheriff we'd meet near the falls."

Lucas sighed as they approached the three horses knotted together near the river's edge. "Sure wish we were riding in the other direction."

Everett laid his hand on his red mare's flank. Crazy Alice had been restless approaching Ol' Whalebones, tossing her head and the reins. She'd sensed that something was off long before he had. He patted her, then seated his rifle into the sleeve on the saddle and swung up into position with the ease of someone who'd spent a lifetime there. As he waited for the others to do the same, he knuckled his ten-gallon hat up an inch on his brow to get a better look at the canyon.

Tombstone was a legend and had been for as long as he could remember. Everett had first seen the mountain lion while camping with his brother, Ellis. Tombstone had watched them around their fire for the better part of the night. No one had slept. Everett remembered how the cat's eyes had tossed the firelight back at them. It was then he'd first seen what distinguished Tombstone from other cats—a missing eye.

His behavior, too, set him apart. Mountain lions shied away from human activity. It was why so little was known about them. In the last hundred years, only twenty-seven fatal cougar attacks had been reported. It was the rattlesnake they had to worry about most on the high desert plain.

But Everett had known that night what it was to be prey. He hadn't cared for it.

He'd seen Tombstone again off and on through the years. Males were territorial and Tombs ruled Eaton Edge's northern quarter and the surrounding hunting grounds.

Everett didn't believe in omens, but even he had to admit that it was strange how every time he or Ellis or their father, Hammond, had spotted Tombs high in the hills, trouble had followed. Hammond's first heart attack, the deaths of Everett's mother, Josephine Coldero, and his half sister, Angel, his sister Eveline's car accident...

Over the last year, Everett had convinced himself the animal was dead...until his father's death over the summer and a ride into the high country where he had seen Tombs take down a small elk.

Everett may be chief of operations at Eaton Edge, but it was Tombs who was king in these parts—and Everett reluctantly gave him his due.

He clicked his tongue at Crazy Alice, urging her to walk on.

"What's the sheriff and deputies think they're going to find up here?" Lucas asked as his neck mimicked a barred owl, rotating at an impressive angle so he could scan the shadows cast by boulders.

"Hiker," Everett grunted.

"Just one?" Javier asked.

"Yep. Kid thought he'd livestream his ascent," Everett said.

"He didn't make it?" Lucas asked. "Seems easy enough."

"The climb's intermediate," Javier noted.

"The broadcast cut off before he reached the top," Everett said. "No one's seen or heard from him in three days. Parents in San Gabriel are worried."

"How old?" Javier asked.

"Sixteen," Everett noted.

Javier made a pitying noise. "Same age as my Armand."

"Shouldn't he be in school?" Lucas asked.

Everett raised a brow. "Shouldn't you?"

"I got kicked out," Lucas informed him. "Didn't my mom tell you?"

Everett pursed his lips. "Your mama told me you were too much to handle and thought I could do something about it."

"How's that coming, *amigo*?" Javier asked, with a sly grin under the shade of his hat.

Everett shook his head. "I have a habit of inheriting problems of monumental proportions."

"Sure wish you had your dogs with you," Lucas told Everett as they crossed a stream. "They'd be able to smell a lion. They'd warn us, wouldn't they?"

Everett scowled, thinking of the three cattle dogs he'd raised from pups. "I'm not keen on putting any of them on Tombs' menu."

"He wouldn't attack them. Any animal would run from their baying. Even a predator."

Everett couldn't predict what Tombs would do, but he had trained the dogs for protection as much as herding. If they scented danger, they'd go looking for it. Everett couldn't think of any circumstance where Bones, Boomer and Boaz meeting Tombs wouldn't end in at least one of them maimed or killed.

"You've got a hot date tonight," Lucas recalled.

"What do you know about it?" Everett barked.

Lucas scrambled. "I heard it."

"From?"

"Mateo. Spencer told him. Spencer heard it from the house. Nobody knows who you're going out with."

Lucas was baiting him, and Everett wasn't willing to share any of his plans for the evening. He gnawed at the wad of gum in his mouth. "What've my plans got to do with anything?"

"We won't make it back to headquarters by sundown,"

Lucas considered. "I figure you'd have sent Ellis in your place to find the guy."

"Kid went missing," Everett reminded him. "If he's camped out somewhere on the Edge, I aim to find him."

The horses climbed to the mouth of a natural arch where the river sluiced and gurgled busily from the mouth of a cave. Water flowed freely now that the snow had melted in the Sangre de Cristo Mountains.

This was the lifeblood of Eaton Edge. The river fed the grass that made cattle ranching in the high desert of New Mexico possible.

As they neared the falls, Everett tugged on Crazy Alice's reins. A smile transformed the grim set of his mouth. The loss of 23's calf had unsettled him. But the sight ahead made the trouble slink back to the corners of his mind. "Howdy, Sheriff," he called. He took off his hat.

The Jicarilla-Apache Native American woman was five feet three inches at the crest of her uniformed hat. Under the two-toned, neutral threads that suited her position, she was built solid. Everett couldn't help but let his gaze travel over the hips under her weapons belt or the swell of her breast underneath her gold badge and name plate.

Sheriff Kaya Altaha's black-lensed aviators hid eyes as dark as unexplored canyons. If she'd take them off, he'd see the usual assemblage of amusement and exasperation that greeted him under most circumstances. She addressed him. "You're late, cattle baron."

"We set out at dawn, like I promised," he assured her, dismounting. He flicked the reins over Alice's ears and led the horse the rest of the way. "Ran into a snag a quarter of a mile south of here."

Her frown quickened. "Trouble?"

"Heifer dropped a calf before dawn," he said, fitting the hat back to his crown. "Something carried it off."

Kaya's frown deepened. "Did you find any remains?"

"Other than a blood trail…" He shook his head. "Cat took off in this direction."

"You think it was lion."

"I know it was. Normally, we don't keep the heifers this far north when the mountain's waking up for spring, especially not during calving season. 23's a wily one— makes a habit of slipping through fences. The big cats are more likely to carry off pronghorn, small deer, rabbit…" He wished she'd take her hair down for once. She kept it knotted in a thick braid at the nape of her neck.

Everett would love to see it free. He'd bet money it was as dense as plateau nights and as soft as the Wapusa between his fingers when it ran down from the mountain.

Something tugged just beneath his navel—a long, low pull that snagged his breath for a second or two.

That wasn't new, either.

Everett had had to come to terms with the fact that he had the hots for the new sheriff of Fuego County. He'd been wallowing in that understanding for some time—since the shoot-out at Eaton Edge over Christmas that had led to her being shot in the leg and, after some recovery, promoted to the high office she held now.

Everett knew what he wanted, always, and he chased it relentlessly. But the last eight months of his life had changed him. He'd been shot, too, in a standoff between a cutthroat backwoodsman and his family. He'd nearly died. Recovery had been a long mental process with PTSD playing cat and mouse with him. He'd found himself in therapy at the behest of Ellis and their housekeeper turned adoptive mother, Paloma Coldero. He'd set aside his chief of operations duties until doctors had given him the go-ahead to continue.

He had hated the hiatus. He'd worked since he was a boy—to the bone. He'd quit high school his senior year to help his father manage the Edge. Everett had never *not* worked.

After Hammond had died in July, work had felt vital. If he wasn't working, he was thinking about the state of his family and the grief he still hardly knew how to handle, even after all his months sitting across from a head doctor in San Gabriel.

Kaya Altaha had been a bright spot. The then-deputy had saved his life in the box canyon last July. Not only that—she'd checked in on him regularly. She'd worked to clear the name of Ellis's soon-to-be wife, Luella Decker.

The first time he'd smiled during his recovery, it'd been with her.

He hadn't known there were feelings attached…until Christmastime, when he'd seen her blood in the hay of his barn. He'd smelled it over the stench of cattle and gunpowder. To say he'd been worried was a damned lie—he'd gone over the flippin' edge.

She tucked her full lower lip underneath the white edge of her teeth, nibbling as she looked beyond him into the hills that tumbled off south. "Anyone get a look at the predator?" she asked.

He had to school himself to keep from rubbing his lips together. "Happened before dawn, as I said. Blood was dry."

"I'm sorry to hear about the calf," she said sincerely.

He could feel her eyes through the shades. He felt them from tip to tail. "I'm not looking forward to telling my nieces. They love the little ones come spring."

She studied him a moment before the professional line of her mouth fell away and a slow smile took over.

He darted a look at the two deputies roving around the space between the falls and the arch walls before he brought himself a touch closer, the toes of his thick-skinned boots nearly overlapping hers. He lowered his voice. "You can't be doing that."

"What am I doing?" Her jaw flared wide from its stubborn point when she smiled.

He'd thought about kissing that point…and a good many things south of it. "Flashing secret smiles at me and pretending I'm not going to do anything about it."

"I don't play games."

"You know what that mess does to me," he said, "and you're betting on me not doing anything about it."

"You wouldn't," she said.

"Why d'you figure that, Sheriff Sweetheart?" he asked with a laugh.

The smile turned smug. "Because I know the only things Everett Eaton fears in this life are bullets and bars. Not the honky-tonk kind—the ones that hem him in and keep him away from…all this." She gestured widely. "Despite how much we both know you like a challenge." She tossed him back a step with the brunt of her hand and raised her voice to be heard by the others. "Hiker's name is Miller Higgins. He's sixteen years of age. Five-eight. Roughly one hundred and fifty pounds. His last known contact was three days ago at approximately 10:23 a.m. The family reported him missing yesterday when they couldn't get in touch with him via cell."

"Cell service is low here," Javier noted. "How good was the quality of the livestream video?"

"Not great, but good enough to establish where he was

and what he was doing," Kaya replied. "If he fell during the hike and injured himself, he might have lost his cell phone or damaged it. That's the working theory. He left his car on the access road to the northeast. Deputy Root will fly the surveillance drone once we get to the top. I plan on combing every inch of this mountain and the surrounding area until we find Higgins. If we need to bring in more search and rescue people, we'll do so."

"Nobody knows Ol' Whalebones as well as me and Ellis," Everett explained. "He'll join us tomorrow, if need be. We'll find Higgins. I'd like Lucas to wait here with the horses since there've been signs of predators about."

She inclined her head. "Fine. Let's split into groups and hit the trail."

Chapter 2

"Ol' Whalebones wasn't always yours," Kaya told the cowboy. It was better than telling him to hold up and slow the eff down. Bastard was like a cat as they hiked toward the summit. She could hold her own athletically. But his legs were nearly the length of her body.

Everett took a glance back. He stopped, planting both feet in the rocky hillside. He extended a hand.

He wasn't even winded. She gritted her teeth as her bad leg shouted in protest and she took the offering. His touch was rough, taking her back to the day she'd been shot.

My hands are only good for cattle branding...

It was hard to reconcile the hard face of Everett Eaton with the pale shell he'd been in his cattle barn that day. He'd been using those hands to stop the bleeding in her leg—or trying. She liked his hands, and she was afraid she'd told him as much as she'd faded in and out of consciousness.

She had saved his life once, too. Hard to believe things had come full circle.

He pulled until she was even with him. She let go of his hand to take hold of the branch of the shrub tree to her left. "Thanks," she said.

"Take a minute," he ordered.

"No," she said. "We'll be losing the light before we know it."

"You can't climb if you can't breathe," he told her. "Here."

He unclipped the water bottle from his belt. She took it when he unscrewed the lid.

He watched her drink. She was aware of him enough to know it. She wondered if he counted the number of times her throat moved around her swallows. It made her hot.

Stop it, Kaya. She was sheriff now. There were those who thought she'd earned the position, and those who didn't. The latter had a strong sense she'd been voted in out of sympathy when she was shot by the former sheriff, Wendell Jones.

She might wear the badge, but she had a lot to prove. There was no time to lust after a long, tall cowboy with issues of his own. She handed the bottle back to him.

He took a sip, too. Then he lowered the bottle back to his belt and fastened it. "I know Whalebones didn't always belong to us. It was Apache."

"It didn't belong to anyone," she argued. "It was a sacred place. The Jicarilla called it Mountain That Breathes Water. Water is sacred to our people."

He grabbed the wrist of the hand she had wrapped around the branch. "Don't use trees for leverage. They've got shallow roots. A branch can snap. If you need to grab onto something, you grab onto me. I'm not going anywhere."

She pushed off the tree. Instead of grabbing him, she clambered her way up the mountain. It was best just to keep going—ignore the low simmer and smooth timbre of his words and what they did to her. "Do you get hikers out here often?"

"Sure. Ol' Whalebones was once the place to go for

camping in Fuego. Ellis and I led a few expeditions ourselves. That all changed when Tombstone established his
territory."

"I looked into it," she admitted. She could hear Everett coming at the same easy pace behind her. She wanted
the lead. His Wrangler-clad buns were too distracting.
"There've never been reports of hikers at Eaton Edge.
Not officially."

"When they do it the right way—knock on the door at
headquarters and ask for permission—we normally give
them the go-ahead. They can't leave any trash, must be
out by a certain date and time and are responsible for any
injuries or loss of gear that happens on the mountain."

"That's big of you."

"It was Ellis's idea. Dad went for it. I had to go along."

"Should've known it was your brother's idea." The
brothers Eaton didn't have much in common other than
height, horsemanship, ranching and the web of laugh lines
they carried around their eyes even when they weren't
amused. While Ellis was easygoing by nature, Everett had
a well-earned reputation for being difficult to deal with. He
was loyal as hell to anybody he thought of as his—family,
hands and the few friends he counted as his own… Anybody else was practically the enemy.

Ellis was a frickin' marshmallow by comparison.

Kaya may have been an officer of the law for a decade,
but she was also a single, red-blooded woman who liked
the look of cowboys. She'd been wondering for a while
why her glands had danced toward prickly over princely.
She liked things that lined up. Puzzle pieces that fit neatly
together. Her clear-cut certainty came from years of honed
gut instinct.

Everett Eaton was a gray area.

She'd been toeing that gray area for a while.

There was nothing certain about him. She hadn't yet had the nerve to cross the line in the sand she'd drawn between herself and Fuego's most storied cattleman.

"Did Higgins contact anyone at Eaton Edge about climbing Ol' Whalebones?" she asked.

"I checked with Ellis and Paloma. Requests normally go through them. Nobody'd heard of him before yesterday."

She climbed to an embankment and stopped to look around. As he climbed to her position, she bent over double, planting both hands on her left thigh. It sang an ugly operetta that made her molars grind. She heard him closing and straightened. "No sign of a hiker."

He stopped, too, and scanned. "No tracks, either."

She took the radio off her hip. "Root."

"Yeah, Sheriff?"

"Status report," she requested, cutting into the hissing static. As she waited for a reply, she took the bottle Everett offered her again and sipped. The breeze was high, cooling the perspiration on her face and neck.

"Javy and I made it around to the east side. We're making our way up to the top."

"Any sign of Higgins?" she asked, passing the bottle back to Everett.

"Not even an empty Doritos bag."

"I want updates every ten minutes," she told him. "Higgins had to climb either the east or south side, and it hasn't rained. Signs should still be there."

"Ten-four. We'll check in soon."

"Thanks." She clipped the radio into its holding on her belt. "Damn."

"What about the live broadcast?" Everett asked. "Didn't the kid say which approach he took?"

She shook her head, shifting her weight to her right leg. "He kept going on about climate change, cultural landmarks... His profile took up much of the frame so there aren't any discernible background features. And the livestream was cut off just before the summit."

Everett assessed her. "You're hurting."

"I'm not," she lied through her teeth. "We need to keep moving."

"Does your leg bug you like this all the time?" he asked as she established the lead again.

She dismissed his worry. "It doesn't bug me anymore. Period."

"Should've left you with Lucas and the horses."

She rounded on him, happy when her feet didn't slide down the slope. "If I'd known you were going to nag this much, I'd have thought better before calling you out to help."

He tilted his head. "My land, my call."

She scowled. It would be so easy to dislike him, as most people did. Why had she never disliked him? She sniffed and caught a strong enough whiff of something foul to distract her. "Didn't you shower this morning?"

The blade of his nose sharpened, and his nostrils narrowed as he took in a long breath, scenting the air. "It's not me." His eyes narrowed, too, as recognition hit his cobalt blue eyes. The pupils grew larger. "That's something dead."

Her head snapped in the direction of the wind. "That way." There was a clutch of trees clinging to the cliffside. She picked her way in that direction, crossing from the trail into the shrubby undergrowth.

"Let me go first," he said, taking her arm.

"Hi, I'm the sheriff. Nice to meet ya," she drawled, refusing to give up the lead once more. "Stay behind me or I'll make you wait here."

Her stomach tightened as she made steady progress sideways across the mountain. Automatically, her hand went to her hip, fingertips brushing the sidearm on her belt. She squinted, trying to see into the shadows of the trees. She recognized the smell. Death, a scent ingrained in the walls of her memory. "Goddamn it," she said under her breath as she narrowed the distance to the grove. "Stay back," she told him firmly, holding up a hand.

"Like hell," came the response at her back. He was coming, too.

She cut the urge to roll her eyes, tilting her chin as she peered into the stand. She took a step into the stubble of thicket that grew at the base of the trees.

It would have taken her longer to find it if not for the flies. Near the center of the stand, a small pile of dead leaves and natural debris gathered. She crouched, narrowing her eyes. Holding her breath, she brushed away the detritus. She hissed at what she found, sitting back on her heels.

Over her head, Everett cursed. "That's a body," he said.

"What's left of one," she confirmed. She pressed her lips together, careful not to breathe too deeply.

"It ain't human."

"No," she agreed. She tried to recognize something of the small animal. "This is something's prey. And it's fresh, so that means—"

Everett cursed again, filthily. He yanked her to her feet. "Get up now!"

"What?" She saw the pallor of his face. It was achingly familiar. "Everett, what—?"

"Look at the trees," he said, bringing the rifle he'd strapped to his back around to his front.

She saw the markings on the trunks. Claw marks. She lifted her Glock from its sheath as her pulse clambered into high gear. "You think…"

"Hell yeah," he confirmed, all but herding her back the way they'd come. "He knows we're here."

"He who?" When Everett continued to push her out of the trees, she raised her voice. "Everett!"

"Move!" he ordered.

Underneath his pallor, she recognized fear. Her response was visceral. It urged her into a sprint. Everett followed close on her heels. Her heart beat in her ears when his hand clamped on her shoulder, keeping her within arm's length.

They made it back to the trail. Everett kept his rifle up. "Look for the ears in the underbrush," he said, pivoting. "You see them first."

Kaya scanned. With everything waving in the breeze, she couldn't detect anything. She shook her head. "Who do you think is out there?"

"Christ, woman. Don't you know this is Tombstone's territory?"

Tombstone. Stories of the one-eyed cat had seemed mythical. "Tombstone's…real?"

"*Hell yeah,* he's real!"

She saw the sweat on his neck and blinked. "You've seen him."

"Saw him hunting in the summer and heard his screams just three months back."

Kaya released a breath before she raised the barrel of the gun to the sky and squeezed off a round. She did it twice, then again. Birds scattered and the thunder of the shots echoed off everything.

Nothing sprang from the grass except a fluffle of rabbits.

She lowered the gun. "He's not here. They run at the slightest sign of humans."

Everett was still tense as a board. "You don't know Tombs. Not like I do."

She observed the tight line of his mouth, the successive lift of his shoulders as his lungs cycled through quick, quiet breaths. She opened her mouth, but the radio on her hip crackled. "Altaha. You read?" came the brisk sound of one of her deputies.

She took the radio out of its holding and raised it to her mouth. "All clear."

"You fired?"

"Three shots. Affirmative. We came across a cougar den. Had to make sure we weren't being stalked."

"Ten-four. You want us to keep going for the summit?"

"Yes," she agreed. "Be watchful and keep checking in. Over." She clipped the radio back in place. "Relax. We're not getting carried off like your calf."

"Yeah," Everett bit off, watching the boulders in the near distance as if one of them would pounce at them if he let his guard down.

Kaya laid her hand flat against the warm line of his back. "You're really spooked."

"I'm not spooked," he said with a deep frown as he lowered the weapon a fraction. He didn't stop scanning the hillside. "I'm ready."

She noted the half step he took toward her, until her front buffered his arm. "You'll have to tell me what that's about."

"You ever seen a cat that size take down an animal?"

"Haven't had the pleasure, no."

"You don't see it coming," he said. "Its prey doesn't see it coming. Hell, the devil doesn't see it coming. It'll wait an hour if it must for its prey to feel secure—for it to get close enough. And it moves like a wraith. It goes for the throat, mostly. Tears out the guts. It feeds. Then it buries the rest for later."

She fought a shudder. "It's an animal, cattle baron. Flesh and blood. Not the bogeyman."

"Let's keep moving. We'll have better visibility from the top."

She pursed her lips when he took the lead this time. Keeping her hand on her sidearm, she followed no less than a few feet behind, her eyes trained to the periphery.

Everett propped the rifle muzzle on his shoulder as he watched Kaya assess the day's findings.

No hiker. No body, either, other than Number 23's calf, or what was left of the spindly little thing. Everett didn't figure Tombs had gotten much of a meal off it. Calves weren't particularly meaty.

As Kaya's gloved hands handled the tennis shoe Deputy Root had found near the top of the east trail, Everett noted the line buried like a hatchet between her eyes. She turned the shoe, checking the bottom, then pulled back the tongue to peer inside. "Men's size nine," she reported to Root as the man took notes. "The tread's new. Very little wear. No tear. Make a note to question the family. See if any of them know if he recently bought a brown pair of Merrell Moabs. Have them check for receipts." She lifted the shoe's opening to her nose. Her studious frown deepened as she lowered it. "Definitely fresh." She placed the shoe gingerly in an evidence bag and sealed it. "This needs to be labeled."

"Yes, sir," her other deputy, Wyatt, said as he took the bag from her.

She pulled off her gloves as she scanned the other evidence bags. They'd found one half-full canteen, one selfie stick, two crinkled foil gum wrappers and one bullet casing. She lifted the bag with the casing and walked to Everett's position. Holding it up for him to see, she asked, "You do any shooting on the mountain?"

"Not in ten years," he replied. She allowed him to take the bag. He laid the plastic-wrapped casing across his palm. "This is newer. Maybe not from the last week, but recent."

She nodded, taking it back. "You know anybody else who shoots on the mountain?"

"No," he said. "We haven't had hikers since last spring, and we make it clear—no shooting unless it's necessary to defend against wildlife." When she continued to measure him, he sighed. "I can track down the waiver the last campers signed. It'll have contact information. I'll have Ellis pass it on to your department."

"I'd appreciate it," she whispered.

He wanted to smooth the line between her eyes away with the rough pad of his thumb. "You got that same funny feeling in the pit of your stomach that I do?"

She blinked, the thoughtful glimmer disappearing as she lowered her gaze to his chest. "I've got questions."

"Like why we found one shoe and no kid."

She nodded. Her lips disappeared as she pressed them inward.

"Sun's going down," he said when her attention turned again to the mountain. "There's no use searching after dark. Cougar's most active between last and first light. We'll hit it again in the morning."

"I know."

Everett shifted his feet when she didn't look any less

discomfited. He spoke in an undertone he knew she didn't want to hear. "You know if that kid's alive, he'd have said something, called for help, after you took those three shots."

"Maybe," she muttered. "Doesn't make leaving for the night easier." She looked back at the shoe Wyatt carefully labeled. "My gut tells me Miller Higgins never left Ol' Whalebones. I can't face his family until I have more."

It'd weigh on her. It'd weigh her down hard. It took everything in him to stand his ground and keep his hands to himself.

Lucas called to him from the horses gathered near the river. "Boss, we should head south for home. Don't you have that hot date?"

Kaya's eyes widened as she looked in the boy's direction. "Who with?" she called.

Lucas fumbled at the sheriff's attention. "Ah…he never said. I just know he was real jazzed about it."

Kaya turned a stunned look back at Everett. "What's that look like?"

Lucas filled in the blanks. "Oh, you know, he's not much a grinnin' man. But once he got word that the date was on, he's been slaphappy."

"I'd like to see that," she mused, scrutinizing every inch of Everett's face. She might've looked amused to anyone else, but he saw the gleam in her eye and his heartbeat skipped. That look was damn near predatory. He cleared his throat and looked long in Lucas's direction.

The boy's smile subsided. "Sorry, boss. Ready when you are," he said before turning away to busy himself with Crazy Alice's bridle.

"Hot date, huh?" Kaya said, refusing to take her attention elsewhere.

"I think so," Everett mused.

"Hmm."

"Sheriff," Deputy Root said. "I put the evidence in your saddlebags."

"Good work," she said. "Mount up. I'm coming."

Everett gave Lucas and Javier the signal to do the same but walked Kaya to her leopard Appaloosa. "Nice horse," he commented, touching its nose. The horse breathed on him, its nostrils filling his palm and warming it with a searching snuff.

"Name's Ghost," she said, adjusting the stirrups. "She likes sweets."

The deputies walked their horses at a safe distance. They were far enough away. Everett felt free to touch her finally, turning her to him. With Ghost's long form between them and the deputies and his own men, Everett filled the space between them. "Are you okay to ride?"

Her smile came slowly. It didn't stretch to fill the ridges of her cheekbones as he'd seen it do at its height, but it warmed. "I was born on the rez. I can ride with the best of them."

"You can find the access road okay?" he asked. "Dark's coming on quick."

"We'll find it," she assured him. She paused, her gaze tracking the line of his throat. Her voice lowered a fraction. "You better get along. Wouldn't want you to miss that date."

"You're not backing out?"

She lifted her eyes to the passing clouds. With the sun low to the west, they burned. "I'll let you know."

"Don't back out," he said.

A laugh sounded in her throat. "Careful. You sound a little slaphappy."

"Lucas doesn't know what he's talking about."

"No?" she said, and she ran a hand down the length

of his shirtfront, making the skin underneath the buttons judder. "Pity."

He caught her wrist before she could feel his muscles quiver under her fingertips. "Eight o'clock, right?"

"Better make it nine, at this rate."

He grinned. "Sure, Sheriff. Sweetheart."

She brought both hands to his lapels and pulled him down to her height. Dropping her voice to a whisper, she cautioned, "Easy on the endearments. I have a reputation to establish."

"I'm aware of your reputation." All he saw...all he wanted...was her mouth under his. "Just as I'm aware it took me three months, thirteen days and nine hours to talk you into going out with me. I'll be damned if I screw this up now." He bent his head to hers and took her mouth.

She made an involuntary "*Mmm*." He released her, stepping away just as fast as he'd swooped, lest he take more than he should with his men and hers within shouting distance. His blood had quickened at the taste, the promise of her. "Don't back out," he whispered.

She pressed a hand to her horse's saddle, touching her mouth. She dropped her hand when she saw him watching. "Ride on. Isn't that what cowboys are supposed to do?"

He tipped his hat to her. "Ladies first."

Chapter 3

Kaya was more tired than she would have liked. And she was worried. She'd expected to find more of Miller Higgins on Ol' Whalebones than his right shoe.

The shell casing bothered her long after she left the station house. She'd stayed long enough to stable Ghost and update the mayor on the hiker's whereabouts—or lack thereof. Then she fielded the phone call from Higgins's mother and arranged for the next search party to meet at the base of the mountain the following morning.

Her house was near downtown Fuego. It was small. She liked to think of it as cozy—cozy enough for one... and that was stretching it. Its one redeeming aspect was the little windowed alcove off the kitchen she used for her round bistro table and as many potted plants as she could squeeze in along the walls. She set her bag down there, taking out the file on Higgins.

She opened it. His smiling photograph stared back at her.

"What happened to you on the mountain?" She wanted to know. He was just a kid—one with strong convictions... But a kid just the same.

She closed the file and told herself to end the questions for the night. If she continued, questions would spring into more before she had a hydra-like situation on her hands. She wouldn't be able to concentrate on anything if she didn't let the inquiries lie.

She checked the time on the stove display and cursed. It was a quarter past eight. She unbuckled her weapons belt and slid it off as she veered toward the bedroom.

As she showered, the questions didn't stop coming.

If it was an accident, what happened? Did he fall down the mountain? Was that why there was only one shoe, the new selfie stick and his half-drunk canteen? Where was Higgins's pack? Every hiker carries a pack. Where was his camera and cell phone? What caused him to stumble? Was it the cougar?

No, Kaya thought. *No*. If it had been the cat, there would have been evidence of that...

Everett's visual came back to her, accompanied by his grim baritone.

...it goes for the throat, mostly. Tears out the guts. It feeds. Then it buries the rest...

There had been no tracks on the summit. No blood they'd been able to see. No remains of any kind...except for the shoe. There weren't drag marks through the brush.

Which brought Kaya's questions around to...

Foul play? Did someone else beat Higgins to the top of Whalebones? Had the perpetrator been waiting? Was their meeting coincidental? If so, why did the perpetrator attack? Was the shoe left behind when the perpetrator carried the body off?

She remembered the absence of blood or drag marks.

Was the perpetrator smart enough to cover his tracks?

Dogs, she thought. They needed search dogs on the summit tomorrow. She needed to call Root, set it up...

She pulled back the shower curtain and checked the watch she had left on the counter. *Eight-thirty*.

She quickly washed the shampoo out of her hair and shut off the tap. She towel dried her hair before she remembered to shave.

It had been so long since she'd dated, she was out of her routine. Placing one leg on the closed commode, she lathered one part of her leg after the other before dragging her razor over it, as carefully as she could manage in a hurry. She nicked herself only once on the knee before she finished. She bounced on the toes of her left leg a bit as she lowered the right back down to the ground. It ached in the center of her thigh. Telling herself to remember to take a pain pill before she left, she went into the bedroom to find something to wear.

The little black dress wasn't new. She shimmied into it, grunting a bit to fit it over the wide points of her chest and hips. She was more muscular than she'd been when she bought it. She tried not to think about her mannish shoulders as she turned to look in the full-length mirror she'd mounted to her closet door.

The dress hit her midthigh. She didn't remember it being that short.

"Hmm," she said as she turned to the side, examining. It was hardly appropriate for someone of her rank.

She thought about her former boss, Sheriff Jones, in something this short and snorted in reaction.

She trailed her fingertips over the gunshot wound he'd put in her. It was completely visible below the hem.

She sighed. That wouldn't do. Nothing halted revelry like a solid reminder that she'd almost lost her life in her date's hands.

She decided on a maxi dress that exposed her shoulder

line and one leg up to the knee in a slit. Seeing that another ten minutes had passed, she rummaged through shoes until she found a pair of wedge heels that matched, then went into the bathroom to find her makeup bag.

"You're sheriff now," she said out loud as she applied mascara, wary of messing it up and having to start over. "Men should take you seriously, Kaya, with or without mascara...whether you're cuffing them...dating them..." Still, the thought of going on this date without mascara... "Nuh-uh," she decided as she switched eyes.

She felt the minutes tick by as she pulled the towel down from her hair. The strands fell to her waist, wet as a drowned rat. "Be late, cattle baron."

The doorbell rang promptly at nine o'clock, causing her to groan at the state of things. Her hair still wasn't dry. There would be no fancying it. "Hold on a minute," she said with bobby pins between her teeth as she knotted her hair on top of her head and hastily pinned flyaways.

By the time she threw open the door, he'd taken to pounding on it with his fist. "Yes," she said, exasperated. "I can..." She trailed off, noting the sport coat over his clean-white button down. His hat was in his hand. His tousled black hair was thick and clean. His dark beard had a nice sheen. He'd trimmed it. "...hear you," she finished, lamely. "Wow. You look...decent."

She'd never seen Everett Eaton look so shiny. Not outside of a wedding or a funeral. And he always looked like his family dragged him to those kinds of things.

"I should hope so," he said. "Paloma threatened to hold me down and shave me." His smile came slowly as he lowered his gaze from her made-up face to her bare shoulders, over the pattern of the dress, down the long slit. "You look fine, Sheriff. Damn fine." And he made a noise in his throat that shot straight through her.

She gripped the door, feeling his eyes everywhere. *Here we go again.* What was it about this cowboy? She made the mistake of shifting onto her left leg in a casual stance. She ruined it by moving to the other leg quickly. Hissing at the pain, she closed her eyes for a moment and touched her brow to the cool wood underneath her hand.

"Hey," he said, stepping over the threshold. "You doing all right?"

"Mmm." She mashed her lips together and offered a nod. He wouldn't get the best of her tonight. If they were going to do this…if she was going to take this leap with him— ill-fated or otherwise—she wanted to be at her best. He'd saved her life, after all. The least she could do was wait for a night when she wasn't worn down. "Listen. I hate to do this. But it's late and there's a lot on my leg… I mean, *my mind.* Maybe we should do this another—"

"Nope."

She jerked her head back. "I'm sorry. 'Nope'?"

"That's right," he said with a decisive bob of his head. "Nope."

He made the *p* come to a point at the end. She narrowed her eyes. "You don't want me tonight, Everett."

He didn't miss a beat. "I beg to differ, sweetheart."

"I'm distracted," she said, ticking the excuses off on her fingers. "I'm tired. I'm a little cranky. I'm more than a little sore…"

"I'll take you any way I can get you. Distracted, tired, cranky… If you're hurting, I'll carry you," he revealed.

"Oh," she said, not at all swept off her feet. "That's nice."

"As for the sore part, I plan to buy a large bottle of wine

for our table when we get to the restaurant for our reservation in…" He checked his big, silver watch. "…a half hour. And I'm not waiting another three months for you to decide that this is right again, so get your bag because otherwise I'm hauling you over my shoulder and we're leaving without it."

She blew out a hard breath. "I'd like a word with whichever barnyard animal raised you."

"Can't," he said. "We sold it for beef a while ago."

When she only stood staring at him, he made a move toward her.

"All right!" she shrieked, dancing out of his reach. She muttered as she went back into her bedroom. "I am the sheriff," she reasoned as she shoved her Glock down into her beaded bag with her wallet and phone, then yanked a sweater off a hanger and stalked back to the door.

"Why wasn't there more?" Kaya questioned. "Why weren't there signs of a struggle? If he fell on the trail, we should have found his body near the trail. Unless something or someone dragged him off…"

Everett bobbed his head in a nod as she went on about the day's search and all the questions that had arisen from it. He poured her another tall glass of wine. At least she was drinking it. He wondered how many glasses it would take for her to forget about work. She was well into two.

He raised the label of the wine toward the light, squinting to read the alcohol ratio. He raised a brow and set it back down on the table.

Kaya Altaha was far from a cheap date.

She'd ordered a steak, like him, and wasn't that just a turn-on? She looked good in candlelight, so good he wondered why he'd taken her out in public and not back to the

Edge where he could kick everybody out of Eaton House and distract her with something other than red meat and wine...

Because clearly those two things weren't doing the job. Neither was the fancy restaurant with its crystal chandeliers, fine china, white tablecloths and overdressed servers. He picked his whiskey glass up off the table, tossed back the contents and savored the burn of top-shelf liquor. Setting the glass down, he leaned forward and asked, "You wanna dance?"

She fumbled in the middle of another question. Her mouth hung open, red as a poppy and glistening, like she'd coated it in gloss. She looked around, as if noting the chandeliers and other well-dressed patrons for the first time. "Yeah, there's no dancing here," she pointed out.

"There could be," he considered. He reached across the table and laid his hand next to hers on the tablecloth.

"No," she decided.

"You're a fine dancer, as I recall." And he smiled at the memory of spinning her around the kitchen at Eaton House.

A glimmer of that memory lit her eyes and shined.

He nudged his hand toward hers so that his first finger grazed hers.

The glimmer faded and her hand retreated. She looked away. "I haven't danced. Not since then. My leg..."

"It's hurting you," he knew. "It hurts a sight more than you let on."

"I get through it," she said, clutching the stem of her wineglass without lifting it.

"Do you take something for it?"

She thought about it. "Not tonight. Damn. I forgot."

He could see a web of pain floating translucent over the powerful line of her brow. He remembered the pain in his chest waking him up in the middle of the night for weeks after Whip Decker shot him and all the mixed-up nightmares that had made it impossible for him to sleep through the night during that time. "Here," he said.

Her eyes widened as he scooted his chair around the table, making enough noise with the legs screeching across the marble floor that the restaurant patrons swiveled toward the commotion. "What are you doing?"

"Gimme," he said, reaching underneath the tablecloth to wrap his hand around the smooth slope of her calf. He pulled it into his lap, edging closer still. Her perfume was heady, and he got lost, so lost he almost didn't see her grimace. "Easy," he murmured, keeping his eyes on hers as he followed the trail of satin skin up the slit of her dress to her thigh. Digging his fingers in, he urged himself to be gentle as he massaged.

He heard the quick, almost inaudible catch of her breath. "You know," she said, "this is more of a third date kind of thing."

He chuckled, then gentled the kneading when he saw the line of her mouth tense. "Are my hands too rough for you?"

"Your hands," she murmured. She closed her eyes. "No. Not for me."

He fought a curse. He was afraid she'd have him panting like a cartoon character by the night's end. "You see someone about the pain?" he asked, diverting his mind elsewhere as his fingers continued to work.

"I'm told it's normal," she said, tipping her head back slightly. Her eyes rolled once before she closed them. "I'm still going through physical therapy."

"Hmm," he said, biting the inside of his lip when she made an agreeable noise. "I'm not a fan of doctors on the whole, but PT helped me." Almost as much as talk therapy, but he didn't mention that. He still had his qualms about telling people he saw a psychiatrist.

"You need to stop," she said, placing her hands over his.

"Why?"

"Because people will think you're doing something else under the table."

"I am doing something."

"You *know* what I mean."

"I don't give a hot damn what people think," he reminded her. He grinned because he could see the touch of pink at the crests of her cheeks. "And as much I like where your head's at, sweetheart, that's not a first date kind of thing, either."

"No?" she asked as he pulled his hands away. She sat up straight, her leg easing off his lap. "Most cowboys expect that sort of thing."

"I'm a bit more refined than your average cowboy," he revealed, lifting a finger to a passing server. He raised his empty glass.

She snorted. "You? Refined?"

He slid her a long look, rattling the ice in the glass.

She licked her lips. Her gaze touched on his wrist. "Sorry."

He saw those dark eyes dart elsewhere and frowned down at his wrist with the expensive watch. Wondering why it made her uncomfortable, he fit his shoulders to the back of the dining chair and tried to read her. Hammond had bequeathed the watch to him...one of the few nice things his father had collected through the years for himself. Like Hammond, Everett was a simple man. He didn't like fuss. But the occasion had called for a bit of shine. He felt the sting of his father's loss as he watched the low light dance across the band.

"Tell me the truth," she asked, carefully. "When was the last time you took someone to bed?"

He tried not to be thrown by the question. "It's been a minute," he mused.

"Not since Decker shot you?" she asked.

"Hell no." He'd been in no place to think in terms of sex or what led to it.

"How long then?" she asked.

"Is this a first date conversation?" he teased as the server brought another glass of whiskey. "Thanks."

"I don't care," Kaya replied.

He raised his hand in an empty gesture. "I don't know. Two…maybe three years?"

Her brows hitched. "Why that long?"

He lifted a shoulder. "Haven't found anyone worth courting. 'Til now, that is."

"You need to court a woman to sleep with her?" she said in amusement.

"Well, yeah."

"Is that why you're here with me—because you're courting me?" she asked, picking through the words carefully.

He bobbed his head and kept her locked in his sights as he raised the glass to his mouth again. "I'd say that's a fair assessment."

She narrowed her eyes as he tossed the whiskey back. "At least he's honest, ladies and gentlemen," she murmured and took a long drink from her wineglass.

"What's wrong with me courting you, Sheriff?"

"It's not the courting I'm worried about," she said with a shake of her head. Dangling the glass with her thumb and two fingers on the rim, she studied him with her cop eyes. "Why me?"

"Why *not* you?"

"That's not really your answer, is it?"

He shifted in his chair. "Cards on the table?"

"I'd like that."

"Fine." He cleared his throat. "I want to find out what this is."

"What?"

He gestured from him to her and back quickly. "This. You know what I'm talking about." When she eyed him uncertainly, he groaned. She was going to make him spell it out in this fancy schmancy restaurant over candlelight and frickin' canapes. "I want to figure out whatever it is I feel—for you."

She stiffened. Her eyes bounced between his in quick succession, but she stayed quiet, waiting for him to elaborate.

He gripped the whiskey glass hard. "During my recovery—" he continued, carefully "—the one person I looked forward to seeing, or even really wanted to see, was you. The one person who never failed to make me grin like an idiot was you. And when the sheriff took a shot at you, I nearly lost that. It scared me more than I thought it could."

"Everett…"

"You wanted to hear," he reminded her.

She settled back, a line digging deep between her eyes as it had earlier that evening.

"I've done a lot over the last several months to eliminate my fear," he revealed. "I've lost people and I'm still dealing with it. It hasn't been easy. It helps, whatever this is. You help…just having you here…lookin' at you. I'm drawn to you, and I want to know why. I want to know you better. I need it."

Her throat clicked on a swallow. "What if…" She stopped, thought about it, then continued, perturbed. "What if I'm a disappointment? You've put me on a pedestal, from the sound of it. That's a tough way to begin a relationship. Expectation's already through the roof where you're concerned."

"The hell with expectation," he dismissed. "My question is, what took you so long to say yes?"

She measured the width of his shoulders. "You're a complicated man, Everett. Some would even say you're a hard man. I'm the sheriff, and you don't have much regard for the law when it comes to your own."

"Who does?" he asked, raising the glass for another drink.

"Me," she replied pointedly. "I do."

"So…you don't want me because you assume I'm not an easy person to live with," he weighed.

"I *know* you're not an easy person to live with," she retorted. "I have it on high authority you're a verifiable pain in the ass." She hesitated, looking down at her lap to fiddle with the cloth napkin she'd laid there. "And I never said I didn't want you," she added quietly.

Why did she have to look away? He wanted those dark eyes on him, always. "Damn, but I'd like to see you with your hair down. Just once."

She closed her eyes. "Don't change the subject. This is serious."

"How long?"

"How long what?"

"How long have you been living with the fact that you want me and keeping me at arm's length?" he asked.

She chose not to answer.

He went a step further, urgency driving him. "I nearly died last summer. I had to watch you bleed. I'm no longer in the business of waiting around to see what life's going to hit me with. I'm tired of getting hit. I see something I want…something I need… I chase it. It'd be nice if you'd let me know how much longer I'm going to be chasing you—because I'm too deep in this to stop."

She propped her elbow on the edge of the table and cradled her temple. After a minute of watching him watching her, she sighed. "All right."

"All right what?" His heart banged in anticipation.

"We do this," she considered. "We see where it goes. But on my terms."

"Name 'em," he said.

She leveled an accusing finger at his chest. "If you brush up against the wrong side of the law while we're together, I'm out."

He offered a crooked smile. "Okay."

"Let's keep this between us. I'm new as sheriff. I'm still trying to gain the respect of certain parts of the community. I don't need talk interfering with that."

"You know how hard it is to keep a secret in Fuego."

"I do," she told him. "Which is why I assume you made reservations out of town."

"I'm banned from Grady's Saloon," he reminded her. "Hickley's BBQ doesn't exactly scream 'date night.' And the steak at Mimi's isn't much to write home about. Third?" he prompted.

"I won't sleep with you," she decided.

He hissed. "That hurts a little."

She held up a hand. "No matter where the courting, as you say, leads… Until I know what we're about…until I'm sure, we keep it PG. Okay?"

He let his eyes rest on her exposed collarbone. Her skin was the color of wheat before harvest and the hollow at the base of her throat fluttered with her pulse. "Can I still think about you naked?" he asked, low.

It shocked a laugh out of her. Smiling widely, she gave an affirmative nod. "Yes," she granted. Then she groaned. "It won't be easy."

"I'm a hard man," he replied, "as you say. I don't do things easy."

"I'm aware of that," she mused. "I'll give it a month. If this doesn't burn out or fizzle and we don't disappoint one another, we'll see if it's worth staying the course."

He raised his glass. "You drive a hard bargain. But I'll take what I can get."

She raised her glass, too. They tipped them together, clinked. "You're worth it," he said as he lifted his glass and drank.

She sipped and muttered, "You'd better be."

As Everett pulled up in front of her house, Kaya unbuckled her seat belt. "Well, this was…something."

He cranked the gearshift into Park. "I'll walk you in."

She grabbed his arm to stop him from turning off the ignition. "No."

"But we're courtin'," he reminded her. "I should walk you to your door like a gentleman."

She leaned into his warmth. "You're not a gentleman and I'm not a lady. We've got something warm and yummy here. You walk me to my door, I'll be tempted to invite you in, despite what I agreed to in that classy restaurant. You'd best stay put."

He raised his hands from the steering wheel. "Hey, you're the sheriff."

"That's right." Grappling for his shoulders, she brought him closer and dropped her voice to a whisper. "Now, I order you to kiss me good night—like you did earlier—so I can go in and think about what I've done."

His quiet laugh blew across her mouth. "You might be a woman after my own heart. Isn't that something?" He gripped the back of her neck, long fingers splaying up into the taut nest of her bun as he tipped his head to the side and took the kiss further, his tongue sliding over her lips to part them.

She caught herself moaning. He made her feel soft, pliant, female. She was so stunned that her mouth parted, and she felt the quick, hot flick of his tongue against hers.

She was practically panting, she found, as his hand firmed against the dip of her waist. She pushed her arms through the parting of his sport coat, all but bowing her torso to his to gather his heat for her own. Her head dipped back on her neck as he took what he wanted, and her hands splayed across the long, firm line of his back.

The big, tough cattle baron had been pining for her— Kaya. Wasn't that a trip?

She was tripping, all right—high on his earthy scent and the sound of his breath clashing with hers in the quiet.

She felt his hand scale her ribs, cruising toward her breast.

She twined her fingers through his before sliding it away. She broke away from his mouth in a faint protest she'd have to chide herself for later. Pressing her lips together, she edged away, toward the passenger door where she'd have stayed to begin with if she'd known what was good for her.

She lived off her mind and her gut and the cool voice of reason. One drink of Everett Eaton and it all turned to ash.

He knocked his head back against his headrest and groaned. "And here I was thinking you didn't want to get all hot and bothered," he said between his teeth. "That'll linger."

"You just hold that thought," she suggested, making herself turn the handle and open the door. She hopped out of the cab.

"I'll see you tomorrow, Sheriff Sweetheart," he called in his distinctive baritone. "Bright and early, like I promised you."

Her legs weren't steady. She blamed it on the wine he'd bought her. "Good night, trouble," she volleyed back and closed the door between them.

Chapter 4

"We've covered most every inch of the east and south sides of the mountain, and we've swept most of the north side as well. It's been two days and we've found nothing else but an old hair scrunchie, two empty beer bottles and some rusty tent stakes," Kaya said. She was back on the summit of Ol' Whalebones for the third morning in a row with her deputies and a ragtag team of professionals and volunteers.

Word of Miller Higgins's disappearance had spread. They'd found a news van from Taos at the end of the access road where they unloaded their horses for the ride to the mountain at dawn. Kaya had forbidden them from coming farther than the eastern trailhead. "If we don't find anything today, we're going to have to bring in a chopper."

Deputy Root's attention was on the screen of his mini-laptop. His reconnaissance drone was in the air, searching the rocky west side of the ridge. "You're comfortable having members of his family come out to help?" he asked.

Kaya shook her head. "Not in the least. If we find remains… And with cameras waiting at the base of the hill… It's hard for people to keep their heads when shock and grief are taking a sucker punch at them."

"The father's a decent tracker," Deputy Root reported.

"With him and Wolfe Coldero, the drone and dogs you had the handlers haul out here, chances are good we'll find something."

Kaya hoped she wouldn't regret involving the Higgins family in the search for Miller. "I put Wyatt and Ellis Eaton with the father and son team. If they find anything first, those two are the most calm and compassionate. I warned the handlers about the cougar den. That's probably going to occupy most of the dogs' attention."

"Is it true about Tombstone?"

Kaya narrowed her eyes at Root. "I never saw him. But I'm told this is his territory. If he's still alive. Seems a bit of a stretch. Stories of Tombstone are older than my niece, Nova, and she's driving now. Still, every team has protection and is on the lookout."

Root paused, handling the drone's joystick. "Is it possible Higgins isn't on the mountain?"

It had crossed her mind. Higgins's mother had searched his room at their home in San Gabriel and found an empty Merrell shoe box with a receipt dated a week prior to the boy's livestream. Size nine. Brown. Moabs. They had one shoe and no Miller. The information fed the deep pit in Kaya's stomach.

Everett had sent men out to the four quarters of Eaton Edge. If Higgins had run in that direction, she could only hope they'd find him alive. It had now been five days since Higgins's last contact. "We can't assume anything until we've searched every inch of the mountain. Is there a clear path to the western part of the ridge?"

He panned and zoomed on his screen. "It'll be a lot more challenging than other parts. You up for it?"

She hated the question but understood it. Three days of hiking had given her a noticeable limp. She'd had to skip this week's physical therapy session, too. "Call a handler and Wolfe Coldero's team. Tell them I want him and half the dogs with us."

Like Everett, Wolfe Coldero was a polarizing figure in Fuego. The tall, dark cowboy was mute, his origins a mystery. He had come to Eaton Edge as a boy, lost and broken, and he'd served time as an adult. It didn't matter that he'd been exonerated of the crime Wendell Jones had sent him up for. Some people still talked of him only in whispers.

Kaya knew him to be a man of exemplary character, if mysterious. He was also one of the best trackers she'd ever worked with. As the dogs yanked their handler onward over the tumble of rocks and boulders that pitted the northern portion of the mountain, Wolfe followed at his own pace, stopping to crouch on and off the path.

When he stopped again, Kaya let the others go ahead. She chugged water from her canteen. While no was looking, she choked down some Advil.

The sun was high so she could discern little of Wolfe's face under his worn, black felt hat other than a contemplative frown and sharp-bladed jaw. His finger had dug a circle in the dirt. He shoved aside a small rock, another, then he raised his head, finally, and whistled in her direction.

She moved to him, kneeling with a short wince. "What'd you find?" she asked.

He pointed to a small object in the soil.

Kaya lowered her head further. "It's metal." She reached into her pocket for her gloves. After pulling them on, she took further precaution by prying the metal object out of its dirt bed with a pair of tweezers. She lifted it to the light so they could both examine it. "An earring," she said.

"Gold. The real thing. It's not tarnished or corroded. I'd say it's been here awhile if you had to dig it up like that."

Wolfe nodded his agreement.

"I doubt it's to Miller's taste," she went on. "But I can't see a situation where a camper would wear something this nice out in the elements." Reaching into her back pocket, she pulled out a small evidence bag. "God, your eyes are good."

He rolled his shoulder in a shrug and stood. When she shifted from one foot to the other to do the same, he grabbed her under the shoulder to help. "Thanks," she said as she put the bag and the tweezers away and pulled off her gloves. "I should catch up."

He walked on with her, scanning the ground.

"How're wedding plans coming?" she asked. "It's only a month from now, isn't it?"

He nodded and sent her a small, sideways smile to show her that plans were going well.

"You and Everett getting along?" she wondered.

Wolfe made a so-so motion with his hand. Kaya made a noise in answer. Everett's long-running feud with Wolfe had only just cooled in the last year when Wolfe and Everett's sister, Eveline, fell in love. Kaya had never known what Everett and Wolfe had fallen out about when they were teens living on the Edge, but it had divided the house, with Wolfe going to live with the operation's foreman, Santiago Coldero. Not long after, Everett's mother, Josephine, had left her husband and three children to join Santiago and Wolfe at Coldero Ridge on the other side of town.

The resulting scandal had lit the touch paper for town gossips and was still the subject of their tongue wagging at times. It was exacerbated by the fact that the events over the last summer had stirred the mystery surrounding

Josephine's and her youngest child Angel's deaths seven years ago.

The sound of a dog's baying carried on the wind, followed by a second and a third. Kaya quickened her pace. She had to climb over a rocky ledge to get to the handler's position. "Did they find something?"

The dogs were straining against the handler's lead. "They won't get away from the edge," he informed her. "Something must be down there."

Kaya tested the ground, looking for cracks. The outcropping hung lengthways over a sharp drop. This side of the mountain more closely resembled the buttes that littered the high desert landscape. "Get them back," she advised, edging closer to the cliff. The wind came up to meet her, teasing the flyaway strands that had come loose from her bun. Holding on to her hat, she turned her gaze down below the outcropping.

"There's another ledge down there," she noted. "I can just see it. Other than that, there's nothing for thirty feet or more."

"There's no way for us to get down there safely," the handler said.

As Wolfe came forward, she asked, "Ever done any abseiling?" At his frown, she course-corrected. "Rappelling?" At the shake of his head, she pursed her lips.

"Could be the dogs smell that mountain lion again," the handler explained. "Though that's a long drop...even for a cat."

Her thoughts exactly. She unseated the radio from its holding on her belt and brought it to her mouth. "Root, do you copy?"

"Ten-four."

"We made it to the north ridge," she relayed. "And we

need your drone. Tell Wyatt to bring climbing equipment. Does anybody have experience with cliff descent?"

Static hissed momentarily, then the familiar timbre of Everett's voice called back. "Affirmative."

She frowned. Of course it would be him. "I need you, too."

A pause hovered before Everett's message came back. "On the way."

"Are you sure you know what you're doing?"

Everett glanced up from the climbing harness Ellis secured around his middle. Kaya's gaze was on Root's drone as it sailed over the cliff edge, scanning. But he knew she meant the question for him. "Ellis and I used to do this every weekend," he told her. "Didn't we?"

Ellis gave a jerky nod. "During the misspent years of our youth, yes."

"Did you do it here?" she asked.

Ellis shook his head. "There're some canyons and cliffs at the state park we liked to hit."

Kaya held her elbows and leaned back slightly—to keep the weight off her bad leg, Everett knew. She met Ellis's stare, probing. "Is he any good?"

Ellis's mouth moved in a small grin. "He's a risk-taker. But he knows what he's about."

"Why does the first part not surprise me?" she said, looking to Everett with an ounce of accusation.

He smiled broadly, feeding the rope through his hands. "You worried about me, Sheriff?"

Root yelped.

Kaya leaned over his laptop screen. "Do you see something?"

"Directly below," he said, making minute adjustments with the joystick. "Do you...see that?"

Kaya's hand came to the deputy's shoulder. "Can you zoom in?"

Everett watched the hand flex. He heard Kaya's breath stutter and moved forward. "What's wrong?"

She held up a hand. "Stay back."

"Why?" Everett asked. "What's down there?"

She raised herself to her full height. His lips parted when he saw that all the blood had drained from her face. "We may have found him."

Kaya had everyone pulled back from the north ridge and a perimeter established. She ordered Wyatt to get Higgins's father and brother to the base of the mountain with a reminder to keep them clear of reporters.

She called in crime scene technicians. It took most of the afternoon for Miller Higgins's body to be recovered from its unlikely resting place.

Along with others.

"Jesus God Almighty." Deputy Wyatt, normally a stickler for professional lingo, swallowed hard as the bag containing the final unidentified victim came into view via a complex system of ropes and pulleys. "That's *four*."

Kaya had seen the bones underneath Higgins's in the drone footage. But she hadn't counted on four, either... "Three unidentifieds."

Root had been reticent since seeing the images on his computer screen. He was several shades beyond pale underneath his freckles. "Where were the birds?"

Kaya narrowed her eyes. "What?"

"The birds," Root said again. His voice sounded dull and his eyes tracked the movement of the techs as they carried the body away. "They should've been here—for Miller, if not the others. He was…fresh."

Kaya lifted her chin, understanding.

It was the medical examiner, Damon Walther, who answered. "The birds have already been here, deputy. They'd finished their job before your search began."

Wyatt blew out a full-length curse, shifting his feet on the uneven ground.

"That'll make determining cause of death more difficult." Kaya knew. "I want this to be priority when you get these bodies back to the morgue. I don't have to tell you what kind of case we might have on our hands here."

Root's lips parted. They were the same color as his skin. "I…I think I'm going to…"

She gave him a light push. "Take a minute. Get yourself together. Miller Higgins's relatives are waiting below. We all need a handle on this before we meet them." She'd be lying if she said that grim feeling she'd had in the pit of her stomach throughout the day hadn't grown. On the back of her tongue, she could taste something bitter and acidic that didn't make it easier to negotiate what was happening in her stomach. She took her hat off as the techs passed by and felt more than saw her deputies do the same.

When the techs had carried the body some distance away, she settled her hat back on her head and scowled at the view from the top. "What the hell happened on this mountain?"

Chapter 5

Everett waited his turn. There was no getting to Kaya through the snarl of people at the trailhead. He waited with Crazy Alice, holding her reins and those for Ghost, who'd been busily munching sweets Everett had stashed in his saddle bag.

He wasn't sure exactly what condition Miller Higgins had been in when Kaya and the others had found him. He'd known by the grim set of her mouth and the appearance of crime scene technicians on the scene that it wasn't good. She'd sent Everett back behind the police perimeter, despite his insistence to stay.

I need you to do this, Everett, she'd told him. *Don't argue with me.*

The words hadn't wavered, but he'd seen what was in her eyes.

She'd seen death. They'd been too late to save the kid.

The choppers had come and gone—not one, but three, which had given everyone at the bottom of the mountain more to talk about. The Fuego police had thankfully separated the kid's father and brother from the small herd of journalists.

He saw Kaya come off the mountain, cutting a swath through the reporters and cameras. She'd gone straight to where police had ensconced Higgins's family and stayed there for half an hour.

By the time she came back to the horses for Ghost, the circles under her eyes were as dark as bruises.

"You okay?" he asked.

She didn't meet his gaze. "I need to return to the station. I'm meeting the rest of the family there. And I need to make a statement to the press. It won't wait until morning. Dispatch called. Apparently, there are more reporters gathered there outside."

"You're tired," he told her.

"I know what I am," she snapped. Then she paused, taking the reins from him. "Sorry. It was rough up there."

"He's dead," Everett said quietly.

She pressed her lips together, unable to confirm or deny. "Listen, if reporters show up at the Edge—"

"No comment," he said and nodded. "I know."

She searched his face, then lowered her voice. "This could be trouble for you. Your family."

"Whatever happened, happened on our land," he stated. "Yeah. I expect there'll be a fair few questions."

Her scanning eyes fell on the buttons on his front. "I can't discuss it any further—with you or anyone. Don't push me."

"No," he replied. "So long as you promise me you're going to eat something when you get back to the station house. You need energy."

She shook her head. "No, I..." For a moment, her lips trembled. She cast a look in the direction of Ellis and Wolfe who were close by. "No."

Everett felt the lines dig into his brow. "Christ. Must've been bad up there."

Silently, she motioned for him to step back so she could mount her horse.

He stood by for a few seconds before reaching out, just enough to brush his knuckles across the tense muscles of her jaw. "Get back safe. You hear me?"

She jerked a nod, placed her foot in the stirrup and boosted herself up, swinging her other leg over Ghost's back. She settled into the saddle, let the Appaloosa shift underneath her, then clicked her tongue. The horse walked on.

Everett watched as Root and Wyatt joined her on their mounts. They broke into a trot, then a gallop.

Ellis's mount, Shy, nickered close behind him as his brother crossed to Everett. "She thinks there's trouble in it for the family?"

"Mmm," Everett responded. He saw Wolfe come to stand on Ellis's far side. His hands moved to communicate in sign language. "What's he saying?" Everett demanded.

Ellis watched his friend's motions. He and Wolfe had bonded soon after the latter had found a home at the Edge. Their friendship had lasted through the twisted forays of their family histories. "He says whatever happened to the kid wasn't an accident."

Everett frowned at the man in the black hat. He didn't feel a lot of warmth for Eveline's fiancé. But Wolfe's instincts tended to be better than others'. "How do you figure?"

Wolfe signaled. Ellis translated, "She didn't talk to the press. Neither did either of the deputies. And why would there be three choppers for one body?" Ellis braced his hands on his hips. "She did tell us, didn't she, that this was going to bring trouble to the Edge?"

Everett picked through Kaya's words. "And here I

thought we'd put trouble to rest with Whip Decker's death and Sheriff Jones's arrest."

"We need to know what happened up there," Ellis countered. "Preferably before reporters come to call. We need to know how to respond."

"Simple," Everett said. "No comment."

"Everett—"

"You heard me." He intervened before his brother could voice any more cautions. "Whatever happened on Ol' Whalebones, I aim for us to pass well below the radar. We've been through enough trouble to last us a lifetime—and Eatons tend not to live as long as others."

"Don't remind me," Ellis muttered. "And you won't be saying that around my fiancée."

Wolfe gestured in agreement.

"It's a bad legacy," Everett acknowledged. "But we don't have a choice other than to live with it." He patted Crazy Alice's muzzle when she nosed his elbow. "If I don't get you home to your women, I'm going to be persona non grata. Let's ride."

Kaya could deal with the press. She could deal with the curious bystanders who'd come to her office, expecting a definitive word on the situation. She could even deal with the questions inside her head and the sick feeling that wouldn't leave her alone.

Sitting down with Miller Higgins's mother, father, brother and sister, however, was something else altogether. This part of the job wasn't easy for anyone in law enforcement. Her emotions played close to the surface. When handling family of the deceased, she struggled even under the best of circumstances.

This was far from the best situation. She had four bodies in the morgue.

When she saw the mayor stride past the press pack and into the station, she allowed herself a lengthy sigh.

True Claymore was all swagger, even on bad news days like today.

His smile didn't quite meet his eyes, as it normally did. He was classed up, as always, in his embroidered black Western coat that was open over a pressed, white shirt complete with all the sterling accoutrements he felt necessary to reinforce his white-collar status—bolo tie with its prominent, engraved *C*, and an enlarged belt buckle with its crossed pistols and the words "GOD, FAMILY, COUNTRY" displayed underneath—up to the buckle of his hat band.

Kaya steeled herself. For all his charm, the good mayor did nothing to whet her appetite for his regular visits. He liked his finger in every pie if they smelled well enough of power and influence, which he'd enjoyed in this town for too long.

Her becoming sheriff hadn't pleased him. He'd done what he could to sway the election a different way.

Chiefly because he knew, unlike her predecessor, that she could not and would not be bought.

He tipped his hat to her. "Hell of a day, Sheriff Altaha. Hell of a day."

"I didn't see you on the mountain, mayor," she stated, "though I'm assuming you know as much as those people outside, which is next to nothing at this point."

"Come now, Kaya, honey," he said, sinking his hands into his pockets. "You know I've got my sources. You didn't find just one person dead on Ol' Whalebones."

Kaya caught the gasp from her assistant, Sherry, at her

desk. Irritated, she jerked her head toward the door of her office.

"Sherry," Claymore said in greeting as he passed her by. "How's the baby?"

"He's doing great, Mr. Claymore, sir," Sherry stuttered.

"Ah, that's fine, real fine," he schmoozed.

Kaya spread the door open. "We're all on the clock here."

As an invitation, it was poor. But the thought of having to deal with this clown inside the enclosed space of her office made her already upset stomach clutch. Claymore's cologne all but strangled her as he moved into her office. She shut the door and went behind the desk to put space between them. "The details of this case are being kept under wraps until we know more. In fact, they're on a need-to-know basis."

He messed with his tie. "That's just the thing, honey." Spreading his hands, he raised his brows. "In order to handle the press and questions from my constituents, I need to know. The bodies were found on Eaton Edge. There's been quite a lot of trouble out that way over the past year. I'd say you should start your investigation there."

"I never said there was foul play involved," she noted. "I won't know that until I speak with the medical examiner."

He rolled his eyes. "Come on, Kaya—"

Her restraint snapped. "It's *Sheriff*, actually. When I held the position of deputy, you never addressed me as anything but that. I don't recall the two of us getting any more familiar with each other over the past three months nor do I anticipate that happening anytime in the future. So you will address me as Sheriff Altaha and when I tell you the details of this case or any other are need-to-know you will take that as my word. Do I make myself clear, Mr. Claymore?"

His good-natured smile slipped. He was too smooth a man to let aggravation take hold, as she had. She knew, though, as the playful light in his eyes dimmed and a muscle in his cheek flexed, that she'd hit the mark. "We'll see about that, Sheriff. Yes, we will see. Have you dealt with the family of the hiker?"

She curbed the urge to club him over the head. "Have I *spoken* with Miller Higgins's father, mother and siblings? Yes. At length. They should be left alone. Instead of focusing on the press and the curious gaggle of townspeople outside, why don't you utilize your mayoral powers to inform people that the Higginses should be left alone? I'm sure they'd appreciate it."

Claymore took in a long breath. "Very well. You will keep me apprised of the nature of this case. It'd be best— for all involved."

He strolled out. Sinking into her chair, she pressed her hands to her temples. She was distressed when they shook. Pressing them between her knees, she willed herself to get it together.

She hated how much True Claymore still rattled her.

Unable to dwell on the reasons why, she opened the top desk drawer and found the Advil she kept there. There was a half-drunk Pepsi can on her desk from the day before. Claymore had left the door open so she called through it. "Sherry?"

"Yes, ma'am... I mean, sir." The woman, who wasn't but a few years younger than Kaya, bustled in. "What can I do?"

"Could you get me a bottle of water?" she asked. "And

maybe something small to eat. Nothing heavy. I'd appreciate it."

"I can run down the street and see if the deli's still open," Sherry offered.

"Thanks," Kaya said. "And you know not a word to those outside…"

Sherry bobbed her head quickly. "Mum's the word."

Kaya tried to fix a smile in place. Sherry had been hired by Jones, so Kaya had inherited her as an assistant. Knowing she had a baby at home, Kaya hadn't contemplated firing her, though she'd been cautious with her, unsure whether she still felt allegiance to her former boss.

Sherry hesitated on the threshold, worrying the pad of sticky notes and pen she carried with her. "Did you really find more than one body?"

Kaya closed her eyes briefly. The images were still fresh in her mind. And after her visit to the morgue, there'd likely be more to contend with. "It's late," she countered. "Once you come back from the deli, you need to go home and see your family."

Sherry handled her disappointment well. "Thank you, ma'am. Sir. I'll be back shortly."

Kaya found herself alone in the station house. Root was dealing with reporters. Wyatt had escorted the Higgins family home to San Gabriel for the night.

She'd seen her share of the dead. She'd been a rookie cop on the streets of Taos where the crime rate was anything but low. Her two years in uniform there might have made her, but they'd also exposed her to victims of overdose, homicide, accidental death and suicide.

She'd learned early that she could either compartmentalize it all, funnel it away or get overwhelmed so she'd done the former—to survive. To keep going because being a cop was the only ambition she'd had that mattered. Failure was not an option.

It still wasn't. She hadn't come back to Fuego County and joined the sheriff's department so that she could take over Wendell Jones's position. She'd had no ambitions there whatsoever. Nor could she turn her back on the people who'd thought she was best suited to the position.

She'd wanted to find Miller Higgins alive. She had needed to find him and return him to his folks.

She flicked open the report on her desk and stared at his photograph, as she had so often over the last few days.

There hadn't been a homicide in Fuego County in well over a year. But she had little doubt that Higgins had been murdered...along with the other three people they'd found with his body on Ol' Whalebones.

Murder had come to Fuego four times, which meant her department wasn't just dealing with a dangerous perpetrator. They were dealing with a serial killer.

Kaya pushed through the doors of the morgue. There was no one at the reception desk. Dr. Walther had volunteered to stay in after hours to see that the bodies were well cared for. Half the fluorescent lights in the lobby had been switched off.

As she turned toward the swinging doors of the examination room, she came up short. Her hand nearly jumped to her sidearm before she stopped it. "Damn," she said as the man just before the doors turned and she was able to see his face in the small amount of light from the lobby. She swallowed the curse because the mystery man was Reverend Huck Claymore. "Sorry. My nerves are on a hair trigger."

"It's understandable," he said in his level voice. The

only place she'd ever heard him raise it was during passionate sermons from the pulpit of the local church.

Kaya had always felt conflicted about him. He was True Claymore's older brother. He'd grown up at The RC Resort, same as the mayor. Neither man had wanted for much. Huck's suit might not be as flashy as his brother's, but even she could see that it was tailored. His tie was silk, and his boots weren't the least bit scuffed. He rarely smiled. She'd never heard him crack so much as a meager joke. He was a sober, weary-eyed man whose presence was a comfort to the citizens of Fuego.

He studied her closely with his unchanging expression. "How are you, Sheriff Altaha?"

She wasn't looking for comfort any more than she'd ever sought any of his preaching. Still, it was a kind, even question she'd be rude to rebuff. "I'm all right," she lied. When he lowered his chin, she sighed. "I've been better. May I ask what you're doing here, reverend?"

He didn't so much as blink. "To pray for the poor souls you took off the mountain this afternoon."

"Right," she said, feeling like an idiot. "That's kind of you, reverend. But we can't allow you beyond this point."

"I understand," he said with a passive nod. "Will the Higginses be returning tomorrow morning to identify their son?"

Kaya nodded. "Ten o'clock."

"I'd like to be here," he requested. "They might need some comfort during this time."

"Of course," she granted.

His lips curved but his eyes didn't track. "Thank you, Sheriff. I hope my brother hasn't been giving you any trouble over your investigation so far. He tends to overstep in these matters."

"I can handle the mayor."

As he regarded her, his eyes followed the path of his smile for the first time in Kaya's memory. Something gleamed to life there that he quickly shuttered. "I have no doubt you can." He reached up and pinched the edge of his white Stetson. "God be with you, Sheriff Altaha."

"And with you." The words didn't come as easily to her as they did him. She waited until she heard the entry doors swing shut behind him before she pushed through the doors into the exam room. "Sorry. I'm behind schedule."

Dr. Walther peered at her through his protective eyewear. He used a scalpel to point to the wall. "Gown. Gloves. Hairnet."

She grabbed what he told her to and donned each, carefully. There was one body on the table. The other victims were likely locked up in the cooler already. The ME's office was small and understaffed. The complete results of each autopsy were weeks out. But she'd wanted to gather any early impressions Walther had as well as view what had been collected with the remains.

The drone had been far enough away to give her only a vague impression of the damage done to Higgins over the last three days. It had given her more than enough, however, to tell her that he was no longer part of the living world. And yet she still felt sucker punched when she leaned over the table and viewed him close-up.

"The wildlife did their work," Walther acknowledged.

"Will you still be able to determine cause of death?" she asked as her stomach flipped the deli sandwich Sherry had brought her.

"After a proper examination," Walther granted. "There are tears and lacerations to the face, arms and torso."

"His family's coming tomorrow," she cautioned. "They can't see him like this."

"His wallet was still in his pocket," Walther revealed.

"Identification and cash?"

"Both," he said, pointing to a tray. "He had upwards of two hundred dollars on his person. Technicians also found a pocketknife with his name carved into the handle."

"What about his phone?" she asked. "He was livestreaming with it or a camera at the time of his disappearance."

"No phone, no camera," Walther answered.

"His pack?" she asked. "Hikers always have packs."

"Yes. Its contents have been catalogued. Would you like to see the full list?"

"I would," she said. "Have you found any other wounds on the body other than tears and lacerations on the front?"

Silently, he instructed her to help him turn Higgins's body onto its right side so the back of his head was facing her. "There's a large wound on the back of his head—a result of the fall, but it also could be consistent with—"

"A killing blow or gunshot wound," she observed. "You'll have him tested for gunshot residue?"

"Samples have already been taken. They'll be sent to the lab first thing in the morning. We'll also be sending DNA from the other victims."

"Maybe we'll get one or more matches with Missing Persons," she hoped. "I hate that we couldn't bring him home to his family alive."

"He was the same age as my oldest, Libby," he mused, nursing his scalpel. He rocked back on his heels, viewing the dead with more compassion than clinical interest.

"Take all the time you need for results. I want the killer found as much as the next person, but you won't get any pressure from my department if it means a thorough report."

"The mayor's going to have something else to say about how fast things should be done."

"I'll take care of True Claymore and anybody else who tries to interfere so you can focus on the dead. I'd like to see the rest of what was found at the scene. Personal belongings of other victims...anything the killer might have left behind..."

"The first tray is what we found on the boy," Walther reported. "The second contains everything else taken from the scene."

"Thank you," she said, veering around the exam table. Miller Higgins's clothes had been bagged and tagged, as had his personal belongings. His library card lay alongside his driver's license. Something about that tugged at her heart. His pack had contained three calorie bars, a half-full hydration pack, a compass, waterproof matches, a minitorch, a machete and its sheath that looked unmarked as if he'd yet to have had a chance to use it, a stick of deodorant, dissolvable wipes and a first aid kit that had never been opened.

The name carved in the handle of the jackknife hadn't been engraved by a professional. It looked like something he might have done himself.

Kaya frowned deeply when she saw the lone shoe among the clothes removed from his person and moved to the second tray.

Her eyes skimmed over one belt buckle, several more boots—these dirty and weathered—a slender wristwatch that was feminine in appearance, one hoop earring that could have been a match to the one Wolfe Coldero had found and then landed on a bracelet. It was a C-shaped cuff that wouldn't have gone all the way around the wrist. It was lined with silver.

She reached for it, turning the face of the piece toward her.

Her heart stuttered.

The cuff was inlaid with turquoise. In its center was the letter *S*.

Her focus narrowed on the simple inscription. She went numb. Her ears filled with distracted buzzing.

She must've made a noise because Walther's gloved hand came to rest on hers.

She jerked. "I…" She was breathing through her teeth. Her pulse was high and the buzzing was incessant. "This piece," she stammered. "I know this. I know who this belongs to!"

Chapter 6

Everett hadn't heard from Kaya in two days—unless listening to her press conference on the local news counted.

...recovered the remains of a sixteen-year-old male. He has been identified as Miller Higgins of San Gabriel. While searching the area, three other unidentified bodies were found...

She'd sent her deputies to the Edge to interview everyone on the premises. They asked questions about the comings and goings in the northern quarter over the last week—casual, routine questions that shouldn't have put his dander up.

But they did. Everett couldn't believe the police thought anyone at the Edge was responsible for Higgins's death. Rumors were rampant in town. Ol' Whalebones had been cordoned off. He and his men had been asked to leave it alone, pending further investigation.

Kaya hadn't said it on the news or otherwise, but everyone from Fuego to San Gabriel had. There was a killer on the loose.

That wasn't the only thing putting Everett on edge. Because the four bodies had been found on his family's mountain, the name Eaton was firmly entrenched in rumor and suspicion. With Eveline's wedding coming around the bend, people were pointing fingers.

There was nothing he disliked more than gossip. Unfortunately, Fuego was the gossip capital of the civilized world.

Even the church on Sunday stank of tittle-tattle.

Paloma always insisted he, Ellis and Eveline attend church with her. She'd somehow won the trifecta this week, roping all three of them into the front pew alongside Luella, Wolfe and Ellis's girls, Isla and Ingrid. Everett passed much of the service ignoring the whispers exchanged behind hands at their backs, swapping folded notes back and forth with his youngest niece, Ingrid, instead. She had a head for mischief and an intolerance for sitting still for more than five minutes at a time—two traits she shared with her uncle.

They had to be sneakier than sneaky to not draw the attention of Paloma who wouldn't hesitate to put a stop to it. Eveline caught his eye once, then subsided when Ingrid placed her finger over her mouth. His sister had smiled and looked the other way.

Ellis was distracted with Luella. She was tense amongst the other townies and with good reason. As Whip Decker's daughter, she'd been branded as troublesome the moment she was born. Whether she deserved the moniker or not, she'd long been branded "Devil's Daughter" by the people of Fuego County.

Everett saw Ellis place his hand on her bouncing knee where he drew circles with his thumb. If anyone could ease Luella's troubles, it was Ellis. He had a way with the woman he'd claimed as his own in high school. She'd slipped through his fingers, and he'd gone on to marry Liberty Ferris. But after the divorce and a fateful winter, Ellis and Luella had come together once more and it didn't look like they would be parting again.

"Psst!"

Everett glanced at Ingrid on his left. He took the note she slid across the surface of the hard bench. Making sure Paloma was still listening to Reverend Claymore, he unfolded the small scrap of paper to find another sketch of a horse.

Ingrid was turning out to be quite the artist.

Everett played along, knowing she was looking for his insight as much as his praises. He picked up the pencil without an eraser he'd found next to the Bible underneath the seat and scribbled, *Nice one. Pass it to LuLu.* He folded the square, then held out his hand as if to shake. She squeezed his fingers, taking the little note as she did. She opened it and read it while he did his best to look uninvolved. Then she folded it again and reached over her father's lap to tap Luella on the wrist.

Both Ellis and Luella looked. Silently, Ingrid did the same faux-shake with Luella she had with Everett, leaving Luella with the folded scrap. She unfolded it with hands that shook only slightly...

A smile bloomed across her face. She swept red curls from her cheek and greeted Ingrid with a soft look. *Thank you*, she mouthed.

Ellis reached his arm around Ingrid's shoulders and drew her close against his side. The child went willingly, casting a grin back at Everett as she did so. He gave her a thumbs-up but stopped when Ellis caught his eye. Shrugging, Everett tried to tune back into the reverend's spiel about sin and damnation and stopping the devil's wicked work in their good community.

Everett glanced over his shoulder, restless. The sanctuary was packed. The question was which of these sinners had been on his mountain. The killer hadn't been on the back of Ol' Whalebones just once. They'd returned over and over and over again. Everett figured it was someone from the county, likely Fuego itself, though he'd thought they'd combed out a fair good many wrongdoers over recent months—Jace "Whip" Decker, Wendell Jones…hell, even lewd Rowdy Conway had been flushed out.

He aimed to do any amount of legwork possible to catch whoever had brought death to Eaton Edge and stop them from killing anyone else there.

His gaze roved over those assembled, searching each face. He knew them all by name. He'd gone to school with some of them. He'd been on the rodeo circuit with others. Hell, he'd raced cars with a few. There were friends and there were rivals.

When his eyes hit the back of the church and Kaya standing near the door, arms crossed over her sheriff's uniform, he felt his heart give a lurch.

She'd been avoiding him. He had no doubt about that. The question was why? Why had she sent Root and Wyatt to question him, his family, his men? Why hadn't she told him about the bodies herself?

Was it because—deep down—like the rest of them, she was distancing herself from everyone at Eaton Edge because she thought somebody there might be involved in the body count?

He turned back around, rolling his shoulders. She hadn't met his stare, but he could feel it like an itch between his shoulder blades. Restless from having sat too long and the strong ache in his chest that he would not name because he knew what was good for him, no matter what had passed between him and the good sheriff of Fuego County, he leaned over his knees, wishing Huck Claymore would just shut up already so he and his family could escape with their dignity intact.

A movement out of the corner of his eye caught his attention. It was a wave from the left of the pulpit where the organist Christa McMurtry sat, watching him.

She was always watching him. She beamed, curling her fingers his way.

"Hellfire." His mutter fell into one of Reverend Claymore's pauses. Heads turned, Paloma leaning clear out in the open to scowl at him. He looked away, up at the pulpit, and saw the elder Claymore eyeing him with strong disapproval.

Join the party, reverend, he thought bitterly.

Everett fought his way to the back of the church once the service was over. He fought so hard, he elbowed several people out of the way and nearly knocked down Turk Monday, the former manager of Fuego's bank. Once he found sunlight and fresh air again, he nearly stumbled down the length of the church steps…

…and found that Kaya had escaped already.

"Ah… Mr. Eaton?"

"What do you want?" He settled down when he saw that it was Nova, a waitress at Hickley's BBQ. She had long raven locks that were straight as an arrow, wide dark eyes narrowed against the angle of the midmorning sun and prominent cheekbones that marked her as Kaya's niece. Kaya's sister, Naleen Gaines, was Nova's mother. "Sorry," he said when he saw her take a half step back in retreat. He sank his hands into his pockets, hoping for a less menacing impression. "Church makes me mean as a woke bear."

The lines of her mouth wavered, and he wondered if

that wasn't amusement lurking beneath. "I've been meaning to speak to you, Mr. Eaton."

"Call me Everett, Nova. I've known you since you were in diapers. And nobody calls me Mr. Eaton," he told her.

"Everett," she said, treading lightly. "I was wondering if you'd consider taking on a new hand at Eaton Edge this summer."

He made a thoughtful noise. "Depends on if they're any good at the kind of work I need them for. I'm already apprenticing one man. Not that he's much of a man…"

"Are you talking about Lucas?" she asked. "Lucas Barnes?"

He groaned. "The pain in my ass." When he heard the last word slip out, he sighed. Now he was going to have to apologize.

She surprised him by laughing. Catching his stunned gaze, she lifted her hand, subsiding. "Sorry. It's just… I know him—from when he was still in school. He gave the teaching staff fits."

"I'll bet he did." He inclined his head. "You know somebody I can take on?"

"Yeah," she said, standing a little taller. "Me."

"You?"

She narrowed her eyes. "Just because I'm a girl doesn't mean I don't know how to herd. Don't you have a sister? Doesn't she ride out with the men?"

"Occasionally," he said. "And it's got less to do with you being a female and more to do with the work itself. We don't just herd. We feed, wrangle, fix fencing, pipes, brand, tag, sort, vaccinate… No matter the season or the weather—hot, cold, rain, high desert sun, snow—we ride. It's tough on a grown man. Much less a teenage girl."

"My stepfather, Terrence Gaines, has been showing me

the ropes at his ranch," she said. "It's a small operation, but we do all those things there, too. And my father...well, my biological father—Ryan MacKay?"

"I know him. He's my stable manager Griff's son."

"He's been teaching me to rope since I was a toddler," she revealed. "And my aunt, Kaya, she taught me to ride with the best of 'em."

"Did she now?" he asked.

"Yeah. She did a lot of trick riding back in the day."

"You don't say." He considered. The girl hadn't wavered when he'd spoken about the work or the elements. "Wouldn't you rather spend your summer raising hell?" When she shook her head, he had to think harder. "Or... at the mall?"

"You don't know much about teenage girls, do you?"

"No. Look... I'm not going to say no to more help. But I'll need to speak to your mother first. I'm not aiming to get on anyone's mother's list, if you know what I'm saying."

"Sure," she said.

"I can't pay you much of a wage," he said. "At least not at first, while you're still learning the ropes."

"I learn fast," she assured him.

"And there's no way in hell you're sleeping in the bunkhouse with the men," he warned.

"Fine by me," she said. "Spring break's coming up. If you'd like, I could use that time to show you my skills. That way, you'll know what you're getting in the summertime."

"Why not?"

The beginnings of a cautious smile touched her mouth. "You're really saying yes?"

He found himself nodding. "I'm really saying yes."

"Wow. My mom said I didn't have a shot in hell." She beamed. "I love proving her wrong. Thank you!"

He was so shocked when she threw both arms around him, the hug sent him back a step. "Whoa." He caught himself, laughing. "There'll be none of that around the men. And you said your aunt was a trick rider?"

She bounced anxiously on her toes. "Uh-huh."

"You'll need to tell me more about that," he advised.

"Why? Are you interested?"

"In your aunt?" He bobbed his head. "Guilty."

"I didn't know the two of you were—"

"We've been keeping it quiet," he said.

"Oh," she said, lowering her voice and darting a look around. "Right. Okay. Well, what do you want to know?"

"How she's doing, for one?" he asked, feeling lame.

Her expression morphed quickly from playful to troubled.

The mob was beginning to file out of the church en masse. He stepped closer. "What's wrong?"

"I shouldn't say. Mom told me it's a family matter."

Everett tensed. "Does it have anything to do with what they found on the mountain?"

"It has everything to do with that."

He nodded. "I don't want to get you in trouble. Just do me one favor."

Kaya put the phone back into its cradle. She called Root and Wyatt into her office. She closed her file drawer with a thud and folded her hands on the desk. "That was the FBI. They're sending a man here."

"They'll shut us out of the case," Wyatt complained.

"We'll have to turn over all the evidence," Root said. "All those bodies…"

She nudged the file on the desk with her hands. "I've been speaking with Walther, off and on. I've also been coordinating with the Fuego, San Gabriel and other county police departments and Missing Persons from each bureau."

"That's a heck of a thing," Wyatt muttered. People tended to go missing in the desert quite a bit.

"Together, we may have turned over some results," Kaya revealed, "but we'll have to wait for DNA to confirm." She picked up the folder and thrust it at them.

Wyatt took it. He flipped it open. "Mescal, Sawni. Missing since... Geez, boss. This woman's been missing for eighteen years."

Kaya nodded. She threaded her hands together to stop them from fidgeting. "She was seventeen when she disappeared. She wasn't native to Fuego. She grew up on the rez."

"Like you," Root said, innocently enough.

Kaya felt it like a blow. "Like me."

"Did you know her?"

Full disclosure. There had to be full disclosure if there was going to be trust. "There's a personal connection," she admitted. "I'm not willing to elaborate much further."

They both exchanged a glance, then let it lie. "Last known whereabouts were—"

"Here, in Fuego," she continued. "After three months, local police and sheriff's departments stopped looking for her. Though her family and others on the rez never have."

"Without DNA confirmation, why do you think it was her?" Wyatt asked.

"It's not wishful thinking, if that's what you're implying. A piece of jewelry was found at the site. It matches one I know she owned and wore often." *I had one to match— with a* K. Kaya had had her mother bring it over from their old house where she'd left it when she joined the police academy in Taos. Her piece and the one at the lab were a dead match. "Her grandfather made it for her and one other that I have in my possession."

"Maybe somebody duplicated it," Root noted.

"Maybe she pawned it before she went missing...or somebody could've stolen it," Wyatt said.

"All good thoughts," she acknowledged. "But the pieces line up...a little too neatly now that there are four bodies in the morgue...one of which could very well be hers."

"If one of the bodies does belong to Mescal and the FBI comes in here and says we're off the case, are you going to allow that?" Wyatt wondered.

She weighed the question and all the implications. "I'm not sure," she said truthfully. She flipped open the next file on her desk. "The other possible is Merchant, Bethany. You probably remember her name from the papers. She disappeared a year before Mescal while she was in her senior year at Fuego High School."

"I do remember this one," Root said. "I was a freshman when she was a senior. Head cheerleader, Miss Rodeo like three straight years in a row... She dated all the high-profile rodeo kids. Terrence Gaines. True Claymore. Sullivan Walker. Everett Eaton..."

Kaya pretended her breath didn't snag on the last. "Eaton."

Root nodded. "Oh, yeah. Real hot and heavy, that relationship. 'Course, then his mom up and left his dad for Santiago Coldero. Everett dropped out of school... Things cooled real fast between him and Bethany."

"Her last known whereabouts were at the Lone Star Motel," Kaya noted from the file. "They found an overnight bag, her wallet, keys, even her shoes in Room 10. The bed was still made, however, and it was between her check-in that evening, which she paid for in cash, and her check-out time the following morning that she disappeared."

"How do we know it's her in the morgue, too?" Wyatt asked, his brows low.

"Something that was not found among her possessions in the motel was a wristwatch, one her mother claimed she never left the house without. It was an heirloom that belonged to Bethany's grandmother and was given to her when the woman passed." Kaya sat back. The chair squeaked beneath her. She closed the file on Bethany's picture-perfect smile. "A watch of the same description was found at the crime scene. The family supplied samples as well as dental X-rays. If it's her, we'll know in due time."

"Which would leave one unidentified person," Root said.

"Did Walther say whether or not he's determined cause of death for any of them?" Wyatt asked.

"Just one for certain," she said, grim. "Our hiker, Miller Higgins. Gunshot wound. His skull was tested for gunpowder residue and the wound there is consistent with a gunshot to the back of the head fired at close range."

Root winced a little. "Sounds mercenary. The others must have contusions on the back of the skull as well. That's why the FBI's coming. If a pattern's been established, they must think we've got a serial killer on the loose."

"I don't have to tell you not to pass on any of this information," she reminded them. "The press is on us as it is, not to mention the public. I've had four separate families in my office over the last few days requesting to know whether or not one of the bodies belongs to their son or daughter. One of them was the Merchants. We must keep as many of the details under wraps as we can so that we can build a solid case."

"And then hand it all over to the FBI," Wyatt said dismally.

Kaya frowned. "We'll see."

It was raining cats and dogs before she left the sheriff's department and drove home. She thought about stopping by one of the takeout places in town and grabbing something, knowing she was going home to an empty fridge. She hadn't had it in her to face the supermarket or its patrons—not yet, anyway.

She wasn't avoiding people, she told herself. She just wasn't hungry.

Messages had been left on her voice mail at her personal number. There, she'd heard the voices of her mother, her sister, the Mescals…and that was hard to swallow.

And Everett. He'd called, twice—once to leave a message.

That was three days ago. Maybe he'd given up by now.

Just as well, she thought, escaping the rain for the comfort of her home. She'd likely be called back in before daybreak to deal with the arroyos that resulted from these spring cloudbursts. She took off her weapons belt and shrugged off her sheriff's button-down so that her shoulders were bare in her black tank top and she could breathe somewhat easier. She put her official phone on charge as well as her radio, ignored the pit in her stomach by avoiding the pantry and poured herself a cup of coffee.

She was watching the steam rise from the surface as it sat, untouched, on the counter when the doorbell rang.

Wary, she didn't move from the space over the brick cobbles of the kitchen. Fuego was small so it was only natural that some of its residents knew exactly where to find her during her off-duty hours. There had been a few who'd knocked on her door during the week, fishing for more on the case. She'd stopped answering.

She picked up her mug when the doorbell sounded again and then again in quick succession. Thoughtfully, she raised it to her mouth and blew across the surface, letting the coffee's scent curl up her nostrils. Maybe it would help settle her, as nothing else had since she'd recognized the turquoise and silver cuff.

Her mind wouldn't leave it alone. She set the coffee back down, tired and heartbroken all over again.

Had she really thought she'd find Sawni alive? After all this time?

She'd been a fool.

The doorbell was replaced by the sound of a hard knock. A voice followed, terse and familiar. "Hey! Sheriff Sweetheart! Open up!"

Kaya found her feet moving toward the door, abandoning her coffee. She crossed the living space. He was pounding on the door so hard, it was rattling on its hinges. She unlocked the dead bolt, undid the chain and turned the knob, then yanked the door open before he could break it down. "What are you doing?"

The porch light spilled over him. He was standing on her stoop under his hat in the rain. The drops hit the raised concrete platform beneath his boots and splatted noisily, breaking apart and coming in the house. He squinted at her. "What's the matter with you?"

Her jaw dropped. "What's the matter with *me*? You're the one about to break my door down!"

"How else was I supposed to get you to answer?" he asked. "Your family thinks you've done well to isolate yourself. You won't return their calls or mine—"

"How do you know what my family—"

He took a step closer to the threshold, crowding it and her out of the doorway. "What'd you find on the mountain that's made you shut down?"

Her teeth were gnashed and anger ground between them. It felt good, feeling something other than the bone-chilling fear she'd been walking around with. "Get off my porch before my neighbors see you lurking."

"You're going to have to arrest me," he challenged. He scanned her. "Christ. Have you slept since I saw you last?"

Had she expected him to be charming? Women who counted on Everett Eaton turning on the charm would be severely disappointed. She convinced herself she wasn't one of them. "Of course I've—"

"Don't lie to me," he said, grim around the mouth. He planted his hands on either side of the jamb. "I'll bet you're not eating much, either. You look like you're about to drop."

"Why are you here?" she asked him, exasperated.

"You're trying to back out," he decided. "You don't want any part of our agreement anymore."

"I've got more important things to worry about."

"At least call your sister and your niece. They're worried sick."

"Why do think I'm going to take orders from you?" she countered.

"Because you're alone and you're trying to keep it that way—however much you might need somebody right now," Everett stated. "Maybe that person isn't me. I can live with that. But the least you can do is tell me—not dodge my calls."

"You're right."

He opened his mouth to argue further, stopped midword and screwed up his face. "I am?"

Kaya closed her eyes. They wanted to stay closed. "I haven't slept. I'll cop to that. The situation on the mountain…it's far more complex than I thought it could be. There's more I can't tell you. It's personal and it's eating at me. I won't even have the authority to finish it or bring closure to the families. The Feds are on their way. They'll be taking over the investigation as early as Wednesday."

"Why the Feds?" he asked. "Your department's small, but you're capable. You won't stop until you've caught this son of a bitch."

He was going to have so many questions, none of which she could answer. "I want that," she said. "More than you know."

He straightened. "Are you hungry, sweetheart?"

She blinked. "I should eat. I haven't been hungry."

He picked up something off the stoop. A to-go container. "This is from Rocko's."

"Rocko's… Pizza?" she asked, bemused. "That's two towns over. Why—"

"Don't ask me to give away my sources," he said, holding the box out to her, "but I was told it was your favorite restaurant."

She felt the warmth of the cardboard box. "You brought me pizza from Rocko's."

"I want you to be okay. I aim to see to it that you are. You take care of the community, everybody in it. But if you need someone to take care of you, you know where to find me. Are we clear?"

She only stared at him, the scent of Rocko's thick crust supreme curling up her nostrils. Suddenly, she was awake, and she was ravenous. "I don't know what to say."

"Say yes."

There was no refusing him. She pressed her lips together.

He didn't waver. "Is there anything else you need?"

You. In my house. In this space. With me. Her face burned as the thoughts hit home. She settled for shaking her head in response.

"Let me know if that changes," he demanded. "And answer the phone."

"Anything else?" she asked, wryly.

"I'd be inside the house if I didn't think you'd tase me for muddying your floors," he said. "The next time I leave the Edge and track you down, I'm coming in."

She didn't think it'd be wise to tell him she didn't care about her floors. She liked the idea of stripping him down layer by layer just so she'd know warmth again.

This man burned hotter than anyone she'd ever known. It was wiser to keep him out—keep him at arm's length, like she'd planned. But his eyes glinted and the longer she looked at him, the more she wondered just how hot his core was.

"Eat," he said in no uncertain terms. "And get some sleep. I'll say good night."

"Good night," she said. He turned away, walked off the stoop. She shut the door. It took her several seconds to move her feet. She walked back to the kitchen, set the box on the stovetop. She opened the lid. Saliva filled her mouth.

Before she could reach for a slice, one of her phones rang on the counter. She glanced over to see the screen of her personal device lit up. Everett's name was splashed across her caller ID.

This time, she didn't hesitate. She picked it up, swiped, then raised it to her ear. "Hello?"

"Just checking," came the sound of his baritone.

A small smile tugged at her mouth. It kept tugging and she gave in to it. "I thought we said good night."

"We're going to say a lot more good nights before this is all over. You know that, right?"

"Yes," she whispered.

"I'm looking forward to the night I don't have to say good night. I'm livin' for that night, baby."

"I can't handle you when you talk like that," she informed him.

"Good. Maybe it'll make you impatient."

"Good night, Everett."

He cursed but said it anyway. "Think of me, sweetheart." Then he hung up, leaving her with an appetite and need that were suddenly and magnificently awake.

Chapter 7

Everett stalked into the hacienda-style ranch house ahead of his dogs after a long day of tagging calves and counting cattle. He wanted to drink a beer, put up his feet and leave the paperwork he knew was sitting at his desk for later. The house smelled damn fine, and his stomach rumbled, needing whatever Paloma had thrown together in the kitchen.

No sooner had he taken off his hat than the dark-eyed housekeeper his father had hired over thirty years ago rounded the corner and snapped her apron at him. "Take off those boots. You're tracking in dirt. Don't you have any sense, or has it all vanished with the altitude?"

Everett hung his hat on the nearest peg and stretched his arms from one side of the mudroom to the other. "I was awake with the cock this morning. I don't need you pestering me when we both know I wiped my feet a dozen times before entering."

"You got witnesses to that?" she asked, eyeing him beadily.

Everett growled low in his throat before he turned, opened the door and stepped out onto the welcome mat. He scraped the bottom of his boots on the coarse fibers in exaggerated motions like a mama cow stamping the ground while he tagged her calf. When he was done, he came back in and slapped the door shut with a resounding thud after letting the dogs in, too. "Satisfied?"

"Turn them up for me, one after the other."

"No," he drawled and stomped around her in the direction of the kitchen. The clickity-clack of the dogs' nails followed him across the hardwood.

Paloma pulled him up short with an urgent hand on his arm. "Don't go in there looking like that!"

"Why not?" He loved her. She was more mother to him than the woman who had made him and run away. But he was hot and drained and all he'd thought about for the last hour was settling down with a beer and his dogs.

"There's a man," she hissed, down to a whisper.

Everett raised a brow. "You got a man in here?" He shook her loose. "Does he know he'll never be good enough for you? Never mind. I'll tell him."

She grabbed him again before he could turn the corner. "Not that kind of man, you lout. And haven't I got enough problems keeping you decent without some good-for-nothing boyfriend hanging around?"

"That's the spirit," he muttered, still trying to get a look around the corner. "Who's the guy?"

"He says he's from the FBI."

Everett stopped straining away. "Say again."

"You heard me," she said, lowering her brow. "Everett Templeton Eaton, don't you go all Clint Eastwood on this one. He's no Sheriff Altaha, or Jones for that matter."

"I'll thank you never to mention the good sheriff and her predecessor in the same breath again," he warned.

"You misunderstand," she snapped, pinning him with an expression he'd come to know well over the misspent days of his youth. "An outside agent of the law isn't likely to give you the sort of understanding or leniency that local law enforcement has. Keep that tongue of yours civil. I don't have the wherewithal to bail you out of federal prison."

It wasn't exasperation that gripped her. Not entirely. She was worried about him—more than usual. He felt himself soften. So few people filed away his rough edges, but she could do it in a look. Without answering, he bent to her level and pecked a kiss on her round cheek. Then he ducked into the kitchen to face the man sitting across the room at the table.

Built like a boxer in a flat gray suit that strained around the points of his shoulders, the fella didn't fool Everett into thinking he was as refined as either his clothing or rigid posture suggested. When he stood to greet Everett, opening his mouth to do so, Everett pivoted for the fridge and opened it. He took out his beer, twisted the top off the bottle and tipped it for a long pull as his dogs Bones, Boomer and Boaz drank from their water bowl under the picture window.

The FBI man cleared his throat. "Mr. Eaton, I presume."

Everett drank until the contents of the bottle were half-gone before coming up for air. He checked what was on the stove. Enchiladas. *This better be quick, secret agent man*, he mused before shutting the fridge and turning to face his latest opponent. "If she invited you to dinner, she's overruled. I'm not in the mood for strangers at my table."

The FBI man looked amused. "The sheriff said you're a real mean cattle king. I was half expecting John Wayne to walk through the door."

"Altaha sent you?" Everett asked.

"She asked me to wait until she could smooth the introduction," the stranger said, talking fast with hints of Boston around his consonants, particularly the *R*s. "But I was keen to form my own impression of Fuego's newly minted cattle baron. This is quite a spread," he added. "I understand you're second-generation. Quite an inheritance for a man still shy of forty."

FBI man would have done better to bring the sheriff with him. Everett lifted the beer for another drink. "Just."

The FBI man took that as his cue to introduce himself, stepping forward. He pulled aside his coat to show the badge strapped to his belt. "I'm Agent Watt Rutland."

"The hell kind of name is Watt?" Everett asked.

"Birth name's Walter," Rutland explained. "Father raised six boys on his own, had monosyllabic names for all of us."

"Now, that's fascinating," Everett muttered, kicking out a chair for himself. He turned it and sat down backward, leaning on the ladder-back rail. After another drink, he hung his arms over it to pet Boaz who came looking for a scratch. "What can I do for you, Watt?"

"I think I prefer Agent Rutland for now," he said thoughtfully, pulling a small pad of paper from the lining of his sport coat.

Everett heard someone clearing their throat from the direction of the door. He turned his head only slightly, knowing Paloma was just out of view. He remembered her warning, the plea in her eyes, and rolled his. Gripping the bottle in both hands, he asked, "Will you be taking some of the caseload off the sheriff?"

"What do you know about the case, Mr. Eaton?" Rutland asked, shifting on his chair. He clicked the button on the top of his pen, ready to scribble on the pad he'd spread open on the tabletop. "Or can I call you Everett?"

"Eaton's fine," Everett admitted. "Just leave out the mister. I'm not my father."

"He passed recently, didn't he?"

"Nine months ago," Everett said. Long time to go without the leathery sound of the old man's voice or the sight of his time- and work-worn boots crossed on top of the office desk. Covering up his grief the way his therapist had told him to stop doing a long time ago, Everett sipped his beer again, then swallowed hard. "I know there were several bodies pulled off our mountain. Three unidentified females and one boy. The kid, Higgins, that went missing recently from San Gabriel. Foul play's involved though nobody's saying how, specifically." He frowned at the stranger across from him. "If the FBI's here, I'd say foul play's been chalked up to murder and it's serious business."

"Is murder ever not serious business?" Rutland asked conversationally.

The casual tone wasn't fooling Everett one bit. Rutland had come to Eaton Edge to study Everett and study him hard. *I'm not going to squirm for you, secret agent man*, he determined. "You've got to look in my direction because you see it as my land."

"Well, isn't it?" Rutland asked.

"It belongs to the family," Everett told him. "So does the business. And there's not a thing going on here that we don't know about."

"If that tracks," Rutland considered, "then one of you knows what happened on Ol' Whalebones. Don't you?"

Everett didn't answer, nor did he lower his stare from the FBI man's. He finished off the beer.

Rutland unclicked the pen and placed it and the notebook back in the lining of his coat. "How's about this? You clean up. Get your story straight. Then you come by the sheriff's department tomorrow morning where my team and I can interview you formally."

As Rutland rose from his seat, Everett raised a brow. "Do I need to bring a lawyer with me?"

Rutland paused. "Representation isn't necessary. But if you've got reason to believe you need counsel, you're well within your rights."

"As a suspect," Everett assumed.

"As a person of interest," Rutland said evenly. Then he stuck out his hand.

Everett didn't bother to stand or shake it.

Rutland dropped it. "I'll note that in my report."

Everett waited until the sound of his high-priced brogues faded before he gave in to a long exhale, trying to release the tension from his shoulders.

Another bottle of beer dropped to the table in front of him. Paloma's hand touched his shoulder. "We got trouble?" she asked, taking the empty bottle from his hand.

"Why would we when I didn't kill Higgins or any of the others?" he asked.

Paloma dropped to the seat Rutland had abandoned. Everett was shocked to see a full beer in her fist, too. To his knowledge, he rarely saw Paloma drink more than champagne at New Year's or wine at Christmas dinner. He recalled the time he'd had to pick her, Eveline and Luella up at the police station where they'd been detained on a trumped-up drunk and disorderly charge after Margarita Night. It nearly teased a smile out of him. She choked the bottle top, twisted off the cap and tipped it to her mouth for a delicate sip.

When he and Ellis were troublemaking youngsters, she'd known how and when to put the fear of God into the two of them. A ranching woman to the core, she could boast as many callouses and scars as either of them.

But Everett had never had any doubt that Paloma was

a lady. She'd tried her best to breed him, Ellis and Eveline to be polite and well mannered.

He'd given her hell. There were times he felt sorry for it. She was the only woman who'd ever loved him for who he was without condition.

"If he's got nothing on you," Paloma considered, "why'd he come all this way to make introductions?"

"To his mind, it's my mountain. He and his team are going to be crawling over this place like ants." It was going to annoy him. Everett opened the new beer. It hissed and the cap clinked when he tossed it onto the table. He crossed his arms over the top of the chair and peered at the view of the barn and corrals from the window over Paloma's shoulder. "They better not do anything to stall operations."

"You don't think he's already looked into you and everybody else here?" Paloma asked. "You don't think he may not like something about your past and was trying to shake something loose?"

The concerned light in her eyes hadn't ceased. Rutland was causing Paloma to worry, and that angered Everett. "He won't find anything, will he?"

"What's this formal interview about tomorrow at the sheriff's then?" Paloma asked.

Everett thought about that. "Hell if I know."

Paloma watched him drink. "You need to call Ellis, Eveline and the others."

The others being Luella and Wolfe, as they were family all but in name as far as Paloma was concerned. "No use getting them worked up, too, over assumptions."

"My assumptions come straight from my intuition," Paloma informed him, "which is rarely wrong where the lot of you is concerned. I'd have thought by now you'd have learned to pay attention."

As she picked her bottle up off the table and got up to leave, Everett waited until she brushed by his chair to reach up and take her by the wrist. He waited until her dark eyes swung down to meet his. "I wouldn't lie to you. You know that."

He saw her lips firm but not before he saw the heavy lower one tremble. "Everett, I know you would kill to protect your own. I've never doubted that. But what happened on that mountain was nothing less than evil. That isn't you. I know it wasn't you. I will not abandon you to this scrutiny. I just wish the sheriff's boys and the FBI would leave us well enough alone. Hasn't this family been through enough?"

He held her for another moment, long after he dropped his eyes. The sight of her unshed tears gutted him. "They won't be looking our way for long," he pledged. "I'll make sure of it."

"Don't do anything stupid, *mijo*," she muttered. She *tsk*ed as she passed a rough hand through his hair. "Get a haircut while you're in town tomorrow or I'll take the scissors to you myself."

"You'll have to catch me first," he warned her.

"Hmph."

As she passed into the kitchen to put plates together for the both of them, the tension jammed taut between his shoulder blades and his thoughts didn't stray far from the meeting with Rutland tomorrow morning.

Kaya tried to gauge Everett's face from the corner of the room. She'd been invited to observe Rutland's interview with him—but not to participate.

He'd had his hair trimmed. The tips had been cut far enough back that she could see the pale stripe the sun hadn't touched at the peak of his brow. There were fine notes of gray there, mixed with black. His hat was hooked over one knee of his Wranglers and his plaid shirt was open over a gray T-shirt that fit him well enough she could see hints of definition underneath.

She steadied herself. She'd known the FBI agent would investigate Everett, his family and his employees. She'd had her deputies do the same. She'd wanted him clear. She hadn't wanted his name anywhere near the list of possible suspects. When Root confirmed that his alibi for the window of Higgins's disappearance had checked out, she'd shut herself in her office to breathe a long, hard sigh.

If she was going to go to bed with the man—and after that pizza business at her house, it felt inevitable—he couldn't be involved in this.

Kaya knew Rutland had to go through the same motions and come to the same conclusion about Everett's involvement. It didn't make her any less wary of what Rutland had hidden in the bland file folder on the desk in front of him.

He'd been working Everett for over half an hour with all the routine questions that Root and Wyatt had already asked. But with the latest news from the forensics lab and Walther's office, there were more questions to be asked.

Rutland reached into the folder and pulled out a photograph of a blonde girl. It was over a decade old. "Do you recognize this woman?"

Everett raised one thick eyebrow. "Her name's Bethany Merchant. She went missing after I left school."

Rutland nodded. "What was your relationship with Miss Merchant?"

"We were involved," Everett informed him.

"Intimately?"

Everett peered at Rutland. "Are you asking if we had sex?"

"I'm just trying to get a more detailed understanding of what happened between you and Miss Merchant before her disappearance."

Everett stared Rutland down. Finally, his shoulders lifted. "We were together. We drank, kissed, partied and yeah, we had sex. Multiple times. You want a list of the places or are you more interested in the positions?"

"There's no need to get testy, *Mr.* Eaton," Rutland said evenly.

Everett tilted his head just slightly and Kaya came to attention when she saw the ready light in his eyes. It meant there was a fight ahead and not a pretty one. "You're the one prying into my personal business. *Watt.*"

She sucked in a breath.

Why was he using Rutland's first name when she hadn't heard him say hers since he'd started asking her to consider him more than a friend?

The hitch of pain came as a surprise. She didn't want it. She wanted nothing but to focus on the remainder of the interview and get back to the county's and the town's needs.

The hurt persisted, nonetheless. And that set her as ill at ease as the realization in the restaurant that he had put her on some kind of pedestal.

It made no sense. Why would he have all these expectations of her and who they could be together...if he couldn't say her name?

Rutland placed another photograph on the table. "Do you recognize this individual?"

Everett frowned. After a moment, he leaned forward.

Kaya's heart was in her throat as he studied Sawni's

picture. *Why?* she thought helplessly as she watched her past and present collide.

Everett shook her head. "No," he answered. "Though she does look familiar. Who is she?"

"Sawni Mescal," Rutland revealed. "She worked in Fuego, not long after Bethany disappeared."

Everett watched Rutland as he shuffled the photos back into the folder. "She went missing, too, I assume." He glanced at the wall. His eyes locked with Kaya's. She felt the impact in her knees. "That's who you found on the mountain?" he asked her.

Rutland cleared his throat. "We can neither confirm nor deny at this time—"

"That's where Bethany's been?" Everett asked, undeterred. "All this time? Her body's been at the Edge…"

The awareness came. Kaya saw it dawn on him. As he trailed off, his chin lifted in understanding. To Rutland, he said, "That's why you think I'm involved. Beyond the fact that Ol' Whalebones is part of the Edge, you think I…what—killed Bethany weeks after I ended things with her and dumped her on the mountain?"

"Mr. Eaton—"

"No," Everett said. He climbed to his feet. "They looked into me. There are files, records that'll show I was cleared after her disappearance." Again, he looked to Kaya. "You still got those files, sheriff?"

"We do," she answered. "Missing Persons cleared you…"

Everett sensed more. "But?"

Kaya stepped forward. "There were rumors that you and her fought at the rodeo the day before she went missing…"

His gaze circled her face. "So?"

"You may not have killed her," Rutland said. "But you

were a man of means, even then. You had enough money and privilege to hire someone to—"

"That's bull," Everett dismissed. "You're talking about my trust fund. If you'd followed through, you'd know that money didn't come into my possession until I was twenty-one. I was barely eighteen when Bethany disappeared. And that wasn't a fight at the rodeo. She came after me, hankering for a dispute for ending things with her after I quit school. I walked away from it. I'd already made my position clear."

"Which was…" Rutland prompted.

"She always talked about going east after graduation," Everett explained. "She wanted to go to college and live there, get out of New Mexico. She had the grades to do it, too. She could've gone to any school, Ivy League or otherwise, and her daddy had the money to pay for anything her scholarships didn't. She wanted me to tag along and start a life with her, wherever she went. But I knew I'd never leave Fuego. I never wanted to. She resented that just like she resented me leaving school because my father needed me at the Edge. I ended things between us because she got her acceptance letter from Princeton, and she needed to know there wasn't anything holding her back."

"If there wasn't anything holding her back, why did she argue with you the day before she went missing?" Rutland asked.

"She was mad because I didn't want to go," Everett explained, "and because I'd told her I didn't love her."

"Did you love her?"

Everett set his jaw. "I don't see how that's relevant."

"Everything's relevant," Rutland explained. "Her parents deserve an answer as to why she was murdered and left on that mountain—a mountain that belongs to your family, Mr. Eaton. Answer the question."

"No," Everett snapped.

"No, you won't answer the question? Or no, you didn't love her?"

"I didn't love her," Everett shot back. "Not enough to follow her across the continental US. Is that the answer her parents want? That I didn't love their daughter the way she wanted me to love her? Is that going to comfort them in their grief?"

Rutland chose not to answer these questions. He'd opened the file again, splaying it wide. Turning it, he revealed the discovery photos and the photos Walther's technicians had taken of the dead in the lab. They scattered under Everett's nose.

Kaya stepped forward, wanting to shuffle them back into the folder where they belonged.

Everett saw them before she could round the table. His hands lifted. The skin of his face seemed too thin. He released a rough breath and stepped back.

He wavered and she dove.

Before he could stagger or fall, she grabbed him by the shoulders. "Sit down," she murmured. Looking around for his chair, she hooked her toe around its leg and slid it closer. "Just sit, okay?"

"Why would you…?" he groaned as she pushed him into the seat. "You think…"

"Quiet." Kneeling, she framed his face with her hands. The skin around his mouth was white. His lips themselves had turned a shade paler than his skin. She cursed, hooking her hand around the back of his neck. "Put your head between your knees and breathe."

"You think I…" he said again even as he did what he was told.

She didn't like how small he sounded. "Put those away," she snapped at Rutland. "He's had enough."

It took Everett longer than he would have liked to pull himself together. It was bad enough that he'd nearly passed out in the interrogation room.

When he closed his eyes, he could still see the photographs of Higgins, Bethany, the Mescal girl…and whoever the fourth person was.

Higgins's brain cavity had been exposed. Bethany's blond hair had still been visible but her skin had faded away from bone—same with the Mescal girl, only her hair had been dark. Nothing remained of the fourth person except skeletal remains…

The images would live rent free in his mind for the rest of his life.

Everett splashed water across his face again in the men's room. The back of his throat was raw. He'd lost the fine breakfast Paloma had made for the two of them that morning before seeing him off with a reminder about getting his hair trimmed…

He felt older, more burdened. He was far angrier than he had been after Rutland's visit the night before and the reasons weren't settling well.

He'd grown up on a ranch. He knew what became of animals left out to die.

But those bodies in the photographs were human.

The image of Higgins's skull floated back to him. Everett ducked his head to the sink and drank water from the faucet. He swished it around his mouth, trying to rid himself of the bitter taste, then spat it out and shut off the water, finally. He ripped brown paper towels from the dispenser to the right of the mirror, wadded them up and dried his face.

His reflection was clear now, but his eyes weren't. They were bloodshot. Pulling the aviator sunglasses from the neckline of his T-shirt, he took his time cleaning the lenses with the open corner of his plaid button-down before he covered his eyes. He tossed the wad of paper towels in the overfull trash can and opened the door.

Kaya was waiting.

He lowered his head and beelined for the door.

"We'll speak again, Mr. Eaton," Rutland called from the open door of the interrogation room.

Everett ignored him. He could see the outdoors through the glass. He pushed through the door, letting the sun hit him in the face.

Before the door could swing shut at his back, Kaya exited, too. "Everett," she said when it closed behind her.

"Nope," he said, shaking his head as he pivoted in the direction of the parking lot. His voice was raspy and weaker than he needed it to be.

Her hands closed around the bend of his elbow.

"You don't want to do this right now," he warned.

She scanned him. "You shouldn't drive."

"I'm fine," he bit off. He felt naked under the glide of her black, knowing gaze and he didn't need her to know it. "I'm walking, aren't I? Now let me go. I'm not feeling peaceable, and I know you don't want to do this dance in town, seeing as you're determined to keep our relationship a secret from everyone."

She didn't loosen her grip. "I'm sorry about what Rutland did in there. It was dirty."

He made a noise in his throat. He extricated himself and took long, retreating strides to the door of his truck.

"I didn't know what he was going to do," she told him. "I wouldn't have agreed to it if I had."

"That's nice," he drawled, opening the driver's door. "I'll see you around, sweetheart."

Before he could boost himself into the seat, she grabbed him again. "Everett."

"I can't do this right now," he growled. "Step away."

She pushed herself farther into his space, taking a handful of his shirt. "I can't let you leave 'til I know you're okay."

"I'm okay."

"You're not."

"Just tell me one thing," he said. "I need to know if any part of you believes any of it."

"Believes what?"

He pointed at the building and what had happened inside. "That I did *that*. That I'm *capable* of that."

"Would I be here if I did?" she asked.

"I don't know anything right now," he replied. "You want me to be okay? Turn me loose."

She hesitated, her eyes doing circles around his face. Finally, her hand released his shirt and she shifted onto her heels.

Everett placed one foot on the running board and settled into the driver's seat. He shut the door. He cranked the truck and gripped the wheel.

He saw Kaya walking back to the door. He thought about rolling the window down and saying something but stopped himself. She'd been in that room. Even if she didn't think he was capable of killing Higgins, Bethany and those other people, she'd stood back while others who did questioned him.

He put the truck in gear and pulled out of the parking lot, unable to deal with what was under the surface.

What had he expected? He was someone who notoriously surrendered to nothing in life. So why had he begun to surrender his heart, of all things, to the goddamn sheriff of Fuego County?

Chapter 8

Kaya didn't want much to do with Agent Rutland, despite their departments working together on the case. She'd spent the majority of time over the last week out of office seeing to her sheriff duties. At some point, she had even stopped checking her personal cell phone. Everett hadn't called or texted once since the debacle at the station.

She patrolled with Root and Wyatt, answering a trespassing call outside of Fuego, which turned out to be a landlord and tenant dispute. That led to a destruction of property charge for the tenant.

A drifter was spotted outside Fuego. When his location was called in to dispatch, Kaya took it. The man turned out to be dehydrated. His shoes were falling apart. When she led him into the sheriff's station to see to his care, she ran headlong into Annette Claymore, the mayor's wife, who had plenty to say about his kind being invited into town. Kaya enjoyed putting her in her place, much like she had put True Claymore in his the day the bodies were found.

"You better be careful," Annette warned her. "If the citizens of this town don't like the way you do your job, they can remove you just as quickly as they appointed you."

"Have a nice day," Kaya said as she led the man into the air conditioning.

There was a medical emergency down the street at the barber shop. When Kaya arrived, Root was performing CPR on one of the cosmetologists, sixty-year-old Mattie Finedale. Paramedics arrived and Kaya helped keep people back so that they could do their job.

Even as Mattie was being loaded into the van, Turk Monday tugged on Kaya's elbow. "When are you going to release the names and cause of death of those poor people on the mountain?" he asked.

It brought attention from others. Soon more questions were hurled at her.

"The Merchants say it was their daughter. Is that true, Sheriff?"

"Was it a serial killer?"

"How close are you to nabbing the killer?"

"Settle down!" Kaya shouted over the ruckus. She heard the doors of the ambulance close at her back as she held up her hands. The siren started up and tires rolled. As its screech wailed into the distance, she shook her head. "People, Ms. Finedale just had a stroke. How would she feel if she knew that before she could be driven off to the hospital, you were causing a scene about a closed investigation that has nothing to do with her? I know you want answers. But there's a reason the investigative team is keeping the details under wraps."

"Do those FBI people think it was aliens?" When others turned to stare openly at Turk, he lifted his shoulders. "What? We're not that far from the rez and Dulce. Y'all know what happened there."

Kaya rolled her eyes as the shouts started back up again. "Quiet!" she yelled.

It worked but for a level voice from the back of the crowd.

Annette Claymore spoke up, asking, "Sheriff, is it true you knew one of the people who died on the mountain?"

Kaya frowned at her. If she wasn't mistaken, there was something smug hidden beneath Annette's careful expression.

"The rumors say one set of remains belongs to a girl named Sawni Mescal," she went on. "Wasn't she a friend of yours? You know, back when you were little rez girls."

...little rez girls...

The words struck Kaya. Her head snapped back as if she'd been lashed. The sharp, cold shock washed over her.

The boss wants you to remember what happens to little rez girls when they don't learn to leave well enough alone!

The shouting that echoed from long ago was loud in her ears, as was the sound of her own screaming.

She'd screamed. She'd thought she'd been so tough, so formidable in her own right. But that day she'd screamed loud into the quiet desert void, and no one had heard— except the man who had hurt her and the other who had held her in place.

She drifted back to the present and realized she was facing almost the entire town in the middle of the street, breathing unsteadily. Sobs...or memories of sobs...she couldn't tell...were packed against her throat. She was drenched in cold sweat and all she could see was the satisfied glimmer in Annette Claymore's eyes.

Does she know? Did Annette know what those men had done to Kaya that day on the road to Fuego?

How could she? That was before she married into the Claymore family.

Back when Kaya was a little rez girl, running after something far bigger and more sinister than herself.

"Well, Sheriff?" Annette piped up again.

Kaya's hands were wrapped around the front of her belt too tight. She loosened them and moved to speak.

"Nobody asked you!"

As heads swiveled to the sidewalk, Kaya spotted her teenaged niece standing tall and defiant there. "I've seen cows with more manners than all of you," Nova added. She looked to Kaya, her stubborn chin high, before fitting a pair of trendy sunglasses to her eyes and cutting through the swath of people between her and the door to the ice cream parlor. The kid, Lucas Barnes, who Everett had hired months before, followed her.

That had once been her, Kaya thought. She saw so much of herself in Nova, or who she had been before that day on the side of the road…before she'd had to work to reclaim her power.

The radio on her hip squawked and she took the opportunity to turn away from the crowd. She walked until their restless murmur was no longer a hindrance and unclipped it, raising it to her mouth. "Say again, dispatch?"

"Two-eleven in progress at Highway 8 and Miflin Road. Officer needs assistance."

"Show sheriff responding, code three," Kaya instructed as she stalked to her vehicle. She engaged lights and sirens, dispersing what was left of the rubbernecking hecklers downtown.

"Do you think people respect you, Sheriff?"

Kaya ground her teeth. Rutland rode shotgun in her truck. She'd left her service vehicle behind at the station. Her business on the Jicarilla-Apache reservation was personal.

Why had she agreed to let him tag along?

Stupidity, she thought. *Complete and utter stupidity.* "Is

this really the conversation you want to have right now?"
she asked him.

"The mayor stopped me outside the steakhouse yesterday evening," Rutland revealed, running a hand down
his tie. The sun was low, and his brows came to a *V* as he
squinted against its rays. "He has some doubt as to your
ability to handle this job."

The mayor can bite me. Kaya wanted to say it. She was
raw. Sawni's memorial was to take place in half an hour
and Kaya was going to have to face her friend's parents.
"I never heard him complain about the last sheriff, and
he was corrupt."

"Might Claymore and Jones have been involved in corruption together?" Rutland asked curiously.

"It's never been proven," Kaya replied. "But Jones was
swayed by Claymore. Jones wouldn't admit to anything
under interrogation."

"Do you think Jones meant to kill you when he shot
you in December?" Rutland asked. "From what I gather,
he wasn't very supportive of his female deputy. It's why
you never advanced within the department."

"He argued before the jury that he didn't want me dead,"
Kaya said evenly.

"He shot you when your back was turned."

She steered the truck over a rise. Jicarilla-Apache land
spread out before her. The view was enough to back the
breath up in her lungs. But that notion of *home* was as hurtful as it was sweet. Gripping the wheel a bit harder, she
noticed the clouds throwing shadows to the west. "He did."

"It's clear to me, whether he stated it for the record or
not, that he had something against you. The question is
whether the mayor still does."

"It's not my job to find out whether the man likes me,"

Kaya told him. "The people in Fuego County wanted me to take this job. So I did. If True Claymore has a problem with that, or me, he's welcome to vote for someone else when my term ends."

"Small-town politics," Agent Rutland muttered. He shook his head. "They're just as messy as they are in DC."

"I won't argue that," she stated. "The way you handled the interview with Everett Eaton." She shook her head. "It wasn't right."

"I got what we needed," Rutland said, unfazed.

"Which was?"

"The truth about whether he murdered his ex-girlfriend," Rutland said. "The victims all had close-range gunshot wounds to the back of the head. My guess is their killer forced them to kneel at the edge of the cliff. He shot them and gravity took them over the edge to the ledge below. He knew their bodies would be hidden there. Any animal other than the birds would have a hard time getting to them, even the mountain lion. As long as no one knew the ledge was there, those bodies would never be discovered."

Kaya pushed the air from her lungs. She didn't want to picture Sawni kneeling on the edge of the cliff, but Rutland had painted too clear a picture. "This is what your profiler says?"

"Some of it," Rutland admitted. "They all died execution-style. It was cold. Mercenary. Nobody who could do that over and over again over time would have fainted or tossed their cookies the way Mr. Eaton did when he saw those photographs." He eyed Kaya's clenched hands over the wheel. "I'm sorry," he said. For the first time, he softened from the dogged, hard-edged investigator she'd come to know. "I asked you to bring me with you to your friend's memorial and I'm walking you through the details of her murder. My ex-wife complains I'm insensitive. Apparently, she's right."

"Why did you ask to come with me?" Kaya wanted to know.

"I haven't been formally introduced to her family and friends, other than you and your sister."

Kaya slowed for the speed limit signs. "You think this is the time and place for that?"

"Grief can be revealing," Rutland explained.

"Or maybe you're just being insensitive," she suggested, turning off the main road as he chuckled. The memorial was being held well out of town. Sawni had loved the outdoors, particularly the small cabin near the river. Her parents had chosen that spot to formally say good-bye. Kaya knew they'd chosen it to curtail any media attention, too. Nothing made saying good-bye harder than a nosy press pack.

"You seem nervous."

Kaya swallowed. "I'm fine."

"I spoke to your sister, Naleen. She said you and Sawni were very close. Like sisters in your own right. After she'd been gone for three months, investigators seemed to give up on finding her. You took up the mantle. She thinks that's why you became a cop—to find Sawni or those who made her disappear. Is that true?"

Kaya didn't want to answer. "It was a long time ago."

"Did you ever find anything?" he asked.

Nothing she'd been able to prove. She'd had to live with that, hadn't she? All these years, she'd lived with it. And facing Sawni's family again was so difficult because of it. She'd sworn to them she would find out what happened. They were still waiting for her to deliver.

Finding Sawni's body on Ol' Whalebones wasn't an answer. It'd only brought forth a whole new set of questions.

Yet Kaya wouldn't stop until she had an explanation. Knowing Sawni had been murdered made her more determined than ever to bring closure to the Mescals...and herself.

At the memorial, the Mescals looked at Kaya like they had for over a decade—with warmth, yes. But with those not-quite-hidden hints of regret. Their mouths said *thank you for coming* and *we hope you are well.*

But the eyes. The eyes said, *Why was it our daughter... and not you?*

No amount of time or reflection could make Kaya believe it meant something different. She was here, and Sawni wasn't. *Why?* Sawni's mother's soft, lined face had seemed to question her as she smiled without meaning.

Kaya was only too glad to drop Rutland off at the bed-and-breakfast on Sixth Avenue when they got back to Fuego in the late afternoon. At least he hadn't felt the need for probing questions or small talk on the way home. She couldn't stomach either. She was drained. She'd been holding her thoughts and emotions together with rubber bands.

Those rubber bands had stretched too far. They'd grown wear lines and fissures and were ready to rupture.

Kaya frowned when she pulled up in front of her house behind an Eaton Edge truck. Putting hers in Park, she spotted no one at the wheel.

Glancing at the house, she groaned.

Everett raised his hand in greeting from his position on the front stoop.

After a week of noncommunication, his timing couldn't be worse.

She didn't see another pizza box. Just a cowboy with a long face and even longer legs taking up space where she'd wanted him, thought about him, practically moped over him since he'd skirted tires pulling away from the sheriff's department days ago.

Bracing herself, she got out of the vehicle and stepped down to the ground. She reached across the seat to the console where the flowers the Mescals had given her, leftover from the service, were tied with a silver ribbon—Sawni's favorite color. She shut the door and crossed the small yard to the house where he was sitting on the stoop. It was so low to the ground that his knees were nearly drawn to his shoulders.

She stopped before him, shaking her keys so they jangled. "You look ridiculous."

"Fine, thanks," he replied. "How're you?"

She found the right key and held it in her hand. "Shouldn't you be castrating something right now?"

"Not until summer," he informed her. He knuckled his hat farther up his brow, gauging her expression. "It'd be rude to castrate a calf just after it's born."

"Kind of rude anyway, don't you think?" she asked.

"You come to the Edge when it's time for business," he advised. "Your perspective might change."

"Maybe." She shook her head. "You want me to ask you in?"

"I've been sitting here for half an hour," he said.

"Why?"

"You drive slow. Nova said the memorial was supposed to end at one o'clock. It's near sundown."

She looked at her front door. He was between it and her. "Are you going to get up so I can pass?"

He made a doubtful noise. "Pretty sure I'm stuck."

She cleared her throat because the urge to laugh filled her—great bursts of it. The grief pushed it, making it more forceful. She didn't give in because she was very much afraid there were tears close behind it.

Her feelings needed to stay in the bottle. There was no collecting them once they broke loose. "I'd make you my new lawn ornament, but people would have too many questions."

"Questions make you uncomfortable," he muttered, reaching out to grab her hand when she extended it.

She went back on her heels to pull him to his feet. He unfolded like an accordion. Ignoring what he said, she unlocked the door, then left it open as she pushed into the house. Laying the flowers on the kitchen counter, she dropped her keys next to them and heard his boots approaching. Trying not to feel insecure about the used sofa or the uneven brick kitchen floor, she watched him come.

The little house felt smaller with him in it.

"Coffee?" she asked, desperate to fill the void as he looked around, trying to get a read on what she surrounded herself with.

"Coffee's fine," he replied.

She snatched the pot from its holding in the coffeemaker and turned to the sink to fill it. "You like it black?"

"As your eyes."

The fine drawl drew the space between her shoulder blades up tight. "Don't do that," she urged quietly.

"Why shouldn't I?" he asked from the other side of the counter.

"I've already told you I won't sleep with you." But she knew exactly how many steps there were between them and the bedroom to the left.

"I'm not always trying to get into your pants, Sheriff."

The pot was full. She shut off the water. It was still dripping but she turned with it to face him anyway. "Why do you do that?"

"Do what?" he asked.

"Why do you call me Sheriff?" she asked. "Or sweetheart? Or Sheriff Sweetheart? But never my own name?"

He paused, frowning deeply. "I've called you by your name before."

"Before it was Sheriff or Sheriff Sweetheart, it was deputy or deputy sweetheart. You *don't* call me by my name, Everett. Why?"

He stared at her and the vehemence on her face. She was breathing hard between them. His gaze skimmed her shoulders, her chest, then lifted up to circle her face again. Dropping his head altogether so his hat hid whatever he was thinking or feeling, he shifted his feet.

She took the opportunity to reel it in—the ready urge to yell at him. The hurt behind the accusations. She did well, normally, to hide these things. She'd had to learn to separate her feelings on the job. She'd done it early and often.

But Sawni's memorial had scattered all that to the wind. And for the past several weeks, Everett had made her feel... well, just *feel*. There was no hiding things. She'd known that from the beginning with him and yet she'd reached...

Stupid, she thought again. *You're so stupid, Kaya.* What a surefire way to get hurt.

Everett lifted his head, finally. His jaw was tight, but he met her gaze and held it. "I never call you by name because..."

She waited. "Because...?"

He licked his lips quickly, then spoke carefully. "...because the people who I love tend to get away from me. They leave. Or they die. So…the ones that matter… I tend to push them away somehow or other."

She made a frustrated noise. "Everett, you wanted this. You told me you'd be damned if you'd mess it up—"

"I know what I said," he acknowledged. "Doesn't mean some part of me isn't terrified you're not going to want this in the long run or something's going to put you so far out of my reach, there's nothing I can do to bring you back. Whatever it is that I want or need, it's hard to move past all that when the people who matter to me don't stay."

Love. In the long run. People who matter. The words dropped into the gulf between them and caused her heart to hammer. She didn't know what to say in response.

She placed the dripping pot back in its holding and turned on the coffeemaker. She should invite him to sit. She thought about going into the conservatory, but he'd look just as ridiculous folded into one of those tiny chairs as he had on her stoop. The used shaggy couch was not an option. So she simply waited for the water to boil and the machine to start glugging.

What felt like an eternity passed before the coffee was ready. She poured it, steaming, into two mugs and passed one over the counter to him.

He lifted it in acknowledgement.

"Don't drink," she warned quickly before he could bring it to his lips. "You'll scald your mouth. Nova told you about the memorial."

"She did," he said with a nod. "She's working at the Edge."

"She told me," Kaya said. "Thank you for giving her a chance. She's wanted this for a long time."

The corner of his mouth lifted. "Girl could be anything. Firefighter. Engineer. Rocket scientist. And she wants to be a cowboy. Your niece wants to ride cattle from sunup to sundown, and she may do it better than half the hands I have on payroll."

Kaya smiled. There was some pride there. Buckets of it. "Naleen wishes she'd move past it, but she's too much like me."

"Then why aren't you a cowboy?" he asked.

"I was," she revealed. "But this isn't about me."

"You're going to have to tell me more, anyway," he told her. "Starting with why finding this Mescal girl's body hurt you so badly you started pushing people away, same as I do."

Kaya nearly denied it. Then she saw the understanding beneath everything. He understood.

"I get what it is to grieve," he explained. "I get shutting everyone else out to do it. Everyone."

"That's not why I didn't tell you about Sawni." Lifting the coffee for a testing sip, she weighed whether she was ready to do this. The liquid was hot, but it didn't burn. She swallowed carefully and leaned over so her elbows rested on the countertop. "This is more than grief."

"Yeah?"

She tilted her head. "Look, if you're not great at listening, then this isn't a conversation you want to sit through."

"I'll sit through anything you've got."

Why did the man who regularly put his foot in his mouth know just what to say to bring her back to him? "Even if it means starting from the beginning?"

"Hey, if I start falling asleep, just kick me."

She snorted a laugh. The bastard. Backing up to the sink, she set the coffee aside and braced both hands on the counter. "Sawni and I grew up together on the rez. We weren't friends—not at first. She was quiet. She let herself pass under the radar in a lot of ways. I think she was afraid of confrontation, even if it was positive."

"And you?" he asked.

"Mmm." Kaya lifted her coffee and found her lips curving over the edge of the rim. She sipped again. "I wasn't quiet, and I definitely wasn't afraid of confrontation. I wasn't an easy child."

"You were a hellion," he guessed.

"That's one way to put it, yes."

Everett stepped around the counter to the other side, raising his mug in toast—one hellion to another. "That's my girl."

Her smile grew to the point she could no longer suppress it. She'd known the telling would be hard. She hadn't known he could make her smile through it. "You and I would have gotten along famously, I think. Sawni was treated as something of a doormat by the other kids. I started standing up for her. She needed someone big and loud and assertive to stand beside. Once she started talking to me, we decided we would be friends, always. It didn't make sense to others that we became so close. I was kind of mean. I could be a bully. She carried around a doll forever. She did everything she was told. I didn't understand why she wanted to be my friend until later. Sometimes the quiet ones will seek out someone stronger than themselves…for protection or…"

"Did you protect her?"

The smile tapered off, slowly. *Not well enough*, she thought. Not when it had really mattered, in the end. "In small ways, I guess," she replied. "Everything was great until we got to high school. Her parents blamed any trouble she got into on me, naturally. And they were right. But then we both started looking outside the rez. We set our sights there. We started going to the rodeo here in Fuego."

"You were half-pint buckle bunnies?" he asked, amused.

"We were spectators," she contradicted.

"I was on the junior circuit for a time," he revealed. "I don't remember you."

"Eaton, your head was so far up your ass you couldn't see past your own nose."

He laughed. Lifting his chin, he scrubbed the line of his neck with a rough, wide-palmed hand. "God, you're right. How'd you know that?"

"Lucky guess."

His grin turned sly. "You knew me. Or you knew who I was."

She raised a shoulder. "Never mind that. It became my single greatest desire in life to ride."

"Did you?" he asked.

"I worked with a trainer on the rez," she said. "Worked my butt off to raise enough money for lessons. Eventually, I joined the junior circuit, too, as a trick rider."

"Apache Annie," he suddenly blurted out, snapping his fingers. He pointed at her. "You were Apache Annie—with war paint and feathers in your hair."

"Yes," she said reluctantly.

"You were the real deal," he breathed. "The other boys and I… We used to watch you. *Everyone* used to watch you. You were mesmerizing."

She blinked at the praise. "I thought the whole life-style was mesmerizing. The circuitous nature of things. We traveled around, never stayed in one place. I wanted that—badly enough that I started lying to my mother. She found out and threatened to send me to Santa Fe if I didn't straighten out. She tried getting me several good jobs in

Dulce so I'd settle down or stay busy enough to keep me out of trouble. I quit every one of them, or never showed up to begin with. The trail riding job at RC Resort was my mother's last stand. It was either that or move in with my dad in the city, which felt like a fate worse than death. She threatened to sell my horse, too. So I started working for the Claymores…"

Everett's mouth worked itself into a scowl. "It didn't work, I take it."

"It worked okay," she said. "But I couldn't stop thinking about riding. So I asked Sawni to take over for me so that I could go train more and compete. As long as the position was filled, the Claymores had no reason to call my house looking for me. The crazy part was that the Claymores are so blind and idiotic that they thought Sawni was me, just because we have the same color skin. They called her Kaya and instead of asserting herself she went along with it."

Kaya lifted the coffee for a long drink. The next part was going to be most difficult. She hadn't talked about any of it for so long. It had lived inside her head. She'd picked through it over the years, combing through every minute detail, trying to find the point where things had changed, where Sawni's disappearance became inevitable. Was it the rodeo? Was it Fuego itself? Was it the resort? Where had it gone wrong? Who was responsible, other than Kaya herself? "She stopped communicating with me."

"Why would she do that?"

"I've never been sure," Kaya said. "For the longest time, I thought it might be resentment or anger. I was at the rodeo. She wasn't. Or the job sucked, and I was responsible for her being there. But over the years, I started to wonder if it might have been something else. She was seeing someone at the time. She never would tell me who. She didn't want to be teased. She stopped sharing little things at first and then…the communication became less and less frequent. No more phone calls. No more meeting after work or school. She just kind of started to slip away. Then her parents reported her missing. At first, the authorities dismissed it. You know how it is. 'She's out partying.' 'She's at a friend's house.' It was three days after that they began to take it seriously. The first forty-eight hours after someone goes missing are the most crucial. By the time they started searching, she was gone."

"You say you were responsible for her being at the RC," Everett recalled. "Sounds like survivor's guilt."

Kaya nodded. "I am responsible. I'm the reason she's gone. Her parents know it. My mother knows it. My sister. Most people on the rez do, too. Her disappearance was a huge story. The entire community came to Fuego to search for her because that was the last place she was seen. There's security cam footage of her walking into the corner store downtown shortly after her shift. The Claymores said she worked the whole day, even though it was a school day. From the store, there's nothing. She didn't have a car. She took the bus, but there's no record of her getting on the bus that afternoon. The bus driver was subbing for the regular one and he couldn't say whether she got on or not. She never made it to the bus stop in Dulce. Somewhere between the corner store in Fuego and Dulce, she was abducted."

"You never bought that she ran away," Everett assumed. "They would have said she did. They said the same thing when Bethany went missing."

"She wouldn't have done something like that. She wouldn't have put her parents through it. She loved them, respected them. She stopped going to the rodeo because they asked her to. Even when I kept going, she stopped. She was the good one."

"Stop," he said firmly.

"Every time her parents look at me, they think 'It should've been you,'" she said.

"Do they say that?" he asked.

"No. But I know that's what they're thinking."

"No, you don't," he argued. "You've been punishing yourself for this way too long, Kaya."

She sucked in a breath. *Kaya.*

When she stared at him, thunderstruck, he closed the small space between them. His hands closed over the counter on either side of her waist. He leaned in, smelling of leather and horses. She could smell his soap, just a hint of it, and wanted to spread kisses up the chords of his neck.

Everything about Everett was long and rough and certain. She wanted every piece, she realized—every little piece of him. Even if it ruined her.

"Tell me I'm wrong," he drawled. "Tell me you haven't been destroying yourself over this for years because you think you put her in the hands of her kidnapper."

"Her killer," she said unevenly. "He killed her. I have to live with that now."

"I don't want you to," he said. "That's not a life. She would've wanted you to do better for yourself. That's why she took the job to begin with—so that you could follow the rodeo and your dream. But you didn't. And it's about time you stopped torturing yourself."

"I haven't told you the rest of it," she said. She hadn't planned to. Oh God, could she? She'd never told anyone... Not her mother, not Naleen, not the police or the men she'd shared a bed with through the years... No one. When he dropped his hand from her face and stepped away so she could gather her thoughts, she realized she could at least make the first steps. "I became obsessed with her case. I led search parties. I knocked on doors. I annoyed the police and sheriff's departments to the point where they'd lock their door when they saw me coming. I hung posters, rallied the community to spread the word. I made websites. It went on for a year or more, long after everyone else had given up on her."

"Did you ever find anything else?" he asked. "Any trace?"

"Nothing solid," she said. "I practically stalked the Claymores. I was convinced they had something to do with it. But I could never shake anything loose, exactly."

"Exactly." He latched onto the word. "What does that mean?"

She felt panic tearing at her insides. It trapped the rest of the story in. She closed her eyes. *Not yet*, she thought. She'd come so far already with him. She couldn't go on.

She inhaled, trying to control the fear. The terror. It was ridiculous. She'd been on the job for so long. But she was still scared, and that was the hardest thing of all to live with.

It made her angry. So angry she could scream. "I became a police officer because I wanted to find her. When the police gave up on her and let the case go cold, I felt like the only one who cared about her or any other rez girl who went missing, for that matter. So I joined the academy in Taos and became a beat cop there. Eventually, I got the job as deputy in Fuego County. I gained access to the case files. I fell back down the rabbit hole again and couldn't stop. I nearly lost myself to it."

Everett ran his hand over her braid, soothing. He did it over and over in a silent caress that salved something inside her.

He spoke low and soft. "You didn't give yourself over to it. You wouldn't be who you are today if you had."

"It was my mother, mostly," she admitted. "She deals well in hard truths. She said even if I was any closer to finding Sawni, I was far too close to losing myself in the process. I had to stop, or Sawni and I both would have been gone."

"I'm glad you're not," he murmured. "I've told you, haven't I—that I'd have been lost without you last summer?"

It didn't hurt to hear it again. "Where would your family be if you had been? They need you, Everett. Everyone at the Edge needs you."

He made a thoughtful noise. "I like your hair this way. Even if it's not loose like I want."

"Thank you," she muttered.

"If you never let it loose, why don't you cut it?" He wrapped his hand around the width of the braid, measuring. "There's so much of it."

"It's part of me," she explained. "It's a part of my story. I don't expect you to get it—"

"I get it."

He did get her, she thought. It was stunning.

"Kaya."

She shivered. It was involuntary and thorough, skating the length of her spine and spreading tingles at the base of her head where his hand came to rest. "Yes?"

"Will you let me take your hair down? I want to feel it in my hands. I want to see it shine."

She placed her hand in the bend of his elbow and followed it up, circling his wrist. "I don't think I can handle that. Not after today."

"Eventually?"

She sighed. "If I've learned anything about the two of us together, it's that it's inevitable."

"What?"

For a second, she couldn't say it. Then she thought about all the other things she couldn't say and pushed it out on a whisper. "Everything."

He sucked in a breath and straightened. "Damn."

She smiled softly. "You were the one who spoke about the long-term."

"I did," he acknowledged.

"You know, I told myself I wouldn't go out with you until I heard you say my name."

"So why did you?"

"You've got nice eyes," she told him. "And a tight butt. And you make me laugh. You're sexy and annoying and you know how to wear a woman down with your big mouth. I may be a cop, but I'm a woman, too. I have needs and feelings and for some inexplicable reason they've both been pointed in your direction for a while."

He removed his hat and tossed it on the counter. His lips moved to hers. He kissed her firmly, cupping the back of her neck as her head fell back and his toes came to rest between hers, the hard line of his body flush against her. She spread her palms against his back and pressed, bringing him closer. She wasn't sure what close enough was anymore. He was beyond that point, wasn't he? But she wanted him closer.

A whoosh of air escaped her when his hands ran down her shoulders and back, over her rear before splaying over the backs of her thighs. He lifted and set her on the sink's edge so they were closer to eye-to-eye.

She wrapped her hands around the counter for balance as his head tilted and his mouth came back to hers for more. She groaned because he was good at this part. His last kisses had lingered for so long. How long would these stay with her?

When he broke away, she started to protest. "I'm sorry," he said on a wash of breath.

"Sorry?" she asked, off balance.

"The other day at the station house," he reminded her. "I was bruised. When I'm hurt or raw, I lash out. It's been that way as long as I can remember, and I'm getting help for it—same as I was getting help for the PTSD last fall. Some habits die hard, and when you stayed silent during Rutland's questioning, some part of me thought it was because your thoughts were in-line with his." When she began to shake her head, he nodded. "I know they're not. You were trying to stay objective. That's your job, whether or not my name's called into question. But I'm sorry."

"It's okay," she said, holding him. "We're okay."

"Yeah?" he asked, tipping his brow to hers.

"Yeah," she answered. She smiled. "Am I still worth the wait, cowboy?"

"Hell yes," he asserted. "I'm not a quitter."

So many men had quit on relationships with her, unwilling to wait for her to give all of herself. Everett was in this, and she couldn't decide if she was terrified or thrilled. "I think I like the idea of being Everett Eaton's woman."

"My woman." He scooped her off the counter and held her so her toes dangled off the floor. His hum of satisfaction vibrated across her lips as his mouth dappled lightly across hers. "You're going to have to come to the Edge. I want to see you ride."

She raised a brow. "Is that so?"

"A horse, sweetheart," he said, but his wicked grin said something else entirely. When her fingers tangled around a hunk of his hair, he hissed and dropped his head back to belt a laugh at the ceiling. "I swear. I meant a horse."

She made a doubtful noise but loosened her hold regardless.

"Your niece hinted at your past life as a trick rider before you did, and I can't get it out of my head—you bareback on that Appaloosa, your hair streaming like a black flag behind you..."

"What is this obsession you have with my hair?" she wondered.

"I'll let you know when I figure it out." He kissed her again, thoroughly.

"Hmm." Her brows came together, and her arms tightened around him. If a swarm of butterflies really was called a kaleidoscope, that was the only way she knew how to describe what happened to her insides when Everett kissed her. "I'll come to the Edge," she agreed. "But only if Paloma cooks us something."

"I might talk her into that," he weighed. "Groveling might be involved."

"Tell her we'll do the dishes."

"She's going to like you so much better than she likes me," he murmured.

She had never understood Paloma Coldero's unconditional love for the eldest Eaton brother...until now. Everett might prove to be as hard to love as others had found in the past, but Kaya liked a challenge. She'd once reveled in them.

She was going to find out what this man was made of. And if those butterflies in her stomach were any indication, she was already too far gone in this particular game of risk.

Chapter 9

The Spring Festival was a chance for Fuego County residents to mix and mingle. It was a boost to small businesses, and it was considered good medicine for all.

Everett thought it was more headache-inducing than watching Lucas and Nova stack hay bales. He'd rather haul manure or square off with a randy bull than talk to Mrs. Whiting from the bank.

He'd rather pay bills, spray weeds or grind feed than talk to Huck Claymore about Our Lord and Savior, Jesus Christ.

He'd clear brush or even sit across from the family's longtime accountant, J.P. Dearing, discussing taxes before chatting up Christa McMurtry, the organist, who for some reason had moon eyes only for him.

"Poor girl," Eveline muttered, seeing Christa's gaze shining in Everett's direction, too. "If she's looking your way, she's a glutton for punishment."

Everett couldn't fight a sneer. "Her father's going to kill me because she looks my way."

"Can I watch?" Eveline asked in a low drawl that nearly made his lips twitch in approval. She took a loud, crunchy bite of her ice cream cone.

He had to admit, Eveline had come back into her own,

comanaging the stable at the Edge with Griff MacKay and recently opening an equine rescue with Luella at Ollero Creek across town.

His sister had come home. She and Wolfe Coldero had found each other, for better or worse. Everett may want to argue with what she was fast building with the man who had once been Everett's biggest rival, but he couldn't argue with Eveline finding herself again—any more than he could quibble over her happiness. "I can't wait until you're Coldero's problem. Not mine."

She wiped a drop of sticky vanilla from her chin. "I'm only leaving long enough to drink daiquiries on the beach and swim naked in the surf with my new husband."

"Washing cats."

"What's that?" she asked.

"I'd rather be bathing Luella's cat than having this conversation," he said.

She hit him in the arm. "You're not getting rid of me. After a week, we'll be back. Then you're going to hire Wolfe for that salary job you've been trying to fill since after Dad died."

He laughed. "I may have agreed to the bastard being my brother-in-law..." He winced, just for form's sake, and had the pleasure of watching Eveline cross her arms and spread her feet in a ready stance. "But that doesn't mean I have to coexist with him any more than necessary."

"Dad gave him a percentage of Edge shares," she reminded him, polishing off the cone and wiping her hands on a thin paper napkin.

"Coldero gave them up. Traded them all for a half-dead horse, as I recall."

"What's mine is his," she added. "And before that trouble with Whip Decker seven years ago, Dad talked about making him foreman."

"Don't remind me," Everett groaned.

"He loved Wolfe," Eveline murmured, "every bit as much as he loved each of us. You know that. You have to know that. He would have wanted you to give Wolfe that job."

"I'm done with this conversation," he replied.

"Fine," she said and rolled her eyes. "Shouldn't we be talking to people like Ellis is?"

"Why?" he asked.

"Public relations," she pointed out. At the sound of his growl, she gestured. "Look. Even Luella's speaking to people."

"She shouldn't have to," he stated. "None of us should have to. Every one of these people whisper about us in church every Sunday. They're the same people who shunned Luella after what happened with her father last summer. They're the same ones who haven't stopped calling our mother a whore though she's been dead for seven years. They made Ellis and Luella's lives hell, circulating rumors about an affair they never had when he was still married. They're the ones who sided with Liberty in the divorce. They wouldn't stop their gabbing after you and Coldero were caught together at Naleen and Terrence's wedding…"

"Of course they gabbed," she said. "We were both in an indecent state."

"That's putting it mildly." He studiously turned his thoughts away from finding Eveline and Wolfe together in the tack room at The RC Resort with their unmentionables down around their ankles. *Changing the tractor's oil. Digging ditches in an ice storm. Falling in a cow patty…*

All things he'd rather do than have this talk. "The point is, we don't owe the people of this town anything, least of all small talk. As far as I'm concerned, Fuego's one big dumpster fire."

"Now you've gone and hurt my feelings."

Everett whirled, bracing himself for what was at his back. Next to him, he felt Eveline tense in tandem with him.

True Claymore beamed from the shadow of his large black hat. His belt buckle caught the sheen of the light and shot sunbeams. The thing was nearly as big around as a tricycle tire. He threaded his thumbs through his belt loops, keeping his wife, Annette's, arm looped through his. "Ms. Eaton," True said, bowing his head to Eveline. "Annette here was just telling me we aren't invited to your wedding next week."

"It's a small ceremony," Eveline informed him. "Family only."

"Word is Javier Rivera and his family warranted invitations," True said thoughtfully.

"He's foreman at the Edge and has been for years," Everett put in. "If that's not family, it's as good as."

"And Rosalie Quetzal is invited," Annette rattled off, counting the names on her fingers. "*And* the Gaines family *and* Ms. Breslin from the real estate office…even a sprinkling of people from your modeling days in New York, Eveline. But not us. You didn't even ask our sweet Huck to officiate."

"Griff MacKay is ordained," Eveline explained.

"You would rather have a grizzly old stable boy conduct your ceremony than a man of the cloth?" Annette asked, round-eyed.

"He's family," Everett said. "It doesn't hurt that his name isn't Claymore."

Annette's mouth puckered, making her look waspish. True's fingers closed over hers, soothing. "Now, Eaton," the man said, shifting his weight. "You've gone and hurt my wife's feelings."

"Didn't know she had those," Everett said philosophically. He didn't back down from Annette's glare. He knew who had started the rumors about his mother, Ellis and Luella, and Eveline and Wolfe and who stoked them tirelessly. He knew what lawyer had put her weight behind the lawsuits and legal claims the Claymores had aimed at Everett and his father through the years, even after he died.

Everett knew who had tried to lure Paloma into leaving Eaton Edge and joining the staff at The RC Resort at his father's wake.

The Claymores had been poaching ranch hands and staff from the Edge since True and Annette had laid claim to it, throwing untold piles of money to transition it from working cattle ranch to luxurious resort and spa. They'd tried to take a piece of the Edge for themselves, crying foul at the informal way their fathers had drawn the narrow margins that existed between Claymore acreage and Edge lands...

Something niggled at the edge of Everett's train of thought. He tried to dismiss it.

The land claim... It had verged on the mountains and the trails. Everett had thought when studying the map that the Claymore's grab for the territory hadn't been about heritage. It had been about hiking. Their spread was flat like Ollero Creek. They wanted to make money off what the Eatons gave hikers free claim to as long as the rules on the mountain were obeyed.

Mountain.

Everett's chin firmed as he looked at True once more. "You son of a bitch."

"Excuse me?" Annette blustered.

True's good ol' boy smile had gone bye-bye. "Better to be the product of a straight bitch than a flaming whore."

Eveline made a disconcerted noise in her throat and stepped forward. Everett grabbed her. "Hold up," he said.

She whirled on him, fury writhing over her fair features. "You cut your knuckles on his real teeth last July for a lot less. You'll let me knock the rest of them out so he has to replace them, too. He won't be able to look in the mirror again without thinking of our family. I call that justice."

"The sheriff'd be a better judge of that," True estimated. Everett saw his nerves in his shifting stance and Annette's readiness in her hard face. "You'll wind up behind bars. There won't be a wedding."

"And won't that be a shame?" Annette chimed.

"Sure would," Everett considered, watching Eveline closely. Goading had always done its job where she was concerned.

Eveline shrugged, bristling his hand off her shoulder. She backed down.

That's right, Manhattan, he thought. *Eyes on the prize.* Whether she married Wolfe or Wile E. Coyote, there would be a wedding at Eaton Edge next week, if only to spite Buffalo Bill and Calamity Jane here. He tipped his hat and said, "Have a nice day, folks."

As he pulled her away, Eveline muttered, "Have you lost the rest of your mind?"

"Everyone's always on me about my mouth and my manners," he said. "I act right, and you still take me to task."

"Do what you want with those two," she invited. "Or better yet, let me."

"You're too skinny to take either one of them," he informed her. He milled through the crowd, dodging plates of BBQ and funnel cakes and pointy metal sculptures from one of the arts and crafts booths. He scanned the crowd, moving on until he neared the sheriff's department. Outside it, under a blue booth, he spotted the two-toned uniform. Picking up his pace, he ignored Eveline's cursing and all but charged.

Kaya crouched in front of a young boy in cowboy boots, smiling as she pinned a plastic sheriff's star to his shirtfront. "You're the real deal now, Officer Lawson," she said as she settled back on her heels and straightened his hat. "Now the first order of business as junior sheriff is to hunt up all the best grub on Food Truck Row. Think you can do that?"

The bespectacled youngster nodded eagerly.

"Report back to me with any signs of doughnuts," she advised. "And make sure to treat yourself to a snow cone. Morale is very important."

"Yes, ma'am," he said, grinning at her toothily before wandering off, parents in tow.

Kaya's smile didn't waver when she found Everett and Eveline. "Well, if it isn't my favorite brother and sister team. I've got some stars leftover. Let me pin one on you."

"Take a break," Everett advised, letting go of Eveline to take Kaya's hand.

She picked up on his urgency. Her smile fled. "Is something happening?"

"Come inside and I'll explain," he said.

She looked to Eveline who shrugged and said, "Don't look at me. He dragged me here."

"I'm on duty," Kaya replied to Everett.

"Handing out buttons?" he asked pointedly.

She let go of his hand to cross her arms over her chest. "It's called public relations, cattle baron. You should try it sometime."

He dismissed her. "I've got no time for that and neither do you. Do you have maps of the mountains north of the Edge inside?"

She nodded. "We have one pinned on the board in the conference room. But you can't—"

"Good," he cut in, starting for the door. "Bring your ass."

"Rude," she said at his back.

He opened the door. Cool air spilled out of the building. "Bring your fine ass," he amended and held the door open for her and Eveline who slapped him in the stomach as she passed.

He merely grunted and moved on. He saw Rutland through the glass in a large room toward the back of the department and rushed the door.

"Everett!" Kaya called. "Don't!"

He ignored her, flying into the conference room. Rutland jumped to his feet. "What are you doing here?"

Everett came to a halt. There were two boards, one nailed to the wall and another that had been rolled in for the FBI agent's use. The grisly images from the crime scene met his eyes. Before Eveline could step inside, he yanked the sport coat Rutland had hung on the back of his empty chair and draped it over the worst of them. He made certain it would stay, then pushed the rolling board with a clatter against the wall behind it so he could get to the map mounted to the other wall. There was a red pin on the side of Ol' Whalebones and another stuck in the location of the state park's parking lot where Higgins's car had been found.

"He can't be in here, Sheriff," Rutland said as Kaya entered.

"I know he can't," she replied. "Everett, I need you to leave. Now."

"Hang on, sweetheart," Everett muttered. "Everybody just hang on." He looked around for a writing utensil and found a Sharpie on the conference table amidst folders and photographs of the victims they had confirmed identification of—Miller Higgins, Sawni Mescal and Bethany Merchant.

He uncapped the marker and followed the lines of the mountain with his finger. He drew an additional one.

Rutland and Kaya made noises of protest. Eveline noted, "You *have* lost your mind."

Everett kept spanning the aerial distance with his hand, using the map scale. He made three more marks before stepping back. Using the marker, he pointed at what he had done. "Claymore."

When the others only stared, he groaned, capped the marker and tossed it on the table. "True and Annette. They wanted the mountain. Last year, they refiled a claim for this section." He stabbed the map over the west side of Ol' Whalebones. "And everything from that point west to their spread."

Kaya closed the door to the conference room. "Are you sure?"

Rutland gripped the back of his chair. "I thought everything north and west of the crime scene belongs to the state of New Mexico."

Everett frowned. "Fine investigative work you're doing here, Watt. How much is the government paying you?"

Eveline joined Everett, scanning the marks on the map. "Everett's right."

"Say it again, Manhattan," Everett requested. "Louder this time."

"Shush!" she hissed at him, then pointed at the map. "From here to here, everything that runs north is state territory."

"Including the river," Everett put in.

"That's how people get to Ol' Whalebones without having to trek across private property. The parking lot belongs to the state park. However, this narrow spit of land between the foot of Mount Elder and Big River Valley, right up to the edge of Ol' Whalebones is Claymore territory."

"My father, Hammond, laid claim to Ol' Whalebones and it was a bone of contention for Old Man Claymore when he was alive," Everett reported. "There's been talk of the Claymores taking it back for years. But nothing formal until my father's first heart attack."

"Which was?" Kaya asked.

"The year I left high school," Everett said. "The year my mother left for Coldero Ridge."

"The same year Bethany Merchant disappeared," Kaya said slowly.

"What if," Everett said, "the Claymores didn't want the mountain because their old man lost it? What if they didn't want it for right of access? What if they wanted it because they needed to cover up evidence?"

"You're accusing the mayor of quadruple homicide," Rutland pointed out.

"Or someone he knows," Everett said.

A shaky indrawn breath filled the quiet. He looked to Kaya who had gone pale. He reached out.

She backed off quickly. "Just... Just let me think it through."

"This could be a break in Sawni's case," he told her. "The one you've been looking for."

Rutland cleared his throat. "We're following other leads, Mr. Eaton. But we will take your information into consideration."

"That's a line of crap."

"Everett," Kaya said.

"Wait a second, sweetheart," he said slowly. He faced the agent. "You don't like me. Hell, you wanted me for these murders. Are you dismissing my information because you're on someone else's case or because it was me who gave it specifically?"

"Specifically," Rutland replied, "the investigative team is pursuing other leads." When Everett swore, he went on. "As you know, details of this case are being kept under wraps for investigative purposes. Which is why, again, you can't be in here."

"Everett," Kaya said again, "let's go."

"You want me to go?" he asked, offended.

"I'm asking you to come with me," she insisted.

There was trouble in her eyes. Scowling at Rutland, he jerked his thumb at the map. "I'll be following up on this, Watt."

"I look forward to it, Mr. Eaton."

Eveline followed them out. "Did he really try to pin four murders on you?" she demanded.

Everett stopped. "I'm clear, okay? He tried to make a connection between me and Bethany's, but it didn't stick. I'm all right," he said again. She shook her head in disbelief. "Don't tell Paloma or Ellis. It's over."

"You should have told us," she said. "How many times

have I bailed you out of jail? Just once, let it be for something I *know* you didn't do."

"Next time," he promised. Then he reached for her, skimming a hand over her shoulder.

"I need to speak to him," Kaya said to her.

Eveline nodded. "Sure." She smiled and lowered her voice. "How long have you two been—"

"None of your business, *hermana*," he told her, firm on that point. "Go find Ellis. Tell him I need to speak with him."

"And Wolfe, too?"

He rolled his shoulders with an impatient rumble. "Fine. Bring the bridegroom. Tell them to meet me at the house and that Bozeman should be there, too."

Chapter 10

"Shut the door," Kaya said.

Everett did as he was told, watching her close the blinds over the window to the bull pen. "What's going on?"

She planted her hand against the wall and leaned. He saw sweat lining her brow when she removed her hat.

"Kaya."

"I need to tell you something."

"Okay," he said bracingly.

"First," she said, "and this is really important, Everett—I need you not to go looking for blood."

He stilled. "This is about the Claymores."

"I need your word."

"Tell me first."

"Everett!" she shouted. "You said you wouldn't wind up on the wrong side of the law if we were together. Your word, please!"

He exerted a long rush of air through his nose, trying to deflate the foreboding built up inside him—the ready tension and anger. "I give you my word," he ground from between his teeth.

"I will hold you to it."

"Just tell me!"

She looked away. "I wanted to tell you before. But I've

kept it to myself for years and it's hard to let go. Even with you." She wet her lips when he fell quiet, anticipating. "I told you after Sawni disappeared that I became obsessed with finding her. I knew one of the last places she was seen was The RC Resort. I wouldn't leave the Claymores alone. I didn't trust that they gave so little information about her and weren't looked into further by the authorities. The police went light on them, likely because they were The Claymores, even then. So I snuck on site and I had a look around. I retraced her actions through what I knew of her day. Then I tried sneaking into the office. True caught me."

"What did he do?" Everett asked. His hands had curled into fists in his pockets.

"He told me he had a way of dealing with 'little rez girls who liked to stick their noses where they didn't belong.'"

Every muscle in Everett's body stilled.

"He took me outside. If True had handled me himself, I would have put him behind bars when I became deputy. Before the statute of limitations was up. But he never touched me beyond hauling me out of there and putting me in one of the resort shuttles. I never even saw him talk to the two security goons who drove me back to the highway. There's no evidence he told them to do what they did."

Words raked across his throat, hot as coals. "What did they do?"

Her hands shook once. Just once. It was enough to make him vibrate with rage. She culled the explanation out in a flat tone, as if reciting the Pledge of Allegiance. "They forced me out of the shuttle onto the roadside. One of the men hit me in the stomach while the other held my arms back. They told me to say I wasn't coming back. When I refused…"

Her voice hitched. Everett wanted to move to her, hold

her, but the vibrations had gone into the bone. He knew, all too well, that he didn't have a handle on himself.

"They grabbed me by the hair," she said. "I wore it loose. It was down to my waist. They made me get on my knees. The first one said, 'The boss wants you to remember what happens to little rez girls when they don't learn to leave well enough alone...' The other one held me while he..."

Everett filled in the blanks. His head nearly split. The images maxed out the capacity of his brain. Every single one of them was gunpowder. They torched his restraint.

Grabbing the first thing at hand, he flipped the visitor's chair on its head. He paced on the spot then faced the wall. It was cinderblock. It would splinter the bones of his fist if he hit it like he needed to.

With his back to her, he zeroed in on a fold of worn tape that had been left behind when a poster was removed. The anger didn't ebb. It was a restless wave pool that beat against one shore, then the opposite one until the swells met in the middle and clashed.

"I'm going to kill him," he said between his teeth.

"No, you're not," she returned.

"You're going to have to let me kill him, sweetheart," he said, revolving back to her.

She shook her head. She was steady, still and utterly calm. He was stunned by her bravery. He was awed by it. She'd had to live with this, on top of everything else. It wasn't long before she'd joined the police force, he knew. She'd come back to Fuego—to chase down her demons. Anybody else would have run from them.

"What about the goons?" he asked. "The men who did this to you. You didn't talk to the police?"

She looked away, her countenance flagging. "I was tres-

passing. I broke into the resort. And it stuck with me—
little rez girls. It followed me everywhere for a time. It was
my word against theirs."

"You came back," he said. "You came back to face
them."

She nodded. "I wanted them to feel threatened. I thought
my mere presence in Fuego in uniform would make them
quiver. I learned soon after I returned that True had replaced the two security goons with others. Worse, there
was no record of their employment with him. Their names
weren't even in the system. They were ghosts in the wind.
The first time I came face-to-face with True, he didn't recognize me. He's never put it together—the little rez girl
and the Fuego County deputy."

"Sheriff," he said, moving to her. "You're sheriff now.
And he should know exactly who he's dealing with. He
should damn well be quivering."

"I've been waiting," she said on a whisper. "I could
never build a solid case against him or Annette or the resort. Every time I got close, Sheriff Jones would shut it
down. After what you said in the conference room about
someone True knows potentially murdering the people on
the mountain... I knew."

"The security guys." He nodded. "True isn't the type to
get his hands dirty. If he'd wanted to put Sawni, Bethany
and the other woman in the ground, he would have used
someone else."

"They were killed execution-style," Kaya said. "One
shot to the back of the head. Mercenary." He heard the audible click of her swallow. "They were all likely on their
knees when it happened...like me on the side of the highway."

He cursed and pulled her to him. He folded around her.

She didn't tremor. She didn't relax, either. She was holding it all in. She'd held it in…all this time. "I want to kill him."

"No," she said, pulling away enough to look at him. "This is my fight. He's going to be my collar. I will gather enough evidence to bring him in. That's why I became a police officer, Everett. To find Sawni and to build evidence and a case around Claymore that he and his wife can never pull him out of. He deserves to rot in prison."

"He deserves to be throttled first," Everett inserted.

"I need you to listen," she said, eyes on fire. "I've waited my entire career to nail True Claymore. He might be looking at kidnap and murder charges if your theory pans out. And I will not let anybody stand in the way of putting that good-for-nothing behind bars once and for all. Not even you."

"God Jesus, you're incredible," he breathed. "But you're *not* alone in this. Not anymore."

"I'm telling you what I need and you're not hearing me," she said. "*Stay away from him.*"

"You mean don't fight for your honor," he amended, frustration stretching against the bounds of his skin.

"I'm asking you to trust me to fight for my own," she pleaded, "and the life and honor of every woman he's taken. I don't know how Miller Higgins is tied up in this. But women were his pattern. We can tie Sawni to him. I'll look for his connection to Bethany Merchant. He dated her, just as you did. We need to know the timing…"

"Rutland doesn't like my theory," he muttered.

"I'll work around him," she said.

"You're going down the rabbit hole again," he cautioned.

"I'm not alone this time," she recalled.

"No," he agreed.

"Promise me," she demanded. "Promise me you won't—"

"Beat Claymore to within an inch of his life?"

"Promise me," she whispered, holding both his arms, "you will not harm a hair on his head."

He scanned her face. Then he nodded, grimly, lips seamed tight.

"I need you to say it."

"Fine," he said. "I will not harm a hair on True's head."

She nodded. "Thank you. Now kiss me, cattle baron. I'm feeling queasy and raw and I need you, goddamn it."

He did as he was told, dipping his lips to hers in a slow motion. He kept it soft. He kept it tender. He felt the give in her muscles. He felt the release. He heard the longing report from the line of her throat and groaned in response, every bit as lost as she was.

"You're shaking," she said, running her hands up and down his arms. "I shouldn't have told you."

"Don't," he bit off. "There are no secrets between us anymore."

She searched his face. "No," she said, understanding. "No more secrets."

He made himself step back. "I'm meeting Ellis and the others back at the house. I'll have Bozeman get you copies of the Claymores' land disputes and any other legal documents they sent our way through the years."

"Everett?"

He stopped with his hand on the door. When he looked back, he didn't read vulnerability. He saw strength. She was strong—stronger than him. Stronger than anyone he'd ever met.

And he loved her.

The realization came like a thunderclap.

He'd known it would never come to this—loving someone uncompromisingly. Men like him didn't fall, not after watching his father's heartbreak over his mother kill him slow...excruciatingly slow.

Yet here he was and so was Kaya, and he loved her beyond doubt or reason.

"I'll see you," she told him.

He felt a quaver as deep as his marrow. Dipping his head to her, he yanked the door open and left.

Chapter 11

Kaya cornered Rutland in the conference room after seeing Everett out. She closed the door, hemming them in. "Why are you dismissing Everett Eaton? Last I checked, this case had run into a wall. We need every possible lead or it's going to go cold again."

Rutland considered the question. He'd taken his sport coat down off the board and was wearing it. Leaning back in his chair at the head of the table, he laced his fingers over his middle. "You're seeing him."

She thought of denying it. But Rutland wasn't going to trust her or her judgement if she lied. "I'm seeing him."

He lifted his brows but otherwise didn't move. "You're trying to earn the respect and authority your office deserves, and you think fooling around with a man who dances in and out of that Mayberry jail cell you've got in the back of your wheelhouse is the way to do that? You're smarter than that, Altaha."

She was still a little bit queasy and more than a little bit raw. She didn't feel stable. She curled her hands around the back of a chair, trying to rein it all in. She would not lose her composure in front of the agent. "My personal life doesn't interfere with my ability to do my job. But you're going to tell me why exactly you're willing to throw away evidence against the Claymores."

He tilted his head. "Are you insinuating something?"

"The Claymores have bought ranking officers for well on a decade," she informed him.

"You claim your personal life has no bearing on your police work," he said. "But it's starting to sound like you have a vendetta against this family. I've read the files from your previous sheriff. I know the Eatons most certainly have one."

"That's why you dismissed Everett?" she asked. "Because he's gone after True in the past?"

"Ask yourself this," he said, leaning forward so that the chair squeaked slightly. He dropped a file on the table. "If you were thinking objectively, wouldn't you have drawn the same conclusion?"

"That's not good enough," she replied. "You said we're pursuing other leads. You lied and tossed his theory out the window."

"I didn't lie."

She lifted her hands. "Is there another lead you haven't told me about? You haven't briefed me on one."

She saw him hesitate. Moving around the table, she said, "You're the one who wanted cooperation between our teams."

"I did say that, didn't I?" He turned his chair to face her. "I was going to brief you this morning. Then the business with the festival. And I saw what Mr. Eaton is to you."

"I'm dating a man you've cleared of all charges in this case and that gives you a right to squirrel evidence away?" she asked.

He let out a breath, then reached for two Baggies on the

table. "These arrived last night in the safe haven baby box at the volunteer fire department on Highway 7."

She took the bags. One contained a standard, unmarked bubble mailer, the kind that could be bought at any office supply store. The flap was open but it had been torn. There was no address or return address written on it.

The second bag contained a small book. Kaya thought it might be a datebook until she turned it over and saw the name written in the bottom corner. "What is this?" she asked in a quiet voice.

"I need to confirm the handwriting with her mother and father," Rutland stated. "But it appears Sawni Mescal kept a diary."

The letters blurred together. "No need," she said, setting the bags on the table. "I recognize it."

"It's her handwriting?"

"It is," she confirmed. "We passed enough notes... I've reread them through the years. Have you opened this?"

"It's bagged and will need to go to the lab for prints," he said, picking up the folder he'd dropped on the desk. "But my team made copies of the pages."

Kaya opened the file when he handed it to her. She had to take a measured breath when she saw the looping strokes of Sawni's handwriting that filled the first page.

"Did you know she kept a diary?" he asked. "Did she ever tell you?"

"She did," Kaya answered. "She let me read others she wrote. This was dropped last night in the fire department's box?"

"It was."

"Someone's had this this whole time... The killer?"

"Possibly."

"Why would they do that?" she asked, flipping through the pages. "When was the last entry?"

"The night before her death," he said. "There's reason to believe some pages were torn out."

She lifted her gaze to his, then went back to studying the final page. "She talks about working at The RC Resort... Nothing seemed to be troubling her."

"No," Rutland said, standing. He riffled back through the diary. "Look at this page."

She scanned the words. Sawni's quiet voice played through her head, as real as it had once been. Her eyes seized on a name. She read through the entry again, coming to the name once more. She shook her head. "I don't understand..."

"You told investigators at the time she was dating someone," he said. "Here she mentions him a week before she disappeared."

Kaya rejected it, offering the file back to him. "That's not right. It can't be."

"Sheriff, you said your personal feelings have no bearing on your work. You're not going to let them get in the way now when the answer may be staring you in the face."

"She's not naming her killer," she said, pointing to the file. "She's naming her lover."

"Wolfe Coldero. He's mentioned no less than thirty-three times throughout her journal. I checked back through her missing person case. No one ever checked his alibi for the day of her disappearance. No one checked him out in the Miller Higgins case, either."

"Wolfe Coldero didn't kidnap or kill Sawni," she stated.

"Why not? He lived in Fuego at the time. He worked at Eaton Edge and lived at Coldero Ridge. He's connected to Sawni through the rodeo. He was a bull rider. That's where and how they met. Why wouldn't either of them have told you?"

Her lips felt numb. She dropped to a chair. "Wolfe's mute. He's never spoken to anyone."

"Did he help with the search effort?" Rutland asked.

Kaya thought back. She combed through memories she'd gone over again and again, looking for clues or clarity or closure… "Yes," she answered. "I remember him being there. His father, Santiago, came. And Everett's mother, Josephine. She and Santiago were having an affair. They brought horses and were part of the mounted search party in the state park areas."

"I'd like to bring him in," Rutland said.

"He won't talk," she reminded him. "Not to you or anyone else."

"He can answer questions in writing," Rutland asserted. "If he doesn't, I can charge him with obstruction."

"He's getting married in a few days."

Rutland closed the file. "With a foreign honeymoon to follow, I hear. He's not getting on a plane until he's cleared."

"Wolfe Coldero isn't a killer," Kaya told him.

"Didn't he do time for shooting a man in the back seven years ago?" Rutland asked.

"Jace Decker," Kaya replied. "Wolfe shot him to stop him from throwing fuel on the cabin fire at Coldero Ridge. Josephine and her and Santiago's daughter, Angel, were inside. Wolfe tried to get them out, but he was too late."

"His record is against him," he said. "He'll be brought in at nine o'clock tomorrow morning. You can sit in."

The door to the conference room opened. Sherry peered around the jamb. "I'm sorry, Sheriff. Agent Rutland. But there's a situation."

"What kind of situation?" Kaya asked, coming to attention.

"It's the mayor," Sherry said. "The luxury vehicle he drives... It's been vandalized. He's agitated. Deputy Root is having trouble getting him to calm down."

"We'll discuss this later," Kaya told Rutland. "Where is the mayor now?" she asked Sherry.

"On Second Street where the car was parked," she said, trailing Kaya through the station. "He discovered the damage after leaving the festival."

"Thank you, Sherry."

The scene on Second Street was nothing short of chaotic. A crowd had formed. Kaya worked through it to the center. She could hear True Claymore hollering before she reached the center of the mass where he and his vehicle were located.

She stopped to assess. The mayor was without his hat. His hair was sticking straight up in places, finger-combed by frustrated hands. His hands flailed and he was on his toes, his red face in Root's. He threw invectives at the deputy, his voice no longer smooth. Nothing about him appeared to be collected.

Kaya walked around the parallel-parked vehicle to the driver's side. Damage had been done to more than the paint job. There was fender and other body damage. The destruction was so thorough, she doubted the vehicle was drivable.

Kaya didn't have to ask what instrument had been used. The offending sledgehammer lay nearby. It was the kind used commonly by farmers and ranchers to drive stakes into the ground. The paint on the front edge matched the color of the car.

"Did the perpetrator flee the scene?" she asked Wyatt, who was standing by.

True whirled at the sound of her voice. "Sheriff! He's done it now! Lock him up! Lock all of them up!"

She raised a hand. "You saw who did this?"

"I didn't have to see it!" True shouted. "He was standing right there with the sledgehammer when I got back!"

"Who was?" Kaya asked, though her gut stirred, and she was afraid she knew the name already. She looked around, searching.

Leaning against one of the closest building's support posts in a neutral stance, Everett stood. His aviator sunglasses reflected the scene. The bend of his mouth showcased nothing—not even amusement.

She knew when his eyes shifted to her. His stance didn't change or his expression, but she felt it.

"Did anybody see who did this?" Kaya asked the crowd at large.

Turk Monday stepped forward. "I saw that Eaton fella there going to town on it."

"He was heaving at it like a raging bull," another man piped up from the crowd.

Other witnesses' voices followed. Kaya rounded on Everett with a glare she hoped singed the fur off his hide.

"White trash, burnout, son of a bitch!" True Claymore yelled, stepping forward.

Root caught him by the arms. "Now, mayor. You're going to need to cool down if you want to press charges…"

Kaya walked to Everett. "Do you deny this?"

"Which part?" he asked. "The white trash, burnout bit?"

"Did you vandalize his vehicle?" she asked.

"That part I'll claim."

She stepped a hair closer. "You promised," she hissed.

He pointed at the mayor. "I promised not to harm a hair on his head. His hair's fine. So's every other part of him. You said nothing about his property."

"Turn around," she ordered. "Put your hands behind your back."

He straightened. "Sure, Sheriff Sweetheart. I know how it goes."

She reached around her belt for her cuffs. "Everett Eaton, you're under arrest…"

Chapter 12

Kaya stayed late at the sheriff's office, long after Rutland had left for the night, her deputies had gone home, and Lionel Bozeman had shown up with Ellis Eaton to bail Everett out of jail. She stayed behind her desk with the pages photocopied from Sawni's diary.

Annette and True Claymore had been there most of the afternoon. They'd railed at her deputies and her in turn. They'd even shouted at Rutland. There was no question Everett would be charged with criminal damage to a vehicle.

They'd threatened her job if she let him out on bail.

Making threats to a sheriff in her own department was a ballsy move. She'd made a note of those who overheard and filed it away, as she'd filed so many other tidbits about the Claymores over the years.

The diary was revealing in ways Kaya hadn't expected. Sawni had dated Wolfe Coldero for much of the last year of her life. They met at the rodeo. When Sawni was forced to stop returning to the rodeo by her parents, there had been meetings with the two—on the reservation and off. Kaya read details about multiple rendezvous at the state park.

It made sense, Sawni and Wolfe, Kaya thought. It made perfect sense, actually. Wolfe was mute and Sawni was quiet. Their similar natures would have drawn them together. Sawni had been curious about boys and men but had never found one she could trust to experiment with…

Until Wolfe, apparently. Their relationship had turned intimate. Kaya had a hard time facing the fact that Sawni hadn't confided her first time to her. They'd sworn they would confide in each other, if no one else.

There was nothing violent about their relationship mentioned in the diary. There was no evidence that Wolfe treated Sawni with anything but care.

Kaya studied the photographs of the diary itself, taken before it was bagged for prints. At several junctures, the binding was ragged. Pages had been torn out. Quite a few of them. That called to question whether Sawni had ripped them or the person who had delivered the diary after all these years.

If it was the killer, why would they hand over the diary? To throw suspicion on someone else?

Someone like Wolfe?

Some of the answers would come in the morning when he arrived for his interview with Rutland. Kaya glanced at the clock. She frowned when she saw it was close to eleven. She closed the file and locked it in her filing cabinet before switching the lamp off on her desk. She changed from her sheriff's uniform to a more relaxed set of jeans and a button-down.

She locked the station door behind her since she was the last to leave. Walking to her vehicle, she got in the driver's seat and cranked the ignition. She pulled out onto the deserted street and started to turn the wheel for home.

She paused. As the traffic light at Main Street and Second changed, she looked down the intersecting road that reached into the black of night.

She thought about the diary. She thought about her bed and the complications she certainly wouldn't find there.

She turned the wheel to the left and followed the road well out of town.

Slowing, she made the turnoff for Eaton Edge and drove up the long, dirt drive to Eaton House. The motion lights flared to life as she parked. She noted the absence of cars in the drive.

She didn't know what she was doing exactly, but she took the path to the front door of the house and pounded on the door.

She expected Paloma to answer. When the door parted from the jamb, she found him instead.

Everett blinked at her in surprise. "Sheriff Sweetheart," he greeted.

When she stayed silent, he released a breath. "Look. I can take a lot. Scream at me. Hit me. You can bust my nuts or gouge me in the eyes. But don't give me the silent treatment. I can't take it."

She walked around him before she could tell herself not to. Beyond the foyer, she found a spartan living room he hadn't changed since his father died. There was a couch with space behind it. There, against the wall off the stairwell, she found the sideboard.

He didn't stop her from lifting the lid off its decanter. She turned an upside-down glass over and filled it with whiskey. She lifted it to her mouth and knocked it back straight.

"I'll take one of those."

She threw a look over her shoulder, quashing his attempt at camaraderie.

"Never mind," he decided.

She poured herself another, then, as an afterthought, a

second. She grabbed it by the rim and pivoted to extend it to him.

He took it, tipping his head to her. "Thank you, Sheriff—"

"Don't you dare," she warned.

He took a drink, instead.

She turned her back to the sideboard and leaned. Sipping, she pointed at him, lifting one finger from her glass. "You know…call me a sucker or whatever you like…"

"I wouldn't call you—"

"But I trusted you," she added, raising her voice over his. "I understand a lot of people have died on that hill, but I thought… I actually *thought* I could trust you."

"I didn't hurt him," he claimed. "Not a hair."

"His hair's gone! It's fallen out! He's so hoarse from shouting at me and Root and Wyatt for letting you out on bail he won't have anything left when he comes at you tomorrow, which he undoubtedly will."

"I'm not afraid of him and his froggy voice," Everett noted. "Though I'm mad as hell he came down on you hard."

"You don't get to be mad as hell," she informed him. "It's my turn now."

"All right," he conceded. He set his glass down. "How do you want to do this?"

"If I was smart, I'd leave," she claimed. "I'd go on with my life and wash my hands of this."

His eyes darkened in understanding. "But you're here."

"Because there's another part of me. The stupid, impulsive part that I never could kill. It seems to think you destroying another man's property on my behalf was sweet and maybe a little romantic, by Western standards."

He chose his words carefully. "You, uh… You like Western?"

"The sheriff in me doesn't."

"What about you?" he asked. "The trick rider. Apache Annie. The real you that ran away to the rodeo and never wanted to go back home."

"I'm here," she said.

His eyes shone, making her stomach flutter as only he could. "Yeah, you are."

She set the glass down with an empty clack. With both hands, she reached for her bun.

"What're you doing?"

"Be quiet, Everett."

"Shutting up," he replied as the pins came down and her braid unraveled, falling to her waist.

She didn't meet his gaze. Not until every last coil had been undone and she'd spread her fingers through her hair to make it spill loose over her shoulders.

Everett backed up until his hips met the back of the couch. He sat and gripped the edge with both hands on either side. "What're you doing to me, woman?"

"I'm not touching you," she said.

"Aren't you?" he asked. There was a bar between his eyes that spoke of danger and longing and her heart began to quake.

She crossed to him. With him sitting, they were nearly eye level. "Put your hands in it," she instructed. "Isn't that what you wanted?"

He made a noise. His fingers lifted to the ends of her hair. He fanned them out, letting the ends pass over the back of his knuckles in whispering strokes. Testing the weight with his palm, he wet his lips before twining one strand around his finger.

Kaya started unbuttoning his shirt. He hadn't changed out of what he'd worn earlier. She parted the chambray shirt over his front, pleased to see nothing underneath it but skin. Pushing the shirt over the hard, round points of his shoulders, she shed it.

In the center of his chest, she found the place where he'd been shot and the incisions where surgeons had opened him up to save his life. She traced the bullet wound, feathering her touch over the damage done.

His voice roughened. "I ain't touched anything as fine as you. Ever."

She smiled, in spite of herself. "Is that your way of telling me you love me?"

He cursed a stream.

"Steady there," she advised, planting her hand over the marks of his chest. His heart beat underneath them, big and forceful. "Steady on, cattle baron. It was a joke."

He shook his head slightly. "I did that earlier."

"You committing a third degree felony was your way of expressing your feelings?" she asked.

His hand came up to cradle the sharp line of her jaw. His mouth said nothing but his eyes, again, talked.

Her lips parted when she took their meaning, too. "Your love language may need a little work."

"I don't know," he considered, giving his attention to the buttons on the top of her blouse. "It's working just fine from where I'm standing."

When he removed her shirt, she stepped in the space between his parted knees. She grabbed him under the shoulders and confronted his smart mouth with her own.

He gathered her against his chest, his hands lost in the thick sheet of her hair. When he unclipped her bra, he tugged it away. Without lifting his lips from hers, he pushed to his feet.

Kaya dropped her head back, closing her eyes. Skin-to-skin, she let him feast on her mouth, absorbing the rough texture of his hands as they cruised over her in sure strokes.

When he unclasped her belt, she shimmied as he pushed the waistband over her hips.

He kneeled, tugging away one of her boots, then the other. The pants pooled at her ankles and his lips found the place on her thigh, the wound that still ached. He traced kisses around her thigh, then up, tickling the place behind her knee that was oddly sensitive.

She didn't stop him when he reached the juncture of her thighs. His mouth opened and pressed against her sex through the thin panties she'd chosen to wear that morning. It was her turn to groan, sinking her hands into his dark, cropped hair. His beard was rough, too. She felt it through the material as she had on her thigh and she shivered, bristled and shivered again as her arousal increased. If he removed the garment, he'd find how wet she was for him.

"Stand up," she directed. When he did, she yanked off his belt, whipping it free from the loops of his jeans. She undid the snap and pulled down the fly and would have reached in for him but met resistance when he took her wrist and held it. He took the other and she hissed at him.

"This isn't going to be fast, Kaya. I don't want you in fast gulps. I want to take my time. I want it drawn out. I want us both thirsty and begging. I want you in my bed."

"Long way to go," she noted absently as he guided her backward to the stairs. The promise of it all was enough to bring her up to her toes. She dragged his mouth back to hers.

Stumbling, they made it halfway up the flight before he turned her to the wall.

She found her cheek against the striped wallpaper and, as he nipped her shoulder, she sighed. "This wasn't on the list..."

"Shh..." His face was in her hair and his touch low on her navel. It cruised down, reaching the parting of her legs.

She planted her hands against the wall as his fingertips sank underneath the edge of the panties. When he traced the seam of her sex with his middle finger, she bit her lip to keep from crying out.

He made a noise when he parted her and found the cluster of nerves at the peak of her labia and the pool of arousal he'd caused. When he stroked, she drew herself up tight, arching her back.

She could feel him through his jeans. He was ready— just as ready as she was. But his touch glided slow, taking her up incrementally, stretching her pleasure to the point of affliction. "Never figured you for a sadist, Eaton," she said brokenly as she dropped her head back to his shoulder.

"You can take it," he whispered hot against her temple. "You can take all of me."

She pressed her hand to the back of his, forcing him deeper. "Don't. Don't make me beg. Not yet."

His laugh fell brokenly across her cheek. He inserted one finger, stroking. Then another.

Her mouth dropped open though she didn't make a sound. It was too divine, this point he was driving her toward. Too bright. She burned, moving against his hand, driving herself right up to the breaking point.

He held her there in splendor. The heel of his other hand pressed against her womb, as if he knew exactly where the heat was building.

She came apart. In diamond-edged rifts and shouts, she came apart in his arms.

He turned her. When she saw his wide grin and the triumph riding high on his face, she raised her open hand.

It cracked across his face. He hissed, but the grin didn't break. Instead, he laughed. "Why you gotta be so mean?"

She placed her hands on the back of his head, urging him down. She kissed his cheek. Then the other. She kissed them better.

He hummed, boosting her up by the hips so her legs wrapped around his waist and he continued up the stairs.

The last step tripped him. The landing came up to meet them. It knocked the wind out of her.

"Sorry, sweetheart," he murmured, sitting up.

"Stay down," she ordered, switching their positions so that he was down and she was up. She yanked at one of his boots, gritting her teeth when it didn't comply. It nearly sent her down the stairs when it loosened. She tossed it behind her so that it bounced all the way to the bottom before doing the same to the other. Then she pulled at the cuffs of his jeans.

He lifted his hips so he could remove them from his waist. Once she had them off, she balled them up and threw them over the railing.

He was fine-boned, long and just dark enough to be tan instead of white. She liked the way the muscles bunched across his flat stomach, the way his shoulders flared outward, defiant, from his collarbone.

She liked the cut of hair down the center of his chest and abdomen that grew thick underneath his exposed waistline. There were other things. So many other things she liked—his long thighs, the definition of his chest and the way he looked back at her with hooded, bedroom eyes, hungry and watchful.

He wanted it slow, drawn out? He wanted them both thirsty, begging? *Fine*. That was just fine...

She scaled the length of him slowly, from ankles to shoulders, dragging the ends of her hair across his front. His knees rose and his skin tightened, and she got to watch him bite his own lip for once. When his hand came to the back of her neck to urge her mouth down to his, she held back, raining kisses over every other part of him she admired. Shoulders, collarbone, neck, pecs and sternum. She traced ribs and abs and waist, letting the dark curtain of her hair cover him as she followed him down, down...

She wanted him as sensitive as he'd made her. She wanted him wild—enough to take a sledgehammer to her enemy's car again. More.

She wanted him wild for her. There was a part of her that reveled in the fact that he'd reached that point. She'd arrested him for it. But that didn't stop the flash of pride or sparkly satisfaction that knowing brought.

She wrapped her fingers around his girth. Passing her thumb over the tip, she grinned when he jerked. "People say you're heartless."

His lungs moved up and down in excited repetitions. He dropped his head back, rising at the bidding of her hand when she stroked. He cursed.

"They're wrong," she considered and caressed. She worked him as he'd worked her. She did it until he was breathless. Then she seated herself over his hips. She took his face in her hands. "They're wrong about you."

He took her hand and placed it over the healed wound on the center of his chest. Underneath, his pulse rocked and clamored and she dropped her lips to that point.

He sat up and grunted as he picked her up and carried her the rest of the way to his door, which was at the end of the hallway.

They made it to the jamb. He propped her against it so he could open the door. He stopped, nibbling on her lower lip before tracing a line down her throat as he discarded her panties and lifted her.

"Now," she said. "Right now."

He obeyed. She took him, all of him. Just as he'd wanted. "Oh," she cried. "Oh, hell yes!"

"I told you," he groaned. "I told you, sweetheart…"

She nodded in quick repetitions. "Don't stop."

"Bed," he grunted and carried her across the threshold, along the floor, then tipped her to the bed. "Just a second…"

She heard him fumbling in the drawer next to the bed. She blinked at the condom he found.

She'd forgotten protection. *How* had she forgotten?

He opened the packet, then fed the rubber to the base of his arousal. When his body covered her again, he uttered an oath, brushing the hair from her cheeks in sweet strokes. "I let you get cold."

"You'll fix it, baby."

His hair messy from her hands, he grinned in a quick, delighted burst. "Baby? I like that."

She smiled, too. It filled her cheeks to capacity. "Make me say it again," she whispered.

"Ten-four."

He was like a furnace. When he joined with her again, she felt like one, too.

Their bodies were already dewy with perspiration. Together, they slid, plunged, tossed. Her ankles crossed at the small of his back and he carried her up to the same point he had before, diamond-bright and stunning. When she moaned, he answered.

The flat of his hands came to the backs of her thighs and he pressed, fitful as he chased his own climax.

When he broke, she pulled his mouth to hers so that when he groaned again, it vibrated across her lips. And when he shuddered, she felt it from the toes up, just like him.

"You won't move," she told him long after he stilled.

"No. I won't."

"Wake up, cattle baron."

"Nah," he said even as Kaya shifted restlessly. His face was in her hair, his arms wrapped around her. At some point in the night, he'd tossed the sheet over both of them, unwilling to let her get cold again. "I'm good."

"The sun's going to be coming up fast," she explained. "Paloma will be here. We both have work. Don't cowboys rise early?"

He smirked. "Which part, Sheriff?" He grunted when she drove her elbow into his stomach. He wheezed a laugh but didn't relinquish her. "Hold still."

He growled his displeasure, turning to his back. He cupped his hands under the back of his head. Why'd he have to fall for a sensible woman? "Don't leave this bed."

She sat up, scooping her hair over one shoulder. She combed her fingers through it. He'd like to do the same once he roused himself enough, he thought.

"We need to talk."

He traced the absence of her easy smile and felt it. "You're wearing your serious eyes."

"Because I am serious," she said. "Are you up enough to talk?"

He propped himself on one elbow with some effort. "Yeah, yeah. I'm up."

"I stopped by last night for two reasons."

"Not to jump my bones?"

"That was a bonus. I stopped here so that I could pick a fight with you."

"I like the way you fight," he said, unable to hide a smile even in the face of her serious eyes.

"I'm not sure you fight fair," she considered. "The other reason I wanted to stop by was because I know who Rutland's going to target next."

He scrubbed his hands over his face and sat up all the way. "Why do I get the feeling I'm not going to like his new direction?"

"It's Wolfe," she told him.

"Coldero?"

"Two nights ago, someone dropped Sawni's old diary in the safe haven drop box at the fire station on Highway 7. It's hers. I recognized the handwriting."

"Who dropped it?" he asked, coming awake in full measure now. "And why did they have it?"

"I don't know," she said. "There were no security cameras. Nobody saw anyone outside. It's at the lab now being checked for prints."

"What does this have to do with Coldero?" he asked.

"There are pages missing from the diary," Kaya told him. "However, the ones that remain primarily talk about Wolfe and their relationship."

"You didn't tell me she was seeing him."

"I didn't know until I read the diary," she explained.

He saw the sadness and trouble on her face. "Come 'ere."

She didn't resist much when he caught her hand. She pressed her cheek to the wall of his chest as he leaned back in the pillows at the head of the bed. "What's all this mean, Kaya?" he asked.

"Wolfe's going to be called in for questioning this morning," she said. "If he doesn't give Rutland the right answers, there's a good chance his and Eveline's wedding will be delayed."

"They're going to lock him up," Everett said.

"I thought you should know. It's your sister who loves him. And you don't mind that as much as you let on."

"I'll warn them," he replied.

"You don't think that he killed Sawni and the others."

Everett frowned and found himself shaking his head. "For the longest time, people thought Coldero killed Whip Decker. He served time for it. But he's no killer."

"He'll need to hear you say it before this is all over," she said.

He made another noise and was relieved when she let him hold her awhile longer before the break of day.

Chapter 13

Wolfe arrived promptly at the sheriff's department at nine o'clock with Lionel Bozeman, Ellis and Eveline in tow. Since Bozeman was to serve as his attorney and Ellis would speak for him, Eveline was forced to remain outside the crowded interrogation room.

Kaya observed the proceedings. Wolfe confirmed his involvement with Sawni but had no memory of exactly where he was the day she vanished or where he had been during the time of Bethany Merchant's disappearance, either. Worse, he couldn't provide a witness to his whereabouts the day of Miller Higgins's death. Through sign language, he claimed he had been working at home. The only witness to that was his father, Santiago, who had moved in with him and Eveline after they built their house on a parcel of land outside Fuego town limits.

Santiago wasn't of sound enough mind to provide a statement. He'd been institutionalized shortly after the death of his wife and daughter seven years ago. Eveline had been working at Ollero Creek with Luella Decker on the day in question. She hadn't returned home until after dark.

"Can't you do something?" Ellis asked Kaya after Rutland requested Deputy Wyatt handcuff Wolfe Coldero and take him into holding.

"I wish I could," Kaya told him. "But if he can't provide an alibi for at least one of the murders, my hands are tied."

Facing Eveline was even more troubling. "How could you let this happen?" she asked, trailing Kaya through the department. "He trusts you. We all trusted you. You think he did this?"

"No," Kaya told her. "I don't think he's guilty, but Rutland believes he is and there's no physical or circumstantial evidence to fight that."

"He and I are getting married in five days," Eveline said. Her eyes were wet. "Kaya, *help him*. Please."

Kaya waited until the Eatons left and the reporters came and went. True Claymore showed up, demanding to know who they had in custody. He was only too delighted to hear it was Wolfe.

Kaya waited until Rutland left for the day before trailing Root back to the holding cells at the back of the building. "Unlock it," she requested when they arrived at Wolfe's.

Root opened the door for her and held it wide. She passed through. "You can close it," she told him. When he hesitated, she raised a brow.

Root gave a short nod. "Yes, sir."

She waited until he'd closed and locked the door before telling him, "Give us some room, please."

Root backed away at a respectful distance. Kaya crossed to the bench where Wolfe sat with his elbows on his knees and his hands together, his shoulders low.

She lowered next to him and stretched her legs. She leaned against the wall behind them, rubbing the spot on her thigh that hurt a little. Studying the strong line of Wolfe's back, she released a breath. "I knew she was seeing a bull rider. She never did say which one."

After a moment's pause, he eased back, too, until his shoulders touched the wall.

"I'm glad it was you," Kaya assured him. "I know you treated her right. She was in love with you." She swallowed because her voice grew thick. "She loved you, and you're being locked up for it."

He took her hand. The hold banked the grief and guilt, somewhat. She felt his anguish, too, in the quiet. "Did you know she was working at the resort?" she asked him.

He shook his head slightly.

"She stopped talking to me, once that started," she said. "Something happened out there. Something happened in the pages of her diary that were torn out. What happened, Wolfe?"

He lifted his shoulders. He had no more answers than she did and just as many questions, it seemed.

Kaya squeezed his hand before letting go. She raised herself to her feet. Passing a hand over her eyes, she made sure they were dry before turning back to him. "I'm sorry about the wedding." When he nodded, she turned away. Root beat her to the door and let her out. As it locked it back in place, Kaya met Wolfe's stare through the bars. "I'm not going to stop until the real killer is where you are."

Wolfe offered her a small smile before he lowered his head again, looking more than a little defeated.

Eveline rode out the next dawn to help tag the night's newborns. Everett was surprised to see her on the mid-morning drive as well. She was quieter than usual, but she and her mare, Sienna Shade, did their job well.

It wasn't until they stopped near the mountains that she came for his knees. "Did you and Kaya have a pleasin' time the other night?" she asked.

He heard the bitterness behind the question and raised a brow at Ellis. Ellis shook his head and moved away to a safe distance, leaving Everett to confront his sister's anguish. "Cut the crap, Manhattan, and say what you're needing to say."

"The man I love is in jail," she stated. "Facing charges *again* for killing someone he didn't."

"He's got a bad habit of being in the wrong place at the wrong time," Everett observed.

She stuck her finger in his face. "*Don't*. Don't accuse him of this. You know he didn't do this."

"I do," he said and watched her fumble into stunned silence. "You tell me what I'm supposed to do about it."

"There needs to be a wedding," she told him. "I *need* there to be a wedding."

"You want me to bring Griff down to the sheriff's department so you can marry Coldero through the bars of his holding cell? I don't see it working out any other way by Saturday."

"Do you love me?" Eveline asked and her eyes filled with tears.

He made a face. "Ah, hell."

"I can't do this alone, Everett. We need to get him an alibi. It was his connection to Sawni Mescal that made them look in his direction to begin with. If we can provide him with an alibi for the date of her disappearance, the case against him won't hold."

"How do you expect us to do that?" he asked.

"By going through Dad's old records," she insisted. "He wrote everything down. He kept everything. You didn't get rid of any of his old file boxes, did you?"

"No." The basement was packed with them, floor to ceiling. "It'll be like finding a needle in a haystack. And that's assuming anything's there to begin with. Wolfe wasn't a member of the family then. Who's to say Dad kept anything on him?"

"Because he wanted to adopt Wolfe when he was found wandering the Edge as a boy," Eveline explained. "He let Santiago care for him only because..."

Everett looked away when her eyes turned implicating. "Because of me."

"I don't know why you rejected the idea of Wolfe coming to the Edge to live," Eveline said, "and it doesn't matter now. What matters is that if there's something in Dad's papers that can help, I need your help to find it."

"Fine," he agreed. "Come to the house for dinner. Bring Ellis and Luella. I'm not promising we'll find anything to clear him..."

"I know," she said quickly. "Thank you, Everett."

"Boss!"

Everett looked around to find Matteo riding from the north. He and Javier walked out to meet him.

Matteo slowed his mount. "Tombstone's been spotted."

"Where?" Everett asked.

"Near the mountain. Seems folks are still hanging around, trying to get a look at the place those bodies were found."

"They need to be headed off," Everett said.

"I'll do it," Javier offered.

"Take your gun," Everett advised. "And Spencer, for backup. Both of you be back to headquarters by dusk."

"Tombstone's back?" Eveline asked as she stood at his shoulder and watched the two men ride off. Fear wavered across the words.

"He never left," Everett said before turning his attention back to their herd.

* * *

Everett was sleep-starved when he entered the sheriff's department the following morning. He'd missed Paloma's fine-smelling breakfast spread with Eveline nipping at his heels to get a move on.

The two of them and Ellis, Luella and Paloma had gone through their father's boxes in the basement. Everett had stared at papers until they were blurry. Not everything had been filed or labeled but most boxes had had the year etched on them.

It had been difficult confronting his father's words, photographs, hand-drawn maps and keepsakes. Because of what had happened over the summer shortly after his death, Everett hadn't truly processed his grief. It had come in fits and starts, dragging itself out over months, not weeks.

It was one of the reasons he'd continued to sit in the therapist's office once a week in San Gabriel after he'd learned to manage the bulk of his PTSD symptoms.

He'd heard Hammond's voice again when he'd confronted his handwriting, his little notes about the day-to-day events that he'd scrawled on calendars... He'd drawn plans on paper napkins and ideas on notepads with conference labels. The low, slow sound of the man's words had filled Everett's head.

Ellis had found wedding photos of their parents hidden in one box. Eveline had uncovered newspaper clippings in another, most of them yellow and soft with age. There were ribbons and trophies that belonged to all three siblings. Hammond had kept the boutonniere he'd worn while escorting Eveline to homecoming court.

Kaya came out of her office when she heard her secretary greet him. "Everett," she greeted. "What are you doing here?"

He felt bleary and not a little clumsy. His better judgement had disappeared along with the possibility of sleep, so he leaned over and kissed her. "Sheriff."

She jumped a bit, then settled. "Good news?" she asked, gesturing to the folder he carried.

"Where's Watt?" he asked.

"Mr. Eaton."

Everett found the agent standing in the open door of the conference room. He raised what he had brought for him. "I'm here to spring my brother-in-law."

Rutland eyed the folder. "I'm afraid it's not going to be that simple."

"Why not?" Everett asked. "I can prove Coldero wasn't with Sawni Mescal or Bethany Merchant on the days of their disappearances."

"Is that right?" Rutland asked.

Everett opened the folder and pulled out a newspaper clipping. "This is from the day Sawni was taken. He was at the rodeo. He won, which is how he wound up in the *Fuego Daily News*. There's the date for you at the top. It says right here that it was an all-day event. I resented him for it, too. The events were lined up one after the other, which tied Coldero up from the early morning until well after dark when he took the final cup. There's his picture with it right there."

Rutland took the glasses from the front pocket of his jacket and placed them on the end of his nose. He assessed the clipping thoroughly.

Everett took out the second piece of paper. "This is my father's desk calendar from the month and year Bethany

Merchant was taken. You can see his notation on the day she disappeared. What's it say right there?"

Rutland bent his head over the page. He tilted it to read the slanted, left-handed scrawl. "'Took Wolfe to auction. New bull bought and paid for. Stayed overnight in Santa Fe. Dinner and overnight at Renaissance Hotel.'"

"I recall that, too," Everett said, "as I wanted to be the one my father took to the auction. But he took Coldero. The man he wanted to be his foreman one day. He saw something in him. When he was gone, my father wanted me at the helm of Eaton Edge and Coldero as foreman. He trusted him. That's why I didn't need proof he didn't do what you're accusing him of. My father saw people for what they were. He saw Wolfe Coldero long before I could bring myself to do so."

Rutland took off the glasses. "That doesn't mean he didn't kill Higgins or this other woman."

"Wasn't that other woman killed close to forty years ago?" Everett asked. "I thought I heard that in the news. That's long before Coldero came to the Edge. As for Higgins, Coldero sent several text messages to my sister and Ellis. Ping his phone. He lives outside town limits. I guarantee there's no record of him being near the tower closest to Ol' Whalebones or the Edge. It'll be the one closer to his and Eveline's house."

Rutland cleared his throat. "I'll need to verify this."

"Before the end of the day," Everett demanded. "There's going to be a wedding at the Edge the day after tomorrow. I don't know if you've met my little sister, but she'll have my ass and yours if her groom is a no-show. You can thank me later for doing your job for you." Leaving Rutland with the folder, he passed Kaya on the way out. "You got a date for this thing?"

A spark of amusement entered her eyes. "I thought I was looking at him. I'll be the one in the black dress."

He winked and saw himself out.

Everett swung the double doors to Grady's Saloon open. The focus on the dance floor and jukebox shifted around to him and his companions. Activity slowed as the patrons came to a standstill.

"This way," he indicated, leading the way to the long line of the bar.

"You sure about this?" Ellis asked, close behind him.

"As a heart attack," Everett replied, locking eyes with the bartender.

Grady Morrison slapped his rag onto the counter. "You're not welcome here," he told Everett. "I told you that years ago. The brawl you started then resulted in over a grand in damages."

"Your memory's long, Grady." Everett had already reached into his pocket. He tossed a hundred dollar bill on the bar top. "How much for a chair?"

When Grady only stared at Franklin's face on the bill, Everett pulled another from his wallet. He flicked it onto the bar with the first. "How 'bout this, huh?"

Grady frowned at the money. Then he peeled it from the water rings it had landed in and stuffed it in his back pocket. He set three glasses on the bar. "What's your pleasure, gentlemen?"

Everett took a seat, motioning for the others to do the same. "Whiskey, straight." He turned to look at the person who settled on the stool to his right. "That all right with you, Coldero?"

Wolfe jerked his chin in affirmation. He took the glass Grady passed across the bar. He lifted it to Everett.

Everett lifted his briefly, then drank.

Ellis tossed his whiskey back in one fell swoop. He released a breath at the burn and set his empty glass down, touching two fingers to the rim for a refill.

Grady hesitated, wary. "Who's driving tonight?"

"I know someone," Everett asserted. "Keep it coming, old-timer."

Grady grunted and fixed Ellis another drink.

Everett watched him walk away. "You think he missed me?"

Wolfe shook his head automatically.

Ellis chuckled.

Everett raised a brow and sipped. He ran his tongue over his teeth and looked around. "I fought you here that night," he remembered.

Wolfe nodded.

"What for?" Everett asked.

Wolfe thought about it. Then he lifted one large shoulder in answer.

"I don't remember, either." Everett screwed up his face. "I don't remember most of the reasons we fought as often as we did."

Wolfe tipped his glass up, swallowing the rest of his whiskey. He eyed the bottom of the glass and shook his head.

Everett shifted on his chair, uncomfortable. "I'm in a pickle. My sister is over the moon for you. And let's face it, if you were going kill anyone over the last twenty years, it would've been me. I've given you nothing but cause."

Wolfe and Ellis remained still and silent.

Everett finished his whiskey, too. "You better make her happy or I'll wipe you off the face of the earth."

Wolfe's mouth slid into a small smile. He signed.

"He says, 'It's done,'" Ellis translated. When Wolfe's hands moved again, he added, "'Thank you.'"

Everett ignored that. "I don't like surprises. Is there anything else I need to know before I let you become an official member of this family?"

Wolfe shook his head.

Everett tapped the counter, signaling to Grady that he was done. He paused when Wolfe started to sign again.

Ellis coughed in reaction. Then he began to laugh again.

"What'd he say?" Everett asked, suspicious.

Ellis cleared his throat. "He says that, come fall, we're both going to be uncles."

Everett stared at Ellis, then Wolfe and the wide grin on the latter's face. His large hand fit to Everett's shoulder and squeezed before he got up and moved to the door.

Ellis grabbed Everett's arm and shook him. "You did good, brother."

"Jesus," Everett muttered, shrugging him off. He straightened. "Actin' like I cured cancer or something."

When Ellis left with Wolfe, Everett stayed at the bar. Grady returned to take their glasses. Everett held on to his. "Another," he demanded.

Chapter 14

The bride wore satin couture and carried a bouquet of desert flowers. Her elder brothers walked her down the aisle to the tune of Fleetwood Mac's "Songbird." Paloma Coldero served as Eveline's maid of honor, looking lovely in full-length chiffon and lace. The groom had been fitted for the occasion in head-to-toe black, including a new felt cowboy hat and snakeskin dress boots.

Eveline and Wolfe exchanged vows under a rustic awning that framed a stunning picture of Eaton Edge. The sun took its last gasp over the distant peak as he dipped her back for a long, satisfactory kiss to a raucous round of applause. They beamed at each other as they came up for air and the wedding party kicked into high gear.

Kaya spotted the security the Eatons had hired to block reporters and photographers—or anyone nefarious—from intruding on the pleasantries. *Smart move*, she thought, sipping champagne on the outskirts of the reception. The happy couple had chosen the wide flagstone patio of Eaton House for the party. Guests spilled down the steps into the yard, milling as far as the white barn with enchanting fairy lights trimming the eaves. She counted four guards, each wearing a spiffy black tuxedo and built like a bulldozer.

She watched the colors change in the sky. Dusk turned

toward night. The hues had softened into lavender, gloaming blue and a soft touch of green in the horizon. The sound of the live band, boots slapping the dance floor and hands clapping split the quiet of the landscape with lively abandon.

"Why aren't you dancing?"

Kaya looked around at her sister, Naleen. Older by two years, Naleen wore her long black hair to one side of her neck in a coiled side bun with a pretty, braided headband. She was several inches taller than Kaya. Her frame was curvy to Kaya's muscly one and she wore a tea-length strapless party dress in navy. "You used to love to dance," Naleen added, holding out her hand.

Kaya tipped the champagne glass to her sister's fingers and watched her drink. "Why is Mom here?" she asked.

Naleen raised a fashionably full brow as she lowered the glass and handed it back. "She was Santiago's nurse when he was transferred to the mental facility and stayed in touch with Paloma and Wolfe through the years."

Kaya raised her chin. "Ah."

"Is that why you're hiding?"

"I'm not hiding," Kaya said, but the words were lost in the echo chamber of the glass as she took another drink.

Naleen's wide mouth curved. "If only the people of Fuego knew how their sheriff cowers at the sight of her four-foot-eleven mother."

"I'm not hiding," Kaya repeated because it sounded good and strong, and she wanted to mean it.

"You're going to have to speak to her," Naleen advised. "Preferably before she finds out you and Everett Eaton are—"

"What?" Kaya intercepted swiftly. "What do you know about Everett?"

"You're having some kind of fling with him and the whole town knows it," Naleen answered. She raised her hands. "No judgement. You and me—we've always had a type."

"What type?"

"The hard cowboy type," Naleen answered smoothly. "The long, tall, gritty kind of cowboy that gets under our skin and doesn't leave. Not until we've been bucked off."

"I don't know what you're talking about."

"Look who's in denial." Naleen sighed as the band slid into a slow song and the bride and groom took to the floor. "I keep thinking about Sawni. Do you think she'd be happy Wolfe moved on and found someone like Eveline?"

Kaya nodded. "If she's watching this, she's seen everything else. The way he and his family searched for her, the way he lost his stepmother and stepsister in the fire, the false accusations made against him, the time he did in jail because of it... After everything he's been through, he deserves a life with the woman he loves. Sawni would want nothing less."

Naleen thought about it. "She did want the best for people." Turning her focus back to Kaya, she added, "She wanted you to be happy, too. You have to know that's the reason she took the job at The RC Resort. So that you could continue with the rodeo."

Kaya shifted from one foot to the other and didn't meet her sister's stare. She watched the others dance. Grief and regret were close to the surface, still. She had thought there would be some resolution to them if Sawni was found. She'd been wrong. She still had to wrangle with them.

"How's your leg?" Naleen asked.

"It's better," Kaya said. "Still sore at times—especially

on days I hike. But I think physical therapy is starting to pay off."

"Good. It's a damn fine wedding, isn't it?"

"They're a damn fine match," Kaya replied, happy to be moving on from the previous subjects. "Nova's got her summer job. Everett says she's a natural cowhand."

Naleen's wistful expression morphed into a fast frown as she found her daughter slow dancing with Lucas Barnes. "I keep telling myself she'll grow out of it—that she'll be burned out by the end of summer. But she's as stubborn as desert weather and just as determined. I'm afraid there's no fighting her nature. Now I know how Mom felt when you ran away to be a trick rider."

Kaya made a noise as she eyed the hand Lucas had low on Nova's waist. She raised the champagne glass to point it out. "Do you think those two are doing it?"

Naleen stiffened. "She wouldn't. She's only sixteen—practically a baby."

"You were sixteen when you lost it to Ryan MacKay," Kaya reminded her. "Then married him before you were eighteen because you got pregnant."

Naleen's jaw tightened. "That's not nice, Kaya."

"It's true," Kaya said. "I was sixteen when I lost it, too. To a cowboy with no more sense between his ears than Lucas over there. Are you sensing a pattern here? Altaha women lose their minds around silly cowboys. Nova's never struck me as a traditional sort, but Lucas's hand is well south of the mark."

"I'll be back," Naleen said, marching off to break up the festivities. Kaya grinned, dangling the champagne glass between two fingers. She hated to throw Nova at her mother's mercy, but Kaya had needed something—anything—to divert Naleen's attention from her.

She heard a growl near her ear and turned around.

Everett caught her by the waist, holding her at arm's length so that he could drink her with his eyes. "That ain't no uniform."

Kaya glanced down at the black dress she'd tried on and dismissed the night of their first date. "Even the sheriff's got to mix it up a little." She glanced over his fancy duds and was forced to take a bracing breath. "Anybody ever tell you you clean up good, cattle baron?"

He didn't take his eyes off her to examine the dark suit jacket with boot stitch that fit the long plains of his shoulders to perfection. Three dogs milled around his legs.

"Aren't you going to introduce me to your posse?" she asked.

He patted his thigh. The one that answered immediately sat at his silent motion to do so then stared, alert and sharp, waiting for the next command. It was an Australian cattle dog. "This is Boaz. She's the leader." As he passed a gentle hand between Boaz's ears, he peered at Kaya. "I have a weakness for strong females."

She smiled softly. He snapped, bringing one of the others around. "Sit," he said until the second cattle dog did so. "This is Boomer. He's four. He likes to herd, like Boaz, and he likes to play."

"Hello, Boomer," Kaya said when the dog's head tilted her way. His tongue lolled out, charming her, and she reached down to pet him.

"This other one's Bones," Everett said, snapping until Bones wound around to his front and sat on his feet. "He's still a pup."

Kaya felt her brow knit as she studied Bones more closely. "Um, Everett?"

"He's learning, still," Everett went on, rubbing Bones's

scruff until the dog's left leg began to mill in circles. "His energy still overrides his decision-making. But he'll be a fine cattle dog in the future, like the others."

"Everett," she said again. When his gaze fixed to hers, she pointed to Bones. "You realize that's a coyote."

Everett quickly cupped Bones's ears under his hands. "He doesn't know that."

She rolled her eyes. "Come on."

"He's not all coyote," Everett explained. "He was three weeks old when I found him in the sagebrush. His mother had been killed and his fellow pups had been eaten, most likely by Tombstone. They were in his territory. I didn't think he'd make it."

"But he did," she considered, sizing Bones up. "Does he yip at the moon?"

"Sometimes," Everett said. He winked. "But then again, so do I."

She pressed her lips together to stop herself from laughing. "And how do I know you're not part coyote?"

He chuckled. "You don't, Sheriff Sweetheart."

She shook her head. In Apache myth, Coyote was often depicted as either the villain or the savior. Kaya didn't think she could attribute either of those labels to Everett. After all they'd been through, she had a pretty good feeling he wasn't going to be the villain in her story.

As for *savior*... Kaya had done plenty of saving herself through the years. And Everett Eaton was hardly a knight in shining armor.

In some legends, it was Coyote who brought light to the world.

And Everett sure did light a fire in her.

When he stepped close again, easing her into his embrace, his eyes traced the seam of her lips and her cheekbones before meeting her assessing gaze. "You've got the night off."

"I do," she admitted. Her stomach clutched. His stare spread excitement in every vicinity.

He nodded. "I plan on making the most of it."

Her pulse rate doubled. They hadn't spent the night together since the evening after his arrest. Since, she'd been unable to ignore the fact that she no longer enjoyed going to bed alone.

"I'd like to dance with you, Kaya," he said. "I asked you once and you were hurting. Is your leg well enough to let me spin you around the dance floor a dozen times?"

He'd had her at the sound of her name. She slipped her hand into his outstretched one.

She'd knocked a full-grown man out with her fist once. But her hand felt small in Everett's. It even felt like it might belong there.

Naleen was right, she thought as her stomach fluttered. "Spin me," she said simply and followed his lead to the dance floor.

"Are you behaving yourself?" Paloma hissed in his ear as the stars came blinking into existence.

Everett flinched. He thought he'd been alone at the buffet table. "Do I look like I'm stuffing crab legs down my pants?"

"I'm more worried about you spiking the punch bowl," she said with a lowered brow. "I heard your little liquor bottles clinking in your vest before the ceremony started."

"Somebody had to calm Coldero down," Everett noted. He picked up a carrot stick. "I've never seen a man sweat his bride showing up to the altar that much." He dragged the stick through the dip bowl and lifted it toward his mouth.

She knocked it out of his hand before he could shove it home. At his stunned look, she snapped, "Put it on a plate, *then* eat it. It's your sister's wedding. The least you can do is act civilized."

He took the plate she handed him and started to pile things on it, muttering, "Jesus God Almighty… I walked her down the aisle, didn't I? I handed her over to Coldero real nicely…"

"Because you know what's good for you," Paloma said, picking up a plate of her own. She used tongs to select a chicken leg from a platter. "The line goes to the left, Everett Templeton," she added when he tried to wind to the right.

"I want the chicken," he told her. When she refused to budge, he groaned. "I want the chicken, *please*."

She used the tongs again to select a breast from the platter. She set it neatly in the center of his plate. "There you are. Now keep the line moving."

"There's no one behind us," he griped. Before she could smack him again, he picked up the serving fork next to the carrots and herded more than necessary onto his plate.

"There's someone you have to meet."

"I don't want to talk to people. I want to dance." He grinned. "I'm taking Kaya onto the dance floor again, soon as I'm done." They had fallen into step together seamlessly. The crowd had split and made room as Everett had found out again how she could answer him move for move and even show him up.

"You should be fixing her a plate, too," Paloma suggested. "The way you two carry on out there, she's going to need it."

"She's already eaten," he replied. He caught Paloma's knowing look. "What?"

"I found a pair of black panties in the upstairs ficus."

He froze, trying hard to look innocent. "They're Eveline's."

"Eveline throws her panties around her and Wolfe's place now," she said, stalking him to the end of the buffet table.

"Luella's then."

"Luella and Ellis moved into the cabin behind the bunkhouse with the girls a month ago," she reminded him, keeping pace easily as he rounded the table to the other side.

He grabbed a roll quickly, fumbling it when it burned him. He caught it, flipped it onto his plate and searched for napkins.

They were behind her. He'd missed them. Cursing, he planted his feet. "I'm thirty-eight years old. I can do what I want with who I want in my own house."

"I'll take it from here, Ms. Coldero."

Paloma subsided, going so far as to smile at the woman who'd decided to intrude. "I warmed him up for you, Darcia. Everett, have you met Ms. Altaha?"

Everett glanced from one woman to the other. The new one had silver-tinged hair. She was less than five feet tall, in his estimation. But her set mouth could raise the hair on a dog's back. Her dark eyes bore into him. He could see her Native heritage in her pronounced cheekbones and her dark skin tone.

The words *It's a trap* flagged across the windscreen of his consciousness. "Altaha," he repeated. "As in…"

"Kaya and Naleen's mother," Paloma supplied helpfully. She smiled as she veered around him. Patting him on the lapel of his Western-cut jacket, she lowered her voice and muttered, "Stand up straight and take it like a man, *mijo*."

Everett cleared his throat as she cleared off, leaving him alone with Kaya's mother. He turned his head on his neck to ease the tension. "It's nice to meet you, ma'am."

She had a stare a mile wide, he discovered when she didn't break it. Everett started to itch around the collar.

"So," Darcia Altaha said, "you're the man who's currently screwing my daughter."

Everett nearly swallowed his tongue. "Ah...not currently. I mean, not right at this second." He cleared his throat louder this time when she only narrowed her eyes.

"I'm no stranger to my daughter's single behavior," Darcia informed him. "She sleeps with men. Sometimes she enjoys them. Sometimes she finds them lacking."

He tried to think of something safe to say and found a minefield instead. "Uh..."

"It seems you're one of the ones she enjoys," Darcia revealed. "You must be very impressive, Mr. Eaton."

"Well, I think—"

Her chin lowered. "You shouldn't finish that thought."

He nodded quickly. "You're right, ma'am. I shouldn't."

"Good man," she said approvingly. "Kaya seems to be enjoying you more than the others."

Everett kept his mouth studiously shut. He was sweating as much as Coldero had before the wedding. If this kept up, he was going to need a change of clothes.

"My youngest daughter, Mr. Eaton," Darcia continued, taking several slow strides toward him, "does not do what she is told. As a child, she was next to impossible."

He felt the beginnings of a treacherous smile warming his face. "Is that right?"

"Kaya is responsible for every gray hair on my head." Her eyes widened for emphasis. "Do you see my head, Mr. Eaton?"

His mouth opened, closed, opened again. "I...think it's very nice."

"It is *covered* in gray."

He thought quickly. "She has a unique effect on people."

"You like to delegate," Darcia said.

He lifted a shoulder. "Sure."

"You're the boss," she went on. "The 'chief,' I believe."

He shook his head. "It's just a title."

"Yes," Darcia granted, "but you are a man accustomed to giving orders and having them followed to the letter."

"Yes, ma'am."

She nodded. "So heed what I tell you. Kaya will not be told what to do. She will not be ordered. She will not follow where others lead. No one delegates to Kaya. She will leave your bed at all hours of the night to put herself in danger, all in the name of law and order. She won't change or be tamed. The moment you try, she will run. This you must know before getting in too deep with my daughter."

He waited for more. When it didn't come, he wet his throat. "Ms. Altaha..."

"You will call me Darcia."

"I will?" When she pursed her lips, he decided, "I will. You can call me Everett, if you like."

"Fine," she granted.

"Your daughter," he said carefully, "is the single most amazing woman I've ever met in my life."

Her arms laced over the front of the beaded, forest green bodice of her dress. "Go on."

"She's powerful," he stated. "Some people may feel threatened by that in a woman, but I find it extremely attractive. She's an exceptional police officer and a far better sheriff than that last one we had here in Fuego. As a friend, you should know she saved my life. As a companion, she's everything a man could want and more."

"Are you everything a woman could want, Everett?" she challenged.

"I hope so, Mrs…er, Darcia. What's more, I hope I'm everything Kaya wants because I'm hers."

He heard it the same time she did. He heard the confession ring with truth. He let out an unsteady breath. "Well. There it is."

Darcia's hand was cool as it twined around his wrist. "It's all right, Everett."

He looked at her, trying to fathom the satisfaction on her face. "How'd you do that?"

"Where do you think my daughter got her interrogation skills?" she asked. "Certainly not from her father."

He let out a breathless laugh. And kept laughing. He was still laughing when he spotted Kaya weaving fast through the crowd to get to them.

"Mom," she said. "Are you playing nice?"

"Of course I am," she said. She smiled at Everett. "If you'll excuse me, I have to go talk to my granddaughter's date."

Everett watched Darcia round the buffet table, still choking on laughter.

"Everett?" Kaya turned him to her. "Are you okay?"

He stopped laughing abruptly. "Your mother scares the hell out of me."

"She left you standing," Kaya considered with a shake of her head. "You must have made a good impression."

He needed a stiff drink. "How does a man survive any of you Altaha women?"

"I've yet to meet the man who does," she explained.

"Is that right?" he asked, measuring.

"Eat up, cattle baron," she said, raising herself to her toes. She brushed a kiss across his cheek. "You owe me a slow one."

I'm hers. He heard it again in his head. Caught between the urge to beeline for the open bar or to fall willingly into her arms like the besotted puppy he was, he trailed her to the dance floor, wishing he'd left the buffet well enough alone.

Chapter 15

Kaya noticed Everett didn't say much after they saw Eveline and Wolfe off. Wolfe had been cleared to leave the country and would be on a plane with his new wife bound for the Caribbean in a matter of hours.

It wasn't until they were gone and the guests had slowly trickled out that Everett grabbed her by the hand and led her into the house.

He didn't say anything as he took off his jacket and toed off his boots upstairs. Well aware that Paloma and other family members were downstairs, she kept quiet, too, as he removed her dress and took her to bed.

The sex wasn't urgent, as it had been before. It felt like something else entirely—not quite soft but crystalline. His rough hands gentled. His strokes were sure but slow. He left the lights off and the windows open so that the desert breeze made the curtains restless and moon beams grazed the sheets.

She didn't realize until after they had both stilled, having rocked each other to climax, that he'd given her something finer than sex—something deeper and far more devastating.

He'd made love to her.

She lay awake thinking about it long after she was sure

he had dozed off. His back was to the window. Moonlight cast his profile into distinction but not his face. She could hear the restful sound of his lungs working. Under her hands, the muscles around his ribs swelled and released, swelled and released in long, languid pulls.

Hesitant, her touch tracked the ladder of his rib cage to his sternum. She felt the little round knot of scar tissue.

She cursed inwardly. He hadn't been touching her. He'd been touching her heart. He'd touched her soul, for crying out loud. He'd looked at her as he'd ushered her over every peak—not watchful and thirsty like last time...

He'd looked at her as if *she'd* brought light to the world.

Everything downstairs had quieted down. In the distance, she could hear coyotes yip and cows low. If she listened closely enough, she could hear the world turn.

He'd split her world in two. He'd broken it like an egg. There was no cleaning up what he'd untapped.

She was done for. It wasn't a comfortable thought. Yet it was a fact and she had to find some way to live with it.

She was going to have to find a way to cope with the strong possibility that she was in love with him.

"What have you done, cattle baron?" she whispered even as she raised her hand into the hair on the back of his head and caressed. She found her lips nestling against the underside of his jaw.

The crack rang out, its report loud. A dog started to howl a split second before the raised pane of the window shattered. Even as Everett jerked awake, Kaya closed her arms around him and rolled as the second shot echoed.

The bullet sang into the wall over their heads as they hit the floor with a jolting thud. "Get down!" she shouted, her hand locked on a hunk of his hair, forcing his head low to the ground. "Stay down!"

The third shot hit the bed. She heard the impact and badly wished for her weapon. Looking around, she saw her beaded handbag where she'd dropped it. Her dress pooled over it.

"Stay," she instructed as she shifted away.

"Where are you going?" he asked, then cursed again as another shot shattered what remained of the glass pane.

"Do as I say, Everett!" She shimmied across the floor, grabbed the bag and took out her phone. She dialed and counted the rings before dispatch picked up. "This is Sheriff Altaha. Shots fired," she reported. "I repeat—shots fired at Eaton Edge. The main house is under fire. Send all available units to this location." She left the line open as she extracted her gun. She found the clip, inserted it in the empty chamber. Using her thumb, she removed the catch and crawled toward the far window.

"Kaya?"

"Stay," she ordered, easing her back against the wall. She stayed out of the slant of light that revealed patterns in the wood flooring. Peering out into the yard, she kept her head clear, in the shadows, both hands gripping her weapon. She worked to slow her breathing, hoping her pulse rate would follow. It raced, walloping her breastbone. Adrenaline surged through her.

She could hear Everett moving around the bed. Knowing he'd left cover did nothing to calm her. Before she could chastise him, another shot rang out, hitting the windows of the room next door to theirs. "Where are the girls?" she asked. "Isla and Ingrid. Where do they sleep?"

"Ellis's house—just over the hill," came his tense answer. He was closer now. "It's Paloma I'm worried about."

She winced as more shots rang out. "There are two shooters," she determined.

"Yeah," he said, listening. "Around the stables."

"Up high," she said. "Is there roof access in the stables?"

"Through Paloma's quarters." Everett made a noise in his throat when the shooting didn't stop. "Kaya. I need to get to her."

"You need to stay where you are," she said.

"The hands. They're all going to come running. Ellis, too. We can't wait for backup. We need to get out there and stop this before my people are killed."

"I don't have visibility," she admitted. "Keep your head down and hand me my dress."

What was worse than walking into a firefight was knowing that Kaya was, too. By the time they made themselves decent and had retrieved his weapon from the safe on the first floor, he realized he was going to have to let her leave the cover of the house.

Paloma greeted them at the door. She fell into Everett's arms.

He smelled her blood before he raised his hand to the one on top of her head. His fingers came away wet and warm. "Those sons of bitches," he hissed, helping her to a seated position on the floor.

"It's not bad," Paloma moaned. "They didn't shoot me. They just knocked me out."

"Put pressure on the wound," Kaya said, handing him a handkerchief.

He covered the gash and pressed. When Paloma gasped, he felt his blood run cold. "I'll kill 'em."

The gunfire hadn't let up. They were hitting the kitchen windows now.

"You go out there," Paloma said, "you're as good as dead. You can't put me through that, *mijo*."

"I'll come back," he promised.

"They've probably got night vision goggles," Kaya deduced as they left through the front of the house. "It's how they knew we were in the room upstairs."

"I shouldn't have left the window open," he realized. As they neared the corner of the house, both gripping their weapons in a two-handed hold, they tensed at the sound of running.

Kaya held up a hand and motioned him back against the wall. They waited a beat, listening.

The sound of a high-pitched whinny split the night a split second before a high-strung colt bolted past in a flurry of hooves. Another followed it at breakneck speed.

"They let the horses out," he growled.

She inched toward the corner, her weapon high. "I need backup to get here. There's light enough to see the roof of the stables, but without cover…"

"I need to get to the barn," he said. At the turn of her head, he went on. "I have to make sure the cattle are secure. Never mind the horses. If they release the herd and open the gates…"

She nodded away the rest. "You go that way. I'll look for a shot."

He gripped her shoulder. It was bare but for the single black strap of her dress. "You be careful, Sheriff Sweetheart."

"You, too," she said before she darted around the side of the house. Everett took off at a run, keeping to the shadows. He ran through the small grove of evenly spaced trees that produced fruit in summer. Grateful for their spring foliage and the cover it provided, he ran hell for leather toward the shape of the barn, hoping his long legs and speed would serve him well.

Someone ran into him headlong. "Hands up!" he yelled.

"It's me," Ellis reported. "What the hell's going on? Who's shooting?"

"Luella. The girls. Are they all right?"

"They're safe," Ellis assured him. "I had her take them into the cellar and lock the door from the inside."

"We need to check the barn," Everett barked. He could hear sirens in the distance. They were closing in. The gunfire still hadn't let up. He thought of Kaya and wanted to scream. "They let the horses go."

"I hear them," Ellis told him. "I can go around the cabins, get farther out of range and make my way around. The men should be over that way, too. They'll help."

"Don't do anything stupid," Everett said, even as he moved in the direction of the stables.

"Hang on, where're you going?" Ellis called after him.

"Kaya's out there," Everett said, pointing. "I gotta—"

Ellis waved off the rest. "Go, then! Go!"

Everett bolted, running toward gunfire. The lights of police vehicles lit the night as he broke free of the trees and crouched low, closing the distance between the grove and the house.

There were holes in the tents on the patio. They flapped, loose, and snapped in the breeze. He followed what he hoped was Kaya's path from table to table. He ducked underneath the empty buffet table. His gaze seized on the front of the house. It gaped at the windows. There was little glass left for the moonlight to bounce off.

There was fear riding underneath the beat of his blood. But anger swelled beneath it, all but incinerating. His father's house, his family's land...his woman.

Pressing his lips together, he eyed the distance between him and the open gate. There was nothing but the night between him and the truck parked on the other side of it.

He took a long, deep breath before taking off like a runner at the starting gun.

Kaya could smell animal. And not just the horses.

She found a decent position behind the water trough and near the fence in the first corral. She kept herself still as she searched the roofline. She ducked back down after counting one, two shapes against the hard slant of moonlight.

Bastards had chosen a three-quarter moon to do their bidding.

Breathing carefully, she eased her weapon around the side of the trough. She peered down the length of the barrel, aiming for the first figure...

The sound of a snort reached her ears. Her finger froze on the trigger as the hairs on the back of her neck stood on end.

She looked over her shoulder.

The bull was huge. Its head was low. She saw the glint of its horns. It struck one hoof against the ground. Dust rose in a plume.

It lowed at the sound of gunfire and shifted, restless. More scared and uncertain than anything, it was lost among the maze of open gates and fences. But Kaya knew she was the only threat it had been able to pick apart from the dark landscape.

Caught between the trough and the open corral, she had nothing but her Glock to stop it if it charged.

It pawed the ground again, bellowing.

"Walk away, big boy," she coaxed under her breath as she raised the weapon. "Just walk away..." She felt a bead of sweat roll from her hairline to her cheek.

A shout split the night. "Hey!" And another, longer. "Heeeeeey!"

Kaya and the bull looked out to pasture and saw the tall figure with arms spread. "No," she moaned. Then louder, "No, no!"

The bull charged Everett. Kaya didn't hesitate. Knowing the gunmen had heard the shout and had made Everett, she raised the gun over the edge of the trough, sighted and squeezed off a round, then another.

She saw the gunman crumple. The second ducked out of sight.

Lowering her head once more, she searched the corral for Everett and the bull. When she saw nothing but grass waving in the wind, she tried not to panic. Shouts of "Police!" and "Drop your weapons!" reached her. She wished for a radio so that she could communicate with her deputies.

Scanning the roofline, she couldn't locate the second figure.

He was on the move.

The stable doors yawned wide. She stood and propelled herself toward the opening.

A man's silhouette appeared in the doorway. She took him down on a running leap at the knees.

A shot went off from his gun before he clattered to the floor.

The man reached for his weapon, but she kicked it out of reach. She grappled with him, going right up against his cloud of day-old sweat. He was big, strong and fought well.

She was a hair quicker. She punched him in the teeth. She hit him harder in the solar plexus. The fist to the groin made him wither.

"Turn over," she instructed. "Put your hands behind your back. Do it!"

When Deputy Wyatt arrived with the cuffs, she had her hands locked around the suspect's wrists. "Second shooter's on the roof," she told him, taking the cuffs he removed from his belt. She secured the attacker's hands behind his back.

"On it," he said. Using a flashlight, he moved into the dark stables, radioing for Root to follow.

"Don't move," she told the gunman, patting his pockets. She found more ammo clips and a flashlight but no wallet or identification.

"Kaya."

She glanced up and found Everett. After picking up the shooter's weapon and unloading it, she stood. "You're okay."

His eyes raced over her. "You?"

"I'm all right," she said. "The others?"

"Ellis," he said in answer.

"He's down?" she asked, alarmed.

He shook his head. "He and the hands are securing the barn."

Relief washed over her. She took a moment to run her gaze across his face and torso a few times. He was dirty and mussed, his hair not at all neat without his hat. She wanted to shove him back a step with both hands. She wanted to gather him to her and hold on until all the little fears...all the what-might-have-beens ceased to exist. "Stupid," she pushed out because she couldn't stop seeing him out in the open waving his hands and shouting like an idiot. It had made her choke with fear. "You were *so stupid*, Everett."

His brows came together. He took a step toward her.

Deputy Root arrived. "Wyatt has the second gunman in

custody," he reported, panting from running. "Says he's got an ID."

"Paloma Coldero is injured inside the house," Kaya stated. "We need to get her checked out."

"An officer's with her now," Root informed them. "She's conscious. They called for a bus, just to be sure."

She helped the suspect to his feet. He had high shoulders and a long face. "You're under arrest. Might as well tell us who you are."

"Fat chance," he grunted, then spit on the ground at her feet.

When Everett whipped forward, Root stopped him. "Take it easy," the deputy cautioned.

"I know you," Everett said, pointing at the gunman. "I've seen you—out at The RC Resort. You work security for True Claymore."

Kaya pulled on the attacker's arm until he faced the moon. Root helped by shining a light in his eyes. Her lips parted. Everett was right. She'd seen the man with the mayor, too.

He was one of the goons who had replaced her roadside attacker from years ago.

"He sent you here, didn't he?" Everett asked, struggling against Root's restraining arm. "This is payback for what I did to his car."

"Don't know what you're talking about," the shooter grunted, lowering his head and closing his eyes because the light in them was too much.

Kaya turned to look back at the house. True Claymore wouldn't be reckless enough to order his men to do something as drastic as this, would he?

Or had the good mayor reached the end of his rope?

Chapter 16

The long drive to The RC Resort might have been scenic if not for the sick taste on Kaya's tongue. It was always with her when she made the trip to Claymore's homestead.

Next to her, Agent Rutland shrugged out of his sport coat and checked the weapon holstered on his belt. "What's the plan, Sheriff?"

She frowned as the ranch house came into view. It was resplendent against a barren desert backdrop. "You're letting my department take the lead on this?"

"As it was you Claymore's hired men nearly shot through an open window, that's fair, I'd say."

Kaya swallowed, tasted bile and lowered her head so the brim of her hat covered whatever emotions were riding high in her eyes. If she was emotional, she couldn't be clearheaded. And she needed to be clearheaded.

She'd sworn she would be the one to lock True Claymore up. She had evidence—enough that she'd been able to secure a warrant. She had the gunmen's confessions. They'd resisted questioning at first, but Rutland had looked at their banking records. A recent bonus of ten grand a piece from their employer had seemed timely.

Everett and Ellis had found the gunmen's horses a half mile away from the barn while rounding up the misplaced horses and few escaped cattle. Their saddlebags had been packed enough for a week's sojourn.

If Kaya and her team hadn't apprehended them, they would be in the wind at this point.

A breath filtered slowly through her nose as she slowed to make the turn under the arch welcoming them to The RC Resort & Spa. "He had to have known the shooting would lead back to him sooner than later. He'll be ready."

"You think he'll make a stand?" Rutland asked cautiously as she eased the sheriff's all-terrain vehicle to a stop in the parking lot. There were a dozen other cars.

Kaya frowned at the shuttle van. It wasn't the same model Claymore's goons had removed her in years ago. But it sickened her to see it, nonetheless. She unbuckled her seat belt and scanned the entrance to the house. "His wife's a lawyer. She normally talks him out of trouble. My bet is he'll hide behind her. If he's desperate enough to fight…" She heard more than saw the second police vehicle ease to a stop behind hers. "…we'll take him down."

"Sheriff," Rutland said before she could open the door.

She glanced. The lines of his face gave her pause.

He inclined his head. "We don't have proof he had anything to do with those bodies on the mountain."

"Not yet," she added.

"Be careful," he advised. "Don't make this personal. If he killed your friend, Mescal, we'll dig deeper. We'll find the truth."

How did she tell him that the anger she felt—the almost blind rage—wasn't about Sawni, for once? It was about Everett.

She hadn't been alone in the crosshairs. Everett's body had been between the open window and her. She'd learned not to think too long about what might have been if the gunmen hadn't missed that first shot.

The texture of the bullet wound on his sternum came to her clearly, as if she were touching it now. She opened the door to the vehicle. The taste in her mouth now burned in her throat. She planted her hand on her belt and waited for Root and Wyatt to join them. "We're here to bring in the mayor," she reminded them. "If you have any problem with that, I'd advise you to wait outside."

"We're with you, Sheriff," Wyatt vowed. To his right, Root nodded.

She scanned them and felt a swell of pride. As a deputy herself, she'd learned to work with them and trust them. As one of the people responsible for Sheriff Jones's fall from grace, she hadn't thought she'd earn their loyalty as sheriff—not right away.

They'd proven their loyalty a dozen times over the last few weeks. They were the best of men. "Follow my lead," she said quietly before heading them and Rutland to the big front doors. She ignored the old-fashioned bellpull that acted as doorbell and knocked in a series of raps. "Sheriff's department," she called clearly. When no one answered, she rapped again.

The sound of the latch grinding put Kaya on alert. She forced herself to relax, outwardly. As the door parted from the jamb, she felt Root tense next to her.

The round face of a housekeeper greeted them, her face riddled with confusion. "*Hola?*" she said haltingly.

Kaya responded in Spanish. "*Buen día.* We're looking for True Claymore. *Está él en casa?*"

She shook her head quickly. "*No, no está aquí.*"

Kaya peered over the housekeeper's shoulder. There

was no one in the foyer that she could discern. "Do you know where he is?"

The housekeeper hesitated for a brief second before shaking her head. "No."

Kaya scrutinized her. She looked worried. "What about Annette Claymore? Is she home?"

The woman bit her lip. She glanced over her shoulder, then shook her head.

Rutland shifted forward slightly. "We have a warrant. Open the door, ma'am, so we can search the premises."

At the housekeeper's knitted brow, Kaya quickly translated. Still, the woman didn't open. "*Por favor*," Kaya added. *Don't protect them. It's not worth it.*

Slowly, the housekeeper gave in. The door opened and she stepped back. Kaya swept in. She nodded to the left and Wyatt went to search the dining room and kitchen. With a motion, she sent Root to do the same in the common area and spa rooms.

"What's back there?" Rutland asked, approaching the back of the house.

"Office," she said grimly. Guests weren't allowed in that part of the house. But she'd gone there anyway once, looking for evidence linking the Claymores to Sawni's disappearance...

"I'll look there," Rutland said.

"I'll sweep the upstairs." She moved in that direction.

At the landing, she began checking doors. The guests that had checked in were out riding or walking the nearby nature trail or shopping in town. The rooms were empty. She located True and Annette's master suite. The fur rugs and grand four-poster bed put her ill at ease. Drawers on the bureau were open. The closet, too, was open with clothes on the floor. There was no sign of a struggle. The bathroom counter was empty.

Where were the creams? The soaps? The lotions?

Kaya frowned as she traced her steps back into the bedroom, across the bear rug. Glass doors opened onto an expansive balcony.

Her radio chirped as she unlatched them. "Sheriff?"

She parted the radio from her belt and brought it to her mouth. "Go ahead."

Rutland answered. "Office has been swept. The desk and file cabinet are empty. The safe is open. There's nothing left."

"He knew we were coming," she replied. From the balcony, she could see the Claymore spread. The little chapel off to the left. The barn used for weddings and dances. Stables to the right.

She could see Root striding off to search the latter. "Who tipped them off?" It was no secret the Claymores had friends in high places. Could it have been the judge? Worse, someone in Kaya's office? "We need to put out a BOLO on True Claymore. It looks like Annette may have left with him."

Root's voice carried through the channel. "Sheriff, you want to get down to the stables."

"Did you find something?" she asked, hurrying back through the parted glass doors.

"The mayor's horse is missing."

She pushed herself forward, leaving the suite. "His horse?"

"The groom said he left on horseback before daybreak," Root replied. "He said he didn't pack light."

"Damn," she uttered, breaking into a run on the stairs.

* * *

The manhunt for True Claymore was the biggest mounted search in Fuego County in five years. But then, it wasn't every day a mayor went missing.

Everett pulled back on the reins, urging Crazy Alice into a walk. "Whoa, girl," he murmured. "Whoa." He patted her neck before swinging to the ground. They'd been out since first light, searching the area north from the Edge to The RC Resort.

Most likely, Claymore would have headed east and there were a dozen or more riders searching the state park area for signs of the man and his horse.

Everett and his team had been mobilized in the southwest quarter of the search area. The border overlapped Eaton territory. His men were spread over the hilly, mountainous region that circled Ol' Whalebones.

Everett led Crazy Alice to the edge of the river. It was shallow at the foot of Mount Elder. As his horse drank, Everett took his canteen off his belt and did the same. The sun had been hot on his back and he'd found no indication that Claymore and his mount had come this way.

He'd been disappointed when Kaya had placed him in charge of the lower region. She knew how much he wanted Claymore's hide. Being the one to find him would have been more than satisfying.

But he was still raw enough—still furious enough— to hurt the mayor for his part in the Eaton House attack. Paloma was still in the hospital. The doctors had assured him it was just for observation purposes, but Everett's gut twisted at the implications. Eveline had come back early to sit by her bedside with Luella. Wolfe had joined the search. He'd been assigned to the team in the northeast quadrant, likely due to his superior tracking skills.

And he was levelheaded enough that he wouldn't throttle Claymore when he found him.

No. Wolfe would bring him in nice and easy. Everett twisted the lid back on the canteen and sniffed, scanning the sky. No birds of prey circled. A hawk kited high on a draft, peering beadily at him.

Crazy Alice lifted her head. She turned it downwind and stilled. Her ribs lifted as she took as exaggerated breath, smelling.

Everett heard her tail swish. Her head arched high and she sidestepped toward him. He laid his hand on her withers. "What is it, girl?" he whispered, stroking in soothing circles. Her breath had quickened. He could feel the tension in her muscles. "What do you smell?"

Sounds carried in valleys. Everett strained to hear over the burbling of the river on the rocks. He heard the chirp of a bird. Then whistling.

The fine hairs on the back of his arms rose. Just like that, his horse's tension was his own. He locked his legs to keep from sidestepping, too. Under the brim of his hat, he searched the slopes of Mount Elder, scanning the sagebrush and boulders.

An eerie scream broke the quiet. It reverberated off the cliffs. Crazy Alice jumped and whinnied.

He grabbed the reins. "Easy, girl," he said, trying to stay calm. His rifle was in the sheath on her saddle. His boots skimmed across the ground as she dragged him with her in retreat. "Easy, girl. Easy."

Her head bobbed. She jerked the reins, but she stilled long enough for him to remove his weapon.

Common sense told him to head in the opposite direction, farther upriver where Claymore lands bisected the Edge. That was where Crazy Alice would flee. She knew as well as Everett they were in the heart of Tombstone's territory.

He clambered up rockfall, trying to reach high ground. He found a position in the shadow of a ledge. The valley spread out beneath him. He didn't need his binoculars to see the lion or its prey.

The horse was down. It lay on its side near the point where rock met river. If it had made it to water, it had died shortly after. There was a pool of blood under its head but no discernable tears in its flank.

The big cat had positioned itself on the cliff on the other side of the water. It yowled and paced, restless. Everett reached into the flap of his shirt and lifted his binoculars. Close up, he saw the lean body lines and the grimacing face with one eye missing.

Everett forced himself to take a moment. Sweat ran from his hairline. He inhaled for a full four seconds. Then he pushed it out, letting his lungs empty. Tombstone was not the harbinger of death and despair Everett associated him with. He was a predator with greater longevity or luck than others in the wild. Sighting him wasn't detrimental to Everett's family, as he'd feared in the past.

That was what common sense said. His stomach cramped, however. The last time he'd seen Tombstone this close—this clearly—his mother and stepsister had come to a horrible end. In some twisted way, Everett had felt responsible.

If he hadn't volunteered to go into Tombstone's territory that day to check the Wapusa's swollen banks after a week's rain and flooding, a part of him was convinced there wouldn't have been a fire across town at Coldero Ridge and his mother and half sister would still be alive.

He hadn't been close to his mother, Josephine. They

hadn't even been on speaking terms when she died. But she was his mother, and that little girl he'd barely known, Angel, still haunted his dreams.

He had to slow down his exhalations until they were twice as long as his inhales, a technique he'd learned in therapy over the last year. He did this until his heart no longer felt like a racing hare. It helped to visualize himself calm. He dropped his shoulders. He couldn't close his eyes to imagine his body relaxing but he worked to forge that mental picture nonetheless and felt his focus sharpening.

No doubt Tombstone would smell his fear over the dead horse if Everett didn't get it well enough in hand.

He changed focus, shifting his view to the horse again. Through the binoculars, he saw no saddle or bags, but the description matched that of True Claymore's mount— the one he'd escaped with in the early hours of yesterday morning.

Everett lowered the binocs to take the radio from his belt. It was slippery in his hold. Mashing down the call button, he said quietly, "This is team three leader. Sheriff, do you copy?"

It took a moment for static to hiss, then he heard Kaya's voice. It steadied him. "Go ahead, team three."

"I've got a dead horse at the base of Mount Elder where it meets the river. Over."

Tombstone's yowling filled the radio silence before Kaya answered back. "Recently deceased?"

"Affirmative," he replied. "Tombstone got here first, but something's holding him up. He won't approach."

"Are you safe?"

He heard the thread of discord in her voice and lifted the radio to his mouth again. "I'm hiding out across the valley. He doesn't know I'm here."

"Hold your position," she told him. "I'll be there in twenty. Any sign of the suspect?"

"Negative," Everett said, searching the valley again. "If it is his horse, he took the saddle and bags."

"Copy. Everett?"

"Yeah?" he said, knowing this was an open channel.

"Shoot if you have to."

It sounded better than any profession of love he'd ever heard. "I'll see you in twenty, Sheriff. Over."

Everett secured the radio, checked his rifle and hunkered down to wait.

Tombstone's frenzied pacing stopped. He leaped from the ledge and down a series of boulders, head low, body tensed, picking up speed.

Everett braced himself as the cougar charged the corpse.

A shot rang out. Between the cliff walls, it was deafening. The lion doubled back, screaming its displeasure.

Another gunshot followed, then a third.

Tombstone retreated, disappearing in the bend of cliff walls and river rocks in full flight.

Everett stayed where he was, keeping his head down. He had another ten minutes before Kaya's arrival.

Someone was protecting the horse's body.

If it was indeed Claymore's horse…

Everett used the rifle's scope to comb every inch of the valley below.

He didn't spot the shooter. But he had no line of sight directly beneath his position where an outcropping offered a respite from the sun.

Cautiously, he straightened slowly to standing. He kept his rifle up, his finger near the trigger as he crept along the slope. He veered around the rockfall. Any loose rock would tumble and alert the shooter to his presence. On firmer ground, he made his way down.

The horse's eyes were locked in a vacant stare. They had gone cloudy. There was a gunshot wound on its crown. Everett scanned its legs and saw the break in the back left. He could smell the decay. With the sun beating down on it and the blood drying, he estimated the horse's time of death to have been sometime in the night.

The gunman's position was right underneath him. Everett inched forward, easing to ground level out of the cave's line of sight. He pressed his back to the mountain, gripping the rifle in hands that were steadier now that Tombstone had retreated. He swallowed once before calling out. "How's it going, Claymore?"

A pause. Then, "Goddamn it, Eaton."

"Toss out your weapon where I can see it," Everett advised. "Don't make me come in there. I want you to walk out. Nice and easy."

"That'd be a fine thing." True's voice was tight. "But I'm not walking anywhere. Goliath broke my damn leg when he fell on it."

Everett's brows lifted under his hatband. "What about Annette? Is she injured?"

"What are you talking about?" True barked. "Annette's not with me."

"Don't lie to me, True," Everett growled.

"I'm telling the truth. Last I saw her, she was screaming at me to man up, stay at the resort where she could protect me. Woman never understood anything. When you're licked, you're licked. That's what my daddy used to say. He left, too. When the Feds came to get him for tax evasion, he made his exodus. He disappeared on horseback. His mount wandered back to us a week later. Nobody ever found any sign of him. Authorities told me he was as good as dead, but he was as hard as iron by that point. Indestructible. He's living on some beach in Mexico to this day."

True was rambling. Everett's frown deepened. "Your weapon. Throw it out where I can see it."

"Ah, hell," True muttered. "What have I got to lose?"

Everett heard the rifle bolt as it unlocked. The cartridges clinked as True emptied the chamber. The slow repetition of the bolt clicking assured Everett that the man was checking the chamber to ensure it was empty. The gold cartridges flashed in the sunlight as he threw them onto the rocks of the riverbed where they bounced and laid still. The rifle followed with a clatter.

Everett eased away from the wall. "Show me your hands," he directed as he swung into the opening, muzzle forward.

True raised his palms obediently. They were empty.

Everett scanned him, kicking the rifle farther from the low opening of the cave. Everett bent over slightly and watched True wave insolently as he sagged against a boulder. His legs splayed in front of him. The left turned outward.

Everett narrowed his eyes. "You got yourself in a state."

"You don't say," True remarked.

"That there's a compound fracture," Everett said. "Must be in a lot of pain."

True's face was flushed like a beet. His breathing wasn't right. It was rapid and ragged. Still, he tilted his head and scanned Everett. "I thought you'd be happier."

"I'd have been happy to find you on your feet."

"You'd have preferred *The Good, the Bad and the Ugly* with me standing on one side of the street and you on the other," True said. He let out a wheezing laugh. "You and my old man have a lot in common. He used to tell me he shot a man in Reno. He said Johnny Cash wrote that song about him. 'Just to watch him die,' he would sing when he'd had too much."

"Why did you flee south?" Everett asked. "That was stupid."

"Was it?" True asked, squinting. "I thought everybody'd be looking in the other direction. State lands. Or farther. Jicarilla territory. Nobody'd expect me to go near that mountain over there."

Everett knew what mountain he was talking about. "Did you kill the boy and those women?"

"You'd like that, wouldn't you?"

"I'd like to see you drawn and quartered after what those men did to Paloma and Eaton House," Everett told him.

"Hey, at least my guys let you and the sheriff finish first," True said. "I wouldn't have been so generous. They're the superstitious sort—assume it's bad luck to interrupt a man while he's laying his pipe."

The muscles in Everett's jaw ground against bone. He saw the horse's saddle propped behind True. He saw the saddlebags. Despite the agony the mayor was in, if True kept running his mouth, Everett was liable to get trigger-happy.

Where are you, Kaya?

"You want to kill me," True guessed. "Take your shot."

Everett found his finger inside the trigger guard. He pressed his lips together. "I won't be the one who puts you out of your misery," he muttered through his teeth.

"Don't be washed up like your old man," True barked at him. "Come on, Eaton. Shoot me!"

"No," Everett barked back. An eye for an eye was fine.

He believed in such things. But before True had been his enemy, he'd been Kaya's.

He wouldn't be the one to kill Kaya's justice. He couldn't.

The sounds of horses reached his ears. He looked around and saw Ghost slowing to cross the river. He and Kaya were leading Crazy Alice on a lead rope.

"Did you lose this?" she called as the horses' legs splashed across the Wapusa.

"I got him," Everett said and watched her shoulders go high.

Kaya nickered to Ghost, bringing him to a stop on the shore. She dismounted. "Tombstone?"

"He ran off," Everett told her. "I got *him*."

She closed the distance. Peering into the cave, she stilled.

True grimaced at her. "Howdy, Sheriff."

She didn't breathe. Everett fought the urge to touch her. "What do you want to do?"

Her gaze crawled back to his. "You didn't kill him."

He ignored the surprise.

Her lips seamed and for a brief flash her dark eyes deepened.

He eyed her mouth. "He's yours."

She blinked several times. "I need to call the chopper. He needs treatment. I have a first aid kit on my saddle…"

He lowered the rifle. "I'll get it."

She grabbed him as he started moving. "Everett," she whispered. When he stopped, she said, "Thank you."

"Later," he promised then moved off to retrieve her kit.

Chapter 17

With True Claymore in the hospital, Rutland and Kaya were unable to question him until he was out of sedation.

Annette Claymore hadn't been seen in over twenty-four hours. Part of her wardrobe had been removed from the master suite closet at The RC Resort. Her suitcase was missing as well as much of her jewelry.

Other than several thousand dollars in cash, they hadn't found the remaining contents of the office safe on True Claymore or in his saddlebags. Their housekeeper had reported that she had seen stacks of cash in the safe while cleaning.

Annette had taken her own exodus. Hers didn't have anything to do with Western glory, like True's. Kaya had a feeling her idea of escape was far more comfortable than riding off into the sunset.

"She doesn't have family in Fuego," Kaya explained to Rutland as she parked in front of Huck Claymore's house. "She's from Colorado and still has family there. But she's smart. She knows better than to go to the first place any investigator would look."

"If that tracks," Rutland said as they alighted from her sheriff's vehicle, "why would she come here?"

"She and Huck are close, from what I understand," Kaya

said, leading the way to the pretty two-story house on Fourth Street where the reverend had resided since taking up the position in the church two blocks away. "He may know something."

Rutland knocked over a small, stone statuette of a praying angel on her knees. He cursed and stopped to right it, then continued to the door.

Kaya's knees locked. All she could see was the angel and the others in the garden of various sizes and expressions on their knees.

On her knees.

Sawni had died on her knees. So had Bethany. Miller Higgins, too, and the oldest woman who had yet to be identified.

She fought a shiver. Hearing Rutland's knock on the door, she moved to his side.

"You all right, Sheriff?" Rutland asked, brows gathered together.

"Fine," she said with a shake of her head. "Just…odd feeling, is all."

The door opened before he could respond. Huck Claymore appeared, a look of vague surprise on his face. "Sheriff Altaha," he greeted, buttoning the cuff of his plain, white collared shirt. It was wrinkled around the shoulders, Kaya noticed. She'd never seen him anything but perfectly pressed. Come to think of it, she'd never seen him outside his robes or his pressed suit. The shirt collar was open at his throat, as if he'd just started dressing. It was five o'clock in the afternoon. "What can I do for you?"

"I'm sorry to bother you, reverend," Kaya said evenly. "I'm sure you've heard about your brother."

He nodded quickly. "Yes. Most unfortunate."

"Unfortunate that he's injured?" Rutland questioned. "Or unfortunate that he was found?"

The reverend peered at him innocently. "Unfortunate that he felt it necessary to flee in the first place instead of taking responsibility for his crimes. I was just changing so that I could visit him at the hospital. My brother may be misguided. But even misguided men need counsel."

Kaya lifted her chin. "Of course. We won't take up too much of your time. You've heard also, I assume, that your sister-in-law, Annette, is still missing."

He stepped out of the house, closing the door behind him. Bowing his head, he gave a nod. "I have heard that, yes, and I'm concerned about her. Greatly concerned."

"Why?" Rutland asked. "By all accounts, it appears that she, too, tried to flee."

"Annette had nothing to do with what happened at Eaton House. Those were my brother's men. They answer to him, not her."

"Then why would she leave?" Rutland wanted to know.

"Perhaps she feared my brother," Huck weighed. "Perhaps he thinks she knows too much about his criminal affairs and she felt she had no choice but to disappear."

"Do you know something about his criminal history that we don't, reverend?" Rutland pressed.

Huck shook his head. "The only thing I have, Agent Rutland, are my suspicions."

"Can you tell us more about those?" Kaya asked.

He glanced over their heads at the street. There were children playing on the sidewalk, a couple walking a dog and several neighbors sitting on porches or puttering around their gardens. "Now isn't the time or place. My brother's expecting me."

"Has your brother ever mentioned the bodies on the mountain?" Rutland asked.

Huck blanched. His lips trembled slightly before he pressed them together. "I don't think so."

"May we search the premises?" Rutland asked, taking a step forward, crowding Huck into his own door.

"Why would you need to search my house?" Huck asked, holding his ground. He was a big man, nearly a head taller than Rutland.

"You and your sister-in-law have a close relationship," Rutland explained. "It seems she may have confided in you. You fear for her safety. It isn't a stretch to assume that you are concerned enough—that you care enough— to let her hide out here from her husband, if necessary."

"But I told you I haven't seen her." Huck looked to Kaya for help. "Sheriff, this is superfluous."

Kaya thought about it. *He closed the door when he came out onto the porch.* Her pulse quickened. Rutland was right. "It'll only take a moment, reverend. Then we'll be out of your hair."

Disappointment tracked across his strong features. His jaw firmed. He shook his head. "I'm sorry. Without a warrant, I cannot let you in. I'm well within my rights to say so."

Kaya took a beat, then nodded. "You are."

"We'll be back with that warrant," Rutland told him as he stepped back slowly. "Have a nice evening."

She waited until they were back inside the car. "He's hiding something."

Rutland buckled his seat belt. "I'd bet my salary Annette Claymore is inside that house."

"If he's that concerned about her safety," Kaya said, pulling away from the curb, "he'll have her moved before a warrant is secure." She waited until she'd safely steered around a clutch of boys dribbling and passing a basketball to one another on the street before she smacked the steering wheel with the heel of her hand. "He knows something about what happened on Ol' Whalebones. I knew there was a connection to the murders and the Claymores."

"And I told you to drop it." Rutland's hand curled into a fist as he brought it to his mouth. "I was wrong." He met her gaze as she pulled up to the stop sign. "I'm sorry, Kaya."

She gave a slight nod. "I'll need to call the judge—the same one that got us the warrant for True's arrest."

"Getting a warrant for a small-town mayor is one thing," Rutland weighed. "Getting one for a minister may be more difficult. Say we find her. We need to hold her. She either fears for her life in regard to her husband or…"

"Or she's hiding because she has information or she had some part in his wrongdoing," she finished. "We have to take Annette into either protective or police custody before she leaves New Mexico."

Everett sat at Paloma's bedside. She was sleeping soundly, but he couldn't unsee the bandage wrapped around her head or what the wound had looked like before EMTs had arrived at Eaton Edge the night of the attack.

She looked white against the sheets. His hand held the lower half of his face as he watched the regular peaks and valleys of her vitals on the screen on the far side of the bed.

Someone touched his shoulder. He looked around to see Luella. Her smile wavered, but she gave it nonetheless. She gave so few smiles that he knew the gesture was heartfelt.

Coming to his feet, he faced her. "She's sleeping. The

doctor says she can go home tomorrow. She's starting to give orders. I suspect they're eager to see the back of her."

"Her vitals are strong. She's doing well. The doctor's right to let her go home and rest where she's more comfortable."

Luella had been a trauma nurse at this hospital before false rumors of her wrongdoing had led to her firing. Everett knew they'd offered the job back to her after her exoneration at the start of the year, but she'd refused. She and Eveline had started Ollero Creek Rescue, instead.

He struggled to trust those in the medical profession and always had, but he trusted her to the bone. "So you're taking the late shift?"

"Yes," she said. "There's something you should know. Ellis told me not to tell you, but that feels wrong."

"What?" he asked, tensing automatically.

She lowered her voice. "True Claymore is being held on the floor beneath this one. He's under heavy guard but is no longer sedated and may even be transferred sometime tomorrow."

Everett took a long breath in through the nose. He rolled his shoulders.

"You can't go near him," she told him in no uncertain terms. "But I felt you had a right to know."

He nodded, then lifted his hand to her shoulder and squeezed. He looked at Paloma. "Take care of her 'til I get back."

"You know I will," she assured him. "But I can handle the morning's shift, too. If you're not going to work, you should see the girls. Have breakfast with them and Ellis. It'll be good for all of you."

He smiled. "Aside from Isla and Ingrid, you're the best

thing that ever happened to my brother. You're good for his girls, too. You're good for all of us."

Her eyes widened. "That may be the nicest thing you've ever said—to anyone."

He shifted from one foot to the other, uncomfortable. "I guess weddings make me sentimental. I'll get over it."

"I don't think it's the wedding that's changed you," she considered.

"Hmm," he muttered when he saw the knowing look on her face. "Would you be willing to take the fall for some black panties Paloma found in the upstairs ficus?"

"That depends," she considered. "What'll you owe me for it?"

He laughed, then quieted himself quickly when Paloma stirred. "Don't marry my brother. You're too good for him."

"It's too late for me," she told him. "And, from what I hear, maybe somebody else I know, too."

He thought of Kaya and released a heavy breath. "I'll get back to you on that, Lu."

"Everett?" she asked as he retreated. When he turned back, she added, "You told me not to wait too long to tell Ellis what I wanted. Don't wait too long to tell Kaya, either."

"I don't know what she wants," he admitted. It sounded plaintive and he regretted it instantly.

"Still," she cautioned, "take it from someone who knows. Life doesn't wait. And these things…they slip away if you're not careful."

He stared back at her mutely before he shifted toward the door again and left.

Kaya stepped off the elevator on the second floor of Fuego County Hospital. She nodded to the guard posted there. "Officer Pettry."

"Sheriff," the young cop returned.

"Everything okay here?" she asked.

"Quiet," he replied. "No activity other than Mr. Eaton arriving about half an hour ago."

"Eaton," she parroted. "Which one?"

"The older one," he said.

Her shoes slapped against the linoleum floor in rapid succession as she rounded the corner to the corridor where Claymore's recovery room was located. She spotted the second officer, Logan, on the door and Everett leaning against the opposite whitewashed wall. As she closed in, Logan glanced over. At her questioning brow, he nodded slightly to show nothing was amiss.

Breathing a little easier, Kaya slowed. "Officer Logan," she said and watched Everett flinch out of the corner of her eye. "Anything to report?"

"Everything's good here, Sheriff Altaha," Logan replied diligently. "Though I hear the mayor's in a good deal of pain."

"Thank you for taking the late shift," she told him before pivoting to face the man against the wall. At the sight of his heavy eyes, she tilted her head. "Everett. What are you doing here?"

He glanced over her head at Logan. His jaw hardened a bit before his eyes returned to her face, weary. "I was visiting Paloma."

"Did you get lost?" she asked, letting amusement ease the question.

Perhaps he was too tired because emotions filed across the windows of his eyes and her heart stumbled in reaction. When his mouth remained stubbornly closed, she turned back to Logan. "Five minute break?" she asked. "I can man the door."

Logan nodded. "Thank you, sir."

She waited until he'd rounded the corner and she and Everett were by themselves in the corridor. "What's wrong, cattle baron?" she asked.

He took a breath to gather himself, unable to meet her eye now. "Since I took over the Edge last summer, I've nearly lost my sister to a madman. We've had a holdup at headquarters. One sheriff turned against us. We've found four bodies on the mountain. My men have been investigated and scrutinized, I've been suspected of murder, my brother-in-law was booked for it, two gunmen attacked Eaton House and the woman I'd call Mom if she'd let me is in the hospital. It hasn't been a year, and that's what's happened on my watch."

Kaya's lips parted as she watched the agony bleed through everything else. She shook her head quickly. "There's been a wedding at Eaton House. An incredible wedding. And there will be another soon. Two new beginnings. Eveline and Wolfe will start a family before the end of the year, from what I'm told. And through all of that, your family and your men haven't gone anywhere. They're more loyal to you than ever. Every single one of them vouched for you when Rutland investigated. Did you know that? And Paloma's going to be okay, Everett. She's okay. You are not responsible for all the negative things that have happened."

"I'm head of the family," he stated. "I'm chief of operations. Of course it's my responsibility."

"You carry too much on yourself," she accused. "Your father did that, too. He bore too much and died too soon. And don't you dare try to tell me one had nothing to do with the other."

Everett didn't say anything. His eyes circled her face instead, thoughtful even if his mouth was grim.

She couldn't help herself. She touched him while they were alone in the corridor, just them two. Sliding her hands from his elbows to his shoulders, she used her thumbs to massage where tension had sunk down deep. His chest lifted with his chin and his dark eyelashes closed halfway. His brow knitted and she could see everything he carried—every burden and worry.

She shook her head. "What is it you're afraid of?"

It took him a moment to answer. His eyes had closed completely. "I can't lose anyone else. I don't have what it takes."

A strong man admitting he wasn't strong enough was a powerful thing. She pulled him into her embrace, wrapping him tight until his face was in her hair, his front pressed to hers and her hands spread across the long, warm line of his back. "It's okay," she whispered, as compelled by the embrace as she was. With his arms circling her waist and the enduring chord of strength humming beneath his skin, she felt small and soft but also like she could take on ten men.

Together, they could take on the world. The certainty was scary and thrilling. It called to the person she was underneath the sheriff's uniform—the person he'd recognized from the moment all this had started between them.

She wavered, letting her palms come up to meet his shoulders again. "I have to question True now that he's awake."

He turned his face away. "I've got to get back."

She let him back away and hated the distance. What she wouldn't give to take him home to her own bed. "You should get some rest before work. There's still time before dawn."

"I'll keep, sweetheart," he said as he headed down the corridor, his hat brim low.

She watched him go and felt her brows arch. *Take care of yourself, cattle baron. Someone loves you.*

If she weren't such a coward, she'd shout it at his back. She'd known she loved him when she'd found True Claymore alive. Everett had wanted revenge. He believed in Old Western justice. He'd proved that many times. The mayor had Paloma's blood on his hands and Everett had needed vendetta for it.

But he'd handed True over to her, unharmed—a gift she'd never forget.

Pushing through the door to Claymore's room, she gauged the man's condition. His leg was bound in a heavy cast. He'd come out of surgery with no complications though his road to recovery wouldn't be short or easy.

How the mighty do fall, she mused at the sight of his baby blue hospital johnny and the crepey skin under his eyes that made him look fragile. His eyes lit on her, alive with pain. "You here to take me to jail?" When she approached the bed wordlessly and pulled up a chair to sit, he reached for the call button. "Hang on. If you're going to interrogate me, I'm going to need another shot of morphine."

"I've got something to say," she told him. "There's no question you're going to jail. You ordered the hit on Eaton House, and we've got the evidence to back that up. But it was sloppy. In the years that I've known you, I've never known you to be sloppy."

He spread his hands as he lifted them from the bedcovers. "What can I say? I finally snapped."

"Why?" she asked pointedly. "It wasn't because Everett Eaton dented your fender. The attacks are disproportionate. Something bigger pushed you to order your men to attack Eaton House. What was it?"

"I need my wife."

"Your wife's missing," she said, her voice reaching for the ceiling now. "Your brother claims it's because she's hiding out from you."

True frowned. "Huck told you that?"

She waited, watching.

True shook his head. "Annette. She's never been afraid of me. Hell, the only person any of us has ever been afraid of was…"

When he trailed off, she had to stop herself from leaning forward. "Yes?"

He looked toward the window. The blinds were shut tight. He shook his head again. "Annette's not afraid of me. I've never done anything to make her afraid."

"But someone else has," she guessed. "Who?"

True's lips thinned, and his eyes wavered with pain or guilt or grief. It was difficult to tell. "You think I killed those women and that boy. The ones on the mountain. You think I'm capable."

She found that she could be truthful. "I do."

"Why?" he asked, his face turning back to hers. "What have I done, Sheriff, to make you believe I'm the monster?"

She needed to break him. And she'd held out for so long. She could hardly breathe as she muttered, "Because even you shouldn't mess around with 'little rez girls.'"

He stared for a full minute. She saw the realization hit. Then the implications. His gaze raced over her, as if seeing her for the first time.

She didn't look away. It was satisfying—so satisfying—when she saw the fear sink in. He was afraid of her, of what she'd experienced. What she knew and had always known about him. "Tell me," she demanded. "Tell me why you had Sawni Mescal killed. I'd like to know that first. Then you can tell me about the others."

Air hissed through his teeth as he braced them shut. He closed his eyes. "I didn't kill her. I didn't kill any of them."

"Not by your hand," she said. "But you gave the order."

"No," he said, shaking his head frantically now.

"True." Kaya stood up. She gripped the raised railing of the bed that caged him in. "Annette's not here for you to hide behind. There's no hiding. Not anymore. You're going to be booked. If you tell me how it all went down—if you tell me the truth—the judge will soften the sentence. You know that."

"I know that!" he shouted. "Damn it, you don't think I know that? But I'm trying to tell you! I didn't kill them! I wasn't the one who gave the order!"

She narrowed her eyes. "If it wasn't you, then who did?"

He took a fortifying breath. "For you to know that, you have to know who my father was and what he did."

"Your father's been dead a long time, True. You can't hide behind him, either."

"My father died the same year Bethany Merchant did," he added. "He was alive for her death and the first's."

"Who was she?" Kaya asked, needing the identity of the first woman. "Who was the first victim?"

"My stepmother." He seemed to wrench the truth out of himself. "Or, the woman who was going to be my stepmother. She and my father were engaged. Her name was Melissa Beaton. She was twenty-two years younger than him."

"He had his fiancée killed?" Kaya asked. "Why?"

"I didn't know how or why until later. I didn't know until Huck told me…"

"Huck knew?"

He didn't so much look at her as through her. "Of course Huck knew. He was the one who did it—who my father ordered to kill her."

Kaya's mouth gaped. She closed it. "You're saying your brother, the reverend, killed the first victim, Melissa Beaton?"

"I'm saying," True said, rounding the words out slowly, "that you found those four bodies on the mountain because Huck killed them there. Because my father programmed him to do so."

Chapter 18

Programmed?

Kaya tried to make sense of what True was saying and wondered if he was speaking nonsense. "Your father couldn't have ordered Huck to kill all four of them. He was dead before Sawni Mescal worked at The RC Resort. Long before Miller Higgins went hiking on Ol' Whalebones."

"My father didn't fight in Vietnam. Do you know what he did instead, Sheriff?" True asked.

"No."

"He was part of a training initiative for special forces," he said. "It was experimental. The theory was that a man could be trained to kill on command. Like Pavlov. If a dog can be programmed to salivate at the sound of a bell, then a man can be trained to execute a command—no matter how ruthless—at the sound of a 'kill word,' as he called it. After the war was lost, he was sent home to New Mexico. He had orders never to talk about or reveal what he did before he got there. He disobeyed orders. Not only that, he kept the program going. He knew Fuego County was rough country. 'Lawless,' as he used to say. He needed a soldier to do his bidding. Huck was born first. If he hadn't been, it would have been me. From the time he could walk, my father started programming him to kill."

The information was hard to take in. Kaya stepped back from the bed and moved away to roam the section of floor between the door and the window. She roved back to the foot of the bed and stopped. "So your father gave Huck the word to kill Melissa Beaton."

"Yes," True said, unable to meet her eye.

"How old was Huck when this happened?"

True's bottom lip shook once, then stopped. "Twelve. Just twelve."

"Why would your father want Melissa killed?" Kaya wondered.

"He said it was because she strayed," True revealed. "I always thought it was because he needed to see if his programming had worked. It's not like he loved her or needed her. My father wasn't motivated by those things. He was motivated by anger and greed. Growing up at RC was like the worst episode of *Survivor* you've ever seen. He made sure I knew what he could make Huck do. It didn't matter how much my brother loved me. If my father gave the word, Huck would kill me—without even thinking, he'd kill me. I couldn't run away and I sure as hell couldn't tell anyone."

"Why is there no record of this?" she asked. "Someone must've noticed a woman was missing from your ranch."

"People who worked there looked the other way," he revealed. "My father bought their silence."

"She didn't have family?" she asked. "Friends? Someone who would have asked questions when she disappeared?"

"She was a stripper from San Antonio. We thought somebody might come looking for her. Nobody ever showed up."

"What about Bethany Merchant?" Kaya asked. "And why did so much time go by between the killings?"

"Huck got away," True said. "Killing Melissa destroyed him. He left school, started drinking. Then he ran off and got a job as a ranch hand somewhere in East Texas."

"Why did he come back?" Kaya asked.

"My father's men found him," True explained. "They dragged him back. He paid for it. Believe me. My father made him pay. He took his pound of flesh. He made Huck bleed."

A shiver went up Kaya's spine. She went to the window again. "This was when?"

"About six months before Bethany Merchant turned up missing," True said grimly.

"Why did your father order Huck to kill Bethany?" she asked. "She was just a girl."

"She wasn't just a girl," True said resentfully. "That son of a bitch made Huck kill her because I loved her. Because I got her pregnant."

When Kaya stared, True nodded. "You know I'm telling the truth now, don't you? The ME would have told you she was a couple months pregnant when she died. The baby was mine. She was hung up on Everett Eaton, but I loved her. I would have gone anywhere with her if she'd have asked me."

"She didn't." Kaya put the pieces together. "She asked him."

"She asked Eaton, and it shattered my heart," True said. "She cornered him at the rodeo because she wanted to meet him at the motel that night she disappeared. She was going to tell him there—that she was pregnant, that the baby was his and he was trapped. He would've had to go east with her to college the way she wanted him to. But Huck met her at the motel instead. My father found out about the baby. After she was gone and I saw how broken Huck was again, I knew he'd given the order. She died because he couldn't abide his line being plagued by the potential of a bastard."

Kaya didn't know if she could hear any more. But she had to. She had to know everything. "Legal records show the first land dispute between your family and the Eatons was around this time," she noted.

"The lines between the RC and Eaton Edge are fuzzy," he explained, "at least when you're out there in the mountains. My father thought the mountain was on our side. After Bethany died, he realized he was wrong. He didn't like lawyers, but he hired one to file a claim before his death."

"Sawni Mescal." She forced the name out. "I need to know why Sawni Mescal was killed. If your father was dead, who was controlling Huck if not you?"

At this point, True raised a hand to his brow. He lowered his head, looking broken himself.

"True," she said gently. He may have kept his family's secrets. But it had haunted him every bit as much as Sawni's disappearance had haunted her. "Please."

He sniffed and lifted his head again. His face had turned red. The words quavered slightly when he spoke again. "I, uh… I met Annette, at college. She was prelaw, from a good family. I didn't want to bring her home. I didn't want her to know what…who I came from. But Dad was dead and I thought maybe everything died with him. Everything but Huck. So I took her home. And she and Huck… They became close. Closer than I expected. I didn't know he'd told her. Not until after the rez girl… She said her name was Kaya."

"You know her name." The response was punchy, but she was no longer in control. She was beyond it.

"Sawni Mescal worked for us for a while without incident," True said. "It was summertime. That's why we needed the extra help. Annette and I had a few months off school and her, me and Huck... We spent it on the ranch. We talked about what it was, what it could be. For the first time, I saw it as something to be redeemed. Something that Huck and I could be proud of. Together, we could make the RC something special. Annette and I even talked about getting married, which thrilled me to pieces. I thought if she and I got married, Huck and I could start over. We could forget everything that happened before—just sweep it under the rug and start clean. But then Annette started to think something was off about Sawni."

"What exactly?"

"Annette thought Sawni wanted Huck," True said. "The girl and Huck were friendly. I didn't see anything deeper than that. There was an age difference, and Huck was friendly with everyone. The girl kept to herself, though, and didn't respond much to Annette's questioning. Annette felt protective of Huck. She seemed jealous, even. I tried not to dwell on it. If she was jealous, it was because she loved him as much or more than she loved me, and after everything that happened with Bethany and Everett Eaton, I couldn't let my mind go there. There were too many ghosts. So I let it be. For weeks. And her hatred toward Sawni festered and whatever she felt for Huck... She became *possessive*. I didn't know until after the girl disappeared and everyone started looking for her that Huck had told Annette everything—about our father, about him, Melissa and Bethany. And she was angry enough...obsessed enough...to use my father's kill code—the one Huck had trusted her with—to snuff Sawni out. Like she was nothing. Dust in the frickin' wind."

Kaya breathed through her nose. Her eyes burned. "So you *married her*, True?"

True turned his eyes down to the hands twisted in his lap. "She knew our secrets. There was no getting out of it at that point. And once she saw how much it destroyed Huck again, she was sorry. She used the trust fund from her parents to send him to a specialist. Someone we could trust. She paid for his therapy. She paid for him to go to some monastery in California where you're forbidden to speak. It was supposed to be healing and he did heal, somewhat.

"When he was done there, he wanted to go to seminary school. He wanted his slate wiped clean. He wanted to be cleansed. The only way he felt he could do that was to become a shepherd of God. So she paid his way. Anything he needed, she sponsored him—on one condition. If he became a minister, he had to return to Fuego. After everything, she felt we had to keep an eye on him. If he'd told her everything, he'd tell anyone else he felt close to. He could have married, Sheriff. Started a family. Started over, finally. But Annette... She couldn't let that happen. If he loved her enough to spill his guts, he'd do it all again for another woman."

"Who kept Sawni's diary and why?" she asked.

"That was Annette. I told her it was foolhardy. Dad burned everything of Melissa's. He didn't take anything from Bethany, either, when she died. He didn't believe in leaving traces. Like I said, though, Annette was obsessed with the Mescal girl. She kept everything in the girl's bag."

"Was it her, too, who turned it in?" Kaya asked.

"Yes," True answered. "She had a row with Huck about it. She showed us the pages she'd torn out—the ones that mentioned her and Huck and me. It was the only thing belonging to Sawni she ever burned."

"What was the point in turning in the diary to begin with?" Kaya asked.

"She thought you and the FBI were sniffing too close in our direction. She got paranoid. She knew Wolfe was mentioned in the pages she left in the diary. She thought you'd start looking his way instead. It worked, for a time."

Kaya spread her feet apart and wrapped her arms around herself. "Tell me about Miller Higgins."

"Higgins was an accident," True said regrettably. "Despite Annette's warnings, Huck started spending time with a woman he met in Taos. They became close. Too close, to Annette's thinking. When he wouldn't listen to her and let the woman go, she took him to the mountain as a reminder why he couldn't be with anyone. They got into a heated argument. Higgins heard everything. Too much. Annette had Huck catch him..."

"She gave the kill order again," Kaya said with an unbelieving shake of her head.

"It was too much," True moaned. "And then the bodies were found, and I knew if any of the three of us made a mistake...a single mistake...you'd know. The Feds arrived and we started to scramble. I started to unravel. Huck talked about leaving, disappearing again, taking the Taos woman with him. Annette wouldn't let him go. I couldn't ignore how much it all hurt—how much she'd come to love him when it was supposed to be me. If she was going to be obsessed with anyone, it should've been me. All my spite and anger came to a head when Eaton did what he did at the festival. Finally, I had somebody I could pin all my frustrations on without hurting anyone I loved."

"If you hadn't ordered the hit," Kaya told him, "you'd still be at The RC Resort. And your secrets would still be yours."

True shook his head. "And none of us... We'd never be free. We'd carry it on our backs for the rest of our lives. To hell with what my wife wants anymore. I can't live like this anymore. And my brother can't, either. His spirit has been traded away by others for too long. If I want him to remain the man he is—the one he should've been—I can't let this go on. If I've got to do time to save him, you can be damn sure I can live with that. My father's sins—his ghost—have been alive in this world too long."

"I need to find Annette," Kaya said. "Agent Rutland and I think she is—or was—hiding out at Huck's house. Do you think that's where she would have gone?"

He hesitated. Then he passed his hand under his nose. "She'd have gone there. But enough time's passed that she's probably up on the mountain or on her way there now."

"The mountain," Kaya repeated. "Whalebones?"

He nodded. "That's where she told me to hide it before I split town. She left me enough to get to Mexico and told me to hide the rest."

"Hide what, True?" she pressed.

"The money," he said. "My father's money. Everything the Feds came looking for when he took his exodus. We saved it for the day we'd need it to do the same. I hid her and Huck's cut on the mountain where the bodies were found, as she told me. If that damned cougar hadn't startled us, my horse wouldn't have broken his leg or mine. Secrets would still be secrets. We would've gotten away with everything. Everything except our souls."

Chapter 19

Everett had Huck Claymore in his sights. The reverend had no idea. Still, Everett kept his finger outside the trigger guard as he followed Huck and Annette's progress on the trailhead of Ol' Whalebones.

As soon as Everett had returned to Eaton House from the hospital in the early hours before dawn, Kaya had called. She was mobilizing the mounted search again. There would be another manhunt—this time for True Claymore's brother and wife. And the most likely place they would be found was the mountain.

The other members of the search party would take time to get into position, but Everett, Ellis and their men were closest.

If you find them, I need you not to engage. Call in your coordinates and wait.

Waiting didn't sit well knowing he was looking at the man who'd killed four people and the woman who had ordered him to do so.

If Annette's with him, Huck Claymore is expected to be armed and extremely dangerous. Do not engage, Everett.

Everett didn't understand Annette's hold on the reverend. But he had understood the urgency in Kaya's voice—the fear behind it.

Something about these two had her spooked. His prom-

ise to Kaya was the only thing tethering him from stopping them before they reached the summit. Once they did,
they would be out of Everett's line of sight.

"Should we follow them?" Javier asked at his right shoulder.

Ellis, on Everett's left, made a discouraging noise. "Orders are we hang back."

"We'll lose them on the ridge," Javier reasoned. "We
could find another position…"

"Sheriff Altaha told us not to approach," Ellis told him.
"Right?"

Everett frowned. Annette and Huck were gaining ground
too quickly.

"Everett?"

Everett lifted his head, staring across the muzzle into
the distance. "You two wait here. I need to get closer."

Ellis gripped him. "What?"

"If they escape on my watch, I'm the one who has to
live with it."

"What do I tell her when she gets here?" Ellis asked,
not having to say her name for Everett to know who he
spoke of.

"She knows I'm a man of my word," Everett returned
before he left the small circle of boulders where the trio
had been hiding. "Tell her I've got her back."

Kaya couldn't hail Everett on the radio. She didn't enjoy
not knowing where he was or what he was planning to do.

He told me to tell you he's got your back, Ellis had said
when she'd located him and Javier in the canyon below.

She and Rutland picked their way over rocks as they approached the place True Claymore had described—close
to where the four victims had been found over the edge of

the cliff. Root and Wyatt weren't far behind. She raised her hand when she heard amplified voices on the wind. Her team slowed. No one had eyes on Huck or Annette anymore. In the canyon below, Ellis and Javier had lost sight of them close to a half hour ago.

"That's Annette," she muttered to Rutland, recognizing the voice if not the harsh tone reverberating off the rocks around them. She glanced back at Root and Wyatt. "Silence your radios. We don't want to alert them."

They obeyed and Kaya reached down to twist the dial on the radio on her belt, muting it.

Rutland leaned toward her. "If they see us coming, you realize Annette could go ahead with the kill code."

"Huck is used to enacting it against a single person," she said. "He never shoots them on the spot. He gets them into position, executes them all with the same shot to the back of the head. He's never faced anyone that was trained in combat, much less four. Root and Wyatt approach from the north, us to the south. Unless you'd rather hang back."

He shook his head, his standard issue already braced between his hands. "I'm with you, Sheriff."

She nodded, then gave the motion for the four of them to spread out.

Everett lay belly-down on the canyon wall, barely breathing. The wind was against him. Any shot he took, he would have to take it into account.

He was alone across the wide gap between the top of the canyon and Ol' Whalebones. The river ran between, its rush audible even at this height. He could see the ledge where Huck and Annette had hidden the bodies. He could see the pair arguing on the cliff edge above it.

His finger tensed near the trigger when he saw Kaya

creeping toward them from the south, Rutland closing on her six.

The shovel in Huck's hand waved as he gestured wildly. There was a mound of dirt at his feet. Annette didn't cower. She grabbed him by the shirt, pushing, inching him back toward the ledge.

Kaya's crouching walk quickened, her feet moving swiftly across the ground, her pistol in a two-handed hold. Rutland followed. When she stood, the wind carried her terse command to *freeze*. Annette pivoted. Huck dropped the shovel. Everything inside Everett did freeze as he watched it tumble end over end over the cliff's edge and fell in a silent arc to the water below.

Kaya watched Root and Wyatt crowd Annette and Huck from the north side. She was aware of the wind teasing her hair and the brim of her hat. She was more aware of the long plunge down the cliff wall to her left. She felt more than heard Rutland behind her. Her eyes moved over Huck's face, trying to gauge his expression.

The debate between him and Annette had reached screaming pitch by the time Kaya had given the order. She'd seen Annette nearly shove Huck off the cliff's edge and had decided to move in.

"Sheriff Altaha," Annette said. Flushed, she was not the polished mayor's wife people in Fuego knew her to be. She swallowed, reaching down to straighten the sand-colored vest she wore over her front. "This is a surprise."

"Show us your hands!" Rutland shouted when Huck's began to reach around his back.

Kaya stiffened even as Huck's hand lifted into the air along with the other. He looked miserable, she thought briefly. He stepped a hair closer to Annette, his toes inching over the edge of the hole they had dug. "You're both under arrest."

"For what?" Annette challenged.

"Huck for the murders of Melissa Beaton, Bethany Merchant, Sawni Mescal and Miller Higgins," Kaya informed her. "You'll be charged in the deaths of Mescal and Higgins."

Annette's eyes widened. "Those are serious charges, Sheriff. Are you sure you have the right people?"

"I have your husband True Claymore's detailed statement," Kaya replied and saw Huck waver like a blade of grass over his feet.

"True says we did this?" Annette laughed. "That's ridiculous. He'll say anything at this point to get himself out of trouble. He's accustomed to talking his way out of sticky situations."

"A search and seizure of Huck's residence turned over Miller Higgins's cell phone. If True's guilty, then what are you two doing at the murder scene? Why are the horses we found at the foot of the mountain packed with a week's worth of rations?"

Annette's mouth fumbled.

Kaya lowered her chin. "Come forward quietly so that we can bring you both in for questioning. Resisting arrest won't work well for you if you're innocent. You're a criminal attorney, Annette. You know this."

Huck's feet shuffled forward, but Annette's arm snapped up to block him. "No."

"Annette." His fingers closed around her wrist in a gentle bracelet. "It's over."

"No!" she shouted. "Not like this! I will *not* see you rot in prison for this!"

"You won't see it," he assured her. His front buffered against her back and his other hand came up to meet the line of her shoulders. "I'm tired, Annette. I can't do this anymore."

Her gaze fused to his. "You can't live with me anymore, Huck? Is that what you mean?"

His shoulders lifted and his expression grew helpless. When he lowered them, his posture caved. "I'm sorry," he whispered.

Annette nodded slowly, jaw flexing. "You won't have to." In a lightning move, she reached around his waist.

"Don't!" Kaya yelled when Annette's grip closed over the butt of Huck's gun. She pushed herself forward. "Hold it!"

Annette threw her shoulder into Huck's chest.

His heel caught on the mound of earth. His hands windmilled as he tipped over the ledge and fell into the open air.

Annette whirled, her gun hand trained on Kaya. "Tell them to get back!" she cried, pointing at the deputies behind her. "Tell them or I'll shoot!"

Kaya lifted her chin to Wyatt. He and Root shuffled backward. "Any chance you had of talking yourself out of murder charges is gone. You realize that, don't you?"

"Not if you let me go," Annette told her.

"You pushed him off the cliff." Kaya shook her head. "Why did you have to kill him?"

"I gave him the easy way out," Annette stated. "He couldn't have sat in a cell for the rest of his life thinking about all the things he's done. He's not built for that. Yeah, he killed those people. But he isn't a killer. He never would've hurt anyone—"

"If not for his father," Kaya finished. "If not for you."

"This doesn't have to end badly," Annette argued. "Huck's gone. He can't hurt anyone anymore. Just back off and stay back and you'll never see me again. I'll leave what's in that hole for all of you."

Kaya's eyes jumped from Annette's right eye to her left and back. "I can't do that."

Annette tilted her head slightly. The sheen over her eyes caught the light. Kaya saw the grief and guilt wash over her about what she had done to Huck.

Kaya lifted one hand from her weapon to motion Rutland back.

"No!" he hissed.

"Just do it," she shot back before repositioning her hands on the Glock when the rocks under Rutland's feet crunched under his careful retreat.

"That's typical," Annette muttered. "My husband disappointed me. Even Huck disappointed me in the end. Now you. I expected more of Fuego's first woman sheriff."

Kaya wasn't going to be like the reverend. She wasn't going to apologize. "I don't think Huck disappointed you. I think he did everything you ever told him to."

Annette's voice broke. "Except run away with me."

"He has run," Kaya told him. "In the past, he ran to get away from all of this. But it followed him. He knew if he ran again, he'd never be free of it. And neither would you."

"The truth wouldn't have set him free, either!" Annette cried. "Don't you understand? That's why he had to die!"

Kaya nodded. "I know what it is to love someone—to love all of him—the good side of him and the bad. I know what it is to live without someone you love—to feel responsible for what happened to them. It tears at the very fabric of who you are."

Tears tracked down Annette's cheeks. "Lower your weapon, Kaya. Please…just lower the gun."

"In order for me to do that, you have to lower yours first," Kaya said evenly.

Annette shifted onto her back foot. The gun lowered by a hair.

"Slow," Kaya murmured, watching Annette's gun turn sideways and her knees bend. She edged forward. "That's it, Annette. Nice and slow."

The gun came to rest on the rocks between them. "Now you," Annette said.

"Step back," Kaya advised. As Annette did so, Kaya released one hand from her weapon. She set it on the ground. Stepping over them, she reached for her cuffs.

Annette backed away, skittish. "You didn't say you were going to restrain me."

"It's procedure," Kaya reminded her. She stepped forward again. When Annette retreated toward the ledge, she stopped, holding up both hands. She didn't know if Annette was desperate enough to follow Huck over the cliff. "All right, look. If you promise not to resist, we can walk out of here together. No restraints."

"Until we get to the bottom of the mountain?" Annette said with narrowed eyes.

Kaya measured her and realized she had no intention of making it all the way to the bottom of the mountain. Not without running. "Yes," she lied.

Annette stilled. She let Kaya close the distance.

Kaya took hold of her arm. "Come on," she said, nodding in the direction she had come.

Annette twisted, attempting to break the hold. She forced Kaya back a long step.

Kaya caught her breath. She felt open air behind her. Annette drove an elbow into her gut. Kaya felt her heels slide back over the ledge.

On the wind, she thought she heard the sound of her name.

* * *

Everett didn't have a clear shot. He hadn't had one since Kaya laid down her weapon and crossed to Annette.

He watched helplessly as Annette tried to drive Kaya back over the ridge. For a second, it looked like she would go over, crashing to the same ledge where Huck lay.

Kaya lunged, grabbing Annette as she did so and shoving her to the ground. She tried to restrain her.

Annette was fighting for her life, arms and legs flailing. She kicked, punched, bit. Her fist closed over a rock and swung it up to connect with Kaya's temple.

"Son of a bitch," Everett breathed as Kaya's head snapped back. Rutland and the deputies rushed to break up the fight. "Hurry up!" he yelled. Why had they left in the first place?

Kaya tried to overtake Annette by pinning her in a reverse hold, but Annette rolled out of it, away from the edge. She scrambled for something on the ground as Rutland lunged for her.

A shot echoed across the canyon and Rutland fell. Kaya had brought herself to her feet, grappling for the Taser on her belt. Annette pointed the gun at her.

Everett felt the trigger, placing Annette in the center of his scope. He remembered the wind at the last second, adjusted his aim.

The rifle kicked against his shoulder as he squeezed.

Kaya watched Annette slump in a limp sprawl on the rocks of the cliff edge. Her Taser was in her fist and her deputies were behind her. Rutland was still down.

Blood pooled beneath the line of Annette's throat. Her body had jerked sideways. Which meant the shot had come from the north...

Kaya looked wildly across the empty space of the canyon to the cliff side a hundred feet across.

She had to squint. The rock to the head had made her see stars and her vision double. She watched a figure and its carbon copy unfold from a sprawl on the flat top of the canyon. As he stood up, she recognized Everett's long lean form. He lifted his hand, waved.

Ellis's words came back to her.

Everett said to tell you he's got your back.

A sob worked against her throat, and she braced her hands on her knees as they loosened. Root grabbed her arms, preventing her slide to the rough ground, while Wyatt sailed by to check Rutland's condition.

As Root asked if she was okay, Kaya's gaze fell on Annette. For a second, she thought their eyes locked. It took a delayed second for her to realize the other woman was dead. She had tried to kill Kaya. And Everett had been quicker.

She looked across the canyon again and saw that Everett had picked up his rifle and was running for the sloping side of the cliff face he'd somehow shimmied up to get to his position. Shrill ringing pierced her ears. Blinking, she struggled to stay conscious—at least until she had a chance to kiss the cattle baron when he arrived.

Chapter 20

"**T**rue Claymore is in custody. Reverend Huck Claymore and Annette Claymore are both deceased. Agent Rutland is in surgery but is expected to recover. Sheriff Altaha was injured, but she is doing well and should be back at work next week…"

"He's doing fine," Naleen commented at Kaya's bedside. Deputy Root's face filled the screen of the television high on the wall opposite the hospital bed.

"He's doing great," Kaya granted. "But I still could've done the press conference."

"The doctor says you have to stay overnight," her mother, Darcia, said as she fussed around the room, straightening the curtains, adjusting the blinds. Turning the chairs so they were angled just so with the bed.

She was driving Kaya crazy. They both were.

Nova breezed in with a large grease-stained paper bag. "I brought reinforcements."

Kaya sat up in bed too quickly and winced when her head split open with pain. She saw little white lights and leaned back on her elbows. "Damn it!"

"You might be the world's worst patient," Naleen considered as she received the bag from her daughter and rattled the paper as she opened it.

Kaya's teeth ground at the noise. "Nova, get out. I'm about to say more bad words."

"You go ahead, Aunt Kaya," Nova invited. "After spring break at the Edge, I feel like I've got them all memorized. Did you know there are over fifty different ways to use the word fu—"

"Do you really think finishing that sentence will convince me to let you work there all summer?" Naleen questioned.

"Do you really think talking at this volume is making me any friendlier?" Kaya drawled.

The door opened again and two people walked into the room. Kaya's jaw came unhinged when she saw Sawni's mother and father.

Mrs. Mescal carried a vase full of flowers. She looked small and kindly behind them as she smiled hesitantly. "How's the patient?" she asked in her familiar quiet voice.

When Kaya remained speechless, Naleen stood up from her chair. "Indignant."

Mr. Mescal chuckled. He was not a tall man, but his presence had a habit of filling any room he was in. That effect had dimmed after Sawni's disappearance. Kaya had noticed that at the funeral as well. But his shoulders were back, and his smile was broad as he scanned the bandage on Kaya's temple. "The headache's to blame, I'm sure."

"It's the captivity," Kaya found herself saying. She glanced at Naleen. "Can you…"

Naleen patted her arm. "Nova and I will step out."

"Leave the bag," Kaya said, snatching it from her before Naleen could escape with it.

Darcia sat down in the chair closest to the window, signaling that she intended to stay. Kaya didn't have the words to tell her to leave, too.

Mrs. Mescal waited until Nova and Naleen closed the door before placing the vase on the bedside table.

Kaya reached out to touch a delicate spray of petals. "Lilies," she said. "For Sawni."

"Our Sawni did love lilies, didn't she?" Mrs. Mescal asked, tracing the shape of another. "The lilies are for her. The peach roses are for you."

Kaya met her eyes and noticed the veil of wet over her dark irises.

Mrs. Mescal turned the vase slightly, fidgeting. "Do you still like peach roses—or do you prefer something else now?"

"Peach roses are fine," Kaya said, her voice breaking up.

Mrs. Mescal's hand found hers. "I'm sorry we didn't keep in touch through the years. I'm afraid you might think it was because we blamed you for what happened. That wasn't the case. Not at all. Seeing you…reminded us of her. So we cut ties when we should have gathered. Nothing heals like community. You needed that as much as we did, and we denied you."

Kaya shook her head. "I denied myself."

"Nonetheless…" Mrs. Mescal patted her hand. "When I saw you at the memorial, you looked so guilty and ashamed—still, after all this time."

"I was afraid I disappointed you." She lifted her eyes to Mr. Mescal who stood now at the foot of the bed.

"Why would you disappoint us, Kaya?" he asked. "You've risen. You've made your people proud."

"You found her," Mrs. Mescal muttered. "You found our Sawni and brought her home. But even if you hadn't, you should know we're proud of you."

Kaya looked to her mother who sat quietly. Darcia nodded in quiet agreement and Kaya had to look away. "Thank you," she said. She reached up to swipe at tears. "Sawni used to get so mad because she'd cry at the drop of a hat and I didn't. Now look at me."

Mrs. Mescal released a sobbing laugh.

"We bend," Mr. Mescal stated, "so that life doesn't break us."

Kaya sighed at the wisdom. "I think I get that now."

Mrs. Mescal leaned down and pressed a kiss to the center of her brow. "Bless you, Kaya Altaha."

Kaya mimicked Mr. Mescal's wave and watched him and Sawni's mother file out. She raised both hands to her head as the door snicked closed. "Did you know they were coming?"

"I didn't," Darcia said, rising to smooth the covers over Kaya's legs. "But I'm happy that they did. You needed that. So did they. Our families have needed each other for some time. Maybe now things can go back to the way they were."

It would be bittersweet without Sawni there, but Kaya found herself wishing the same.

The door crashed open, knocking against the wall. Darcia jumped at the sudden noise and the man that charged into the room. "Are you all right?" Everett demanded to know when he found Kaya lying in the bed.

Her heart stuttered. The wash of her pulse made her head ache in time with it. Still, she hadn't seen Everett since the rescue chopper had arrived to transport Rutland to the hospital. He, Root and Wyatt had insisted she go, too. She cleared her throat and tried to sit up straighter against the pillows stacked behind her. "I'm fine. Why wouldn't I be?"

He swept an arm toward the door. "There's people crying out in the hall like there's somebody on their deathbed in here."

"No one's on their deathbed," Darcia assured him. Her tone dripped with both frustration and amusement. "You silly man."

"You're fine," he repeated, eyes drilling into Kaya, hands propped on his waist.

"Yes," she insisted. "The doctor wanted to keep me for observation through the night as a precaution."

"There's nothing wrong with you?" he stated in question.

She pressed her lips together because she was very close to smiling. "No."

He nodded faintly before he flicked a glance at her mother. "Darcia."

"Everett," Darcia volleyed back.

"Nice to see you again."

"Is it?" she asked mildly.

He shifted, uncomfortable.

Kaya took pity on him. It was nice to know she wasn't the only one who withered in her mother's presence. She lifted the bag from the bed. "Do you want a burger?"

"I could eat," he weighed. He looked around. "Do you have a drink?"

"I don't," she realized. "Nova forgot to grab one."

"What do you want?" he asked, sidestepping quickly to the door. "I'll get you something."

"A coke is fine," she replied.

He grabbed the handle of the door. "Darcia? Can I interest you?"

"You interest my daughter enough for both of us, thank you," Darcia retorted.

He grimaced, then pinned his gaze again to Kaya. "Do you need me to do anything else?"

She started to say no, then stopped. "I need to get out of here."

He lifted his chin and a mischievous grin lit his eyes, turning the corner of his mouth up in a crooked smile. "Oh, I'll get you out of here, Sheriff Sweetheart. Don't you worry."

Kaya didn't realize how wide her smile reached until she looked at Darcia. She shrank back into the bed. "What's with the look, Mom?" she asked bracingly.

Darcia's half-lidded stare was more incisive than usual. Her lips parted a moment before she spoke, as if she were weighing her words or whether to say them. "You've been waiting."

"For…" Kaya prompted.

"For redemption," Darcia said with a wag of her chin. "The Mescals have given it. You always had it, but it took them visiting here today for you to believe that."

"Okay," Kaya said, unsure.

"You've been waiting for something else," Darcia continued. "Something you've probably never been aware of. I've always found it so curious how Naleen could fall so fast and dive into relationships with hardly a second thought and you never could bring yourself to do so."

Kaya had to fight the urge to roll her eyes. She fought it hard. "Mom. Naleen and I are hardly the same person—"

"Very true," Darcia agreed. "But I know now—what you've been waiting for."

Kaya narrowed her eyes. "Care to clue me in?"

"You've been waiting for a warrior."

A laugh burst out of Kaya. "A warrior? How Apache princess of me," she said derisively.

Darcia looked at her until her amusement faded, and Kaya was left to contemplate the seriousness of her expression. "He's a warrior like you," Darcia continued. "You've never found your equal—until now." She stood. "If he's returning, I think I'll take a walk. He won't want me staring daggers at him while he mashes food into his hairy face."

"Why did you tell me all that if you don't like him?" Kaya wondered.

Darcia closed the flaps of her long sweater over her front. "I don't mind him. But you'll allow me to resent the man who's stolen the heart of my youngest daughter. You may be the sheriff of Fuego County, Kaya Altaha. But you are still my child." With a nod, she left the room, leaving Kaya to grapple with her thoughts.

Before daybreak, the kitchen at Eaton House stood silent and still. The rest of the house lay quiet, too. The boards over the windows blocked the faint stain over the mountains, buttes and cliffs that heralded another long day of working cattle. The windows would be replaced later in the week. Repairs were still going on at Eaton House, off and on, but it was slowly coming together again. Soon, the ambush would only be a bitter memory.

In the dark, Everett pulled on his boots. He didn't bother to button his shirt as he crossed to the counter and the cubby where Paloma kept the coffeepot. He took down mugs. Pouring the coffee, he left it strong and black and lifted the mugs by the handles. No sooner had he turned than he hitched at the sight of the figure hovering in the doorway.

"Jesus Holyfield Christ!" he exclaimed, touching the mugs safely down to the counter next to him as the liquid sloshed over the rims. He grabbed his heart like it was going places. "You can't do that to somebody who's had his chest opened up in the last ten months."

Paloma clicked her tongue, tying the belt of her quilted, scarlet robe as she entered the room she'd ruled for the last three decades. "You're jumpier than usual. Not that that's a wonder." She grabbed the hand towel draped across the handle of the oven and tossed it to him.

He dried the piping hot liquid that ran in between his fingers.

"She's upstairs," Paloma said, eyeing the pair of mugs.

He tossed the towel onto the counter. "She fought me tooth and nail about not letting her go home. But I couldn't sleep. Not without knowing she was okay."

"You stole her from the hospital sooner than doctors advised," Paloma reminded him.

"I did it because she asked me to," Everett responded. "I'd do anything…"

She lifted her chin knowingly when he trailed off. "You'd do anything for her," she said, laying it out for him.

He pressed one hand to the countertop. Paloma saw everything. She saw him better than most.

She sighed. "Oh, *mijo*—"

"What are you doing out of bed?" he intervened smoothly. "You shouldn't be up."

"I feel fine," she assured him. "I'd feel a sight better if you children would stop fussing over me and let me get back to my work."

"You don't need work," he argued. "You need rest."

She grabbed him by the open flaps of his shirt. "Look at me, Everett Templeton. Look *here*." When he obeyed, she widened her eyes. "I am fine. Paloma's fine. *You*, on the other hand, are a basket case."

He sneered. "Now you're just being mean."

"You're not blind," she said gravely. "Nor are you stupid. You know what it is to love someone. What it *means*."

"How do you know?" he asked, uneasy.

"You love your brother," she told him. "You love your sister, despite what you have to say about her. You loved your father more than any son has."

He frowned but couldn't argue.

"You love your men," she went on. "And you love me. We've had our spats. But you were my child long before Ellis and Eveline decided to be. You chose me first."

He dropped his gaze from hers. Yes, he'd chosen her. Like a lifeline, he'd reached. She'd answered. He wondered if she knew, by doing so, that she'd saved him. He shifted his feet and cleared his throat to block the emotions building in the back of his throat.

She waited until he stilled. Then she said, "I never thought the day would come when I would have to point out to you that you've chosen someone else."

"Yeah," he whispered because his voice was somehow lost. "Me neither."

"She's worthy of it," she told him. "She's worthy of your heart."

"That's not what I'm worried about," he admitted.

"What are you worried about, *mijo*?"

He shook his head restlessly. "I don't know if she wants it."

Paloma nodded, drawing a long breath. Lovingly, she gathered the flaps of his shirt together. "You watched your father get his heart broken. It broke when your mother left. It broke a little more when she married my brother, his friend. It broke when she had another child—someone else's. It broke every time he saw either one of them in town. They say people don't die of a broken heart, but in the end, there was no doctor in this world who could fix it, was there?"

Everett was unable to contemplate the lengths to which his father had suffered. "We buried him with it. Why did we do that? You don't bury a man with the gun that killed him."

"The heart defines the man," Paloma insisted. "The same heart loved you and your siblings with every beat. It forgave your mother and my brother. Every betrayal, big and small."

"He was a fool for that," Everett stated.

"He could have been bitter," Paloma spoke over him. "He could have gone off like a demon—like that Whip Decker—and killed them both for it. He could have shut out what remained of his family, given up your birthright and fled. He didn't do those things because he was no fool. He did them because his heart was strong."

"Why're we talking about him?" he asked. Talking about Hammond hurt. Would it never not hurt?

"Because now you're the one who has to decide how your heart defines you," Paloma asserted. "Starting with your woman upstairs." He opened his mouth, but she stopped him. "She's your woman, Everett. There's no denying it."

"I'm hers," he granted. "She hasn't told me yet whether she wants to be mine. Not in the long run. She hasn't told me whether she wants this life with me. And it was me that told her I wasn't easy to live with. She knows all too well that this life is hard."

"Life's hard with or without the person you need most in this world," Paloma explained. "What do you want?"

"I *know* what I want," he said through his teeth.

"Does she?"

He hesitated long enough for her to pounce. "Tell her," Paloma told him. "Tell her, *mijo*, so I don't have to watch you live the rest of your life with regret. Never mind your heart. Do you think mine could stand that?"

He ran his eyes over her face. A smile grew on his. "You like kicking my ass, don't you?"

"What do you think gets me out of bed every morning?" She laid her hands, one on top of the other, over the center of his chest. "Be a good man and try not to plague us both to death."

"No promises," he replied, then added "*Mami*" and watched her eyes grow damp. She drew him into her arms and, for once, he went quietly.

Kaya woke facedown in a bed that was not her own with her head about to implode. She rolled slowly to her back, reaching up to hold her head on her shoulders.

She felt like she'd been hit with a rock much bigger than the one that had concussed her.

Going back to sleep seemed like the safest option. If she slept through the headbanging, she wouldn't have to learn to live through it.

As she tried to slink back into the deep, empty chamber she'd just climbed out of, the aching in her head crescendoed and she realized there would be no respite until she took something for the pain.

Groaning, she dug her elbows into the flannel sheet and propped herself up part of the way. Her neck muscles screamed, and she wished for a hammer to knock herself out with.

A hand gripped her shoulder, preventing her from rising further. She angled her head back.

"Stay down," Everett instructed.

"I have things to do," she grumbled at him.

"Such as?" he asked, lifting a single brow.

"Where'd you put my phone?" she asked. "I have to call Root and Wyatt and check in…"

"Nope."

She sighed, dropping her chin to her chest because her head felt heavy. "Not this again. I'm sheriff. I have responsibilities…"

"Not today," he informed her. "Not tomorrow, either. For the next few days, you're not the sheriff."

She frowned. "I'm just your sweetheart?"

His hand slid from her shoulder as he stepped away. "No. You're Kaya. And that's enough."

She raised her hand to the back of her neck, trying her best to ignore the pancake-flippy feeling his words placed in her stomach. "Do I smell coffee?"

He thrust a mug into her face.

She grabbed it like a lifeline.

Everett piled pillows behind her. "Slow," he told her when she began to scoot back.

"I'm not an invalid," she informed him. Clutching the mug in both hands, she let the heat seep into her fingers and closed her eyes, breathing in the aroma. "That's nice."

"Drink," he said as he sat on the edge of the bed with his own mug. "It's been sitting for a minute."

She did and found the temperature to be just right. Scanning his profile, she swallowed and waited until the warmth spread to her belly. "How long have you been watching me sleep?"

He drank in answer.

"Hmm," she muttered thoughtfully. "Just so I know— how long do you plan on doing that?"

He lowered the coffee. His voice delved deep. "Until I'm certain you're going to keep waking up."

"I'm fine."

His eyes roved over the bandage on her temple and what she imagined were bruises starting to color her skin. "I nearly had to watch you go over a cliff and get shot again. You'll let me worry about you."

He'd come close to watching her die again. He'd saved her life—again.

She closed her eyes. "Thank you."

"It's just coffee."

"Not for that." She shook her head. "For having my back."

"Always," he said softly.

She looked away because it was too much. He was too much.

His mug clacked onto the bedside table. "I've got things to say to you."

She wasn't sure she was ready to hear them.

"Right now, though, you need something to eat. You can't take those pain meds the doctor sent you home with on an empty stomach. Paloma was making you a plate when I left the kitchen. I'll go see if it's ready. When you've taken something, you can go back to sleep and rest some more."

As he moved to the door, she wanted to call him back but saw the stubborn line of his shoulders and forced herself to stop. When he closed the door, she slunk back down into the covers and pulled them over her head, overwhelmed by all that was inside her.

Kaya could only take so much coddling. On the second day, by the afternoon, she was out of bed and wouldn't hear refusal from Everett, Paloma or Luella—who Everett had brought in to do regular checks on Kaya as a nurse.

That evening, close to sundown, she ventured out onto

the patio, settled into one of the wooden Adirondack chairs and wouldn't hear a word spoken from any of them about returning indoors until the bugs started to bite and the cool night air began to nip.

Upstairs, Paloma drew her a hot bath. Soaking felt divine. Parts of Kaya ached from the skirmish with Annette—not just her head. She didn't mind so much when Paloma lingered nearby, as if she were afraid Kaya would drown if she left the room. She even helped Kaya wash her hair without getting the bandage on her temple wet.

"Thank you," Kaya murmured as Paloma helped her dry and dress.

"It's no trouble," Paloma replied. She handed Kaya a fresh stack of clothes. "Your sister brought these for you."

"It *is* trouble," Kaya argued. "You've all gone to way too much trouble—"

"Kaya Altaha," Paloma snapped, "out there you may be the sheriff and you may have to care for everyone else. But under this roof, you are in our care. It's my duty to care for Hammond's children, his grandchildren and the ones they choose and that pleases me. You've done enough. Our troubles are over because of all you have done. All we ask is that you let us take care of you now. *Por favor.*"

Kaya held the knot under her collarbone that kept the towel closed around her and the clothes Paloma had given her with the other hand. "*Si, señora,*" she murmured.

A smile touched Paloma's eyes but not her mouth. Reaching up, she brushed the hair back from Kaya's face. "*Buen.*"

Kaya responded by taking her hand. "Paloma?"

"What is it, *niña?*"

"Does it take as much strength as I think it does?"

"To do what?"

"To…" Kaya pressed her lips together. Then she closed her eyes and made them part again. "To love him the way that you do…for as long as you have…"

Paloma blinked in surprise. "It takes strength to love anybody." When Kaya bit her lip, she straightened her shoulders. "But he isn't just anybody. Is he?"

Kaya shook her head silently. She felt open and tried to make her expression unreadable.

Paloma squeezed her hand. "I have loved him—even when I thought he would never change. But he has changed. Do you know why?"

"No," Kaya replied.

"Then you are blind," Paloma said simply.

Kaya searched the woman's face. She started to shake her head again, then stopped when Paloma eyed her in warning. She released a breath. "I haven't changed him."

"He did some of the work himself," Paloma admitted. "He was forced to open himself—to grief. To acceptance. That is how love found him. But we do not love him because he has changed."

Kaya thought about it. "No," she stated.

Paloma nodded. "That is how you know it is strong. That is how you know this has what it takes. Do you think he is strong enough to be your man—through everything, good and bad?"

"I do," she realized with no hesitation. She could see it—him and her, through thick and thin, together. She heard herself gasp. That was the answer, wasn't it? To all her questions. "Do you do this every day?"

"What?"

"Change people's lives," Kaya said softly. She jumped a bit when Paloma laughed in a loud, genuine burst. Then she laughed at herself and pressed her fingers to the center of her brow. "I'm sorry. I'm a mess."

"If this is you at your lowest, Kaya, may I just say," Paloma said, "you handle yourself with more dignity and strength than anyone in this house before you."

"Never meet me when I'm sick or hungry," Kaya asked and laughed much more easily with Paloma the second time.

Everett had finally gone from watching her sleep to sleeping beside her. The bags under his eyes had started to pop. He'd come to need rest as much as he said she did.

Kaya found herself sleepless. The pain had slunk back to an irritating level. She was no longer buried by it. She hoped tomorrow it would be mild enough that she could manage a trip into town. The desire to speak with her deputies had only escalated. She'd checked with the hospital to hear Rutland's status. Surgery had gone well, and he was recovering.

The fallout for Fuego would be long. The mayor was facing charges. The reverend had killed four people, at the behest of his father and sister-in-law. He and Annette Claymore were dead.

Kaya had to get back on patrol, if only to show the people of Fuego some measure of assurance.

She just had to get past the big tough cattleman first.

He looked soft when he slept. His breath whispered across her face. She lifted her fingertips to feather across his lips. They parted at the motion and she licked her lips to stop from kissing his. *Let him sleep*, she told herself, despite the need. It kindled, insistent.

She knew what flowered with it. She knew what she felt beyond need and want. And she knew how loud that voice screamed whenever he looked at her. Like she was still on that pedestal he'd put her on at the beginning of all this. It didn't matter how broken or bruised she was. He looked at her, and she believed—in herself. In him. Everything.

True to routine, Everett stirred near dawn. He raised one arm over his head and opened his eyes to find her sitting up in bed.

"Thirsty?" she asked.

"You have no idea."

He sat up slowly, letting the sheet fall to his waist and he took the drink she handed him. Together, they drank in silence.

He judged her constitution. "You're stronger today."

"I think so," she said. When he raised one knee and drank again, she bit her lip. "You said you had things to say to me."

"When you're ready."

She waited until he'd finished his coffee before she admitted, "I think I'm ready to hear them."

"Better be sure, Sheriff Sweetheart," he warned.

"I'm sheriff again, it seems," she observed.

When she didn't break eye contact, he took the mug from her. "You think you can handle getting dressed?"

"Why?" she asked as he got out of bed.

"Because we're going for a ride."

The horses shambled. He wouldn't hear of them going faster.

"We could've walked faster than this," Kaya informed him.

"If you'd stop complaining for a few seconds at a time, we could do something crazy like enjoy the sunrise," he stated.

She didn't so much settle into silence as bristle at it. The light coming into the world did draw her gaze, however, and hold it. Day broke the grip of grim night, painting Eaton Edge and its river, hills and mountains in nature's watercolors, one after the other, until the sun's golden fingers grasped for its first hold of the sky.

Kaya had no words, so she let Everett and Crazy Alice lead her and Elsie, the gentle, sweet Haflinger he'd put her on, down a dirt trail a mile to the west of Eaton House, past Paloma's vegetable garden, past the orchard with its neat rows of trees, beyond the bunkhouse where the hands were beginning to stir and the cabin Ellis and Luella shared with the girls... They rode until the buildings were far behind them.

Finally, when the sun had rounded over the top of Ol' Whalebones, Everett tugged on the reins to bring Crazy Alice to a halt. Kaya did the same. "Where are we?" she asked, frowning at the ponderosa pines surrounding both sides of the trail.

He walked around Crazy Alice to grab Elsie's bridle and ran a hand over her long neck. "Attagirl," he murmured. Then he reached out a hand for Kaya's.

She ignored it. She'd gotten on the horse without his help. She could get off it, too. To prove it, she nudged her right toes out of the stirrups and swung her leg over Elsie's back. Gripping the horn, she lowered smoothly to the ground.

The change in altitude made her head spin. She stumbled as she brought her other leg down.

He caught her, gripping her upper arm. He cupped the back of her shoulders to keep her off the ground. "You said you were ready," he said near her ear.

"Stand me back up," she instructed, gritting her teeth. "I'm ready, damn it."

He made a noise in his throat but helped her steady herself. After several long seconds in which he watched for signs of weakness, he asked, "You good?"

She jerked a nod. He didn't let go of her arm, she noted, as they walked off the trail and into the trees. "Where are we?" she asked again.

Winding his way through the long shadows of the ponderosas, he hooked a right and guided her into an open glade.

The headstone gave her pause. It was centered in the safety of the dell. She opened her mouth to say something, then stopped because Everett released her and moved closer to the stone.

She watched as he crouched in front of it and tugged weeds from its base, then tossed them away before standing again. "This is where we buried him."

Kaya walked around the stone to stand at his side. It rose out of the ground to the height of her shoulders, coming to a point. The shape of a ten-gallon hat was etched just beneath the crest, followed by the name "HAMMOND WAYNE EATON" and the dates that marked his birth and death. The words "LOVING FATHER, GRANDFATHER & FRIEND" were carved in the center.

She read the words by Virgil inscribed in small italics below. "'May the countryside and the gliding valley streams content me.'" It felt sweet and so sad. She twined her fingers through Everett's and felt his hold tighten.

"He stands alone here," he muttered.

The breeze rustled the leaves. A hawk called from the distance. Otherwise, there was nothing here but the stone.

It felt lonely. She made sure her eyes were clear as she raised them to his. "Why are we here?"

"Because that's not what I want." He paced away. Tracing an unseen path around the glade, he lowered his hat with one hand to drag the other through his thick hair once, twice and again, mussing the waves thoroughly.

When he ceased the restless roving, he faced her, planting his feet. "Until he died, I didn't give dying alone a thought. Then something happened." He pointed in accusation. "You."

Her lips parted, but he spoke again before she could. "I don't need much in this life. I never needed to be the boss or the man everybody looks to when the day's starting. Before last summer, all I wanted was to know that my family was going to be okay—that we'd survive because life keeps swinging at us. I thought that was all I needed. All I'd ever need."

Her pulse was high, she realized, when he paused. She was starting to feel heady again. There was nothing to grab but the headstone so she crossed her arms over her chest. "Until me?" she asked.

"You're damn right until you," he muttered, holding his hat in two hands.

She watched him bend the brim, misshape it. "Why does that bother you so much?"

He stopped and quashed the hat over his head again. Planting his hands on his hips, he looked at her long under the shadow of it. "Because I need you to marry me."

Kaya realized after half a minute that she was gawking at him. She looked around—at the circle of trees, the empty glade—and shook her head. "You're proposing."

He made a face. "The hell did you think I was doing?"

She held up a hand, trying to get a grip on the situation. "You're…proposing to me…in a graveyard." And she started to laugh.

She laughed herself silly. She laughed until it hurt and she was bent over double, her hands on her knees, eyes tearing. "Oh, Christ," she hooted, swiping the back of her hand over them. She raised herself back up to standing, throwing her head back to peer at the sky. "That's good stuff."

"You 'bout done, sweetheart?"

She saw the deep-riddled scowl on his face and sighed at him. "Oh, I'm done. Believe you me."

He smacked his lips together unsatisfactorily. "Fine." He turned sharply on his heel and walked away.

She tailed him. "Wait a minute. Where're you going?"

"I know when I'm licked," he tossed over his shoulder.

She sprinted to catch up and grabbed her head when it protested. "Stop, please!"

He whirled back around just as fast as he'd left. "Look, I'll get on my knees."

"Everett—"

"Is that what you want, Kaya? You want me on my knees for you?"

"No!" she shouted when he started to kneel. "Get up!" Grabbing him by the shoulders, she yanked until he straightened to his full height again. She hissed when her head sang an aching tune.

He cradled the side of her head gently.

Who knew he could be so gentle? Yet another reason she loved him. "I don't want you to kneel for me," she told him. "Life's brought you to your knees one too many times before." Before he could open his mouth, she clapped her hand over it to make sure he listened for once. "And my answer isn't no. It was never no. It's yes."

As she lowered her hand, he blurted, "Yes?"

"Unequivocally yes," Kaya breathed and beamed at his utter confusion. "It may kill us both, but I'll be your wife." She framed his face in her hands and stroked his bearded cheeks. "You won't have to walk this world alone any-more—or the next one."

He lost his breath. His hands met either side of her jaw and he lowered his brow to hers. "It's a yes."

"Yes." She would've closed her eyes if he had. But un-derstanding started to gleam there and she saw relief rid-ing behind it. She threw her arms around him and buried her face in his shoulder. "I told you, didn't I—that I was your woman?"

"Christ," he breathed in disbelief. "Mine."

"I didn't think I was strong enough," she admitted.

"You're the strongest person I've ever known," he said. "I'm in love with you—and have been for a while. Sorry it's taken me so long to say it. I guess I wasn't strong enough, either. You make me stronger."

She sighed, taking a moment to savor it all. He loved her. He wanted to be with her, always. "I love you, too." She swallowed. "I love you so much, I'm overwhelmed by it. You're not walking away, and neither am I. This is it."

He nodded. "This is it," he whispered in agreement.

"I'm in, Everett—all in. Do you see that?"

"I see you," he assured her. He swayed with her over the grass. His arms gathered her against his chest. "I see us." He touched a kiss to her cheek, then the high point of her brow and her other cheek. He grinned and she felt his happiness and her own radiating through her. "To the very end."

In the quiet glade, in the shadow of the trees, she felt Everett's warmth and for the first time in her life, she knew something beyond life's uncertainty. She was certain they would be together. She was certain they would love each other truly, uncompromisingly.

To the very end.

* * * * *

Romantic Suspense

Danger. Passion. Drama.

Available Next Month

Guarding Colton's Secrets Addison Fox
Her Private Security Detail Patricia Sargeant

....

Murder At The Alaskan Lodge Karen Whiddon
Safe In Her Bodyguard's Arms Katherine Garbera

....

LOVE INSPIRED

Cold Case Tracker Maggie K. Black
Her Duty Bound Defender Sharee Stover

Larger Print

....

LOVE INSPIRED

Yukon Wilderness Evidence Darlene L. Turner
Hidden In The Canyon Jodie Bailey

Larger Print

....

LOVE INSPIRED

The Baby Assignment Christy Barritt
Uncovering Colorado Secrets Rhonda Starnes

Larger Print

Keep reading for an excerpt of a new title
from the Intrigue series,
WHISPERING WINDS WIDOWS by Debra Webb

Chapter One

The Light Memory Care Center
Lantern Pointe
Chattanooga, Tennessee
Sunday, April 21, 10:00 a.m.

"Are you certain you want to do this, Reyna?"

Reyna Hart smiled—as much to reassure her friend as
to brace herself. She was going to do this. "I absolutely do
want to do this."

Eudora Davenport's eyes shone with excitement. "I knew
you'd never be able to resist." She placed a frail hand against
her chest. "You don't know how much this means to me."

Reyna had a fairly good idea. She had been visiting
Eudora, a sweet woman she'd enjoyed getting to know, for
nearly a year now. Each Sunday from 10:00 until 11:00 a.m.,
sometimes until noon. Generally, they sat in the two chairs
positioned to take in the view out the one large window in
her room. Their tea on the table between them. They had
become friends. Good friends.

"There aren't many who will talk to you," Eudora reminded her. "Others will say plenty just to hear themselves
talk." She drew in a deep breath. "Some will attempt to
mislead you. Folks don't always tolerate change very well.
Particularly if that change prompts the unknown."

"I'm aware." Reyna considered herself a good judge of character. When she'd been pursuing her original career dream, she'd spent most of her research time interviewing people—and Eudora was right. The best interviewers learned to recognize the difference between a thoughtful and forthright person and a conversational narcissist. Reyna had spent most of her life, even as a child, watching people. Her mother always said that particular skill was one of the things that made Reyna so perfect for the art of storytelling. She was a natural at slipping into the thoughts and dreams of characters.

Reyna had certainly expected she would spend her life writing fiction. She'd been writing short stories since she'd been old enough to string sentences together. The first contract had come quickly and somewhat easier than she'd anticipated. Her debut novel had made a brief and distant showing on the bestseller lists. Not so shabby. But that book had been the one and only.

Just call her a one-semi-hit wonder.

The marketable ideas had stopped coming, and her publisher had moved on.

For a while Reyna had drifted—career wise. She'd held on to her New York City apartment that was about the size of a shoebox for another year, and then she'd opted to take a break from the dream and spend some time in reality.

Not so much fun at first. Coming back to Chattanooga to start over hadn't been easy. She'd tried out a few different career hats—none worth remembering. And though the process had been painful, the timing had turned out to be important: her beloved grandmother had been diagnosed with Alzheimer's. From that moment there had been no looking back for Reyna. She'd become her grandmother's primary caretaker even after she'd had to move to this very facility. Throughout the remainder of her life, her grandmother's greatest fear had not been of dying but of forgetting who she was and what her life had been before, so she'd asked Reyna to write her story. Then, anytime she wished, she could read her story and remember.

Reyna would have done anything for her grandmother, so she'd thrown herself into the task. The story, mostly a narrative written in first person, had given her grandmother much pleasure the final months of her life. When she'd passed, others at the facility had pleaded with Reyna to write theirs. So, she'd decided to give the possibility a go.

Now, two years later, work was steady and surprisingly lucrative. Reyna had been featured in the *Chattanooga Times Free Press*, and several other newspapers had carried her work in their lifestyle sections. She'd even received an award from the city for innovation in supporting quality of life for the elderly.

"You've decided how to start?" Eudora asked, drawing Reyna out of the past.

"I have." She gave her friend a nod. "I'm starting with Ward Kane Senior."

Eudora's thin gray brows rose. "He may not talk to you. At the ten-year anniversary of the disappearance as well as the twenty, he refused to give an interview. He's a stubborn man."

Reyna had heard this from her before. "He's also the only remaining father."

Eudora's gaze turned distant. "Sometimes I forget how much time has really gone by." She sighed. "Thirty years. It's hard to believe."

Eudora Davenport remained a beautiful woman even at eighty-two. Her hair was that perfect shade of silver that required no dyes or anything at all to give it luster or to add thickness. She wore it in a French twist with pearl pins. At this stage she spent much of her time reclined in her bed or in her favorite chair, but her loungewear was always tasteful and representative of her elegance and class. Eudora insisted aging was a gift, one that should be respected and embraced with dignity.

"I will call him," she said then, her tone determined. "Perhaps I can persuade him."

"It couldn't hurt," Reyna agreed. "I've read everything about the case that has been released for public consumption. Anything he hasn't shared could prove helpful. The FBI agent who assisted the sheriff's office in the investigation has passed away, but the deputy detective, Nelson Owens, who worked the case, has agreed to meet with me tomorrow."

Eudora picked up her cup of tea from the table between them and sipped. When she'd set it aside once more, she searched Reyna's face for a long moment before speaking. Reyna hadn't quite decided why this case was so important to Eudora. She was not related to one or more of the three men—the Three, as they were called—who had disappeared, nor the wives and children—if any—they had left behind.

The only thing she had told Reyna when she'd commissioned her to write the story that was technically not even hers was that she wanted to know the truth before she lost herself completely or died—whichever came first.

Eudora stared straight ahead for a long moment, her gaze reaching somewhere beyond the window. There were times like this when she stopped speaking and drifted off. Sometimes for minutes, others for hours. Her grandmother had done the same. Reyna had learned to be patient or to come back another time.

"She never comes to see me anymore," Eudora said, her voice as distant as her gaze.

"Who?" Reyna asked, though she wasn't sure the eighty-two-year-old was speaking to her or if she was still aware Reyna was in the room. It happened more and more lately.

Her pulse reacted to a prick of emotion. She truly had begun to consider this woman family. There was little left of Reyna's. She still had her mother, who had remarried recently and was quite focused on her new husband. Not that Reyna resented this one little bit. Her mother had been madly in love with Reyna's father, and his death had devastated them both. It had taken a decade and a half for her mother to even consider having dinner with a romantic interest. Now she was happily married to the second love of her life, and Reyna was incredibly grateful for her second chance.

Reyna, however, was still waiting for her first chance. But she had time. Thirty-five wasn't so old.

Wasn't so young either, an evil little voice chided.

"Eudora, who do you mean?" Reyna prodded.

Eudora blinked, turned away from the window to meet Reyna's gaze. "I'm sorry—what were you saying?"

"You said she never comes to see you anymore."

A frown lined the older woman's otherwise perfectly smooth brow. The woman had beautiful skin with so few lines one would think she'd had multiple cosmetic surgeries, but when asked, Eudora always laughed and insisted it was simply good genes. "Just an old friend. No one important, dear."

"Well." Reyna stood, walked over to her chair, reached for her hand and gave it a little squeeze. "I should be on my way. I can check in at the bed-and-breakfast after lunch. I'll spend some time getting the lay of the land, so to speak."

Eudora held on to her hand when Reyna would have pulled it away. "No matter what happens, I so thoroughly appreciate that you have agreed to do this for me. Please know that if you don't find the answer quickly enough or at all, don't despair. Knowing what happened is important to me, but it is not your fault if I go first."

Reyna smiled and gave her hand another squeeze. "I'm sure you'll be fine, and if I can uncover the truth, I will revel in writing the story."

Eudora released Reyna's hand and clasped hers together in her lap. "Oh, I have no doubt you'll find the truth. From the moment I met you, I was certain you would know exactly how to do what no one else could."

No pressure.

"I'll talk to you soon," Reyna promised before leaving.

This lady had a great deal of faith in her. She surely hoped she wouldn't have to let her down. A thirty-year-old missing persons case that no one else had been able to solve was a tall order.

In time, evidence grew faint, disappeared, as did memories. But there was a flip side. The passage of vast amounts of time often loosened tongues and added to the weight of guilt. Reyna exited the facility and drew in a deep breath of cool spring air. So much had started to bloom already—it gave her hope that anything could happen.

Even solving a very, very cold case.

Whispering Winds
1:00 p.m.

LEGEND HAD IT that the air in Whispering Winds was never still. The small community was an old one, nestled against the state line, nearly in Georgia. The tourist guides called it one of Lookout Mountain's lesser-known gems. Like most of the small niche communities on the mountain, the tiny town proved a powerful draw for tourists with its incredible views and ghost stories that were nearly legend in themselves. Not the least of which was the story of how three young men—Ward Kane Junior, known as JR, Duke Fuller and Judson Evans, ranging in age from twenty-eight to twenty-nine, all three with wives, one with a child—had just vanished into thin air, never to be seen again.

Reyna turned into the small parking area of the lovely historic home that had been turned into the Jewel, a bed-and-breakfast located right as you entered Whispering Winds. The house was the first of many grand old residences that had been well maintained and remained occupied. A bit farther down Main Street the town shops and offices lined both sides. Tourism kept the little shops thriving. Many of the residents worked in Chattanooga, but there were a good number of retail and service jobs available locally.

The sheer number of thriving little communities on the mountain had surprised Reyna. There was Dread Hollow and Sunset Cove, and both had their own tourist draws. Funny, when Reyna had returned to Tennessee she'd expected to end up in Nashville after spending some time with her grandmother, but fate had seen things differently.

Now she owned her grandmother's cottage in the city's historic district. Growing up, Reyna had found the little cottage filled with hidden treasures and treats. Since Reyna was the only grandchild, her grandmother had loved creating little treasure hunts and mysteries to solve whenever she'd visited. As a child, Reyna had been convinced her grandmother had secret fairy friends. She was also certain she had inherited her creativity from her dear grandmother.

The city wasn't so far, and Reyna could have opted to drive back and forth for the next few days while she did this deep dive into research, but in her experience, there was no substitute for living among the folks from whom she wanted answers.

Reyna parked her vintage Land Rover—also inherited from her grandmother—in a spot reserved for guests and climbed out. Owning a vehicle in New York City had been far too much trouble. The better route had been just to rent one when needed. But here, in the South, a vehicle was a must. Reyna had always loved the Land Rover, and her grandmother had insisted she take possession of it as soon as she moved back home. Even for a vehicle nearing forty years old, it had very low mileage and was in pristine condition, aesthetically and mechanically.

She grabbed her bag from the back seat and headed up the walk. Spring flowers were blooming, and the trees had sprouted new leaves. The world was coming alive, her grandmother would say, after its long winter's sleep.

The porch was exactly what one expected of a grand Victorian home. It spread across the front and wrapped around one side. More than a century old, the home stood three floors high and covered better than thirteen thousand square feet. Lots of stone taken right from the area made up the foundation and the walkways. But it was the fountains and gardens that took her breath away before she even reached the entrance. Truly beautiful. So well-thought-out.

Stepping inside, Reyna found exactly what she'd anticipated. Soaring ceilings and grand chandeliers. Furniture made during a time when craftsmanship had carried a higher standard. Shiny wood floors and well-loved woven rugs.

The registration desk was staffed by the owner. Reyna recognized Birdie Jewel from the website's About page. A lovely woman of somewhere in her late seventies, with the gray hair to prove it. Her hair hung in a long, loose braid. She looked up and smiled, and her eyes were bright in a face that showed a light hand toward cosmetics. As natural as Birdie Jewel's gray hair and minimal makeup suggested she might be, her style in clothing was the show. Flamboyant fabrics in brilliant colors. Lots of exotic jewelry that tinkled as she moved around the counter to meet Reyna.

"Welcome. You must be Reyna Hart."

Her voice was as musical as her jewelry. Pleasantly so.

"Hello." Reyna dropped her bag at her feet and shook the woman's outstretched hand. "This is genuinely lovely." She gazed around the lobby.

Birdie's smile widened. "Oh, I adore hearing guests say so. Come sign the guest book." She hurried behind the counter once more and turned the large guest book around to face Reyna. "We do things here a little on the old-fashioned side. None of your personal information will be in the book, but we do love for you to sign your name. Even if only your given name."

"Love that." Reyna accepted the pen and signed her name on the next available line. She passed the pen back to the owner.

"Now I'll need your credit card."

"Of course."

Once the paperwork was done, Birdie grabbed a key from one of the numbered boxes behind the desk. "Follow me," she said.

Reyna picked up her bag and trailed after Birdie, who

led the way up the grand staircase, her bohemian skirt flowing around her. It wasn't until they neared the top that Reyna noticed the older woman was barefoot. Her toenails were painted a bright orange. Reyna smiled. She preferred bare feet herself when working at home.

The owner paused in front of room seven. "This one is for you. It has the balcony that overlooks Main Street."

"Lovely." Some might prefer one of the views provided from the elegant home's cliff-side location, but she was interested in what was happening among the people, so a view of Main Street was perfect.

"Make yourself at home," Birdie said as she placed the key on the table near the door. "If you need anything at all, just let me know. I'm always here. Breakfast is served each morning from seven until nine. Snacks are always available, but we serve no other organized meals."

"Perfect," Reyna assured her.

When the lady had gone, after closing the door behind her, Reyna quickly hung up the clothes she had brought along. She put away her suitcase and left her toiletry bag in the bathroom. The claw-foot tub was center stage in the room. Very romantic.

Reyna walked out onto the balcony and simply stood there for a long while. She watched the slow pace of the cars moving along Main Street and the even slower stride of the pedestrians. The small town had a very sedate air about it. Peaceful, content. And yet thirty years ago the Three had disappeared without a trace.

The wives left behind remained, to this day, widowed. For thirty years all three had stuck with their stories of having no idea what had become of their husbands. Never a single deviation, not even a little one. Those closest to the families had given mixed messages, according to the many, many articles Reyna had read. Most were certain the couples had all been happily married. Churchgoing, deeply in love, happy people with no financial issues or other known troubles.

The men had been lifelong best friends. Different jobs, different family backgrounds. As adults they'd remained friends, and the women they'd married, Lucinda, Deidre and Harlowe, had been best friends their entire lives as well. They'd attended school together, parties, vacations, and they'd all married the same summer—only days between their weddings.

So strange that the men would abruptly disappear together and the women would know nothing of the reason. Not one had ever remarried. Not one had ever spoken against the other.

Reyna walked back into her room, closed the French doors to the balcony and decided she would drive around a bit and get the lay of the land.

Tonight she would call Eudora and tell her all that she'd seen. The woman couldn't wait to hear everything.

Eudora was such a good storyteller in her own right that developing her narrative would be incredibly easy. Reyna had videoed their sessions using her phone's camera, as she did with all clients, and then she would use those to help bring their voices to life.

The sun was shining and the temperature was perfect for a leisurely stroll, but Reyna wanted to drive to a number of locations first thing, so she opted to head out to the Land Rover. She'd grab some lunch somewhere before returning to the Jewel.

Excitement had her belly tingling as she descended the staircase. To tell the truth, she hadn't felt this much enthusiasm for an endeavor since her own book. She enjoyed all her work, but this was the first time she had felt so drawn toward a project. She wanted to find the answers that no one else had. When she'd written her novel, a mystery loosely based on an actual event, she had loved the research aspect. The digging into the dirty details in search of previously unearthed facts.

Perhaps that was what had put the fire in her blood this time. Her goal was to find the answer to a thirty-year-old mystery. Had the young husbands taken off for parts unknown in search of wealth or new love? Had they met with untimely deaths from someone to whom they had been in some sort of debt?

Or were the Widows actually murderers who had decided for whatever reasons that their husbands had to die?

The Widows of Whispering Winds. The perfect book or movie title. For the first five or so years after the disappearance of the Three—no remains had ever been found—there had been lots written on the Widows and the long-lost husbands. But the story had eventually fizzled as they all did. Once in a great while a retired cop or private investigator or investigative reporter would come to town and dig around. But no one had ever found an answer.

Reyna refused to allow that reality to dampen her spirit. In all such unsolved cases, there were no answers until someone found one. It was only a matter of time and interest. And maybe luck.

She had the time and the interest. Just maybe she would get lucky.

The idea that this could be more than the memoir for Eudora dared to flirt with her thoughts. This could be Reyna's next book.

Eudora herself had suggested as much.

"Don't get ahead of yourself, girl."

Reyna started her Land Rover and prepared to back out of the parking lot. A knot tightened in her stomach. She wasn't getting her hopes up about anything more than what was. She would write the memoir and dig as deep into this mystery as necessary to find answers for her client.

Nothing more…for now.

If more developed…well, that would be incredible. For now, all her focus needed to be on finding answers.

The knot loosened, and Reyna eased the Land Rover out onto Main Street. She surveyed the lovely shops and the happy-looking pedestrians. It was all picture-perfect. Like a Norman Rockwell painting. The quintessential little village filled with the best of what life had to offer.

But there was something unpleasant or perhaps evil hidden here.

All Reyna had to do was find it.